SANGSTER'S PARCEL

David Allen Rice

Copyright © 2024 David Allen Rice
All rights reserved.
ISBN:

DEDICATION

This book is dedicated to anybody who will flatter the author merely by picking it up, let alone reading it.

REVIEWS

(Note: not one of these reviews is necessarily authentic)

•

I do not know why I was asked to review this dreadful book. How is this puerile trash supposed to relate to the modern feminist? Undiluted male chauvinist claptrap, it epitomises the work that yet needs to be done to combat toxic masculinity and destroy the rule of white male supremacy. No woman should ever even lift this book.

**Jenny Bulldyke,
Women's Hour Book Club**

•

Every woman should lift this book if wishing for an insight into how the male psyche works. A game-changer for male/female relationship-building. Written by an alpha male for alpha males (gollygosh, don't we all love an alpha male), it features some spiffingly-well-crafted characters, a jolly intricate plot and highly fluid prose. Yummy!

**Lady Clarissa Hermione Phuuk-Trumpit
Horse & Hound**

•

Poorly crafted characters, practically zero plot. Adequate punctuation. But well-intentioned in its treatment of the inevitability of the descent into a life of crime caused by poor social housing.

The New Statesman

•

At last we have a novel written by an author of laudably indeterminate gender, which portrays with empathy a strong female lead in trying circumstances, dragged down by the dysfunctional, cis-gendered, dinosaur family of the supporting male character, whilst emphasising the sisterly struggle of oppressed women (such as myself) eternally battling to break through the glass ceiling.

**Duchess of Sussex
Archwell Podcast Book Reviews.**

(Ed: You were meant to review *this* book, not your effing husband's)

•

For once, a crime thriller with a strong, gay lead character showing that, as that icon of camp, David Bowie once said, "We can be heroes." With homophobic scorn glancing off him like Ping-Pong balls off a disco glitter ball, our hero forges ahead, to triumph over overwhelming odds and find true love.

OUT! Magazine

*

At $4.50, a very good read for the money. Contains some excellent hints for those choosing handguns for their spouses this Christmas.
Guns & Ammo

•

At £4.50, a very good read for the money. Contains some excellent hints for those choosing handguns for their spouses this Christmas.
Liverpool Echo

•

Documentary-style novel. Deals in part with homophobia and the trials and tribulations of coming out. Embraces the gay lifestyle in a very tender and sympathetic way. But is let down by its lack of racial and gender diversity. Would make a good one-off television drama if the lead character was more representative of the diverse society in which we find ourselves, say, a Somalian hermaphrodite.
BBC Book Club

•

At last a novel that portrays rugby players as the sensitive and caring people that we truly are, rather than the knuckle-dragging, frequently drunken, sexually predatory and violent thugs that we are purported to be.
RugbyPass.com - The Home of Women's Rugby

•

I cannot recommend this captivating document highly enough: multi-faceted in its brave approach, it illustrates the high drama and nerve-jangling tension of government. Beguiling and groundbreaking, this visionary instrument aptly illustrates the chicanery, dodging and weaving that has to be done just to keep the voters placid and stay in power. This manifesto is a new Mein Kampf for our time.
The President
(Sec. of State: Mr President!? Can I have minute please?)

•

A literary tour de ~~farce France~~ Forth.
The Grauniad

•

I get a lot of film scripts across my desk, and I must say, on a first reading, the tangled, confusing and impossible to follow plot is right up my street. But if I filmed it, there'd need to be a lot more blood.
Quentin Tarantino

•

A superb story about a working class hero mired in a life of crime. Set against the oppressive, class-ridden backdrop of Scotland's capital, the so-called "Festival City", where I once played to an audience comfortably into double figures.
Billie Braag
Folk Singer, Activist, Millionaire, Cunt.

CONTENTS

Prologue	2
Chapter 1	6

Zombie Dawn 6; Post Mortem 8; Epiphany 14; Gentlemen, Start Your Engines 21; Matheson 25; Lockerbie 28.

Chapter 2	30

Hermens 31; Angela 33; Seedy 39; The Park 41; Bryson 50; Meeting, Parting 52; Pigeons 58; Greg Patullo 66; Mackenzie 69; Berwick 70; At the Paullos' 77; Hermens Aftermath 82; Matheson Aftermath 88; Gym 96

Chapter 3	98

Divorce Writ Large 98; Matheson 101; The Patullos 108; Bryson 110; Hermens 111; Glasgow 113; Julian 127; Gym 131; Grand Theft Auto 132; Wee Hammy 135; Robbed 139.

Chapter 4	151

Wee Shady 145; The Car 15o; Shopping 153; Impact 160; Conscious 164; McShaed 171; Countryside 173; Hospital 180.

Chapter 5	190

Hospital 183; Bryson 195; Hospital 196; Angela 203.

Chapter 6	215

Hospital 206; Hermens 213; Brenda 214; Removal 217; Julian and Mackenzie 223; Matheson 225; Hospital 229.

Chapter 7	240

Hospital 234; Bryce 250; The Car 250; Lockerbie 251; Visitors 253; Ash's flat 258.

Chapter 8	274

Hospital 263; Campbell and McColl 267; The Beatties 270; Car Higher 278; McShaed 279; Highway Patrol 280; Hospital 285.

Chapter 9	302

Lockerbie 290; The Patullos 298; Tooled Up 303; Deirdre 303; The Farm 316; Water 322; Payback 331; The Stick-up 338; Deirdre 345; The OK Coral 365; Hermens 371; Bryson 373; Deirdre & Nisbet 375; Hospital 376; Leith 377.

Chapter 10	396

Mackenzie 380; The Office 385; Sngster's Parcel 388; Bryson 390; Matheson 390; Hermens 391; Rogoff 392; The Patulloes 393; Ten days 394; Six months 395.

About The Author	398
Thank You	399

PROLOGUE

"Yes," said Aaron Rogoff QC, putting his Mont Blanc ball-point pen to the Telegraph crossword. "I've had to do that sort of thing too. But not on quite the same scale."

Rogoff felt slightly impatient with his friend. He always started the working day at eight o'clock with a coffee and the Telegraph crossword. It got his nimble mind ready for the day ahead. Matheson had interrupted the process. And more annoyingly, had called him via the practice reception.

He filled in six across, 'Evil kept in purse'. It was 'repulsive'. So was his friend's line of talk on the other end of the line.

Rogoff had the long slow accent of the old Etonian. Even to another member of the bar, a professional peer, it was delivered in the secure knowledge that by dint of wealth and upbringing, social superiority was assumed. And Rogoff, like many an old Etonian, cultivated it: as a weapon to be used carefully, to beguile, befriend or belittle. Even his friend Matheson's private schooling at Sedberg hadn't been enough to elevate him to Rogoff's social stratum. It was a north, south thing too. But they were friends, nevertheless, from university, kind-of.

"I have a friend in that line of business," said Rogoff, in that stifled, patronising way that lawyers have, breathing in as he spoke, as if he'd been holding his breath for five minutes.

"Oh, excellent!" said Matheson.

This was helpful to Matheson. Rogoff had some inside knowledge. Rogoff was one of Matheson's oldest acquaintances, in the same line of business. They had studied law together at Cambridge and kept in touch. One looked up to the other, the other didn't. But they shared the same interests: shooting, sailing; the same stock broker (money: legitimate money, had to be kept somewhere) and even, sometimes, when Matheson was in London, they shared the same tarts.

Whilst Rogoff's law practice was, of course, straight, he had kept his fingers in many pies: the stock market, Futures, Options. He was a wealthy man, ambitious, successful, multi-talented and diligent.

And crafty.

"Well," he went on, "I do have relatives in that line of business, but I wouldn't want them involved. This fellow I have in mind is not so much a friend as an acquaintance. You know how it is Roddie. But he'll keep you on the, ehm … straight and narrow, so to speak. He's in the, what you might call "carbon futures" business. At the, ehm, blunt end. He's based at Hatton Garden. He probably won't touch it with a bargepole, but he'll know somebody who will. Oh by the way, if I was you, I'd expect to factor in say, as much as twenty percent commissions along the way."

"Twenty?" said Matheson. "That's a lot."

He hadn't bargained on that amount, but in uncharted seas like these, he was in no great position to bargain.

An affirmative, "Mmmm," was drawn out at the other end; a patronising sigh, meaning, to all intents and purposes, "What did you expect?"

Rogoff thought he'd better comfort his friend.

"I wouldn't worry about commission or finder's fees, Roddie. Diamonds are on the up, soaring. So is gold. Everybody's running from the pound, it's the right time to get in, you'll make your costs back in a year, and then some."

Matheson, a successful QC, but from the provinces, always felt a bit like a country yokel when his Greys-Inn, high-rolling friend took charge like this.

"Oh well if that's what it takes, that's what it takes. Thank you Aaron," he said. "Can you email me his contact details?"

"I will *Royal* Mail you his details," said Rogoff. "I'll need a name."

"Just give him my name."

"Roddy! …"

Again the voice had the almost, but not quite, imperceptible, disappointed impatience of a dad talking to a naughty ten-year-old.

"Oh, I see. Ehm, just say, ehm Sharky," said Matheson.

The White Shark was the name of his sailing boat, referring in his mind, to his white hair and his predatory skills in court. To his earth-mother, hippy wife, he might have chosen some other kind of fish for the boat's name. She, lacking the decorum of a dear friend, had suggested, with a nod to his performance in bed, The Flounder.

"Ah, I see. Your boat," said Rogoff after a moment. "Apt. I'll be in touch. Goodbye ... Sharky."

The call ended. Rogoff sighed affectionately. His friend Roddy Matheson had no doubt been up all night wringing out the sparse sponge of his creative juices before he bought the boat, eventually to come up with that grim nugget of a name.

"*If boats could blush,*" thought Rogoff.

At the other end of the line, Matheson put his phone down and pumped a little 'score!' fist as if he'd just, well, scored. Things were starting to take shape.

In London, Rogoff fished a small, well-fingered leather notebook out of the bottom drawer of his desk. Always keep certain information in a form that can be fed into the jaws of a document shredder or a wood burning stove. He looked up a phone number and called an office near the London Diamond Bourse.

"Hello Manny, yes, it's Aaron, long time no see."

They exchanged a few pleasantries, then Aaron Rogoff got down to the facts.

"Look, I've got a friend who has some money to invest ... yes, a fairly long term investment, tuck it away for quite a while. ... Yes he needs to, ehm, put his ill-gotten gains somewhere safe."

"And he wants to invest in carbon futures?" This was the fashionable insider code for diamonds, an allotrope of carbon. "Why not send him over to your uncle, or that cousin of yours?"

"Wouldn't touch either with a bargepole. Never do business with family or friends."

"I thought you said this was a friend."

"Well, it's not really business. It's a favour. I'm not really involved."

"I see. So just exactly how ill-gotten are these gains?"

"I wouldn't know. As ill as it gets, probably. I don't care and it doesn't matter. I suppose he just wants to hide some loot from our friends in the Treasury or, for all I know, the boys in blue."

"And how much does he have to invest?" asked Manny. Rogoff told him. He whistled. "I see. Well I do know somebody who'll know somebody. I'll put them in touch. It's quite a lot of money, shall we build in a finder's fee?"

"Madness not to," said Rogoff.

"Lump sum or percentage?"

"Whichever is the greater."

"I thought you said he was a friend."

"Nothing makes the earth seem so spacious," drawled Rogoff, "as to have friends at a distance."

"Ah … Thoreau, wasn't it? … the American poets. I flunked English Lit," said Manny.

"I know," said Rogoff.

-----------oOo-----------

CHAPTER 1

Zombie Dawn

An Edinburgh suburb. Thin, lace-filtered, spring morning sunlight through leafless garden birch branches etches twig shadows on the pale peach bedroom wall, nervously touching it like dead men's fingers on young skin.

The struggling, rising sun competes with cold, LED, energy-saving light bouncing its bleak environmental smugness from the stucco-ed ceiling. The clumsy Art Deco pastiche of this bedroom struggles to waken from its terminally desaturated pastel palette.

Carefully, 'carelessly' scattered, pseudo-art deco artefacts inhabit this place: Clarice Cliff-style prints for the curtains, framed Klimt prints for the walls. Deep pile apple-green' carpet, upon which self-conscious, pseudo Rennie Mackintosh furniture cringes. Industrial strength twee: a porcelain cowboy hat on the floor by the dressing table, chiffon scarf about its brim; thematic incongruity here and there for contrast: a red silk rose on the dressing table mirror, a body on the bed.

A body, naked except for jockey shorts, lies very, very still, floating motionless amid the rolling ice blue surf of a fifteen-hundred-tog, goose down duvet. A male body it is, unshaven and white. No, very white, cadaver white. The blue-grey white of un-sunned skin bereft of life. Pity really. This might have been a good body at some time, a useful body. It might once have been an athlete or a sportsman, but it's now slightly too soft, puffy around the edges. And slightly too cadaverous. Sadly, former athlete or not, this cadaver has a large metal object protruding from the left side of its skull.

Lying supine, the body is almost perfectly symmetrical. The legs slightly splayed, the bare feet splayed a little more. The hands lie on the belly, either side of the naval, fingertips almost touching, their weight impressing permanent, rigor mortis digit dents in the cold-stiffened, subcutaneous belly flesh. The body lies symmetrical, except that the weight of the rusting metal object draws the dead head down slightly to the left, giving the formal, funereal arrangement of the cadaver an air of relaxation that belies the stiffening limbs. Sightless eyes, half open, are dry slits around which the puffed flesh has gathered, wrinkled in a sickly, sallow, yellow-grey corona, bracketed beneath by the blue bags of recent heavy drinking.

Through the blank birch tree in the bare, suburban garden, the slowly brightening spring dawn continues to slide its cold, skinny fingers through the lace curtains, now challenging the opaque glass bedroom uplighter for command of this morbid scene. But the eyes cannot see it.

Still the body lies, as the mortuary-cold, LED-tinged sunlight spreads around the room.

An adrenalin shock! A finger twitches, the eyes blink. No! Surely not a sign of life. Just a reaction, a last hopeless, lifeless twitch from an autonomic nervous system winding down to oblivion. It lies still again.

Many minutes pass and still the body lies. A deep, deep cold has penetrated the lifeless flesh and the rigor of it sets the joints stiff and immovable, lifeless, even though this household's central heating has gasped into pre-programmed life: on for two hours while you get ready for work, then off until tea-time.

Then shock again! Suddenly and swiftly the cadaver's left hand moves. Grasping the shank of the rusted steel bolt, the zombie fist wrenches the corroded thread from the cranium, drawing with it an adhesion of addled brain tissue. The torso rises suddenly like a swiftly opening submarine hatch, the lifeless legs still gravity-anchored to the bed like pale, water-logged mooring rope. Upright now, the sallow zombie face gapes and blinks as twig-shadows finger the numb white skin.

"Jesus Christ Almighty! What a fucking hangover!"

--------oOo--------

Post Mortem

Nisbet Sangster looked at his empty left hand and groaned. Because being awake was a living nightmare. The rusting bolt in his head had been drawn out and was gone but the pain in his head remained. What a fucking night. How could he be in this condition after so much to drink? Was it not true that you could drink yourself sober? No, as it turned out, apparently it was not true.

No human being could be expected to endure such cranial agony.

"*On a scale of one to ten,*" said the physician in Nisbet's head, "*what level is your pain at now?*"

"*Level thirteen,*" said the pain in Nisbet's head. "*But I can do you a few pulses of fifteen, I you like.*"

He looked for the rusty bolt to shove it back in again. It was, however, gone: his hand was empty. He groped at his head. Nope, no bolt, but it certainly felt as if it was back in place, rotating, twisting itself in and out, spinning like a brass monkey, screwing its way through to the other side. The pain of it was unspeakable. Jesus Christ Almighty! He had to get up and find the paracetamol.

Careful to make no sudden movements that might echo their way up his spine to his fragile cranium, he swung his mooring-rope legs over the edge of the bed and his feet fell to the bedside rug with consecutive thuds like the exploding of not-too-distant canon shells. A death-ray of intense and exquisitely focused agony ran, as expected, like a tectonic shockwave, up his spine into the aforesaid fragile cranium, and burst like a Hogmanay firework in the dark, hostile, pain-filled firmament of his skull. He waited while the multi-coloured firework sparks of pain floated down from the black sky of his brain to trickle back down the drainpipe of his spine. Jesus Christ Almighty! What a hangover!

Rising as carefully, as gingerly as he could, he eased his way across the "apple green", or as he lately called it, "public toilet green", deep-pile bedroom carpet to the designer en-suite bathroom, switched on the light and waited the obligatory twenty minutes for the twenty-year-old energy-saving bulb to get over the electric shock of being asked to lighten the fuck up.

Stumbling across the bathroom floor, he opened the bathroom cabinet. The paracetamol were easy to find now that the clutter of toiletries, cotton buds and the rest of his recently estranged wife's cosmetic paraphernalia had gone. He grabbed the packet of painkillers and his waving, zombie hand brought with it his bottle of Paco Rabanne aftershave. The heavy glass bottle exploded against the edge of the porcelain washbasin and the bulk of it bounced into the toilet bowl.

Nisbet, even in this state, could see the horrible comic irony: the Paco Rabanne was in the back o' ra pan. Oh how we laughed. The smile seized up half way across Nisbet's face and the twisted grimace winked back at him from the bathroom cabinet mirror.

As he looked at this strange Quasimodo face, his eyebrows came down to meet his wrinkling nostrils. It was too ugly to bear and anyway, the tension of flexing facial muscles was causing stress fractures in his skull. Gradually, and with great care, he relaxed his face back into the zombie repose with which it was most comfortable and let his facial muscles hang from his forehead like melted pizza cheese. Now the bathroom stank like a gay bar and there was glass everywhere. The fumes lightened Nisbet's head a little so he braced himself on the washbasin and breathed a deep draught of the perfumed vapour hoping that it would lighten his head a little more.

The head-lightening effect of a lungful of aftershave vapour was not what he anticipated. His head spun as if he'd taken a left hook from Mike Tyson, inducing a vertical dose of the whirly pits. He took the standing count. Waves of nausea.

He swayed in a circle like a dying gyroscope. His white knuckles gripping the basin, he waited for something to change. Nothing much changed, but after further basin holding, the nausea subsided a little but did not leave entirely. Would there be pills for nausea? Peukatemol?

He looked again for the packet of painkillers and found them still on his hand. Sadly the paracetamol packet contained only a few pills and the massive, suicidal overdose he was contemplating would have to be postponed. He reached for the glass shelf above the wash basin, grabbed the pseudo-René Lalique glass tumbler which held his toothbrush and evicted it with a flick of the wrist. It too went the way of the aftershave bottle and landed in the toilet bowl. The implications of this were not immediately obvious to Nisbet as he ran cold water into the manky tumbler. He popped the pills from their foil packaging and began to flush them one at a time down his throat with peppermint flavoured cold water, just spotting the bobbing weeks of fluffy dust that had gathered in the glass. It slipped into his mouth and was gone forever along with the pills. Gone forever eh? Well we'll see about that.

Waves of nausea. Then a nausea tsunami.

The fourth of the planned nine painkillers never made it to his stomach. It met the previous three on their way back up to the surface, still suspended in the cold, fluffy, stale, peppermint water in which they had been dispatched. Nisbet dived to the pale peach porcelain of the toilet bowl and presented the contents of his stomach for inspection.

First came the four pills in the cold water, then colourless fluid, then horrible green slime. Slime, which strangely bore no trace of, the giant, lager-flushed tandoori horror story of the night before. It erupted from the gaping caldera of his mouth like a Vesuvian pyroclastic flow, scalding his throat cruelly and corroding the enamel of his teeth. As his mouth spouted in wretched, retching instalments, so did his tear ducts and pores. Gastric lava spewed from the volcano of his gob. It was impossible to breath and much too dangerous. To breathe would be to risk inhalation of this painful, rasping, acid brew. He couldn't breathe through his nose, stuff was coming out of it too. As the spasms convulsed his little-used diaphragm into a concertina seizure, he farted. And considering the colossal volume discharged, unaccompanied by any satisfying sphincter-flapping rasp, he knew for a certainty that he had just shat his pants.

"*Jesus bloody Christ,*" he thought, "*Can it get any worse?*"

Yes indeed. This would become apparent soon.

This wretched retching carried on for some time without any help from Nisbet. He was caught in the vengeful grip of his body as it purged itself of the frightful alien filth that it had nurtured overnight.

Kneeling, foetus-like, with his acid-scalded throat on the cool rim of the toilet bowl, his face gaping into it like a cathedral gargoyle, every orifice of his upper body was on full warp drive. Sweat poured from every pore until he felt greased up like a Channel swimmer. And every bit as cold. How could you sweat with hypothermia? He puked again and was sure he could even feel the wax escaping from his ears.

The puking continued, although it seemed way beyond anything a single stomach could contain. Soon he would be a shriveled, evacuated shadow of his former being. His naked empty shell would be found on the bathroom floor, a mere notion of its former substance like a discarded snakeskin. A discarded snakeskin with skid marked underpants. Only the pain and guilt would remain for forensic scrutiny, hovering over his shabby remains like the Ghost of Curries Past.

He looked into the toilet bowl and saw the bristle end of his toothbrush bob to the surface.

"*Shite! Ma bloody toothbrush!*" he thought, inasmuch as thought was possible, which, clearly it wasn't, not good quality, clear thought anyway. Clear thought would have seen the sense in hesitance. Unhesitant, he reached for the toothbrush, and puked on his wrist.

When this particular spasm passed he held his wrist, hand and toothbrush up to the light. It looked like the inside of a calzone. He dropped the toothbrush back in the toilet and rested his fiery throat on the soothing cold porcelain of the toilet bowl once more. The toilet seat, which, it transpired, he hadn't raised fully, now made its way back where it belonged and smashed onto the back of his neck.

"*Typical,*" though Nisbet. "*Absolutely bloody typical.*"

He stayed still, a cathedral gargoyle with a toilet seat horse collar.

Time passed, maybe a minute, maybe a geological epoch. Nothing much was being emitted now. The frequency of the spasms began to diminish, but only slowly. Would they ever stop entirely or did they have a half-life like decaying plutonium? Diminishing, but never gone entirely, still faintly detectable after a million years.

Nisbet, still kneeling in a foetal position with the horse collar halo of pastel plastic around his head, and still with his throat cooling on the cold porcelain of the toilet bowl, took the chance to wonder what had become of the rest of the giant tandoori horror story which had punctuated the previous evening's drinking. On reflection, maybe he hadn't puked up as much as he had eaten or drunk. After all, he and his pals had eaten and drunk enough for an infantry brigade. Each.

Now that the retching was dying down and he had time to ponder, he realised what had prompted him to think of it. It had insinuated its presence into his subconscious while his mind was otherwise unoccupied. Transmitting on a long-wave frequency from deep within his pelvis like muted whale song, its pulsating rhythmic message was clear. It wanted his attention.

Shit! It had his attention. And it was at the point of no return. He tried to stand up but was restrained like a rearing pony by the horse collar of the toilet seat. His eyes bulged for a second, then he ducked out from under it and pushed it back upright. The whale song was now coming directly from the launch pad of his colon.

"*Holy shit,*" he thought, "*Mah pants!*"

Rising to a crouch, he whipped them off and yes indeed, he had sharted them. He threw them into the washbasin and spun, Travolta-like, to rotate his bum toward the puke-blocked toilet bowl. Over-rotating by half a turn and almost succumbing to the temptation of following through for a full three-sixty. For fear of another fly past, or worse, a triple salchow, instinctively, his arms extended, slowing the rotation. Aha! He knew that GCSE Physics shite about conservation of angular momentum would come in handy one day. He could just see the toilet pan in the corner of his eye.

His backside rotated back anticlockwise of its own volition like some kind of automaton until it was aligned with the bum-pan docking zone. With the slap of high speed flesh on a polished surface, he sat heavily on the cold porcelain, and only just in time. No effort required now. No time to stand up and get the toilet seat down. Once again he was caught in the awful grip of gastric vengeance.

Blast-off! The full Cape Canaveral, sheik kebabs for rocket fuel, vindaloo afterburners on max. Fasten seat belts, kindly do not leave your seat. But you have to, there's a stinging pain in your left arse. But you can't, arse central is on warp drive. Oh God, he was going to throw up again. The basin was four feet away. Either he'd have to puke in the basin and shite on the floor, or vice versa.

No, he couldn't puke in the basin, his pants were there, complete with a skid mark the size of a Cornish pasty, and anyway, the projectile vomiting had passed and could no longer be relied upon for range, trajectory or overall accuracy. He looked down. Only one course of action was open to him: he would have to puke in the toilet. With his arse still glued to the cold porcelain, he spread his knees, and closing one eye, he aimed for the triangular aperture between his thighs and the toilet bowl. He puked. And missed. Blimey! Look at that! Surprisingly, considering his rugby club past, Nisbet had never puked on his wedding tackle before, interesting outcome though it was. Direct hit.

"Jesus bloody Christ," he wailed, "Ah've puked on ma pubes!"

He waited, elbows on knees, head in hands, for maybe an hour, maybe a week, until it was all over. His head was pounding, and sick was drying into his pubic afro. His post-curry arsehole pulsated like a grilled sea anemone, his left buttock was stinging like a third-degree burn, his throat rasped like a gravel-rashed arse while his head was on tumble dry.

He swayed upwards to his feet. Puke was everywhere. Blood was everywhere. Blood everywhere?! Had he shat his guts out? Oh no. Oh yes. He remembered, the stinging pain in his left buttock. Nisbet stood upright and pulled a piece of Paco Rabanne glass from the back of his upper thigh. He held it up: a chunk of green glass coated in red.

He stood still for a while. His bum was bleeding, his head was still bursting - the rusty bolt must have returned. It definitely wasn't imaginary. It was exerting its mechanical advantage over his neck muscles and he could feel the weight of it drag his pain-riddled skull onto his left shoulder. In this position he got down the last five paracetamol in the packet and stood at the ready to see if they would stay down. They did.

--------o0o--------

Epiphany

Nisbet surveyed the disgusting physical wreck in the mirror. There was no bolt jutting from its head, or rather, jutting into it. But it felt like it. Looking back at him was the ugly image of a hung-over slob. His stomach rumbled again and he stood there, braced for action, waiting for more bad news from the gastric volcanism department. This time, however, the pills stayed put in the swirling vortex of his stomach. He hoped they'd make their way to the swirling vortex of his head very soon indeed. He ran his tongue around his mouth. His mouth was like a badger's arse. And not a particularly nice badger's arse at that. The arse of a very dirty badger that never cleaned its arse.

His teeth weren't in good shape either. They were sticky - sticky in the way that public bar linoleum is sticky. He clenched his teeth for a moment and they stuck together. He had to consciously heave his jaws apart. They juddered open, sending a few thousand volts up through his skull. Amazing! He had discovered a new two-part adhesive. A new wonder glue made from badger's arse and puke. He'd better clean his teeth.

The toothbrush, where was it? He looked at the wash basin. Nope. His single functional memory cell made faint radio contact with the solitary operational consciousness cell that had turned up for brain duty this morning. Rousing a few more brain cells from their coma, the brain responded and he looked in the toilet bowl. The awful meaning of the inch of green plastic and substance-encrusted bristles bobbing from the horrific volcanic slime in the toilet was clear: he'd had puked and shat on his toothbrush. He flushed the toilet and waited. He flushed it again, just to be sure. Everything went except for the toothbrush, too long and stiff to escape round the u-bend.

Without any input from Nisbet, his brain instinctively ran an unsolicited cost-benefit analysis on the toothbrush situation. What remained of reason was able to dismiss the idea of washing it. He decided to grit his teeth and bare it. He gritted them for a moment and even as his jaws relaxed again, his pub-floor teeth stayed obligingly gritted, stuck shut like a catatonic clamshell.

Sad and deeply alone Nisbet got into the shower and turned it on full. Oblivious to the cold (he already had hypothermia anyway) he played the icy water on his head, his buttock and his arsehole until it (the water) eventually ran hot. The head, the arse puncture wound and the arsehole continued also to run hot. He shampooed his wedding tackle, picking mushy bits of half-digested curry from his pubic hair. Funny, he couldn't remember sweetcorn. His penis meanwhile, shriveled in terror, peeking from its hairy bunker like a pink octogenarian bower bird, keeping well out of the way for fear of another attack from the lava flow monster.

Dried now, and swirling around his shoulders a fresh white towel, newly polka-dotted with blood-red spots, he stood on one tiptoe with his other knee on the washbasin to try and see his arse in the bathroom cabinet mirror. Aiming, or rather guessing, he stuck an Elastoplast on his buttock in the same post code as the cut. He looked in the mirror. In his white and blood-red polka-dot outfit, he looked like the Tour de France King of the Mountains.

He went back to bed, bled a little on the duvet, and hoping for a fatal stroke, he lapsed into the welcome miasma of another coma.

Time passed and he inched his way to the bathroom again, his bladder having roused him from his stupor. Still hypothermic, probing for his terror-stricken dick he caught it, and pissed all over the toilet seat. Brenda had trained, or rather terrorised him into always replacing the toilet seat in case she sat on the porcelain in the dark. Her nagging had worked because this he had done. So now there was piss, puke, aftershave, blood and glass on the floor. Fuck it. Did Brenda and he have a mop? Had Charles Rennie Macintosh taken time to design mops? If he had, Brenda would have bought one. Perhaps she had taken her designer mop when she left, along with the four-acre television?

Bollocks! He had more to worry about than piss, puke, aftershave, glass and blood on the bathroom floor. The hangover had by now assumed control of his meagre existence and he lapsed once more into semi-consciousness, standing in a sadly slouched position, swaying in small circles like a top losing its purpose. Perhaps it was only the gyroscopic action of his whirling brain that was keeping him upright. He'd never had the whirly pits standing up before.

He found himself on the bathroom scales, his head still bolt-weighted to one side, looking down the length of his left arm at the dial. Brenda's fixation, over the course of their married life, with weight and diet had him programmed for activities other than merely replacing the toilet seat: he was also trained to weigh himself regularly; part of her Nisbet improvement program.

His weight, much to her disappointment, never changed. Neither did his waistline. She had served him healthy, upwardly mobile, whole-food, low-calorie dinners in the evenings to get his weight down, not that it needed to, but he got it up (his weight) the next lunchtime by consuming proper food like pies, cheese rolls and pints. This had been another of the things about Nisbet that had perplexed and frustrated Brenda: he had not allowed her to improve him. It was another manifestation of his ingratitude.

Funny that: she hadn't taken the bathroom scales with her when she cleared out - she'd watched them as much as she did the television and she had taken that. Perhaps it had only been a weapon with which to torture him, a weapon of man destruction. And now that she had left, she'd left the utensils of her black art behind to haunt him, laughing up her sleeve at the thought of him, still programmed for self-esteem reduction.

"*Fuck 'er,*" he thought and he took some small pleasure now from the piss, puke, aftershave, blood and glass on the floor. That lot would have driven her clean up the twist. Daft bitch.

Interested to know how he had got home, wrapped in his King of The Mountains red polka-dot bath towel, he walked to the spare bedroom window and looked down on the drive. The car was in the drive, but it solved nothing. Had he driven home, or had he been driven home? And by whom? And where were the keys? If he could find them it might mean that he had been driven home because he always mislaid things when he was pissed. Good thinking. Towel-wrapped, he scanned all the usual places for the car keys, the bedside cabinet, the dressing table, the table in the hall. He lifted his jeans from the bedroom floor. Nope. His jacket, where was his jacket? He must have had a jacket on last night. Christ! He'd left it in the curry house no doubt. But the keys must be somewhere. If he'd been driven home by one of his mates, whoever drove him home must have put them somewhere - or maybe still had them. Bollocks, he had a spare set in his desk, in the box-room.

He went downstairs, got a bucket, found the mop, lifted an old tee-shirt from the dirty laundry and set about cleaning the bathroom. It wasn't as bad as it might have been, apart from the blood and the pee, most of his mess had made it to the toilet, although it had taken more than one flush to get it all round the u-bend. At the last flush, all that had been left in the bowl was his toothbrush. He fished it out of the (thankfully clear) water in the toiled bowl and held it up to the light. It looked ok but he'd chuck it out. Meantime, he laid it on the glass shelf above the washbasin and continued mopping, careful not to lean or kneel on any Paco Rabanne glass.

Nisbet was still worried about the awful picture he had seen in the mirror. He was a slob, but now that he didn't need to be one as a matter of principal to get on Brenda's nerves, he hated himself for it. It wasn't that he was excessively overweight; he was still in pretty good shape, sort-of. He did go to the gym, went for a five mile run at least once a week. It was just that, despite that, he felt like an out of condition pile of crap. The bedroom mirror said it all. Was he becoming one of those slack, ageing dick-heads at the rugby club to whom he had always felt superior? A has-been, ready to join the blowhards propped at the bar, sneering at young talent, always knowing better. Except that now he hardly ever went to the rugby club. Where was the lightning-fast winger? The complete, eighty-minute rugby-playing animal? Five seasons in first class rugby. Well, the animal was here, and it was full of shite.

Maybe a soak in the bath would help.

Holding his hands to his ears to dull the Niagara pounding from the bath taps, Nisbet watched the steaming water crash into the bath. When he thought it was full enough, oblivious to the obvious hint extended by the steam, he stuck a foot in the water and stood his full weight on it.

"Oh yaaah!"

Lying on his back on the bathroom floor, inspecting the rapidly reddening and stinging end of his leg, he reflected with pride that he might be an out-of-condition pile of crap, but his reactions were as sharp as ever they had been, hangover notwithstanding. He crawled to the taps to run the cold water and knelt on a stray piece of Paco Rabanne glass. There was pain, but there was worse: more disappointment. More self-recrimination. It was harder to bear. He held his lobster-pink foot under the cold tap.

With the bath water, and his foot now down to a tolerable temperature a few degrees below boiling, he lowered himself millimetre-slowly into the water. He had run the bath in the hope of some return-to-the-womb solace but now, submerged, looking along the surface of the hot water, his self-esteem was ebbing to zero. A trickle of red ran down to the surface of the water from the cut on his knee to meet a spiral of pink rising from the cut on his bum. If he didn't stop bleeding soon he'd be found dead in a bath full of coagulated blood like a giant black pudding with a head sticking out of it. Should he get the oatmeal, black pepper and salt from the kitchen to finish the recipe?

He felt like shite and the view of his flaccid naked body in the bedroom mirror had confirmed that he looked like shite. His one-time beach-ready body, the rolling undulating hills of his six-pack, could only faintly be recalled beneath a coating of flab.

Fully immersed, his white over-fleshy belly protruded slightly from the surface of the water like a South Pacific coral atoll, the remnants of a half-arsed volcano with the deep, extinct crater of his belly button dark, shaded and bottomless, flooded to the brim.

The view was pretty bad so he did his best to sink it, drawing his belly downward. But even drawing his belly down to the risk of asphyxia, the flabby island didn't quite disappear entirely. He inhaled before he asphyxiated and let the volcanic tropical island of his belly rise again, with tectonic slowness, as if the tide was going out. Now all it needed was a palm tree and a castaway.

He wondered if he would have had to sink it further ten, or even five years ago. Or was it just that he was taking shallower baths? Probably not. He was just an out-of-condition, low-self-esteem twat and it had to change. He was at the crossroads. He had to change his ways, get fit, give up the booze, go back to circuit training and get back to where he had been before he got married: back in the firsts. He'd do it by degrees: resolve and dedication would get him back to where he should be - and he knew he could do it, he'd always been able to train hard, even on his own.

For now, however, the way to measure physical condition, obviously, was with a ruler. He would fill the bath to the same level each time, get in (after testing the temperature) and measure the distance between the surface and his belly. Maybe he wouldn't even lose weight. He would train his flab into muscle, remain the same weight and have the sunkenest bath-belly coefficient in the universe. Brenda could stuff the bathroom scales up her arse. This would be the turning point. He would get back to where he should have been if he hadn't married Brenda. If a twat could have an epiphany this was his. His road to Damascus. Or rather, since he was going to use the bath-belly-level fitness regime, his road to meniscus.

A faint recollection of the previous evening's proceedings snuck into his consciousness. He'd gone to the rugby club for the first time in weeks. The welcome had been warm and the congratulations on the news of his likely divorce were enthusiastic. It seemed that the whole club had predicted it – before the wedding.

"I knew that wee whitsername would drag ye away from yer rugby," Vinnie had said. "Spoilt wee shite. Never let a woman get between a man and his rugby, it never works out."

And they all drank several pints to that undeniable truth, at which point four large between-marriages men, led by Beastie the tight-head Cave Troll, had peeled off out of the rugby club and had several more pints in Diggers. Then, as all self-respecting rugby players will do, they'd headed like homing pigeons to the nearest Balti house to let Vinnie 'Vindaloo' McCallum, the club gourmet, order a massive and virtually unending flow of South Asian health food. Nisbet could remember the dishes arriving at the table but that was about it. But it had been good crack. An evening of having the piss ripped out of him had reminded him of what friends were for.

Pondering this taste of his former self and having seen the light dawning over his disappointing desert island belly, he saw a faint ghost of his old self shimmering in the steamy air of the bathroom. He could almost grasp it, almost hold it again. Briefly, a déjà vu notion of last night's comic encouragement from his pals to get back in shape, get match fit and 'get a game' sniggered its way through his aching brain like a humorous birthday card. It felt good for a minute or two lying in the hot water there, at once cathartic and comforting, and also setting him a challenge. He accepted the challenge.

But he'd better get a move on. He had to get to the office and earn money.

Moving slowly, like a man with a flask of nitro glycerin for a head, he washed, shaved in the bath, cut himself shaving, then rose, rose pink as a boiled-lobster from the matching blancmange-pink, bloodied bath water. Shit! He must have lost two pints by now! He stepped unsteadily onto the banana skin of the bath mat and hit the floor in a heap. The nitroglycerine went off between his ears.

Maintaining three points of contact and only moving one limb at a time, he free-climbed the washbasin until he was near vertical. With his fist belayed safely around a tap and his toes trying to suck themselves to the floor like an Amazonian tree frog on a wet leaf, he groped in the cabinet for the sticking plasters. One went on the hole in his knee and one in the same post code as the hole in his bum. Oh well, a fifty percent score was pretty good all things considered. Satisfied with that, he stood and let himself lapse into his usual morning robotic rhythm. He lifted his toothbrush, squirted some toothpaste onto it and began to brush his teeth. He finished scrubbing the last of his molars, withdrew the brush and spat out the mouthful of peppermint foam.

Looking down at his toothbrush, his mind's eye overlaid it, Photoshop-like, with the image of this very same toothbrush bobbing up to the surface in the toilet.

"Aw Christ!".

He threw it back where it belonged, in the toilet, grabbed the fluff tumbler, rinsed his mouth out several times and followed it with half a pint of mouthwash.

Much to his surprise, looking at his watch, which he found on the bedside cabinet, it was not as late as it felt it ought to be. Time only flies when you're having fun. However, enough of the euphoria of his in-bath epiphany remained to steel his resolve about getting into shape, so he dug his gym kit out of the bottom of the wardrobe, stuffed it in his hold-all and threw it down the stairs so that he wouldn't forget it. Conscious that whatever he did today, he didn't want to do it with his arse bleeding through his breeks, he went downstairs and fixed up a field dressing large enough to accommodate his poor aim: three sheets of toilet paper, a large dollop of ointment and held in place with half a yard of duct tape. At least he could be confident that the hole in his bum would be somewhere beneath that lot.

He got dressed, and since he had decided to make a new start, he got out his best 'smart-but-casual' kit: the Boss slacks, the Church loafers and the Armani leather jacket. No point in having high self-esteem, or even merely adequate self-esteem, if you were going to dress like a twat. He checked himself in the mirror, approved of what he saw (except for the navy blue bags under the eyes, the cadaverous complexion and the hint of a spare tyre hanging over his belt), spun on his heel and spare car key in hand, made for the door. The bang as the door closed behind him nearly split his aching head apart and was enough to point out that he might have his spare car key in his hand but that his door key was with his normal car key. Shite! He was locked out.

--------oOo--------

Gentlemen, Start Your Engines

Nisbet could see the from the lock pins sticking up inside the Beamer windows that the car had been abandoned unlocked. Bloody hell!

Never mind, it hadn't been stolen. If it had been stolen, that would have been the shitter of the century. He loved his BMW, a collector's item Alpina B10 in mint condition despite the seventy-odd thousand miles on the clock. He climbed into the car and tried to stick the spare car key in the keyhole, to find his car and door keys there, where he had left them: in the ignition.

Jesus! He had driven home shit-faced and he had absolutely no recollection of it. A chastening shiver ran up his spine. If he'd been nabbed by the cops as pissed as that he'd have been looking at a three-hundred-year ban and a stretch in the HMP Saughton mailbag factory. Absolute ruin would have ensued. A brief nightmare scenario flitted across his aching brain: he'd have got out of the choky to a new career in media distribution - selling The Big Issue. Even worse, his arsehole of a soon-to-be ex-father-in-law would have seen to it that his mates inside HMP Saughton ensured that he got regularly rodgered up the arse by some cave troll from the swamps of Peffermill. Nisbet didn't know if the bastard had any mates inside the slammer but it was a racing certainty that a two-faced, twisted, nasty bastard like him *would* have mates even further over the fence from the right side of the law than he was himself.

Even more chastened than before, he turned the ignition key and nothing ignited. No starter motor, no nothing; barely even a light on the dashboard.

"*Gentlemen! Start your engines!*" said the resident self-recriminatory voice in his head. "*Apart from you Sangster ya wanker! You left the bloody headlights on, you twat.*"

He turned off the lights, let the hand brake off, got out, and leaning against the door pillar, straining his mooring rope legs, curling his tree-frog toes inside his shoes, the better to get a grip on the designer pink granite gravel of the drive, tried to push the car backwards out of the drive. Then he got back in and let off the hand brake. He got out and pushed again. His car was in gear, but his brain wasn't. He leant in and knocked the gear lever into neutral.

Straining once again on the door pillar, he managed to push the car backwards out of the drive and across the street. Turning the wheels downhill he gave it a little forward push, got in and rolled off, the whole thing a practiced move, learned long ago in his youth when the battery of whatever jalopy he was driving left him, and it, flat most mornings.

His Beamer was a very nice motor indeed, but for so long, in his formative years, had he driven one decrepit motor after another, the downhill bump start was second nature to him. He dipped the clutch, stuck it in second gear and let the car accelerate downhill. At about fifteen miles an hour he let in the clutch. Nothing. Just the judder of unelectrified cylinders in a high-compression, fuel-injected engine. He rolled off again and dropped the clutch again. More nothing. About twenty feet from the bottom of the brae where it would be too late and he'd have to go home and phone the AA, he spotted his mistake, turned on the ignition and dropped the clutch. This time the car caught, jumped, fired. He revved, u-turned back up the brae and drove off at a brisk pace in the direction of town and the office. Lanark Road felt weird this morning, surreal. Jesus! he was still a bit pissed. You could fail a breath test, so he'd heard, up to twelve hours after a piss-up. He slowed down, the chastening shudder of realising that he'd driven home shit-faced last night ran up his spine again.

Plainly, it was a cracker of a spring morning and despite his hangover he was sorry to have missed a chunk of it. He put on his Ray Bans. The sunshine might be uplifting for his sprits but it was doing his head in.

Another slight downer about this morning's lateness would be Angela's disapproval. Some architects had secretaries that were ruthlessly efficient; others had secretaries that were squirmy, giggly, sexy and flirtatious. But Nisbet had one that was like a plump big sister. Anyway, she was a worker, was very charming and could be truthful to clients in a much more appeasing way than any palliative lie that Nisbet might concoct.

As he eked his way through the park, the midmorning sunshine started to work its magic on him because he began to feel quite disproportionately well. Well, better than he deserved to feel, all things considered. Things that is (apart from his slowly diminishing hangover) like how his wife had walked out a fortnight ago, had taken the Land Rover Discovery, which was hers (or rather her bastard of a father's), the TV, which was technically Nisbet's but to which she was emotionally umbilically joined, and the Brat which was hers (definitely, because he had seen it pop out of her front bottom), but which he hoped might not be his because the child was a brat of colossal proportions: a tiny human with all the empathy of a preschool Joseph Stalin.

Actually, the child definitely was his - Brenda' wasn't the sort to flirt with other men. She didn't even do it with Nisbet. The problem with the child was genetics. The baby he had once been besotted with had grown into the spoilt, girning little puss-nodule of a three-year-old that she was now? Obviously the poor child took after her grandfather, the megalomanic, girning, psychopathic, self-made arsehole.

And now, having walked out, Brenda, with her arsehole of a father's help would probably sue his pants off and get everything from the house right down to the fillings in his teeth. At least Nisbet thought he would contest any claims on his teeth because the nasty old bastard hadn't stumped up for his dental work - like he had Brenda's share of the house.

Turning his red BMW into the crunchy grit of Summer Street he pulled up outside the red brick, slightly crumbling thing that was his office. The sun was hammering down hard on the brass nameplate on the door but it only glowed humbly in reply. Nisbet determined to go to the Co-op and get a tin of Brasso so that Angela could give it a good shine as soon as her huff was over. After all, if he couldn't read that this was the office of The Nisbet Sangster Partnership, Architect, Civil Engineer and Project Management, how were rich property developers going to read it? Even if this alley was too narrow for a rich property developer's Bentley.

Nisbet Sangster was a shite name. He'd always hated his first name. But on a brass nameplate at least it quite, kind-of, a bit, sounded like, a big partnership. Why the hell had his parents called him Nisbet? All through school even the bullies had had trouble thinking up something novel to ridicule about such a patently ridiculous first name. He couldn't even hate his parents for it. His dad's name was Stan and his mum' name was Senga. Stan and Senga Sangster. Shite names ran in the blood.

Probably, he wouldn't have the balls even to say the word Brasso to Angela for fear of another huff and as usual it would go on the long list of things to do that never got done, the composition of which had yet to begin. Procrastination: a lifestyle choice you can make tomorrow.

The brass plate had barely been cleaned since Brenda had rubbed it red hot in the first flush of pride at her new husband having joined the ranks of the upper middle class, self-employed professional. Sod it; maybe this was going to be a day of new beginnings so he would polish the bloody thing himself for sure. And make that list.

--------oOo--------

Matheson

A plain envelope lay on the doormat of Roddy Matheson's town house when he got home the following evening. He picked it up and looked at it. First class stamp and the handwriting was the neat, flowing cursive of his classically educated friend. He opened it. Inside was an A4 sheet of paper, blank except for a telephone number and the single initial A. Presumably this number was the contact that Aaron had promised. He laid it on the coffee table, went to the bedroom, stripped off the chalk-stripe suit he'd worn for court today, tossed his shirt and underwear into the laundry basket and stepped into the tiger skin onesie that his occasional 'mistress' had bought him for his birthday - with his money. He was expecting her round soon - no sense in wearing too much. He poured a large malt whisky, picked up his 'private' pay-as-you-go mobile phone and dialed the number on the sheet of paper. It was answered immediately.

"Who's this?"

"It's Mr Sharkie."

"How do you do Mr Sharkie," said Eric Hermens. "How can I help you today?"

Matheson began to explain his need to disappear a substantial amount of cash and Mister Aich, as he described himself, explained that he would be able to help. Matheson began to go into detail in suitably furtive, conspiratorial, monosyllabic sentences while Hermens patiently took note. As he spoke, Matheson heard the front door open and close and his guest for the evening came in. He looked up. Tight, black leather skirt, high heels, dark, seamed stockings. Blimey! His dick said blimey too.

She poured herself a decent malt whisky from Matheson's large collection while he carried on discussing his project with Mr H. She laid her large Versace bag on the floor, sat down beside him and unzipped his onesie as he spoke to Hermens. She put her hand inside the tiger-patterned onesie, ran her fingers downwards and grabbed his dick. Matheson grunted into the phone.

"Ehm, sorry Mister Aich. No I didn't mean anything by that, my secretary just handled me…, sorry, *handed* me something."

He completed the conversation with a promise to be back in touch and hung up. His plan was coming together, life was good, even if this evening's entertainment was going to cost him most of a grand.

Matheson explained his plan to his son. He got a frosty reception.

"Honestly dad, you don't want to be getting too close to these people. We don't know them."

"We-ell, you know, they check out. I have friends in London who…. Look, it's a simple matter of handing over money for goods. I can just fly down there, collect the goods and fly back."

"Dad, are you nuts?" said the young Matheson. "It's a cash deal, and it's a lot of cash, to say the least. How would you get it through airport security?"

"Well I wasn't meaning to fly down in a bloody aeroplane Julian. … I mean, not a British Airways aeroplane. I'll take a plane from the flying club, the Beachcraft."

This sounded like a very bad idea. His father was a bad driver and an equally poor pilot, having only scraped his pilot's license after a decade of lessons. Julian had been in the passenger seat of a Cessna as his father flew the small plane, bouncing around the Pentland Hills like a sycamore seed in a hurricane. It had been an unnerving experience. He imagined a light aircraft stuck nose first into a field, somewhere in the home counties with the wind fluttering a large part of his inheritance to the four corners.

Acknowledging his son's nervousness, Matheson volunteered a new version of his plan: "Ok, I'll get Beaton to fly, I'll ride shotgun."

This was a slightly better proposition, Beaton was the flying instructor and at least he could navigate. But it didn't dispel the young Matheson's fears.

"Can you imagine what it would look like if you got stopped with that much money on you? The idea is to salt this money away, safely, from the revenue and the police. It's bloody nearly impossible to disappear money these days, or spend it without attracting attention. And what are you going to tell Beaton the trip's for? A visit to Madame Tussaud's?"

"Alternatively," said Matheson, thinking out loud, "if you don't like this idea, we have somebody in police headquarters in Organised Crime. We could simply ask him to divert attention."

"And the revenue? What about the inland revenue?"

"What's it got to do with them, they'll never know?"

Matheson was tired. He was getting too old for this crap. He wanted things simple, and anyway, he'd been up all night shagging. And his backside was a little bit tender too. He was hoping to retire to the British Virgin Islands. This was a considerable top-up to his pension. His pension was measly, even though he'd stacked it to the gunwales over the years. He wanted to retire in luxury. Luxury didn't just mean a home somewhere in BVI, it meant a home in BVI and a yacht, a bigger yacht, parked on the private jetty with a few tarts in micro bikinis lounging around on the foredeck. All he had to do was get through a couple of years before the mandatory practice retirement kicked in and he could pull the pension. If he could make regular investments of loot from his other line of business, come retirement, he could dump his scatter-brained wife and piss off.

A system for disappearing the occasional half million every now and again over the next few years would allow him to bugger off and leave his dizzy, earth-mother, hippy wife with enough money for her to meditate herself into tantric yoga oblivion with her pot-smoking, new-wave, Hare Krishna friends. He had no intention of parking the money somewhere for Julian to squander on coke-snorting parties with his chums. "No pockets in a shroud," as his gran used to say.

"Not good enough dad. We're the customer. Let me deal with it, you shouldn't get further involved. I'm an accountant - remember? I'll sort it. We'll get *them* up *here*," his finger tapped the desk for emphasis. "And do the exchange on our turf."

"You think so?"

"Yes dad. Bryson can handle the money, I'll arrange the swop."

"Ooooh well. If you think that's the right way forward."

"It's the professional way forward, dad."

"Oh well. If you're sure. OK son, go for it."

He gave Julian the contact's phone number.

"You'd better get yourself a pay-as-you-go mobile phone. I'll tell my contact to deal with you."

"It's ok, dad. I'll call him right now."

Sadly, Matheson's son, so he thought, had taken after his wife: bright enough to qualify as an accountant and run his father's finances but altogether a bit too effete. He was crafty, he thought, crafty at tax, but not … gritty enough for a life of crime. He himself was a lawyer, so a life of crime was a neat fit. Also, he was worried about his son's social circle: it included no women. Maybe he should have sent him to Gordonstoun instead of Fettes College. "Fettes for wetties," was the saying amongst the former pupils of all the other fee-paying schools in Edinburgh.

Julian, on the other hand, couldn't give a toss what his dad thought about the company he kept. He set off, already concocting how he'd set up the meeting to exchange the money for goods.

--------oOo--------

Lockerbie

"Do you really think so daddy?" asked Brenda Sangster.

"Aye, Ah dae," replied Tom Lockerbie, warming his backside on the Aga. "Ye dinnae want tae be rattlin' aboot in a big three-bedroom hoose ower in Balernae oan yer ain. Ye're faur better back here wi' us. And yer mammy can help ye look efter the bairn. When yer divorce is a' sorted and ye've settled doon we can look fur a nice wee place fur you and the bairn, maybes here in Colinton."

The truth was that although the house was in his daughter and son-in-law's names, he had stumped up more than half of the total purchase price on his daughter's behalf. He could well do without two hundred grand sitting doing nothing, tied up in a half-empty house.

"But what about Nisbet's share? What if he doesn't want to sell?"

"Well he'll just hae tae buy ye oot and Ah dinnae think he's got the money, no wi' that pishy wee business o' his. Onywey, he'll hae enough tae worry aboot wi' lawyer's fees." He rubbed his hands together.

"I don't think it's such a bad business," put in his daughter. "After all, he designed and built this extension - and did all the planning ... and your warehouse extension and ..."

"Yon's just draughtsmanship at best, the rest's just a case o' getting' brickies an' joiners in ... naethin' but project management. He's no a real architect."

"He's a qualified architect *and* structural engineer."

Brenda was sticking up for the qualifications, not the man.

"He's an arse. He just mairried you coz yer faither's got money."

Brenda knew there wasn't much point in discussing anything when her father was in this sort of mood, which he was, almost all of the time; completely fascinated with himself. She decided to change tack.

"Daddy, what you said about lawyers. Nisbet and I decided we were just going to make a clean break, keep it amicable, we don't need to get lawyers involved."

"Aye, that's whit he *wid* say, cheapskate bloody ... arsehole."

He clenched his fists, his teeth, and his buttocks, and seethed for a second or two, his usual posture and frame of mind.

"See pet, ye cannae dissolve a marriage wi'oot a reason, ye need grounds for a divorce. That's why ye need a lawyer."

He rocked back and forward from toe to heel again, his mood becoming more positive at the notion of doing somebody wrong.

"Irretrievable brekdoon of the marriage … due tae mental cruelty," he mused.

"But it's not like that daddy, we just …"

"Well then, wis there anither woman?"

"No, we just haven't been getting along for a long time. Nisbet's so … it's just the way he is … he's just …"

"An arse," interjected her father. "And if he's been an arse, then it's mental cruelty. Did he ever knock ye aboot?"

"No! Nisbet's not like that."

She didn't mention that she'd decked her husband a few times.

"Then it's mental cruelty. That'll dae it. I'll phone the lawyers."

He walked off.

Brenda Sangster sighed. There was no arguing with her father when he'd made up his mind. He'd never liked her choice of husband. They had never been on good terms, her father continually making remarks, sniping, sneering, occasionally, indeed frequently pointing out that he'd stumped up for half the house *and* the extension *and* half the furniture. Then once, after Nisbet had politely asked to be paid for the umpteenth job that he was being asked to do for her father's property business, or for one of his dodgy pals, Lockerbie had gone completely apeshit, calling Nisbet an ungrateful bastard, screaming directly into Nisbet's face. Things hadn't been going well in the marital household, but after that, what had been a downhill slope became a precipice, with Brenda's loyalties to her father gradually growing in proportion to a decaying marriage she knew was on the road to nowhere.

From the sitting room, she could hear her father on the phone to the lawyers, using his usual diplomatic style.

"Get me Mister Berwick. … Then get him out of his meeting! … Then get him tae phone me when he comes out! … Lockerbie! … *Mister* Lockerbie! *Thomas* Lockerbie! … Bloody Lockerbie! L-O-C-K-erbie. Jesus bloody Christ! It's no that hard is it?"

--------oOo--------

2

Hermens

Eric Soloman Lutoslawski-Hermens rose early. He needed no alarm; his body clock was as precise as every other aspect of his being and he awoke precisely at six o'clock every morning. Even the biennial irregularity of British Summertime's waxing and waning had no effect upon the cadence of his sleep. His body clock adjusted, entirely in harmony with the changes. It seemed that the very act of adjusting his watch, adjusted his sleep pattern.

Of Polish Jewish extraction, he was London born and bred. His grandfather, a Holocaust survivor had made his way to Holland intending to cross to England. But in Amsterdam he'd met other displaced survivors. Befriended by a small-time diamond trader, he was taken under his wing. The young Lutoslawski had applied himself with a fanatical zeal and a focus that can only come from the burial of nightmares and together he and his mentor built up a respectable business. By the mid '50s, they'd opened a modest office in London and the young Lutoslawski moved there to be closer to the London Diamond Bourse. With money in hand, he married well, taking a Dutch wife and settled into middle class English life, paying only occasional lip service to the synagogue.

So it was that his grandson, Eric after his grandfather and baptised Hermens, his mother's maiden name (it would be helpful to the boy not to appear altogether too Jewish), Eton-educated but of no great academic merit, had grown to be a lynchpin in his grandfather's business. Ignoring his less diligent father and learning from his grandfather the intricacies, the politics, the excitement of the shady underbelly of the London and Antwerp diamond trades, he diversified. Not for Eric the smiling, fawning role of the retailer, the mind-numbing tension of cutting and polishing stones, nor the drudgery of the wholesaler.

No, Eric Hermes delighted in the thrill of dealing in diamonds: legal diamonds, illicit diamonds, stolen diamonds, blood diamonds, even industrial diamonds, he knew them all and nobody, he prided himself, knew better how to melt stones, illicit or bona fide into the market leaving nothing but a good profit for him and his chain of contacts. Any diamond of any size, any quantity, measured by carats, of course, but for all he cared, ounces or pounds if the trade was good enough. And so it was also, that insinuating himself into the London Diamond Club, rubbing shoulders with the old guard in the London Diamond Bourse he cultivated a more, middle-England, slightly less-public school accent. In the diamond community of Hatton Garden it was easy, on the one hand, to be an establishment trader and on the other, to hide his other activity in plain sight.

Strangely, it was not simply the money to be made that drove Hermens, although profit was needful. He liked the planning, the control, the meticulous attention to detail. These things fascinated his studious mind more than anything, more than friendship (he had no close friends, only business acquaintances and relatives); or love (he didn't need it and had little to give); more than sex, more than money (he was comfortable). Eric Hermens was useful to people but he had no friends, and he had no friends for two reasons: he didn't feel the need of friends and people did not seek out his company. The thing was, Eric Hermens was not a very nice man.

So this morning he rose, ignoring as he always did the inevitable distraction of his morning erection and went to the en-suite toilet. He looked in the bathroom mirror as he peed. Even his sleeping attire was precise: his pyjamas were barely wrinkled, his hair barely disheveled. He always slept alone, mainly upon his back, hands upon his belly, but he never snored. He had never married because he had never given the possibility any thought whatsoever; it was just that it was not relevant to his lifestyle and aside from that, he did not, as a general rule, find the company of women to his liking.

The hotel, although he could afford better, on this occasion, was perfect for both his personal and his business needs, anonymity being the key factor. That it catered for the many budget-minded visitors to Edinburgh made it all the more private because he could simply float through the throng of bus-party culture freaks, ruck-sacked students and travelling salesmen in the hotel lobby without catching anybody's eye.

He'd arrived last evening, by train. The hotel was just off a busy main street and the room was nice enough: clean and quiet, en-suite. As usual, he spread his toiletries out across the fake marble surrounding the washbasin and enjoyed his fastidious personal hygiene routine. In point of fact, he really didn't enjoy it any more than a pilot enjoys a pre-flight check or any more than most people enjoy breakfast. His pre-flight check was a necessary routine and breakfast the mere taking on of fuel. For him, personal hygiene performed the same kind of life preserving function. To be other than meticulously clean, was to be slap-dash with one's personal well-being.

This morning, however, required an entirely different type of fastidiousness. Quite the opposite in fact. This morning he had to be quite as un-fastidious as he could be. Quite a chore for a fastidious man. Accordingly, he went back to bed, and with the self-confident, statesman-like ease of an Eisenhower or a Churchill, slept soundly for another three hours.

At nine, he rose again and removed from his wheeled overnight bag a suit of clothes entirely different from the Saville Row city clothes in which he had arrived. He opened it. On top lay the Google Maps screen grab of the part of Edinburgh he'd rehearsed: Lothian Road and Princes Street Gardens, his preferred route marked in pencil. He tore it up. He already knew it.

--------oOo--------

Angela

Nisbet got out of the car and went into the little white-oak reception area to face Angela's arctic sneer.

"Hi!" he croaked, "'Been at a client's."

Angela looked him hard in his rose-tinted eyes. Then looked at the bags under them. There was a long pause.

"So The Diggers is a client now?" she enquired.

Angela had brought the drop-dead tone of voice to the level of an art form. She could tell just by looking at him that he'd been out on the piss.

"Or, wait a minute, don't tell me, ... The Guru Balti on Dundee street? They'll be a client now too? I'll create an account for them."

Black-belt sarcasm.

He might as well 'fess up'.

"Actually, the boys at the rugby club took me out to celebrate."

"I know, Beastie's been on the phone already. Worried about you. Anyway, celebrate what?"

"Me and Brenda separating."

"I wouldn't think that's anything to celebrate."

"Well *they* thought so. Anyway, I got hammered, totally hammered."

"I kind of got that impression," she said. She held her nose, rotated the desktop fan in his direction and switched it on.

"That bad?"

"Yup. You smell like road kill. You have umpteen emails," she said, digitally, like a Dalek, without breaking the rhythm of her typing on the computer.

Nisbet wasn't providing her with enough work to keep her busy full time, but Angela had a very active other life on Facebook.

"Aye. I've not had a chance to check my mail this morning."

"Two clients want to see their drawings, you have Hamish Morrison just after lunch, and a Mister Berwick called and said he wanted to see you. Something concerning you and your wife. He's made an appointment for four this afternoon."

"*How come Angela's got access to my personal email?*" thought Nisbet. "*How do these things come about?*"

"He sounds like a lawyer," said Angela.

"Christ Angela," said Nisbet, "Could you not ...?"

"No, I couldn't. He just said he'd be here at four and hung up before I could ask. He was quite abrupt."

"Oh well. ... Anyway, there's no such thing as me and my wife anymore. Is the kettle on?"

Angela was beginning to spoil the day. It had started out bad and

Nisbet wanted, at the very least, to keep it that way because there was always a danger it could get worse.

"It was."

This meant, "Get your own bloody coffee, I'm your secretary not your housemaid."

She paused, then with a softer tone she asked, "Did you hear from Brenda over the weekend?"

This was Angela going into her big sister routine. It was a genuine enough enquiry because Angela had a special type of woman's intuition which had guided her across a perfectly uneventful marriage of her own to a spectacularly uneventful Health Board Clerical Officer called Colin, and she knew the real truth that, although she liked Brenda a lot, Nisbet should never have married her. She knew, as did Nisbet, that Brenda should have married a wealthy double glazing tycoon with a gold bracelet and a gold Rolex, and that Nisbet should be living with a sporty young flibbertigibbet in a nice little terraced cottage somewhere in a wee village.

"What's there to hear?" replied Nisbet.

He went through to his office pursued by Angela's concern about his relationship with his daughter Samantha. Samantha Sangster for God's sake! Sammy Sangster. Jesus Christ Almighty! What kind of a name is Samantha if your second name is Sangster? What was wrong with Jean? Or Carol? Or bloody Susan?

Brenda had caught him in a weak moment. Her puss-nodule of a father had been so convinced that the child was going to be a boy that everybody had given up on the notion of a girl and no girls' names had even been mooted. So when, to everybody's disappointment but Nisbet's, a girl had popped out of Brenda's nether end, she had come up with a name that she felt reflected her middle-classness. And her disappointed guttersnipe twat of a male parent had approved, there being nothing he could possibly disapprove of about his daughter other than the fact that she wasn't a son - and she was married to Nisbet.

So it turned out that ludicrous names continued to run in the Sangster family. Names are like mercury in the bloodstream. Nothing you do will ever rid you of the family curse of shite names. Nisbet was about as daft a first name as anybody could possibly come up with.

He'd often thought about changing it by deed pole, to something less ludicrous, like Stalin Sangster, or maybe Hitler Sangster.

Out loud, he said to Angela, "Samantha hates me. I'm the only person in the whole universe who treats her like a child. Everybody else treats her like the dowager empress of bloody Balerno."

"You love her really."

Angela was now shouting through from the kitchenette. Having made her point, she was putting on the kettle to make a fresh pot of real coffee, the sort of coffee usually reserved for clients.

"I love her Angela," Nisbet shouted back. "But I don't like her. She's an extortion racketeer. Brenda and her bloody parents have her so spoilt, they're afraid to go for a crap in case she bites her own arm off. Brenda's measure of good motherhood is how terrified of your offspring you are."

"I'm sure she'll turn out all right when she grows up."

"Well she'll grow up no matter what happens."

There was a pause, then, "Don't forget, you've got a meeting with Hamish Morrison at half past one," said Angela.

"Aye, I nearly forgot about that." said Nisbet. "It's just a preliminary for that care home in Niddry. No panic, Hamish is a mate - we used to work together."

"You'll run out of mates one day," said Angela.

"You better hope not," retorted Nisbet. "Or we're both out of a job."

Nisbet turned to his computer, fired it up, ignored the huge stack of email - only two wouldn't be spam and they'd be hate mail from clients. He started work on an extension to a bungalow. The client wanted the cheaper option, a flat roof. It would leak inside ten years and Nisbet would be back designing what he should have had in the first place.

Nisbet was ambitious but he didn't like hassle and he quite liked to be liked. So when it came to acting the ruthless businessman, he often got walked over by bolshie clients. He even got walked over by mousey, apologetic clients. To begin with, his ambition had been fulfilled when he had qualified and got his job with the council. There you could sit up in your office block with a bloody good salary and help design council houses with tiny rooms that made people's lives miserable, sure in the knowledge that they would be pulled down in fifteen or twenty years so that you could build new, different but equally horrible new-age starter homes for a new generation of unhappy people, by which time you would be a head of department, stoke up your pension, and nobody would bother you. Meanwhile you could make a tidy wedge on the side doing homers, designing dormer windows for bungalows in Broxburn and lean-to extensions for 'Right to Buy' council houses that you'd designed in the first place. In the council offices, architects' and civil engineers' mobile phones rang continuously as the team answered calls from their private clients. They were all making a decent living and Nisbet, being single, was doing ok. He had a nice flat, a cool car and no worries other than staying in the first team at the rugby club.

But that was then and this was now. Then he met Brenda: attractive woman, nice figure and, as it turned out, two twats. One was a nice place to pass the time, and the other was her nasty twat of a father. But they were happy, for a while, until they moved to Balerno and Brenda's arse-faced office-equipment tycoon father and brain-dead, nodding donkey simpleton of a mother were close by in Colinton. Poor old Brenda's mum. Her life had been one of brow-beaten terror. She'd been emotionally lobotomised by her psychopathic bully of a husband, and had become a compliant automaton agreeing to anything to keep the peace. But she was a nice lady, or must have been, once.

In truth, much of the ambition for this business venture had been Brenda's. She had married a well-balanced, rugby-playing, happy-go-lucky guy and had decided to transform him into a badly balanced, non-rugby-playing successful businessman with poorly-balanced accounts.

In fact he wasn't doing too badly, building a reputation, the business came in and he usually got paid fairly promptly - except for work he had done for his wife's bastard of a father. After he'd married Brenda, the bastard had regularly preyed upon Nisbet's good nature, having him spec. up property renovation work, handling planning applications, project managing the work. The bastard never paid him for a single job.

The bastard had a very successful business selling office equipment and computer systems to businesses in Edinburgh and the east of Scotland, and with time on his hands, he had turned his hands to property development and private letting. And when Nisbet had met Brenda the bastard's dreams had come true: a tame architect, engineer and project manager all rolled into one, and one that he'd never have to pay. The man was a complete and utter bastard: a greedy, foul-tempered sociopath.

Nisbet put those thoughts to the side and worked as contentedly as he could, considering his throbbing hangover, for an hour or so.

Angela called through from her desk, "You haven't forgotten you've got an appointment with Hamish thingy at half past one have you?"

He had a meeting at the city chambers, a preliminary, fact-finding meeting prior to bidding for the design of some sheltered housing in one of the less desirable post codes in Edinburgh. He had a good shout at getting the business, or at least onto the short list for it. His pal Hamish was in charge of the project and he knew that Nisbet could do it and would also bring in the full QS inside budget.

He looked at his watch; bags of time. He lifted the bundle of masonry samples he'd gathered to show Hamish – just something to talk about: small slices of masonry stuck to cardboard and a similar sample swatch of Marley roof tiles.

Hamish probably wouldn't even look at them but Nisbet didn't want to go empty handed. Most likely they'd just talk about rugby, knock back the city of Edinburgh's putrescent coffee for an hour and Hamish would put Nisbet on the short list - he hoped. He lifted his laptop bag, took the laptop out, laid it on the desk and shoved the bundle of samples into the bag, then slid his neatly bound proposal into the document pocket and zipped it shut.

"I'm off to the City Chambers, Angela. I'll get something to eat on the way."

"Get something to drink too - like a bottle of disinfectant. Don't breathe on anybody important."

"Thanks Angela, it's always nice to have one's self esteem massaged."

--------oOo--------

Seedy

The little man walking along Morrison Street towards Lothian Road was unlikely to be noticed. He was perfectly unnoticeable. Maybe a retired clerk, or a teacher. Despite the nondescript, even slightly seedy look he had, nevertheless, taken great care with his appearance: the worn, grey, Matalan car coat, the dark grey flannels and cheap shoes were nicely complimented by cheap wire-framed spectacles and whispy hair poking out from beneath a trilby, the sort of trilby that only bald men with a comb-over wear to keep the wind from creating tonsorial havoc.

In point of fact, he wasn't all that small, it was just that Hermens had perfected the look, the demeanour and the gait of a person of utter insignificance. And it made sense to behave like this because to appear to be a person of low worth was perfect camouflage when carrying tens of thousands of pounds in diamonds across city streets.

Nowadays it was Hermens' habit, with this outfit, at the end of the day to fold it, although, not all that neatly, pack it in polythene, and confine it to the floor of his wardrobe until next time. Anyone idle enough to take the trouble to give him a glance today would have had trouble maintaining their focus for long, he was that uninteresting.

Thus attired, he made his way toward Lothian Road with his carefully aged, retired-person gait and modest posture, toting his agéd laptop case.

He headed up Morrison Street towards the centre of town. It was a bit of a risk, a seedy little man with a shabby laptop case because he could easily have been mugged for the computer that it might contain, but that was what had been requested by the client.

He'd never have risked such a stupid format himself but he was going along with the plan and anyway, he'd temporarily attached the laptop case to his wrist with a loop of nylon cord. The bag wasn't heavy, he could endure it for the brief walk. But as he went, he found the strange, furtive arrangements increasingly irritating.

He crossed Lothian Road and cut along Bread Street. Here he gave the laptop bag a slight heft as if testing the weight to reassure himself that the contents were as they should be and perhaps gave the only signal so far that he had anything to occupy his mind whatsoever, far less to be nervous about. Neither did he need to hurry. He had timed the walk to the dropping point to the second so that he would be waiting for the shortest length of time: just enough time so as to appear only to be a casual visitor to the park but not so little time as to hurry the rendezvous.

His impression of the people he was to make the drop to today, however, had led him to consider the possibility of some kind of cock-up. He had a dim view of provincial savages like the Scots. At best the Sots were yokels. At worst they were self-destructive idiots who never stopped complaining in their ridiculous accents. In all likelihood, his contact would be late and the messenger would be some kind of ethnic cretin. Like all people from the south-east of England, he was sick to the back teeth of the Scots: they were hillbillies, bloody amateurs, idiots who never stopped complaining. They were shit at football, shit at rugby, politically duplicitous, shit at macroeconomics, and ought not to be trusted to run a cold tap, let alone their own country. The Glaswegians, he had heard, were bad, but this Edinburgh bunch looked like they would be equally incompetent. His contact in Edinburgh had sounded like a precious young Gen Z prick, and maybe a bit of a left-footer. But it was hard to tell with the funny accent.

From Bread Street, Hermens zig-zagged his way from Spittal Street to the top of Lady Lawson Street and at the traffic lights took the opportunity to look behind. The street was empty. Down Lady Lawson Street and along Castle Terrace, this was enough of a circuitous route to give him plenty of street crossing opportunities to look right and left and spot anybody still there who shouldn't be. It wasn't paranoia: there was absolutely no chance of him being followed, but there was no shame in cultivating the extreme caution and attention to detail upon which he prided himself.

Back on Lothian Road, he walked to the corner of Princes Street and turned right down the slope, past the public toilets and headed east towards the National Gallery end of Princes Street Gardens.

Just past the Royal Scots Greys monument, a few benches along from the gate onto The Mound, he sat down casually and placed his laptop bag beside him on the ground. There was an odd looking couple at the other end of the bench but after a moment, they got up and left, not liking the look of their new neighbour. He checked his watch, the contact was late. Bloody savages.

--------oOo--------

The Park

Nisbet put on his classy, outrageously expensive tan leather jacket as worn by incredibly cool successful types and strutted down to Mahmoud's corner shop and sandwich bar for a couple of rolls, a can of Coke and The Scotsman newspaper. Above the shop was a boldly painted sign proclaiming "Khan's Korner". Mahmoud Khan had tried simply calling it "The PakiSannies", but the council had asked him to take it down on the grounds that it was racist. Mahmoud had resisted on the basis that a) that's what his customers called the shop with no malice whatsoever and b) he'd already been asked to take it down by the mosque, a higher authority, and his mother, a higher authority still. But eventually he bowed to pressure from all sides, including Nisbet, and it became Khan's Korner, Minimarket and Sandwich Bar.

"You're lookin' a wee bit rough big man," said the broad Glasgow accent from behind the counter, a moment after the bell announced Nisbet's entrance. Mahmoud Khan was born and bred Glaswegian.

"Been oan the tropical fish then?"

Weegie rhyming slang. Mahmoud had a Masters in mathematics and a perfectly middle-class upbringing, but he liked to turn the authentic working class Weegie up on Edinburgh eejits like Nisbet. They both enjoyed the crack.

"No half," said Nisbet. "Totally mangled last night, so Ah wis."

Nisbet's native West Lothian dialect kicked in but it was no match for Mahmoud's Weegie.

"Rugby? Yon's a game fur jessies. They're aye cuddlin' up every chance they get," said the shopkeeper, the world's most loyal and committed Asian Celtic FC supporter.

His ambition was to go to an Auld Firm game at Ibrox or Parkhead but even he knew that a brown face in a green and white hooped jersey might be too much of a temptation for the imbecilic elements of Rangers or Celtic. He should have been a cricket fan like his dad, but cricket, as far as Mahmoud was concerned, was "a game for jessies".

"Ah dinnae dae much of that cuddling Mahmoud, just the occasional ruck. Ah'm a winger, or an inside centre, or used tae be."

"Inside centre? That sounds a bit bent."

"Aye," said Nisbet, "it does a bit."

"So does a ruck. Is that rhymin' slang? Or a misprint? An' ye's a' dae that scum. That cannae be healthy."

"Scrum," corrected Nisbet.

"Same difference. So ye got hammered eh?"

"Aye, then we went for a Ruby Murray," continued Nisbet.

"A curry? Where did you go?" Mahmoud asked suspiciously, dropping the over-egged Weegie in favour of his genuine Bearsden accent. He knew nearly every curry restaurant in both cities and was either fiercely loyal or unforgivingly critical depending upon whether the owners were kin. As well as their property portfolios, his brother and his dad ran a restaurant near Tollcross. Mahmoud and his mum ran the shop. They all worked their arses off.

"One of your enemies."

"What? A Rangers curry? An English curry?"

"No, an Indian ya tube," said Nisbet.

"Indian curry?" said Mahmoud, rising to the challenge. "Navaho or Apache?"

"Well, you're frae the wild west."

"Very funny Niz. Just buy something and clear off ya rugby-playin' Embra tosser."

If Mahmoud's mother came in and heard him talking like this he was dead meat, albeit halal dead meat, but dead anyway.

"Ok, I'll have two ham rolls." This was pushing it a bit.

Mahmoud looked him in the eye. "Get lost."

"Cheese then."

"What kind of roll?"

"A bagel."

"Get stuffed," said Mahmoud.

Mahmoud started making up the cheese rolls.

"By the way Niz, mah ma's made thur sheik kebabs," said Mahmoud, nodding towards the cold counter. "They're braw."

Nisbet eyed them up, they looked perfect, just what he needed for a post-curry hangover: more curry.

"They look like dog jobbies," said Nisbet, keeping up the crack.

"Aye, she's got the look right but no the flavour. Ah think they need a bit more essence of labrador."

"Ok," said Nisbet, already salivating at the thought of them. "Ah'll have a kebab."

"They come in pairs," said Mahmoud. "Or, if you only want one, it's one for the price of two."

While he continued chatting to Mahmoud about his hangover, Nisbet had a look on the rotating book stand and on impulse picked out a Stephen King novel that he hadn't read: The Stand. It was about three inches thick. That would keep him going for several nights of empty-bed insomnia. He went to the counter, got the cheese rolls and a couple of Mahmoud's mum's sheik kebabs. It was a giant stack of food for a mere lunchtime snack but his hangover demanded carbohydrates, saturated fat and E numbers. He produced his debit card. Mahmoud shook his head.

"It's ok Nisbet, Ah owe ye big time - for the plannin' application."

"This book says four fifty," said Nisbet. "Plus the rolls and stuff, it's too much, just take the money."

"The book was four fifty - back in nineteen eighty four. That's a book an'a, by the way."

"Pardon?" said Nisbet.

"Nineteen Eighty Four. Aw forget it ya numbskull. Anyway, my brother gets the books for next to nothing. Besides, we've had it in stock about four years already. Just forget it."

"Thanks Mahmoud," said Nisbet.

"Here's another book fur ye," said Mahmoud, bending down to a box beneath the till and handing it to Nisbet. It was the Koran.

"You gave me one already," said Nisbet.

"Take it anyway Niz. It might come in handy. Have ye read it?"

"Aye," said Nisbet, truthfully. He had. Well, a good portion anyway, out of loyalty to Mahmoud. It had made as much sense to him as the Old Testament. Or the new.

The Khan's planning application had taken Nisbet two evenings working late, but he didn't mind. Mahmoud's dad, Ashad was a nice man and like many Pakistanis he invested his hard-earned surplus in property. He had an as-yet-undisclosed number of rental flats in Edinburgh, and a pile of mortgage debt so big it was, according to Mahmoud, the biggest man-made object you could see from space. Nisbet didn't know how Ashad managed the amount of debt he must be pushing around but then, they didn't spend much on frivolity. It was Ashad that was letting out Nisbet's old flat for him. He only took ten percent and the rest was paying off Nisbet's original mortgage at warp speed.

When Ashad had heard about Nisbet and Brenda splitting up he'd been horrified and genuinely upset. It's what comes, he'd said, with genuine sincerity, of not letting your parents pick your wife for you. The way things had turned out with him and Brenda, Ash had a point. If it had been down to Nisbet's dad, he would have picked wee Sandra MacKay from Glebe Street whose dad worked beside him. Looking back, wee Sandra MacKay would have done just fine – compared to Brenda, she was almost completely hang-up-free.

With nothing better to do until his appointment with Hamish, and with the spring sunshine splitting the paving stones, he got into the car and drove up to town to watch the pretty office girls sunning themselves in Prince's Street Gardens. Now that he was very nearly single again he felt he needn't have any guilty feelings about eyeing up girls, and Princes Street Gardens was the place for that. Spring was rising in Nisbet's soul and you never knew your luck, something other than Spring might get a rise out of it too. He had bags of time before his meeting.

In town, Nisbet crossed The High Street, cruised down Bank Street to the top of The Mound and turned into Market Street looking for a vacant parking space.

"*Pure spawn,*" he thought to himself.

There was a vacant parking space half way down from the top of the street. Three quid in the ticket machine would do it, although at Edinburgh parking prices, it was probably only good for thirty seconds.

Walking back up to The Mound, it crossed his mind that he probably, in fact definitely, hadn't bought enough time on his parking ticket and the car would get booked. But he decided to be cool, not to give a toss and walked towards Princes Street Gardens looking as confident, casual and successful as he could. But he would get booked though, and he knew it. But Nisbet decided to be the cool successful type, not care about a ticket, and not pay it until the last minute. Mind you, he reflected, he never paid them until the last minute anyway, and only after Angela nagged the hell out of him.

His steps faltered near the gate into the Gardens - this lunch was probably going to cost him about fifty quid in parking fines. Explain that to Angela! Maybe he should move the car and have a legally parked lunch. No. Bollocks! He looked at his watch; twenty to one, he would risk the twenty minutes or even half an hour eating his lunch in the sunshine. He was now in total control of his own destiny.

He turned into Princes Street Gardens and skipped down the steps past the Floral Clock, which wasn't floral yet. The only blossom on display was a neat row green gardeners' arses, up in the air getting it ready for planting because, of course it was spring. And now that he was in the Gardens, he realised that the spring sunshine had conned him into believing that summer was here. There wasn't a pretty girl in sight. He'd had, in his mind's eye, the picture of pretty girls lying about in the warm sunshine escaping from the salt mines of Edinburgh's legal offices and banks. This was an encounter he had made many years ago and he remembered now that the disrobing office workers he had seen then had, of course, been sunning themselves in July, not April.

Now that he gave it some thought he couldn't ever remember seeing goose pimples on all those thighs protruding from all those panties he had ogled all those years ago. Indeed, it was bloody cold in the partial shade of the still-leafless trees and the spring sunshine only slanted through them dappling the embankment that sloped down from Princes Street. He wandered along, looking down onto the frosted grass on the lower level of the Gardens. The frosty air in the hollow of the gardens bit through his leather jacket and goosed up his skin. Thinly clad office girls were going to be thin on the ground.

A few people, mainly elderly folk, or tourists, wandered past enjoying the spring day but most of them were wrapped up warmly, and Nisbet was reminded that his designer leather jacket might nearly have bankrupt him but it wasn't going to keep him warm. Apart from nearly four hundred quid, the price, he reflected, of looking hypercool, was hypothermia.

He missed a couple of park benches occupied by elderly folk and tourists stuffing their faces from Pret a Mange sandwich wrappers. Seeing in the distance the danger of being shat on by thousands of pigeons being fed by the people farther along, he took the first vacant seat. And he didn't want to get much farther from the car because he had a feeling the cold would drive him back to it pretty soon.

The only occupant of this bench was a sorry looking man at the far end, dressed in cheap clothes with a shabby laptop bag between his feet. Nisbet sat down at the far end of the bench, laid his own laptop bag containing the cheese rolls, book, kebabs and Hamish's samples and proposal on the bench beside him and looked at the headlines in The Scotsman newspaper. The chancellor of the exchequer had announced more stringent cost saving measures and warned of tougher times ahead for everybody, except his pals in the City of London, who had just cranked interest rates. Bloody brilliant. You no sooner elect the bastards than they're shagging the population up the arse. Further down the page it seemed that a terrorist bomb had gone off in Brussels. There was utter carnage, people blown to pieces, and he wondered what things were coming to. What would it be like to be near that? It made him shudder. Or was it the cold?

After a minute or two, out of the corner of his eye Nisbet saw the little man shuffle his creepy arse along the bench until he was less than an arm's length away.

"*Jesus Christ,*" thought Nisbet. "*I pick the only bench in the whole of Princes Street Gardens with a weirdo.*"

The weirdo leant a bit in Nisbet's direction, shuffled a little closer, leant forward, and looked Nisbet directly in the face.

This was a bit too creepy for comfort, so for something to say Nisbet came up with, "Chilly for June!"

He immediately felt like a prat. Only a complete dork would use an expression like that.

The creepy little man continued to look at Nisbet for a few long seconds. He gave the creepy guy his best friendly-but-firm negotiating eye contact and looked back at his newspaper to read on about the Brussels bomb.

"About right for the time of year," said the man, apparently not phased at all by Nisbet's attempt to psyche him.

His accent was odd, the regionless, slightly posh accent of somebody educated somewhere in England, outside the state system.

"Well one doesn't does one," said Nisbet, wondering why he was replying in this deranged pseudo-posh manner.

The weirdo was still looking hard at Nisbet when quite suddenly, his whole manner changed. Rising up from the bench he stood facing Nisbet. He was taller and looked less fragile than he had seemed at first. In an utterly contrasting tone to his earlier bird-like style he said, and this time with the clipped consonants and rounded vowels of the public school mixed with the nasal drawl of North London.

"You were late you ill-mannered oaf! And why did this trade have to be so theatrical? You won't make it in this business," said the weirdo. "Amateur! You're all bloody amateurs."

Hermens' cool demeanor had departed.

"*Amateur*?!" thought Nisbet indignantly.

Indignant or not, obligingly, his current questionable self-esteem and lingering hangover made him feel like an amateur. This weird individual was having a bad effect on his current wafer-thin optimism, and just as he wished the man would go away, he did. He turned and strode off west along the promenade of the gardens. As Nisbet watched him the confident stride deteriorated into a nondescript shamble which ceased to hold Nisbet's attention.

"Edinburgh," said Nisbet to himself, "is full of bloody weirdos."

He opened his newspaper again, finished the remaining four column inches about the bomb, wondered if terrorists would ever hit Edinburgh, comforted himself that they probably didn't know where it was, and turned the page. He read his newspaper for a few minutes more, then feeling the pangs of post-bender, E-number and saturated-fat deficiency reaching its nadir, he reached out sideways for his laptop bag containing his cheese rolls. It was gone. He looked hard at where it had been. It remained gone. That little creep had run off with his bloody cheese rolls! He looked again, this time under the bench. His laptop bag definitely had gone, cheese rolls, kebabs and all, and worse, with his client's samples and his proposal in it. But wait, a minute! The weirdo had left his own laptop bag on the ground there, where his feet had been.

Nisbet considered this for a moment. Was it a bomb? Like the Brussels bomb in the newspapers? Would he make it to the road before it blew up? Preposterous. Be decisive. Be macho. If you were going to let a terrorist bomb off you'd go for a bigger score than one bloke on a park bench in Princes Street Gardens.

On the other hand, maybe the chap was new at it, getting in some practice before he went for the full suicide vest job - blow up an embassy or a crowded disco. Gingerly, he picked the laptop bag up. It was a well-worn laptop bag too, the handle was frayed and the nylon weave of the fabric pretty grubby. It wasn't heavy and by the appearance of its weirdo owner, it would, like Nisbet's own laptop bag, only contain a packed lunch - aside from an effing client proposal which he'd have to do without unless he could get online at Hamish's office. With no packed lunch to enjoy, he stood up to see if he could spot the weirdo and get his bag back. But with the Gardens filling with tourists, he concluded that he'd never find such an insignificant wee shite in this throng and sat back down to check out the fellow's laptop bag.

He unzipped it. Inside there was a rectangular parcel, not quite as long as a house brick, wrapped very neatly in classy, watermarked brown paper and sticky tape. There was nothing else in the bag. He couldn't imagine what a funny wee man might have, wrapped up in such a parcel, but since it was so nicely wrapped he figured it couldn't be a bomb. After all, why wrap a bomb up as nicely as that, like a birthday present, if you're going to blow it to smithereens?

A moment's contemplation - well, it *could* be a present. He figured that even an insane, creepy person might have someone to give a present to. Maybe a present for his mum. Nisbet felt sorry for him. The poor guy would be upset to lose his mum's present. With the parcel held against his ear there was no suspicious ticking and nothing rattled so was it safe to assume that the owner hadn't intended to bomb Nisbet? Or his own mum for that matter?

The parcel wasn't heavy, but it had a nice, sort-of birthday present feel to it, probably not a bomb. It was wrapped in high quality brown paper with a sort-of, shiny etched pattern on it. It looked expensive. He lowered it back into the laptop bag and stared down at it, still a bit suspicious. Could it be a bomb? but the guy didn't look like a terrorist. But then …

Up on the castle wall, Edinburgh's famous One-o'-Clock Gun went off with a colossal boom. Nisbet leapt off the bench about a foot.

"Bloody hell!" He'd nearly shat himself for the second time today.

The pigeons further along rose to the sound of the blast, but better used to the One-o'-Clock Gun than Nisbet, soon settled back at the feet of the tourists.

--------o0o--------

Bryson

"There's too much effin' subterfuge," said the big man in the passenger seat of the huge Mercedes parked on Queen Street.

"Aws ye huv tae dae," he continued, "is meet up somewhere quiet, dae the trade, an' bugger aff. A' this subterfuge is a loady pish. These English bastards take theirsel's too effin' serious and so does the boss's laddie - the wee ... ."

He flicked some fluff from the seam of his trousers.

"Christ all Mighty!" he continued. "If the thing was weel-enough set up in the first place, they could just post it tae us."

"Maybe the boss's laddie disnae want tae gie them his address. And they widnae ken we'd send the money," said wee Mackenzie, who always did his best to be smart, even though he was dim.

"Look son, Ah'll dae the thinking. You just get the motor in the right place at the right time. Right?"

"Aye Alec. Hanover Street taxi rank, eight minutes efter ye enter the park. How eight minutes?"

The big man's voice was deep and throaty, well hard, "Because Julian paced it oot. He reckons that's the time, apparently, that it'll take tae go intae the park frae the Art Gallery end, go tae the fourth bench frae the west gate and meet some prat dressed scruffy-like. Some Big Issue-sellin' wee retired bastard wi a hat and a black laptop bag."

"Then what?"

"We swop passwords. Somethin' like, *"Chilly for the time of year."* Then the Englishman, whoever the fuck he is, goes, *"Not if you expected better."* Or something' like that."

Bryson continued, "Honestly it's like a fuckin' John Le Carrier bloody spy novel." Not that he'd ever read one. "Whit's wrang wi' a bit o' auld fashioned, straight-forward shady fuckin' dealing, oan the level? Meet up in the fuckin' pub carpark, or oot in the countryside. Money for goods, handshake, fuck off. On the level, nae jiggery fuckin' pokery. The trouble is, the boss's laddie thinks ye're no in the crime business unless ye're awash wi' fuckin' intrigue. Fuckin' retard. Fuckin' wee ... public school ... shirt lifter."

"He likes to be discrete. He did say no tae take the Merc."

"Look son, the reason Ah've got a S-Class Merc and, by the wey, a gold Rolex an' a fuckin' Armani leather jaikit is because Ah ken how tae dae crime!" said Bryson, his gravelly, bass-baritone voice rising to tenor, and notching up a few extra decibels.

He lowered his voice, "Unlike yon Julian."

"Ye can get they jaikits in TK Marcs 'n' Sparcs," said MacKenzie.

"TK *Max*," corrected Bryson, not that he'd be seen dead there.

"Aw, forget it, ya wee dimwit. Listen wee man. Yon Julian's just a jumped up public school squirt straight oot o' fuckin' university and he kens eff all about onything ither than gettin' shagged up the erse by wan o' they bent-shot posh mates o' his. The auld man widnae normally hae gone in for a' this spy-versus-spy shite. He's just been indulgin' the bairn."

"Aye, but Julian's still the boss's laddie, so we better dae whit we're tel't."

"Look son, if ye dinnae want tae choke on yer fuckin' front teeth, keep yer gob shut."

"Ok Alec," said MacKenzie.

Bryson looked at his gold Rolex.

"Gie me that fuckin' laptop bag," he snapped, snatching it from Mackenzie. He opened the car door. "Park near the tap o' the taxi rank."

"I'll get asked tae move."

"It's a black fuckin' S-Class Mercedes wi' tinted windaes! Naeb'dy'll come near ye, if they dae, tell them tae eff aff."

"It's a'right fur you Alec, you're big, Ahm no."

"A' right, pit thur Rae Bans oan an' dinnae even open the windae. Just look at them, hard like."

"How dae ye dae that?"

"If somebody chaps the windae, ye dinnae react, ye just sit there. They chap the windae again; ye just sit there, starin' oot the front windae. They chap the windae again, ye turn yer heid – very slow; ye look straight at them; ye dinnae move a muscle, ye just stare."

"Then whit?"

"Nothin'. They'll fuck off. Even if they dinnae think you're big, they'll ken somebody or somethin' big is comin'." He opened the door. "Ah'll no be mair than a couple o' meenutes."

--------o0o--------

Meeting, Parting

Alec Bryson got out of the Merc on Hanover Street, headed downhill to Princes Street, crossed over to the esplanade beside the gallery, cut past the ice-cream stall and turned left into East Princes Street Gardens at exactly one-o-clock and, like all Edinburgh natives, checked his watch as the huge blast of the One-o'-Clock Gun from the castle ramparts echoed round the capital's busy lunchtime streets.

"Utter shite, this rendezvous lark, needless fuckin' cloak an' dagger pish," muttered Bryson, walking angrily into the gardens.

Mackenzie sat, patiently counting down the minutes on his watch. A traffic warden knocked on the driver's door of the Merc. Mackenzie did as he was told: he stared straight ahead. More window knocking. More staring straight ahead. More knocking. Mackenzie slowly turned his head and stared through Bryson's Ray Bans at the traffic warden. Twenty-seven seconds went past, and Mackenzie was getting a stiff neck. The traffic warden left.
"Ya beauty!" shouted the diminutive Mackenzie, pumping his fist. He felt well hard. He'd never before successfully pulled off a hard-man move in his life.
The traffic warden came back and knocked on the window again, waving his computerized, automatic car-booking doofur at Mackenzie. Mackenzie drove off.

Not too far away, but far enough to matter, Nisbet's 'weirdo' was indeed, as Nisbet predicted, going to be upset about losing his parcel. In fact, more upset than Nisbet could possibly imagine. More upset than the weirdo himself could imagine.

When Hermens left his leather jacketed and obviously terminally thick Scottish contact, he headed off in the direction of the public toilets at the west end of the gardens to check inside the laptop bag and count the money. The bag just did not feel as if it had the right amount of money in it unless it was in larger denominations than was usual. But it was not safe to draw attention by stopping and counting money in a public park. Something about the whole thing just didn't feel right, *and* the bastard had been late.

The One-o-Clock Gun went off up on the castle ramparts. Hermens nearly came out of his shoes.

His instinct was that there had been a terrorist bomb. His pulse rate dropped to normal again as he remembered about Edinburgh's One-O'-Clock Gun. No town clocks in the square or on the buildings, no church bells, just a one-hundred-and-five millimetre howitzer cuckoo clock on the castle wall. Like most Londoners of public schooling, he had been drilled in the facts of UK geography and anthropology: the Welsh were all crooks, the Irish beyond the pale, and the Scots were a bunch of ungrateful, drunk, illiterate degenerates who kept their coal in the bath and their porridge in a drawer. The One-O'-Clock Gun confirmed it: none of them, apparently, could afford a watch and had to be told when lunchtime had arrived by using WWII artillery.

At the far west end of Princes Street Gardens he climbed up the stairs to the public toilets pondering how only in Scotland would the stupid bastards put a public toilet at the top of a flight of stairs. What do you do if you're disabled? Not that Hermens could give a shit about whether disabled people could get a shit. He just needed more reasons to hate these northern barbarians.

Inside, he waited for a cubicle to free up, entered and locked the door. In his life, he hadn't crapped in a public toilet more than about twice. His obsession with good personal hygiene prevented it - but here was the only private seat in town. He hung the laptop bag on the coat hook on the door, and spent a few minutes carefully laying a hygienic security cordon of toilet paper around the toilet seat. He dropped his pants, got hold of the laptop bag and sat down with it on his bare knees. A crap might help to ease the uneasy feeling he had had all morning.

He relaxed and let it go. That was better. He opened the laptop bag and his hand met Nisbet's sample cards of decorative stone. His eyebrows came down as he withdrew the card and stared at the stone samples; he held the card up in the dim light of the cubicle.

"Oooooh!" he groaned. "Oh no..oh." This looked bad. "Pieces of stone!? Pieces of bloody stone!?" he said, his voice rising, tense and puzzled.

The two American tourists at the urinal turned and stared at the door of the cubicle where the anguished voice was coming from.

"Kidney stones?" said a puzzled Marty to his pal.

"Aaahh!" said the voice in the cubicle as Hermens lifted out another sample card.

"Jesus Christ! Tiles?! Bloody tiles?!" The pitch was now two octaves higher.

"I think he means piles," whispered Rick from Tennessee, doing up his fly.

"Yeh, he's got a steech imdepiment," joked Marty.

"The Koran? The bloody Koran? Bastards, bastards, bastards!"

The cubicle voice rose through another full octave and fifty decibels of pain and anguish.

"Well at least he's not a terrorist," said Rick, washing his hands, lie a good American. "I mean, he wouldn't swear at the Koran."

"Two cheese rolls!? Two kebabs!? And two books!?" wept Hermens in horrified astonishment. He looked at the title. "The Stand? The bloody Stand!" He'd read it.

"You should get help buddy."

"Yeah buddy," said Marty, you need to watch your diet."

"Yeh, if you're gonna eat books, try the Reader's Digest."

More anguish came from the cubicle as Hermens lifted the second book from the laptop bag.

"And the Koran!?" The voice was perplexed. He certainly hadn't read that. "The Koran!? Jesus Christ Almighty."

"Wrong book for Jesus my friend," said Rick. "Y'all wanna try the Bible."

Hermens seethed so much, that a loud fart and a splash came from the cubicle as a deeply embittered and confused turd hit the water.

"Wow!" said Marty. "Sounds like he just shat an encyclopaedia."

Hermens would kill those double-crossing Scottish bastards. They would die horrible deaths. If he'd had a gun they'd die today. So would those bloody Yanks on the other side of the door. He reached for the toilet paper. None left. He'd used the last of it coating the toilet seat. He looked around the cubicle. No spare toilet paper to be seen. Bloody savages! They would die horrible, horrible deaths.

He used the paper bag from the rolls and was left with the books. Atheist though he was, the Koran was out of the question, so he dropped it back in the laptop bag, ripped three pages from The Stand and wiped his arse, appropriately, with the Contents page. He dropped the book on the floor. Still in a daze of fury, he hauled his trousers up along with most of his toilet paper security cordon which had stuck to his arse.

"A lousy packed lunch!" he cried, looking at the cheese rolls which were now in the toilet. He flushed it. He was left with the kebabs, and instinctively knew that they wouldn't flush away. The thought of leaving unflushed debris in the toilet was too much for his fastidious mind. Consumed with hatred for Nisbet's laptop bag, he booted it. It bounced off the toilet pan and slid along the urine-soaked floor to the cubicle next door.

Bursting out of the cubicle with the sheik kebabs in his hand, he shoulder charged one of the Americans back against the urinal and then stood at the exit in a daze of fury, sheik kebabs in hand.

The Americans watched as this weird, angry Limey bastard stood there with a deranged expression on his face and what appeared to be a turd in his hand. Hermens held the sheik kebabs up to the light and stared at them with utter hatred.

He yelled, "Bastards Bastards, bastards! Dirty heathen bastards!" at the sheik kebabs, took two vicious bites from the ends, threw them back in the cubicle and raced out of the toilets and down the steps.

"Jesus Aitch Christ!" said the Americans in unison, and gingerly stepped out of the public toilet door to see the weirdo tearing back along the gardens heading for the rendezvous point, municipal toilet paper flapping from beneath his jacket.

"Did you see that? He just ate his own turd!" exclaimed Marty.

"This is one freekin' weird country," said Rick.

"Yup, but I don't think he was Scatch, I think he was definitely a Limey," said Marty.

"No wonder the Scatch hate 'em. My gramps was stationed in England during the war. He said the Limeys were assholes and their food was shit. I didn't think he meant they actually ate shit."

"Yeah, if Rhonda ever mentions oral hygiene to me again, I'll tell her about that Limey."

In the next door cubicle, a startled Malaysian tourist cowered, too afraid to leave for two reasons: a psychopath had just left the cubicle next door, and there was no toilet paper.

He contemplated the laptop bag that had just slid beneath the cubicle divider. Desperate to get out of the toilet alive, but also with a clean arse, he gingerly opened the bag in the hope of finding something resembling toilet paper. He flipped the bag open on the floor. He lifted the Koran. Perhaps it was a sign from the Prophet. He slid it into his jacket pocket, and had a look in the bag's document pocket. He pulled out Nisbet's A4 proposal. The cover read:

EDC Project 1476/B

A Proposal for the Design, Development and Implementation of

a

Care Home for the Dependent Handicapped and Elderly

The Nisbet Sangster Partnership

Architect, Civil Engineer, Project Management

This meant nothing to the tourist. The cover was stiff, shiny paper, so he ripped out Page 2, the Contents page, and wiped his arse with it. He used two more pages, including the one with the full colour site illustration. He pulled up his trousers and left the toilet, unaware that his arsehole was now navy blue and black. It would itch later in the day.

Nisbet gathered himself together, shot through with adrenaline as the canon blast echoed around the Gardens. He looked back at the parcel in the bottom of the bag. When he lifted his face out of the laptop bag he noticed that a squadron of pigeons raised by the canon-fire from the castle wall had settled around his feet and were lobbying confidently for some cheese roll.

"Your out of luck boys," he said, opening his newspaper again to hide from the pigeons. "You'll have to go and find that wee weirdo. He's got the rolls, and my book ... and Mahmoud's Koran."

Nisbet imagined the perplexed face of the strange little man as he opened the laptop bag, only to find some stone samples and the Koran. He had no idea just how perplexed.

But by now, Nisbet's stylish, cool-guy, pretty-girl-oggling, chill-out, spring sunshine lunch was completely blown and instead of chilling out, the air had him chilled to the bone. And aside from that, the One-o'-Clock Gun had blown his system's adrenaline count clean off the scale. He decided to return to the car before it got a ticket.

He looked at his watch. He'd better leg it or he'd get booked for sure. With the stranger's laptop bag in hand, he jogged back towards the Floral Clock gate, past the upward arses of the gardeners, and rounded onto The Mound to head for his car. The more nervous of getting a parking ticket he got, the faster he jogged until he was powering up the hill at about the same speed, he imagined, that he'd once have come onto the park as a half-time sub.

Oh well, cool or not, he needed the exercise and the steep gradient of The Mound was fairly getting his pulse rate up and straining his calf muscles. So it was with some relief that he turned into the Market Street downhill stretch towards his car a hundred or so yards away. On the far side of his car Nisbet spotted a traffic warden heading in its direction with his automatic car booking gadget drawn like a six shooter. Putting on a final sprint, Nisbet skidded to a halt, unlocked the car, leapt in, threw the weirdo's laptop bag on the passenger side floor and drove off before a parking ticket could hit the windscreen. In the mirror all he saw, with great satisfaction, was a frustrated looking traffic warden. He hadn't seen a well-filled leather jacket giving chase for the last hundred yards.

--------oOo--------

Pigeons

Alec Bryson was a big man and he looked every inch the professional thug that he was. He drove a flash car and wore expensive clothes because he had money and wanted respect. He wanted respect because his money was as good as anybody else's. In point of fact, as often as not, it *was* somebody else's. So by logical deduction he should get the respect that other pillars of society got who also wore expensive clothes. Unfortunately, Bryson didn't know this: they had taste and he didn't. So poor Alec Bryson often had to resort to intimidation to get the respect that he felt he deserved. When it came to intimidation, however, Alec did get the respect that he deserved: when the need arose, which it often did, he could be very intimidating indeed.

Even when he was at ease in your company he was more frightening than many men of similar size would have been when angry. The difference was that Alec Bryson would not have minded trading the pleasure of your company for the pleasure, if you annoyed him, of rubbing your face off on a roughcast wall. When the need arose, and often when it didn't, he could be a nasty, rotten, sadistic, humourless bastard.

Bryson was not unusually tall, six feet four, but he was naturally powerfully built. His monstrous gold sovereign ring would have been even more tasteless had it not looked like a farthing on his huge hands. His expensive blouson leather jacket would have been stylish if he hadn't filled it with little room to spare, and his silk shirt would have been exotically sophisticated if there had not been dark hair peeking from the collar and cuffs.

He spent hours every week in the gymnasium, convinced that his physique would make him more attractive to women and more intimidating to men. Sadly, and he didn't know this, it had precisely the opposite effect so that the women he hoped he'd attract, found him grotesque and more than a little scary, and a certain type of man found him quite scrumptious.

A natural athleticism and an inclination to be muscular, combined with early years competing in martial arts, had given him the well-honed physique of a heavyweight athlete so that for all his lack of culture and sophistication he had an animal-like poise and grace. For his size he was light on his feet, nimble and quick.

As he entered East Princes Street gardens from the Art Gallery end, pigeons and people fluttered from his path. Most people would guide their steps through the throng of pigeons but Alec Bryson's gate never faltered and his large, Gucci-clad right foot caught one of the pigeons amidships. It rolled over, gathered itself and flew off. One or two other birds went with it, but the pickings in the park were too good to miss for the whole flock to leave on account of one bird's unlucky encounter with Alec Bryson's foot.

He prowled along to the forth bench where sat an apologetic-looking little man with a rather shabby black Cordura nylon briefcase-cum-laptop bag on the ground beside his feet. Bryson sat between him and a young Japanese couple. The swarm of pigeons reconvened its feast of breadcrumbs behind him but the people kept to their wide berth. Multilingual in the body language of intimidation, Bryson gave the young Japanese couple one of his hard-man, intimidating, you-need-to-fuck-off looks. They did.

The little man on his other side had a handful of bread and was casually flicking pieces to different open parts of the pavement so that he steered a small colonnade of pigeons around like radio-controlled toys. He appeared not to notice Bryson but concentrated fully on the task of keeping the pigeons in constant search of the next tit-bit. The point seemed to be to get the one dominant pigeon to explode from overeating while the others died of exhaustion.

Already Bryson did not like this little creep. Supercilious wee English shites like this always got on his tits. The rude little bastard hadn't even acknowledged his arrival.

After interminable seconds of watching the pack of pigeons, and waiting for some kind of reaction from the wee man, he said, impatiently, "Chilly weather for the time of year eh pal? No? Eh?"

This was done with the standard Scottish hard-man tone,

understood across all social divides in the land, and from a man like Bryson it always got a reaction. The little man started slightly and turned to look at Bryson through his wire-rimmed glasses, interrupting the steady flow of bread to the pigeons. The lead bird stopped for a breather.

"Oh, I beg your pardon." said the pigeon man quietly.

Bryson stared him hard in the face, his look of distaste quite undisguised, "Ah says, 'Chilly weather for the time of year!'"

The pigeons had gathered expectantly around Bryson's feet and were pecking the gold decals on his Gucci shoes. He kicked them away.

"Oh I expect so," said the little man apologetically, but quite politely. "But then you'd expect it still to be cold at this time of year."

The big man looked expensively dressed but a bit on the heavy side. He was bursting out of his jacket. Entirely not the sort of person you'd expect to meet in the park on a day like today.

"You can't even get the fucking script right can you? Too much fucking intrigue and no enough common sense," said Bryson.

"My dear boy ..."

But Bryson was up and away, pigeons and pedestrians fluttering out of his way, the laptop bag looking half the size swinging in his huge fist.

"*Oh well,*" thought Greg Patullo. "*People are a major pain in the arse these days. Can't even exchange a few polite words about the weather.*"

That big guy was probably one of those Care-In-The-Community early releases from the psycho wards. A paranoid schizophrenic or something. Or just a prick. It was why he'd been happy to take early retirement from the university. He was tired of teaching architecture to a bunch of entitled snowflake students, and for half the money they were likely to earn in their first year in a job.

He flicked a few crumbs of bread to the pigeons and reached for his laptop bag. It was gone. That big weirdo must have taken it, with the slate samples and his notepad. Instead, there was another laptop bag lying on the bench.

"*Sod it!*" he thought, "*It doesn't matter, don't need the samples anyway. What's this here?*"

He reached for the new laptop bag which had materialised beside him. It was a big laptop bag, an expandable one, with the expansion zip undone. Probably for one of those fifteen or seventeen-inch laptops the yuppies bought. Wankers. And it was quite heavy, he nearly pulled a muscle lifting it from the bench. Maybe it contained a nice new laptop. Maybe an Apple Mac Powerbook, he'd always wanted an Apple Mac. Mind you, it would probably just be the big idiot's packed lunch. But it was too heavy, and too thick. With his luck it would be one of those crap laptops that you get out of PC World that ruin your life, lose your data and hang every two minutes. Then ask you to click OK. He already had one of those.

He partly unzipped the bag and looked inside. What he saw was not a laptop but two large rectangular parcels filling the corners of the bag. Each was maybe two inches thick, wrapped in brown paper. Not sandwiches anyway, that's for sure. And they were heavy like books are heavy. Two big, thick encyclopaedias? He was lost for ideas. Two new laptops? Who buys laptops two at a time? Nope. Books, probably. Maybe a couple of those big glossy coffee table editions. Nice big, glossy books with beautiful photography. But the big guy didn't look like the bookish type, didn't have the look of an avid reader, if he could read at all.

Presents, surely? Who wraps stuff this neatly in brown paper unless it's a present? One you're going to send parcel post? Oh dear, somebody wouldn't be getting their birthday presents. He looked along the garden to see if he could see the big fellah coming back for it. To his relief there was no sign of him, and he really didn't want to chase after the crazy big bastard. And he'd never find him in the throng around the gallery. Sod it. A fair swop, his old laptop bag with some slate samples in exchange for a couple of big coffee table books - finders keepers, the guy was an arse anyway.

Greg Patullo zipped the laptop bag shut and checked his watch, which told him it was time to go for the bus. He grabbed the laptop bag, got up from the bench, poured the last of the bread crumbs onto the ground, stuffed the empty paper bag into his coat pocket and went for his bus. He took his ancient iPhone out of his pocket and called Moira to say he'd be home in fifteen or twenty minutes. No, he hadn't eaten and yes, a nice bacon sandwich and a cup of tea would be perfect. The two of them could have a flick through these books while they ate lunch. Moira always made a nice lunch for him now that he was at home so much. He didn't miss the university refectory food but he did miss the company, and the crack with his colleagues, and he missed the money. A lousy pension from thirty years of lecturing. At least he still had the odd homer.

Climbing back up to Princes Street, the bag felt pretty heavy: definitely books or something.

--------oOo--------

Bryson tapped his foot impatiently as the Merc cruised back down Hanover Street towards him. The bag felt heavier than he'd expected but he hadn't dared look inside it. All he'd wanted to do was get the fuck out of there and get this stupid scenario over with. Too much effing subterfuge, and here he was, standing in the middle of Edinburgh in full view of the law-abiding public with a bag of loot in his hand worth a king's ransomed.

"Where the fuck have ye been?"

"I caught all the lights Alec," said Mackenzie.

"Whit fuckin' lights? There's nae lights oan in your heid ya daft wee shite."

"Ah'm only hauf a meenute late."

"Fucking shut up and get us the fuck oot o' here!"

He got in and pulled the door shut, still enjoying the way that an S-Class Merc's door closed. It closed with the same satisfying, quiet thud that a fist made when driven upwards into a solar plexus.

Mackenzie schmoozed the big Merc back up over George Street in the direction of Queen Street and the boss's lockup garage in the mews lane behind his townhouse.

"You should hae seen the wee shite. Disguised as a fucking pensioner. I ask you. Wee beaky-nosed, wee Sassenach, kindae wee

Jewish-lookin' bastard."

"Did you get the stuff Alec?"

"Shut the fuck up and drive."

Bryson undid the laptop bag's zip and looked inside it for the first time. There was a parcel in it, something comfortingly heavy, rolled up in bubble wrap. It was dusted with breadcrumbs. Feeding the pigeons for Christ's sake! The contact had taken blending into the surroundings to a ridiculous length.

"Too much fucking subterfuge," said Bryson, thinking out loud. "This crap is all Julian's fucking idea. The boss should hae sent him tae art college tae dae a degree in fucking fashion design or something like that insteed o' accoontancy. Get the wee public school poof oot the wey in some gay bohemian, twenty-four-seven arse-bangin' commune. Insteed he's went an' brought the wee shirt-lifter intae the faimily business an' now we're a' actin' like fuckin MI5."

"Aye," said Mackenzie, happy to agree with Bryson. "Julian's a stuck-up erse."

"Ah think he gets it stuck *up* his erse," said the naturally homophobic Bryson absent-mindedly as he lifted the laptop bag.

It felt a bit too heavy for what it should contain. But maybe that was normal, a bit of disguise or something, maybe in a metal box or something. He had no experience of trading in anything other than recreational chemicals, of the smoke it or inject-it-for-relaxation kind, or the inject-it for-muscle-building kind. He unrolled the bubble wrap and found himself staring at four pieces of roofing slate. They were slightly different colours. His heart leapt and his stomach sank. He looked back in the laptop bag. Nothing, just more breadcrumbs, a relatively new, A4 spiral-bound note pad and a copy of True Crime magazine.

"Jesus!"

He plunged his hand into the other compartments and rummaged around. Zilch. The full horror began to dawn on him.

"Aaaw Naaaw! Aaaagh! Stop the car! Stop the fucking car!"

The car heaved to a halt on its massive disc brakes and a taxi swerved around it with its horn blaring.

"Naw keep gawn, keep gawn. Awe Jesus, awe Jesus! Naw, burl roond, burl roond! Back tae the gairdens."

Mackenzie swung the wheel and booted the throttle, spinning the huge car around in its length, cutting up cars, vans and taxis to go back up Hanover Street. Bryson, his heart pounding, thumbed through the notebook. Only two pages had anything on them. Just numbers, meaningless scribblings, and symbols, what did they mean? And the odd short column of figures.

"Aaaaagh!" he screamed. "We've been screwed, fuckin' screwed! Get back tae the Mound!"

The Mercedes powered back up Hanover Street, jumped the lights on Queen Street, cut through the throng of cars on George Street, and surged downhill towards Princes Street.

"Bastards. Double crossing bastards! True Crime Magazine!? True Crime?" His voice rose another octave. "Sarcastic fuckin' double-crossing Sassenach bastards! Ah'll gie them true crime!"

The comic irony was entirely lost on Bryson. If he'd had a sense of humour he'd have seen the funny side. As the car reached the traffic lights at the top of Hanover Street, Bryson, his pulse rate now at two thousand, looked to his left and was about to jump out of the car to go and look for the double-crossing wee bastard. Instinctively he looked to his right, around the bus that was blocking their exit, his eye caught something strange. A man, a fairly big man, dressed very like himself, and carrying a black laptop bag, appeared from West Princes Street Gardens at the Floral Clock gate and, apparently in a big hurry, ran off up The Mound, full tilt. Bryson did a double take and thought for a minute. It was too strange, too weird a coincidence to be a coincidence.

"Get roond that fuckin bus!" he yelled at Mackenzie. "Jump the lights, up The Mound!"

Mackenzie had several goes at circumnavigating the bus but was blocked by traffic, marooned at the junction.

"Ah cannae, Alec, there's a row o' buses in front o' him."

Bryson got out of the Merc and started running diagonally across the junction; for a big man he could shift. He vaulted the bonnet of a hatchback and made it across the junction to join The Mound pavement at the Floral Clock gate. The man in the leather jacket was a hundred yards ahead by now and also quick on his feet. Bryson put his head down and sprinted after him.

Near the bend at the top of The Mound, Bryson's quarry cut across the road and dodged between the traffic into Market Street. Bryson powered after him. He reached the top of Market Street in time to see a red BMW pull out of a parking space and drive off down towards Waverley. Bryson thought he got some of the Beamer's number. N15 something, something T.

--------oOo--------

Hermens ran back along Princes Street Gardens promenade, by now looking, and feeling, dangerously deranged. He passed some tourists who gave him a puzzled look. The festive banner of toilet paper still fluttered out from beneath his jacket. He rounded the post of the Floral Clock gate just in time to spot his leather-jacketed contact, about seventy or so yards away, running fast up The Mound. He gave chase and was gaining fast as the leather jacket rounded the corner into Market Street. The man's dress looked familiar but something about him wasn't quite right. He got to the corner to see the man just standing there, fifty yards away. A bit further down the steep Market Street gradient a red BMW was pulling out of a parking space. Hermens caught a bit of the car's number: something, something, something, BET. Or was it 13ET?

The game was up, Bryson turned around, out of breath, head down, dejected and apoplectic. He started to head back up Market Street to The Mound to look for Mackenzie when he lifted his head and saw a mature chap in shabby-looking clothes standing there looking directly back at him, not thirty yards away. Their eyes met and instinctively each knew who and what the other was, and Hermens knew immediately that this leather jacketed monster might be similarly dressed, but he wasn't the contact he'd swapped bags with, and he knew a thug when he saw one. He could be a hard bastard when need be, but he was no match for this freak.

Bryson worked it out too: something was well weird. He'd get hold of this wee creep and beat the facts out of him. Like an enraged grizzly he charged back up the hill towards Hermens. With an athleticism that belied his aged look, the fellow turned and bolted back down The Mound. Bryson, pretty-well done as far as sprinting was concerned, gave chase. Cutting in front of a black cab and causing the driver to hit the brakes hard, Bryson did not hear the harmony of impact inside the cab as two tourists walloped into the cab divider. He almost kept pace on the downhill stretch to the bottom of The Mound, bouncing tourists like skittles into the iron railings as he charged down the pavement. Inside the Gardens, for a hundred yards he kept going but the old guy was quick. Plainly, he wasn't all that old.

Alec Bryson was fit but he was never a distance runner, too heavy, and with the other guy putting more distance between them he slowed to a walk, sweat running down between his considerable pectorals. He knew when to pack it in, when to get the hell out of it. He'd attract even more attention than he had already.

A hundred yards away, aware that the race was won, Hermens slowed and turned. Bryson stood and held the other man's distant gaze for a moment, trying to size him up, then turned and walked unhurriedly back to The Mound to find Mackenzie parked at the Floral Clock gate. A traffic warden was bending down speaking into a one-inch aperture at the top of the driver's door.

Bryson straightened the traffic warden up by his collar, "Get the fuck away frae mah motur," he said, selecting his well-practiced, dangerous psychopath tone.

It was enough to stop anybody in their tracks. The traffic warden simply looked at the pavement like a child approached by the school bully. Bryson rounded the Merc, still watching the traffic warden with his total death stare. He got in the passenger side.

"Get us the fuck oot o' here wee man."

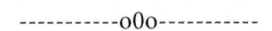

-----------oOo-----------

Greg Patullo

Greg Patullo sat upstairs on the near-empty bus heading toward Haymarket. A Mercedes Benz cut in front of the bus causing the driver to brake sharply. Patullo shook his head; everybody was such a total arsehole these days.

When the bus reached Haymarket and began its creeping way round the one-way system, Patullo thought he might as well have a look at these big books, or whatever was in the parcels in the laptop bag. It definitely looked like they contained a couple of those big coffee table-type books, a couple of hardbacks or maybe a few big glossy paperbacks at least. He couldn't think what else it could be, but it had the dense feel of paper. With the laptop bag on his lap, he ran the zipper round the perimeter. Inside were the brown paper parcels with what indeed, now that he saw them again, might be two, well-wrapped, very solid and heavy books. They seemed flexible, so maybe they contained some of those big coffee-table-type paperback books. With his luck they'd be some of those cookery books his wife got every Christmas from her sister: "*Nigella Lawson's 101 Things To Cook While Snorting Cocaine*", or "*Jamie Oliver, Fifteen-Minute Vegan Crap for Millennial Wankers to Spend an Hour Cooking.*"

He raised the end of the top package. It was carefully, meticulously wrapped in heavy brown paper and Sellotaped so that there was no loose paper to pick at. It looked to be about a foot by thirteen or fourteen inches. He took out the tiny Swiss Army Knife key fob that his daughter had given him three Christmases ago - he knew it would come in handy one day. Gently sliding the tiny, razor-sharp blade into the paper at one corner, careful only to slit the wrapping paper and tape, he opened a couple of inches of the brown paper. Couldn't see inside.

He slit open a few more inches of the brown paper wrapper. All he could see was a layer of thin cardboard then the neat edge of the pages of a book. Surely not a glossy coffee table book with that cardboard cover. He wondered what it was because the edges of the paper didn't look all that clean; not a new book, that's for sure – well-thumbed. He slit open a few inches of brown paper along the adjacent side and bent back the rough cardboard to try to see the book's title. He was met with a number 50. Tearing a little more of the paper revealed a portrait of Queen Elizabeth smirking back at him.

Blimey! A book about money? But this wasn't the glossy, heavy paper of a large paperback book. No, it looked too much, in texture and colour, too much like money, not that he could recall what a fifty pound note looked like, everything he bought these days was with his debit card. Couldn't be fifty-pound notes, could it? His pulse hit the bell for round two.

He pulled apart more of the brown paper wrapper, this time looking around himself to see if he was being watched. He wasn't; the bus was nearly empty. He ran his finger down the pages of 'the book'. The Queen was smirking back at him from all of them.

He looked out the window of the bus for several seconds. Then he looked back into the bag. He had been right the first time. Bundles of fifty-pound notes were staring back up at him. And this was just one parcel. He put his hand in the bag and ran his thumb down the corner of the top bundle. There were hundreds of them. Hundreds and hundreds of fifty pound notes.

Greg Patullo looked around again to see if anybody had been watching him. No, thankfully. He re-packed the parcel's brown paper as best he could, snuggled it back into the laptop bag, zipped it shut and sat as comfortably and calmly as he could as the bus stopped at a bus stop. He looked out the window, watching people get on and off. They seemed to be in slow motion. His mind raced, his head swam, his pulse rose and his knuckles whitened. The bus pulled away again.

He shook his head to make sure he was awake rather than in some weird dream. He had on his lap, a laptop bag with two large parcels in it. In each parcel, he calculated, were several pounds weight of fifty pound notes. Each bundle was as thick as, well, a thick paperback book. Like say, War and Peace. Or The Stand - a couple of inches thick, say four hundred pages, two hundred leaves of paper. Say, two hundred, fifty pound notes. Times two, times maybe four. Two hundred thousand-odd pounds maybe. And there were two parcels, the same. That thug had left him a bag with four, maybe five hundred grand in it.

On Glasgow Road, just past Corstorphine village, a number 21 bus stopped and the driver ran up the stairs. A student had reported that a mature gentleman was being sick on the upper deck. Greg Patullo made his apologies, got off the bus and walked his puke-splattered shoes the last few stops to North Gyle Road with the laptop bag held prisoner in his arms as if it might struggle free and bolt, like a cat heading for the vet.

--------oOo--------

Mackenzie

"I ken't it was a fuck-up frae the stert," said Mackenzie, trying to sound knowledgeable, as he drove sedately down Hanover Street towards the boss's lock-up garage.

"Aw did ye?" said Alec, through his teeth.

"Aye, I ken't we should hae been mair careful. The boss is gawny kill us."

"Aw is he?" said Bryson, apparently calm now.

He was having trouble containing himself. Any minute the red mist would come down. All he needed right now when things had gone terribly wrong was an *I-told-you-so* remark from a worm like wee Mackenzie.

"He's going to go Radio fuckin' Rental Alec, so he is."

The red mist came down.

"Tell ye whit son, pull ower a meenit," said Bryson, calmly, through the red mist. "Stop the car."

"Dae ye want tae drive Alec?"

"Aye, in a minute."

The kid stopped the car and depressed the parking brake with his left foot. Alec's left fist smashed into the kid's face and rattled his head off the door pillar. Blood fountained from his nose and Alec mopped it up with the kid's anorak before it dripped on the Merc's cream leather upholstery.

"Ah think Ah'd better drive son. Ye're in nae condition. Hae a wee rest in the back seat. Dinnae bleed oan nothin'."

--------oOo--------

Berwick

When Nisbet got back to the office after his meeting, he was starving. He dropped the laptop bag with the weirdo's parcel onto the reception coffee table and headed for the biscuit tin. Angela was just back from shopping and had made a pot of tea. She obviously had warmed a little towards him since this morning and had a mug ready for him as he came in.

"Thanks," said Nisbet, already making a pig of himself with the digestive biscuits. "Any mail?"

"Not so far. How did it go at the City Chambers?"

"Aye, fine," said Nisbet, "I think I'll get it. Hamish gave me the nod that we're well within budget." He thought for a moment, "Maybe I've underpriced it."

"No," said Angela, "let's just get the job."

Angela was as much involved in all of the project management and delegation as Nisbet. She could be that hard-nosed with his sub-contractors that she occasionally scared even Nisbet.

"Remember, you have that Mister Berwick coming to see you shortly."

"Oh him, I wonder what he wants. Really Angela, you – we should find out what people want."

"If I wasn't here, nobody would know what anybody wants."

This was true and Nisbet nodded sagely.

"He said it was about you and your wife, remember? Besides, it's not my business to pry. Who's is the laptop bag?" continued Angela, prying. "That's not your laptop bag. Where's yours?"

Christ, Angela missed nothing.

"Oh that. I found it in Princes Street Gardens. This little creep mistakenly took my laptop bag with my samples *and* my cheese rolls and left that. Bloody lucky I never took my actual laptop with me," he said, stuffing the last of a digestive biscuit into his mouth and taking a sip of his tea.

"I had to go and see Hamish without my samples and my proposal."

"How did you get through your meeting without your proposal?"

Angela was inspecting the laptop bag.

"There's a parcel in it," he mumbled from a full mouth and pointing at the bag with his tea. "The proposal's in the iCloud. I emailed it to him from my phone while we had a coffee. All we did was talk rugby. See that's where relationships get you. You can still do business with people when they know that you're …"

"A numpty," said Angela.

She opened the laptop bag and looked inside. Lifting out the brown-paper parcel, she shook it at her ear.

"It's awfully carefully wrapped. That's really nice brown paper. Wow! It's got a little Harrods' logos all over it. That's expensive paper."

Nisbet hadn't noticed the tiny Harrods' logo's

"It's probably a present," continued Angela. "You should hand it in to the police."

"No fears! He's got my cheese rolls and my book, and Hamish's samples, and a couple of Mahmoud's mum's kebabs," said Nisbet with his bottom lip out. "I was looking forward to those kebabs. Let's open it."

Nisbet grabbed the parcel from Angela and began picking at the Sellotape.

Angela grabbed it back. "You'll do no such thing, it's probably a present. We'll hand it in to the police."

"What about my book?" pleaded Nisbet petulantly, knowing that Angela could not be swayed on matters concerning "doing the right thing".

"Too bad," she replied. "The poor chap lucked out. Cheese rolls and some stone samples wasn't a very good swop."

She popped the parcel into the bottom drawer of the filing cabinet. Nisbet went off to his work station feeling like a greedy ten-year-old.

About four o'clock, Angela came in and announced that Mister

Berwick had arrived, and showed him into Nisbet's office. Nisbet always hated this habit. He felt that Angela should keep people waiting to make it look more professional: make it look like he was very busy with important stuff. He got up from the design workstation, went the few steps to the door and held out his hand, already drawing the impression from the visitor's bulbous, fleshy jowls and sullen expression that this was not a very engaging individual.

"Good afternoon Mister Sangster. My name is Berwick, from Robb, Styles and Chatham."

Berwick looked familiar but Nisbet couldn't place him: ugly, but familiar. Berwick held out his hand and Nisbet automatically took it to shake it. But it didn't shake. Berwick's hand was limp, warm and clammy to the point of being slimy. Nisbet barely suppressed a shudder and his heart sank as it began to sink in that this would be his dog-puke father-in-law's solicitor. Robb, Styles and Chatham were known colloquially in Edinburgh as Robb, Steal and Cheat'em, a soubriquet by all accounts, that they wore with pride.

Despite Berwick's superior air and obviously expensive three-piece suit, there was a distinctly unwholesome feel about the man, as if some deeply hidden but substantial part of his mind was occupied with some very unsavoury thoughts indeed. Would you leave your thirteen-year-old daughter alone in a room with this guy? No.

At all events, either Berwick was buying his suits a size too small or his body swelled up when it got clammy. His body had to be clammy if the handshake was anything to go by, and Nisbet had been careful to wipe his hand on the bum of his slacks as soon as it was free from Berwick's sweaty, limp and ever-so-slightly over-lingering grasp. He knew he wasn't going to like this podgy, pompous git and he knew also, that Berwick wasn't going to mind that Nisbet didn't like him. He'd be well used to being disliked, it seemed to Nisbet, so unlikeable did he seem.

"You were lucky to get me in. I'm quite often out at a client's."

"We had an appointment," said Berwick emphatically. His life revolved around appointments and he plainly didn't believe Nisbet's appointment story any more than Nisbet did.

"Mister Sangster, I have come on your wife's behalf in order to discuss your separation."

"Oh?" said Nisbet. He knew this already, but now it was confirmed that the rest of the afternoon was definitely going to be a complete pisser.

Brenda had left fairly unemotionally with a parting comment that they should just sort things out amicably, to which he had wholeheartedly agreed. But it was a sure-fire bet that her sack-of-shit father had got her moving.

"Can I get you a coffee?" he offered trying to sound friendly.

"No thank you," said Berwick, wrinkling a fat nostril as if the coffee would be unhygienic, and proceeded to fill the vinyl-covered occasional chair which Nisbet proffered.

Even if Nisbet was going to come out of this looking like a complete prat he would get what little he could out of it. He knew that every time Berwick moved his clammy arse, the vinyl seat would make giant farty noises. It was why he never sat on it.

"Mister Sangster," said Berwick, leaning forward, "I'm sure we are both very busy men so I will get straight to the point." ...thrrp.

"Quite."

Nisbet would endeavour to be as pompous as he could every time the interface between Berwick's arse and the vinyl chair made a farty noise.

Almost immediately however, Berwick took the upper hand.

"As you may be aware, Mrs Sangster is concerned about the future of her daughter..."

"Our daughter. "

"... now that you have separated."

Berwick had not come to beat about the bush: Robb, Steal and Cheat'em were known amongst the Edinburgh legal community as a bunch of blood-thirsty, ruthless, unscrupulous bastards.

Nisbet sat with his elbows on the last few remaining exposed inches of his desk as this awful man went straight onto the attack. Brenda's father was not short of disposable income and there was nothing he liked better than to rip another human being to shreds, legally, financially or physically, not with any good reason, but just because he could. And he had plenty of reason with Nisbet because he had never liked, and now absolutely hated his son-in-law.

Considering the speed at which Berwick had gone on the offensive, Nisbet wondered if there could be a couple of heavies lurking outside to take over when he tired of the sound of his own voice. By the sound of the fat, slimy bastard, Nisbet would have several hours to go before Berwick did tire of his own voice. Now that Nisbet knew the dual purpose of the ensuing diatribe, (Berwick listening to the sound of his own voice and berating Nisbet), he slouched a little and, unable to form any kind of resistance, resigned himself to hearing the fat bastard babbling on and bloody on.

It was depressing, not just because of its content, which deepened his anxiety as it unfolded, but mainly because it went on and bloody on. Berwick produced some papers from his briefcase. Nisbet rested his chin on his clasped fingers. Berwick's liking for the sound of his own voice meant Nisbet was in for the long haul here.

Berwick was a tape-deck on loop: Annulment, Custody, Mental Cruelty, Maintenance, Alimony, Child Support Agency, on and bloody on in the same drab monotone, like a stuck Leonard Cohen record.

Hypnotised by the pounding of Berwick's chant, he began to feel completely displaced from his normal reality. It was like one of those out-of-body experiences he'd heard of. He felt like a stranger in his own office, a voyeur. He looked round vacantly. It was pretty bad.

"Alimony, Regular payments, Failure to pay, Child Support Agency. Direct debit." On and bloody on.

It was pretty bad. His chin sank deeper into his hands and his heart sank deeper into his abdomen. Direct debt more like. He looked round his office with his out-of-body-experience eyes and saw it the way strangers, the new clients, not enough of whom came, must see it: it was a bit of a tip. Piles of papers, a dirty coffee cup on the filing cabinet, slightly grubby carpet. Files on the floor, dust. Was it that way because he was lazy? Or too busy? Both, probably. The office was like Nisbet's life nowadays: a right mess.

"Swift settlement, sensible mature conclusion … ."

By now Nisbet's head had sunk far enough for his nose to rest on his thumbs and he peered through the diver's mask of his hands at Berwick. Ugly bastard. He had scaly skin too, like a big pink fish. One of those drab fat bastards hanging around the coral reef scavenging on the brightly coloured but poorer inhabitants.

He swam his gaze round the sunken wreck of his office, past the waving reefs of paper and the rocky outcrops of junk until it alighted once more on Berwick. Suddenly he knew where he had seen Berwick before: the thick lips, the bulging eyes, the sallow complexion and the rapidly retreating forehead escaping down the back of his fat neck.

"*As we reach the depths of the coral lagoon,*" said Attenborough, in the back of Nisbet's head, "*we meet the Giant Grouperfish. Ugly though he is, he is relatively harmless. He seems to be saying to us …*"

Nisbet sniggered at his own humour.

"Mister Sangster this is a very serious matter!"

Berwick leant forward again and his arse thrrrped the vinyl seat. Nisbet sniggered again.

"I must say that I really don't appreciate your attitude."

Plainly, Berwick was a mind reader and took exception to resembling a fat, slimy fish. You'd think he'd be used to it by now – fat and slimy was a lifestyle choice for him.

Nisbet, currently low in self-esteem and suddenly almost bereft of all hope, scraped the bottom of the barrel containing his pride to find a handful of his old self. He grabbed it and sat back. Notwithstanding Brenda's departure, he was sure, well a bit sure, well, optimistic, that Brenda wasn't feeling this vindictive and this was all her suppurating pussnodule of a father's doing.

"Mister Berwick, before we go any further, when did my wife engage you to act on her behalf?"

"Mister Sangster, now that the marriage has ended, we are concerned about the future of Mrs Sangster's daughter."

"Mister Berwick, when my wife and I separated, she was very keen to keep things as amicable as possible, so I'm surprised to hear you coming on so strong. I think it would be best if I speak to her before we go any further."

"Mister Sangster!" Berwick's voice was tense now. "My client is adamant tha ..."

"Exactly," said Nisbet, finding some moral fibre. "Your client is adamant because your client is actually Thomas Lockerbie and not my wife."

Nisbet knew that this would eventually amount to the same thing because Brenda's bastard of a father would brow-beat her into going for Nisbet's throat. He stood up, finding, to his surprise, that he was angry, something that practically never happened, except maybe from a no-arms tackle. But it felt good. If this had been on the rugby park he'd have decked the bastard. But then he'd have been red-carded. Anyway, he didn't care if he got red-carded right now.

"Mister Sangster," said Berwick, raising his voice.

"*Thrrrrp*," said Berwick's arse on the vinyl seat.

He didn't seem to notice. Perhaps his clammy arse, and ears, were inured to clammy-arse vinyl-farting.

"I think you'll find ..."

"No Mister Berwick, I think *you'll* find ... the door ... over there. It's time for you to leave, wee man. And don't bother coming back."

Overall minute self-esteem notwithstanding, Nisbet was actually quite a big bloke and riled as he was, he loomed over the flaccid, fat, flabby, arrogant little bastard. He opened the door. Berwick stood up and gathered his briefcase in his arms. At the front door he turned and stared up at Nisbet, looking him straight in the eye with the air of someone who, although physically intimidated, is yet consumed with utter hatred.

"You'll regret this Sangster. Nobody speaks to me that."

He turned on his heal and quivered his gelatinous body from the office.

"Don't bother giving my regards to your client, Mister Lockerbie," said Nisbet as Berwick exited the reception lobby, slamming the door behind him onto his own ill-coordinated, flabby ankle.

There was a grunt as the ankle was withdrawn. Nisbet felt quite pleased with himself. He had been accommodating his bullying, sarcastic, and manipulative psychopath of a father-in-law for too long and he had enjoyed dealing with his lawyer in the proper mano-a-mano manner. Even so, as he walked over to Angela's desk and perched his buttock on the corner, he almost shat himself to think of the consequences of riling Brenda's male parent's lawyers. Shitting yourself twice in one day would be a real bummer.

"I take it that didn't go well," said Angela.

"Aye," said Nisbet, "that would be an understatement. Brenda's father's bloody lawyer. I tell you what Angela, you might think it's a shame me and Bren splitting up, but I won't be sorry once that vindictive arsehole's out of my life for good."

"I thought it was all going to be quite amicable," said Angela. "I mean, I had Brenda on the phone a couple of days ago."

Nisbet looked at her. He wasn't surprised - they'd become quite good friends and Brenda had precious few real girlfriends. Her reptilian male parent had scared them all away, either with his appalling manner or, as Nisbet suspected, his forthright fingers. Most of Brenda's friends were the wives and girlfriends of Nisbet's pals.

"What was she on about?"

"Nothing much, she's a bit down, but apart from that, just the usual girl chat, mum stuff, you know, the usual Brenda."

"Unfortunately, the 'usual Brenda' includes her father," said Nisbet. "Anyway, might as well pack it in for today Ange, it's nearly five anyway and I can't be arsed after that crap from Berwick, it did my head in. I think I'll go for a pint on the way home, maybe get a bar supper." He slid off Angela's desk. "In fact, I'm off to the gym first. See if I can get a game next season."

"Oh the bachelor life," said Angela, light-heartedly.

"Aye," said Nisbet, getting his jacket, "the bachelor life." He laughed, but it wasn't that funny. "You lock up and I'll see you in the morning."

"What time? Early? Eleven? Twelve?"

"Piss off Angela,"

--------o0o--------

At the Patullos'

Heading up North Gyle Road, Greg Patullo took off his cap, rolled it up, stuffed it in his coat pocket, letting the breese waft his comb-over up in the air and down over his ear. He slipped the coat off and folded it over his arm so that it covered most of the laptop bag. He had a sneaking feeling that certain people might be on the look-out for somebody of his description carrying a big laptop bag. He turned into North Gyle Loan and a minute later, was home at their bungalow.

Letting himself quietly into the house, he was warmly welcomed by their ten-year-old German Shepherd. Unusually, he ignored it and went into his 'study', the box room, opposite the front door and slid the laptop bag between the wall and the side panel of his flat-pack, Ikea desk. He hung his coat over the swivel chair and went into the kitchen where his wife, Moira, had her face in an illustrated cookery book

"*Damn,*" he thought, "*This'll most likely be something from 'Jamie Oliver, Fifteen Minute Dog Puke.*"

In fact, she was in creative contemplation of the business of churning out more culinary tedium for her gastronomically gutless husband.

He snuck up behind her and blew in her ear.

"Jesus Greg!" his wife squeaked, coming back down to land. "I didn't hear you come in."

"Sorry honey, I thought I'd surprise you." He kissed her on the cheek.

"You could surprise me by peeling the tatties for dinner."

"Ok. Bacon sanny for lunch?" He took out the tattie peeler.

His wife gave him one of her looks, getting the bacon out of the fridge. "You look a bit flushed, are you ok?,"

"Aye, just hauling those slate samples up the brae probably."

"Yes, How did you get on with Sandy?"

"Och, it's a dawdle. But he doesn't need an architect, he should get a kit house from B&Q."

"Do B&Q do kit houses? I never knew that."

Her husband rolled his eyes.

"Just joking. But he should just go to one of the kit home builders, - save a lot of bother, and money.

"You could charge him for the work, he's not short of money."

"Och, Sandy's a pal, I'd end up doin' it for nowt anyway."

"Sandy takes the mickey out of you."

He changed the subject. "Listen, I've been thinking, do you think I should do away with this comb-over?"

She put the bacon down and looked at him in utter astonishment.

"Ye…es." She didn't want to hurt his feelings with an over-enthusiastic response. She'd missed her chance to deal with the comb-over twenty-odd years ago.

"Maybe it's time to go bald gracefully."

"You're already bald."

"I suppose so. You wouldn't mind? What about the moustache? Should I shave that off?"

"Well, it might take a few years off you."

She couldn't believe what she was hearing. He must have stopped off at the hospital for a frontal lobotomy on the way home.

"That's what I thought. Ok, I'll do it then."

"Ok." She gave him a kiss and a hug. "What brought that on?"

She was already planning a trip to the shopping mall to young-up his style of dress. In her mind's eye she could see the seagulls at the city coup shitting on his knee-bagged, brown-corduroy trousers, the suede loafers and the rest of his style-disaster, British Standard university lecturer's outfit.

"Oh, nothing, I just thought it was time for a change."

What he really had been thinking was, if there was ever a time for a change of style, this was it. If ever he ran into that big hard-man again he had better look substantially different, totally unrecognisable.

"Do you fancy a holiday?"

"Yes," she said, emphatically. "Take the caravan somewhere nice, like, Argyll, or the Lake District. What's the point about being retired if you can't take some holidays?"

"Well, we could get one of those last-minute deals, I was thinking more, sort of, maybe, the Algarve, or a cruise."

In other words, maybe it was time to get a haircut, a shave, some different clothes and get out of the country sharpish for a few weeks, then come back tanned like a Glaswegian sunbed junkie.

"A cruise? Too expensive, when did you get rich?"

"Hmm ..." enough said. "Gimme a minute, while I tidy up my notes for Sandy's house."

Twenty minutes later he came back to the kitchen, still a bit flushed.

"What about a safari holiday, Tanzania, lions and tigers, giraffes?"

"There are no tigers in Africa," said Moira. "Too expensive. Besides, we'd need jags. I'd rather have midges than mosquitos. The caravan will be fine."

"Ok, I'll go and make a list of stuff to check."

"No hurry," she said. "I'll just make the bacon sannies and we'll decide where we're going."

"Ok, I'll go and finish Sandy's stuff, I'll just be five minutes."

He went back into his study, sat down at the desk, lifted the laptop bag and unzipped it fully. He pulled out the package he'd opened and slit it a bit further open to get a better look. He removed one of the bundles of fifties. It had a paper band round it. On it was written, "100 x £50". There were eight bundles of notes in this layer, all with that on their label. There were five such layers, separated by thin white card. There must be the best part of two hundred grande in this parcel. And if the other parcel was the same? Jesus, there might be four hundred thousand quid or more in this laptop bag.

He put the money back in the bag and slid it into the filing cabinet drawer of his desk, behind the suspension files marked "Housekeeping"; "Homers" etc. He leant back in his chair. He could feel the pulse in his temple banging away. He was sweating like a pig, his head was a clutter of competing issues. This could only be crime money, organised crime money. He must have been mistaken for somebody else. Bloody hell! Whoever they were, they'd be after it, they'd turn over every stone to look for him.

Should he give it back? Who to? How would he find them? Then they'd do him in just for knowing. Turn it in to the cops? Bugger that! They're even more bent.

His head churned with ideas. It wasn't his money. He was an honest man. But it was crime money. Screw the criminals. Screw honesty, screw good citizenship. Nope, he'd keep it.

But some very angry people would be looking for this money. Mind you, they couldn't possibly know who he was. His laptop bag had only contained Sandy's samples, a new A4 notebook and his copy of True Crime magazine. Nothing to identify him. But he'd have to make himself scarce nevertheless, never look like himself ever again. He'd have to disappear good and proper, a change of image. But he was damned-well going to keep this money.

He got up and went into the bathroom, picked up his electric razor, flicked open the beard trimmer and with a trembling hand, buzzed off the moustache, then shaved off the stubble. It felt weird, cold. He'd had the moustache for twenty-five years or more.

"Bacon sanny's ready!" his wife shouted from the kitchen door.

"O.K. pet," he shouted.

He wiped his sweating face with a tissue, did his best to compose himself and went back into the kitchen.

"You alright?" asked Mrs Patullo, putting the teapot down on the kitchen table. "You seem a bit out of sorts. Not your usual chatty self."

"Might be getting a bit of a cold." He paused. "I think you're right about Sandy, by the way. I'll just tell him to get a kit house. He wouldn't likely pay me enough for the work."

"Suddenly, you don't think we need Sandy's money?"

"Ehm ... no, not really, don't suppose we do."

Bloody right they didn't.

"Oh well ... Anyway, where shall we go with the caravan?"

"Cornwall?" he offered.

"Too far."

"Not far enough", he thought and furrowed his brows wondering how to manage four hundred-odd grand in cash. How could you bank it?

It was going to be difficult to explain to his wife how they could suddenly afford things they never could before. A wave of panic ran through him, not because he'd come into possession of a pile of somebody else's money, but more because, now that he had a huge pile of money, he didn't want to lose it.

"Do you think we should get a burglar alarm honey? CCTV, for while we're away."

"Never mind that," she looked him in the face for the first time and spotted the missing moustache.

"Good grief Greg! You weren't joking about the moustache! What's brought all of this on?"

"Oh, I don't know, I just felt I needed a change of style."

She poured him a cup of tea then leaned over and kissed him on the lips. It felt weird.

"Mmm, that's nice. Let's get your hair cut. Then we'll go into town and get you some nice clothes for the holiday."

No way was he going to go back into Edinburgh in case he met that big bruiser, who would now be going mental looking for his money.

"What about that big shopping centre in Livingston, you can get parked there?" It was fifteen miles west of Edinburgh. "They have a big Marks and Sparks."

"O.K," said his wife.

The removal of the grey, salt and pepper moustache took about twenty years off him. If the comb-over and cap went he'd just about look like the man she'd married. Minus the hair.

--------oOo--------

Hermens Aftermath

Roderick Matheson QC's "other" mobile phone rang and he nearly jumped out of his skin. He sat and looked at it for a minute. The number was withheld. Nobody ever phoned him on this mobile so it must be some call centre trying to sell him something, although he thought he'd managed to keep that number sacrosanct.

He lifted the phone and said, in as flat a tone as possible, "Hello."

"Sharky?" said the voice at the other end. Cold-calls didn't usually start like this.

"Who is this?"

"I think you know who this is. You treacherous bastard. Who the hell do you think you're dealing with?"

A string of invective ensued, through which, Matheson recognised the voice of his London contact.

"Just hold on a minute …"

But the diatribe continued, including phrases like "double-crossing bastard" and "regret this for the rest of your life".

He was used to this from some of his less apologetic (or less grateful) criminal clients but he'd never experienced it in his other line of business. Politeness and good manners amongst potentially violent criminals was de rigueur. He'd learned this from Bryson.

"I'm terribly sorry, but I do not have the slightest notion what the devil you're talking about."

But he was getting the message loud and clear: something had gone terribly wrong with the "meeting", and his supplier hadn't got his money. He turned on his congenial courtroom charm and dug a little deeper. He didn't have to dig much deeper at all.

"*Hell's teeth!*" he thought. "*The bastard's handed over the stuff and come away with no money. How did that happen?*"

On the face of it, this sounded like an exceptionally good deal. Bryson was some operator, it looked like he'd made off with the goods and kept the money.

"Look," he said, in the tone usually used by rip-off merchants whose work has malfunctioned. "I don't know what's happened here but I'll certainly look into it and get back to you as soon as I can."

This was followed by more invective and then there was a pause and the voice picked up in a calmer tone. What Matheson heard was quite sobering and it somewhat took the shine off the frisson of pleasure he'd got from the notion that Bryson had made off with the goods without parting with the money.

"Ok, very well, I take your point, we'll get back to you … no I've got your number. I'll get back to you." He hung up.

Just then, Bryson came in, looking deranged.

-----------oOo-----------

Hermens was awash with fury, but the walk back to the hotel had gradually calmed him enough to do some cold reasoning. Not a word that Matheson had said to him when he'd eventually called him back was in the least believable. It just wasn't feasible that they'd been shafted too. Nobody knew about this, so either it was an inside job by one of their own people or, more likely, *they*, had decided to shaft him simply because he was a sole trader and they thought they could. But one thing was always true regardless of your line of business, straight or crooked, and even more true if it was crooked: don't screw with people.

Hermens was a hard bastard, at least in terms of the sort of resolve it takes to walk both sides of the law, but he didn't get involved in anything other than commerce; he couldn't as long as he remained a sole trader. However, he'd just been shafted, shagged clean up the arse by a bunch of provincial, small-time crooks and he wasn't going to take it lying down, no matter what it cost him.

Back at his hotel he stripped off the shabby outfit he'd been wearing and showered, mostly to try to rid himself of the feeling of dirt that had overcome him: the dirt of having been shafted. He showered, dressed in his business suit, sat at the small desk in the hotel room and opened the packed lunch he had brought all the way from London. There was no way he was going to eat the sort of muck he'd heard that Scots eat. Haggis? What the hell was that? Something made from the parts of sheep that most civilised people wouldn't even feed to their dogs. Wiping his lips with the linen napkin he'd brought with him (Hermens was nothing if not fastidious), he tidied the desk ready to make a few phone calls. He lifted his mobile phone. It showed only one dot - there was hardly any signal in his room. Third-world bastards! They don't even have decent mobile phone coverage! He'd have to go down to the hotel lobby.

Downstairs, was a mob of young tourists. Chinese or Japanese culture vulture students. Some guys in suits, low-level sales reps. What a shithole of a country!

Finding a quiet corner of the bar and now with a large vodka (there was no way he was going to drink the native spirit of this disgusting, treacherous, vulgar, dishonest backwater ever again), he began to sift through his notebook. Dozens of contacts in the trade, on the fringes of the trade, and on the fringes of the fringes, anybody that might have a contact. He needed help. An hour on the phone and two referrals later, he ended back where he'd prefer not to be: on the phone to his cousin Aaron. He was a QC, and as much as, if not more of a wide boy than any lawyer in Greys Inn. Aaron had fingers in pies all over the place, the shifty bastard. He'd surely have contacts.

Aaron Rogoff's phone rang.

"A Mister Hermens for you," said his secretary.

"Well I never Eric," said Rogoff. "I don't even get a Christmas card and here you are wishing me good afternoon."

The voice on the phone was the slow, can't-be-arsed Etonian drawl. Hermens hated it, and his cousin. "Well, I don't suppose you called me simply to extend your best wishes. What can I help you with?"

Hermens' cousin, Aaron, had been a couple of years above him in school, and he'd been either a patronising shit, or bit of a bully. Consequently, Hermens hated that whole end of the family.

He gritted his teeth, swallowed his pride and said, "I was wondering if you had any contacts that could help me."

"In what way?" drolled the patronising old-Etonian voice.

"Well ...," and Hermens gave him a little of the background.

"In Scotland you say?" He said the word as if it was something unhygienic. "And you've been swindled out of a substantial quantity of diamonds. I take it, Eric, that this deal was never entirely, what one might call, above the law?"

"Possibly. I just trade in diamonds. Money for goods."

This had a strangely familiar feel to Aaron Rogoff. Had his introductions to the diamond trade and its money laundering potential led his friend Roddy all the way to his very own cousin?

"My goodness Eric," he said, with only a modicum of sarcasm. "And I had always thought that you and your grandfather ran a *very* respectable office in Hatton Garden."

"We *do!* But there are other ... routes to market than ..."

"Yes, I can imagine," interrupted Rogoff.

Actually, Rogoff knew it well, but he wouldn't have touched his cousin with a bargepole, especially if he'd known he was in this parallel line of the diamond business. What an irritatingly small world it was.

"So you want somebody who can supply some ... investigative muscle ... somebody who has contacts in Scotland."

"Yes ... please."

"As it happens, I do have a client that might be helpful. He ... well let's just say, he rather owes me a favour - in my debt so to speak. I'm meeting him tomorrow morning. He's on remand. The Scrubs. What you might call, senior management level."

"Is that the quickest you can get somebody? This is vital, vital!" Hermens voice was rising up the chromatic scale, his dark side, the biggest side of him, beginning to show again.

"My dear Eric," said Rogoff, easing back like the QC he was, his instinctive judo-like negotiating technique cutting in: if the opponent pushes, don't push back, pull.

"I am very happy to help, if you'd like me to. But I do think," now the voice was patronising again, like a father with a recalcitrant teenager, "that under the circumstances you might have to make do with what you've got, unless you want to try somebody else."

Hermens didn't. After never needing friends, now he needed some help from, of all people, his stuck-up bastard of a cousin. He breathed a sigh. Being astride the law was all very well but it meant that he had no real, deep, loyal contacts in the old-fashioned underworld of London.

"No, I'll sit tight here until you call." His voice was shaking. "Give me a call in the morning, I'll be right here. Goodb..."

"Eric! I'll need your number. And it won't be in the morning, I have a meeting in the morning. With somebody who might, as luck would have it, be able to help you."

The voice was once again patronising, and now impatient.

Hermens gave him the number of his pay-as-you-go mobile.

"Very good, I'll call you on that number, please don't call me at the office again. Oh and Eric, you do know that this won't come cheap. These sorts of people don't lift a finger unless you lever it up for them."

The signal clicked off. Hermens went back to his room.

His nerves jangling, his stomach churning and his pride burning like a well-spanked buttock, Hermens lifted the hotel phone at the bedside, called reception. He'd kept the room for two nights in order to have a base to work from if he needed it, but had booked to get the sleeper to go straight back to London. Now he had to stay there and wait for Aaron to call him. And he might need another night now, just in case.

Reception answered. Could he keep this room for another night?

No, said the receptionist, we need that double room for a party of Koreans, but he could move to a single smoker, it was all they had if that would be ok. And could he check out and check back in now please? He said it would and put the phone down.

"Fuck, fuck, fuck bastards!" he said, smashing his fist onto the tiny hotel desk. He almost never swore, but now he needed to. Swearing out loud felt good. And then it felt as if he was letting himself down.

He packed and went to the elevator. He queued at reception for what seemed like an hour, behind a bus party of foreign students, Dancing from foot to foot, he wished he'd gone to the toilet before he quit his room. At last, with the contents of his bladder at the point of no return, he went to the toilet at the far end of the concourse. He took the urinal between two men in suits. They looked like Mormon missionaries. Indeed, the younger man had The Book of Mormon under his arm. He looked at Hermens, both still peeing. He got a sickly-sweet, artificially wholesome smile as both of shook off and zipped up. The sort of smile, he imagined, that perverts gave to young teenagers in toilets. It made him shudder. Another reason to hate Scotland: the toilets were all full of American bastards and perverts.

"Y'all look troubled brother," said the young missionary, his voice professionally empathetic.

"Good God!" said Hermens, "Is there a Yank pervert in every public shitter in this shit-hole of a country?" He stormed out of the toilet.

"Y'all need to not approach people in toilets," said his mentor to the younger missionary, as Hermens exited the toilet. "It can alienate even some of our neediest. It can give the wrong impression."

Hermens head came back round the door, "Pervert!" he screamed, and disappeared back towards the queue at reception.

"I guess you're right," said the young missionary. "That Limey got very alienated."

The alienated Hermens rejoined the queue at reception, looking over his shoulder for approaching missionary creeps, they didn't appear.

"Probably still in the toilet touching up some student," he thought.

Eventually, his turn came at the reception desk. He checked out, checked back in again and went up to a room that smelt like an ashtray. Sitting down on the bed he put his face in his hands and wept tears of hatred, frustration, shame, anguish, and more hatred. Never in his life had he ever felt sorry for himself and here he was, swindled by some provincial hicks from a shit provincial city in a backward, third-world country. He'd been patronised by his stuck-up cousin, plagued by American perverts in two consecutive public toilets and was down nearly half a million quid's-worth of his hard-earned diamonds. Or, to be fair and more accurate, a box of largely cloudy, second-quality, cut diamonds to the tune of approximately half that value. Well, he had to make a profit.

---------oOo--------

Matheson Aftermath

Matheson sat at his desk in his 'other' office, with his face in his hands. This was the office from where he conducted his 'other' business, two hundred yards along the lane, behind his law offices.

At first it had looked like a nice fat bluebird had landed in his lap: he had both the goods and the money. Now it had turned out to be the exact opposite: he had neither. All Bryson had collected was a laptop bag full of slates and a copy of True Crime. All the supplier had, apparently, was a laptop bag, also with some stone samples and a cheese roll. It was all too much to believe. What was the significance of the slates? Or the stone? Or the Koran for that matter? The Koran? Was he dealing with an Asian gang? Some weird gang of evangelical Muslim con artists?

"Fuckin', treacherous bastards, when Ah get ho'd o' yon wee, effin' Sassenach, effin' wee Jewish-looking wee bastard, Ah'll effin', kill them a'."

Bryson looked like he would punch a hole through the wall at this rate: he was incandescent, his craggy, pock-marked face as red as an apoplectic raspberry.

"Alec," said Matheson, in a disappointed and quiet tone, like a father to a son who has just picked his nose at the table. "I told you, I've already spoken to them on the phone, twice. They got stung too."

Matheson was as immaculate a dresser as Bryson but at the other end of the scale. His chalk-stripe suit, cut-away-collared shirt and old-school tie were typical off-duty queen's council garb. He had just come from lunch at the New Club, the crusty gentleman's club on Prince's Street from where, if he'd had a mind to, he could have overseen the whole of the failing proceedings below in Prince's Street Gardens. He had been celebrating a not-proven verdict with his adversary. Matheson had promised to buy the common little shit lunch at the New Club if he won the case, which he had, and after which, he did.

"How?" barked Bryson. Meaning, in the Edinburgh vernacular, why, where, when and by whom, but not necessarily how.

He went on, his voice rising to as much of a pitch as his bass baritone could muster. His massive fists were clenched like two pale, tattooed barn weights. It was an intimidating sight, even for his indulgent boss.

"Ah dealt wi' the wee shite in the park: wee, fuckin' Jewish-looking', auld, shabby bunnet. Shabby wee shite wi' a fuckin' shabby laptop bag. He ken't the fuckin' password an a'."

"So do you it seems," said his boss sarcastically. "He looked

Jewish, you say?"

"Well, maybes aye, maybes naw. But it is diamonds we're dealing' wi'. So Ah just assumed he'd be, ye ken, Jewish."

"But would whoever swindled both of us necessarily be Jewish?"

"Dinnae ken. Onywey, Jewish or no, Ah'll kill the bastard when Ah get mah haunds oan him."

"You'll do no such thing."

Matheson could see Bryson was about to explode.

"Alec, we'll sort it out, it wasn't your fault." He paused for several seconds to think and let Bryson calm down. "We should have handled it the normal way: your way."

This was cold comfort for Bryson. The deal had been screwed up. He was in charge of expediting it, even if the ludicrous subterfuge had all been the concoction of the boss's son – the wee, stuck-up, public school pansy.

"As I said, they've been on the phone already," continued Matheson. "They got stung for the goods. They're blaming us."

"Jesus fuckin' Christ! Ye're jokin'?" gasped Bryson. He looked at the boss's face. "Naw, ye're no jokin'."

"No. It's true enough. Sadly."

Plainly, they had been taken to the cleaners from both ends. They'd been outclassed. Both men were quiet for several more seconds while their brains whirred: Bryson's in a turmoil of shame and fury and Matheson's in as good a representation of analytical thought as he could manage, considering he was down four hundred-odd grande.

Then Bryson, without much enthusiasm for the notion, because it had probably just been a coincidence, said, "Ah seen some bastard comin', oot the park, hurryin' like. In fact, he ran for it. Big bloke an' a'. Leather jaikit an' a' … like …"

"Like what? asked Matheson, culturally unable to get the hang of a modern idiom that ended every sentence with "like".

"Like mine's. Ah legged it efter him ontae Castle Terrace but the bugger could shift. He jumped in a rid Beamer. N suhum, suhum, suhum suhum T. Maybes N fifteen. No a new Beamer. Auld yin ah wid think."

"Very observant!" said Matheson, writing it down, "N something, something, something T, or fifteen."

"Naw it wis N maybes fifteen, maybes eighteen. Then suhum, suhum, suhum."

"Got that. Very observant, You should have been a cop Alec."

"A cop? Aye, very funny Boss. You should hae been a lawyer."

"That's what my partners say. No money in it anymore."

Well, not the kind of money that satisfied Matheson's lifestyle. The dullness of being senior partner in a criminal law practice had long ago decayed into mind-numbing tedium. Except for the defence of his cohorts in crime, all he seemed to do these days was get hopeless junkies probation and domestic violence practitioners a standing count before they engaged combat again.

"So let's get this as straight as we can," continued Matheson. "Some ... person, who is impersonating our ... ehm, supplier ..."

"Aye."

"... meets you, swops the goods, or rather a very sarcastic bag of trash, for the money. Some other ... person, impersonates you and swops a bag of ... similar stuff ... for the goods from our southern friend."

"Aye," said Bryson. "That sounds aboot it. Maybes. Plus a' they weird messages."

"Messages?"

"Aye, the stanes, the tiles, the magazine, the Koran," said Bryson. "Who the fuck goes in fur that kindae stuff? Is it a code?"

"Indeed, who the fu... Sorry, who the devil goes in for that kind of thing?"

Matheson looked at Alec with impatience. He hated to swear. He usually delegated that department entirely to the expletively-talented Bryson and let him get on with it from his vast lexicon of filth. It was part of his raw animal charm. Unfortunately, the man's talent and shear stamina for profanity made it catching.

"So who, just who are we dealing with?"

He picked up the copy of True Crime magazine and flicked

through a few pages. It looked like quite a fun diversion: stories from the annals of crime and punishment. His own life story.

"Insiders?"

Both of them considered this. Other than their contact, nobody but the two of them and the boss's son Julian knew what the plan was. There was a pause while they looked one another in the eye, both thinking the same thing about Julian: one nervous that his son might be at fault and the other happy to allocate blame where it very likely belonged.

Bryson changed the subject. "It cannae hae been a leak frae wur London contact. At least, ye widnae think sae. He's a sole trader, apparently, accordin' tae Julian.."

"Indeed. That's how we were introduced. But nothing's ever out of the question. He was apoplectic on the phone," said the Boss. "And I assured him that at this end, nobody but you, Julian and I knew what was going on. Somehow, somebody got in between us and them and got wind of the handover instructions."

"He could be takin' the pish, like. Makin' it look like he got stung, but is just fuckin' aff wi' the dosh."

"Could be that, but he's a bloody good actor, he's got some tongue on him."

"Angry wee bastard then?"

"To say the least. Foul-mouthed, vitriolic, caustic …"

"Caus.. whit?"

"Caustic," repeated Matheson. "You know, like acidic only … different."

"Awe aye. Acidic. Wan o' they acidic Jews?"

Bryson nodded, picturing a small bearded man with ringlets and a black hat.

Matheson rolled his eyes. Bryson was smart, but poorly educated.

Bryson contemplated for a moment.

"Naw, Ah dinnae think sae boss, nae black hat an' ringlets, just yer ordinary sort of geezer, dressed like a wee nurd. He could run though. Fit bastard."

Matheson sighed, "What makes you think he's Jewish?"

"Well, diamonds. See, they basically run that trade, dae they no? Plus the guy on the park bench. He looked kindae Jewish."

"Hardly a monopoly Alex, I got the contact from one of my barrister chums in London. Anyway, it doesn't matter whether he's a Muslim a Jew or a Jehovah's Witness, if *he* got screwed and *we* got screwed then somebody found out what we were up to. But who? Only you, Julian and I knew what we were up to."

"Aside frae yer pal in London," said Bryson.

"Well, I hardly think so, he's in the same line of business as me."

"Whit? He does crime?"

"No Alec, he's a barrister."

"Same difference," said Bryson. He thought for a moment then said what had to be said, "So, ehm, Jules couldnae hae let it slip tae wan o' his ... his chums."

There was no inflection of sarcasm in Bryson's tone but "*chums*" was not a word in common usage in working class Edinburgh, so it had, at best more than enough irony. The Boss looked up at him anxiously.

"Naw, right enough," said Bryson. "It wid be a' ower Facebook in ten minutes."

He let that lie for a few seconds and resisted the temptation to observe that, apart from anything, Julian would probably have been biting the pillow, so he wouldn't have had the opportunity to 'leak' information to his 'chum'.

"We could stert wi' yon guy Ah seen comin' oot the park. Him that went aff in the red Beamer. At least tae eliminate him. Get yon number plate checked oot. There's no that many red Beamers like that aroond. It wis quite an auld yin, braw motor. Ye could trace it wi' just the letters we've got. Ye could get that wee bent shot frae Fettes tae look intae it."

The Boss looked at Alec, quite shocked at his faithful servant's apparently treacherous, and possibly homophobic view of his son.

"Bent shot? Fettes?" he said defensively.

Matheson knew that Alec thought that Julian was gay and he himself had had sleepless nights worrying that his key henchman might be right.

"Yon wee *cop* at Fettes polis headquarters," said Bryson, spotting the scope for ambiguity.

Both of them let their shoulders relax in a silent sigh of relief that the 'bent shot' from Fettes had been identified as Moss, one of a small clutch of, if not totally bent, at least malleable cops. And the Fettes in question was Lothian and Borders Police HQ, just next door to Fettes College, Julian's old school.

"That wee turd Mossie in Organised Crime, whitever they cry it."

"I'll get hold of him, but he'll be on duty right now."

Unlike those actually involved in organised crime, their police counterparts in the Organised Crime section, only worked day shifts. They mainly did paperwork and worked the same hours as the Inland Revenue, their principal partners in chasing the proceeds of crime.

"Whit are we peyin' him?" asked Bryson, irony, sarcasm and curiosity rolled into one.

"Good point," said Matheson and lifted the phone. "He can take his tea break now."

"Good idea. Ah'll pit the kettle oan while ye're phonin' him.".

Matheson nodded, contemplating how endearingly domesticated Bryson was for a professional thug. Bryson went out to the hall and told wee Mackenzie to make some fuckin' tea and went to the toilet.

After several attempts Matheson got hold of Detective Constable Moss at Lothian and Borders Police HQ.

"Yes, I understand. Thank you Moss."

Matheson put the phone down, finished writing on his leather bound notepad, carefully laid his Mont Blanc fountain pen on the desk in front of him and looked Bryson in the eye.

"This will take some sorting Alec. I want that money back. I *need* that money back. Or the goods."

The Boss's earlier calm demeanour had wilted. Unlike Bryson, who could work himself through fury and beyond into a cold efficient focus, the Boss could sink himself into a well of negativity. To top it all, his tea had gone cold while he waited for Moss's call.

"So dae Ah Boss, so dae Ah," said Bryson. "Ah'll sort it oot fur ye

Boss. Wan wey or another, Ah'll mak it up tae ye Boss."

"I appreciate that Alec, I really do," said Matheson, and he meant it. Bryson had paid his dues over the years to substantially more than that. "But it's nearly half a million. That's a big hole to back-fill Alec."

"Aye," he nodded glumly. "Did that fuckin' treacherous wee twat Mossy get the number traced?"

Alec Bryson hated cops, but he hated bent cops even more. For all his faults and his thuggery, Bryson believed in loyalty. Bent cops were useful but they were still disloyal, parasitic bastards. He contemplated his contempt for the likes of DC Moss for a few seconds.

"The two-faced wee bastard."

The boss looked over his reading glasses disapprovingly. Bryson's language was really his only fault. He was totally loyal, utterly trustworthy, cunning, stealthy, endearingly ruthless, frequently colossally violent and for the most part, completely without remorse. If he'd been slightly (but only slightly) more of an intellectual, or even simply better educated, he'd have made a good lawyer.

"He said that he can do it but that he'll need to make it look as if it's a legitimate part of a legitimate case," he said.

"So how long?" Bryson's voice was getting tense again.

"He's not on shift again until the morning, he'll sort it then."

"This cannae wait boss." The voice was now very tense indeed: clenched up like his fists.

"We'll get to the bottom of it soon Alec." And then after a nervous few seconds, "Look, I'm due in court in an hour, you hold the fort."

He stood up, his hands on the desk, pushing himself up from his chair. He turned to take his coat from the stand behind him. Bryson got to it first and like a valet, held it while his boss slipped into it.

"By the way, what happened to Mackenzie's face? He looks like one of those American creatures, two black eyes ... ehm ... raccoon."

"Eh? Mackenzie? Ra coon? Whit coon?" It dawned. "Aw aye. Dinnae ken, he must hae walked intae a door or somethin'. Ah'll ask him," replied Bryson, and left the office.

Alone in his office for a few minutes, Matheson, still happed in his camel hair coat, picked up the phone and dialed Rogoff.

--------oOo--------

Gym

There was hardly a soul that Nisbet recognised in the gym. It was a testament to how seldom he'd been working out. Anyway, he was resolved and steeled himself for the self-induced weeks of torture to come. The trick with rugby training, he well knew, wasn't to get fit by going to rugby training on a Tuesday and Thursday night. If you want a game for anything other than the beer-belly-bumpers fifteen, you get match fit long before you even start going to training. But at least, with it being the end of the season, he had the whole summer to get back in shape and at nearly thirty, it would take a bit longer than it had at twenty.

Knowing that he could bust something by over-taxing his flabby muscles, he started off with twenty minutes on a treadmill, having carefully selected one well away from a cross-trainer occupied by a pretty girl. Besides not wanting to look like a creep, looking at a pretty girl's arse would distract him from the job in hand: self-induced torture.

After his twenty-minute warm-up he got into his own 'Pure Dead Mental' sprint interval training system, a self-induced torture that he'd conjured up himself after investigating ways to get match fit without spending your whole life in the gym. It worked, but it was purgatory and it got worse the fitter you got. Ten minutes into the routine he was sweat-drenched, gasping, deep in oxygen-debt and lactic acid. Only ten minutes and it was all he could take. And he'd eventually have to run that routine up to twenty minutes or more.

He jogged it out for five minutes until his pulse rate got down below two thousand, then leant on the arms of the treadmill until he felt he could step off it without staggering around like a drunk. Half the folk in the gym were sitting on cycles reading books. Tossers!

He cleaned up the giant lagoons of sweat that he'd splashed all over the treadmill, then did some work on the weights and finished with several dozen crunches. Then onto the mats for some stretching, careful to make sure that his tackle didn't fall out of his shorts.

"That wasn't as bad as expected," he thought, as he showered.

He was feeling quite pleased with himself, and on the way back to the car he started to get that after-training mood lift, partly from endorphins but more from the smugness of the reformed sinner. He'd pay for it tomorrow and for days after when his muscles stiffened up, something else to look forward to. But it felt good to be back in the saddle again, training properly.

Stranded at the traffic lights on the Lanark Road, he once again reflected how daft it was having an office on the wrong side of town. He'd been browbeaten into it by Brenda and her psychopathic bastard of a father, mainly, he suspected, because it was closer to the bastard's house in East Lothian, and he was always wanting something done or to inflict his lifestyle- and successful-businessman-opinion on the two of them. Now the bastard had moved to a big house in Colinton, just to be nearer his daughter and make their life a misery. Nisbet could just as easily have operated from the spare room. But then, he wouldn't have a star like Angela to keep him pointed in the right direction. Or a brass plate on the wall.

He'd avoided thinking ahead regarding Brenda's departure, but Berwick had forced him to confront it. Where would he stay if the house was sold? He still had his old flat but it was rented out and he'd have to get Ashad to give the tenant six months' notice. He didn't want to throw his tenant out on the street, she was good tenant, but he supposed he'd eventually have to. Even so, he got a little lift from the thought of moving back into his flat. Oh the bachelor life indeed. It sounded quite attractive. Feeling positive and dynamic now, he let the clutch out and booted the car, enjoying the way the seat hit him in the back. It was a bloody fast car. Fifteen minutes later he turned into the pub car park and parked, as he usually did (or usually had until he got married to Brenda) in the far corner against the wall where only one side of his car would be exposed to the danger of door clanging from whichever transit van would park next to him.

He went into the pub and ordered two pints: one of orange squash to replace the sweat, and a pint of heavy to ease his aching muscles.

--------o0o--------

3

Divorce Writ Large

Nisbet arrived early the next morning, even before Angela, and took a call from Hamish at the City Council. He'd got the job he was bidding for. That lifted his spirits no end and he worked the morning feeling quite good about himself. Amongst other, bread and butter stuff he had going, he now had a lucrative, big-time contract. Added to that, he had no hangover, no wife and no loveless, shag-free marriage (at least he was part of the way there) and almost felt as if he could take the divorce situation in his stride. Things were looking up.

The previous evening Nisbet had left the pub after a pint and a half (for safety), then another pint (just to be sociable) and gone to the chip shop. The hour at the gym had got his appetite up so he'd bought the full horror story at the chippy: a twelve inch kebab-and-pepperoni pizza and a large bag of chips. With the ketchup and the salt from the kitchen, two beers from the fridge, he'd eaten this anti-Brenda concoction in the sitting room, on the priceless leather sofa, something that would have incensed Brenda. Two Rambo movies later he'd sloped off to bed and slept like a baby. Oh the bachelor life.

At lunchtime, just about to step out to Mahmoud's for some more saturated fat and carbohydrate therapy and a bit of crack with Mahmoud, he was careened into by a leather-clad motor cycle courier barging into the reception, helmet still on, visor down.

"Can you take your helmet off please?" said Angela, still at her desk behind Nisbet. She was nothing if not security conscious.

"Are you Mr Nisbet Sangster?" said the muffled helmet, a few inches away from Nisbet's face.

"Can you take your helmet off please?" insisted Angela, out of her seat and standing behind Nisbet.

The visor went up to reveal a face pinched into a pucker by the crash helmet's padding.

"Wull this dae? Are you Nisbet Sangster?" This was not a polite and friendly helmet person.

"Take your helmet off! Please! Or get out of this office!" repeated Angela, and she slid her ample curviness between Nisbet and the courier.

Both men took a step back. Nisbet wished he had Angela's sangfroid.

The helmet came off with very poor grace. The face slowly unpuckered.

"Are you Mr Nisbet Sangster?" repeated ex-helmet person.

"Who wants to know?" said Nisbet, over the top of Angela's head.

"Me," said the biker and dipped into a satchel that was filthy from many weeks of road grime. "Here. Sign here."

He held out a rubber-bound document pad and like an automaton, Nisbet reached round Angela, took the pen from under the gloved thumb and signed it while into his other hand was thrust a thick A4 envelope.

"Cheers," said the biker and left.

Nisbet looked at the fat brown envelope. It was headed, Robb, Styles and Chatham. His stomach sank, and he sank, into the easy chair in the corner of reception.

"What is it?" asked Angela.

"It'll be from that fat slimy bastard from Rob, Steel an' Cheat 'Em. He didn't waste any time, the slimy little reptile."

"Maybe you should have been a bit easier on him?"

"Gimme a break Angela," said Nisbet, tearing the envelope open. "He was here on Brenda's father's say-so. Nothing to do with Brenda other than letting herself be browbeaten by that psychopath - like her poor mother."

"Brenda's ok," said Angela.

She liked Brenda and could sympathise with her. Much as Angela loved Nisbet to bits, he could be a bit annoying, from a domestic science point of view.

Nisbet pulled the thick pad of documents from the envelope.

"Fuck me, he didn't waste any time at all, he must have had this ready before he even came here yesterday."

He began to flick through the paper.

"Christ! Brenda's already filed for divorce - at the Court of Session!"

Nisbet didn't really know what the Court of Session was but it sounded bigger and meaner than the Sheriff Court. "*Session*" seemed to imply long hours in court accompanied by a lawyer at a thousand pounds a minute.

"This is definitely Lockerbie's doing. Brenda would never have moved this fast on her own. I mean, she's hardly been out the house for a fortnight!"

"Apart from two weeks in January, a few days in February, a..."

"OK Angela! Christ, whose side are you on? ... No, don't answer that."

Angela had always been quite friendly with Brenda: Brenda had Nisbet for a husband, a likeable guy with merely (from a wife's point of view) acceptable levels of ambition. Angela had a husband with a civil servant's non-existent levels of ambition; they could swop unsatisfactory husband notes.

"I think you need to get a lawyer," said Angela. "Here, let me have a look."

She sat her big motherly bum down on the arm of the easy chair and Nisbet handed her the wad of paper.

"I suppose I do need a lawyer," said Nisbet. "More bloody money."

"Do you know any good lawyers?"

"No," replied Nisbet. "Except for Wee Hammy at the rugby club. He's some kind of a lawyer."

He thought about that for a minute. Wee Hammy was a six-foot-seven, second row forward and although a complete psychopath on the field of play, he was a typical second row forward: a big softy off the rugby park. And off the park was frequently where he was with referees' increasing use of yellow and red cards.

"Maybe I'll get hold of Wee Hammy. Or maybe he just does house conveyancing – or some other sort of legal stuff."

"Do you have his number?"

"No, but he'll be on Facebook. Or, if not, I'll get hold of him at the rugby club."

Angela put the kettle on and nipped down to Mahmoud's for a Scotch pie to comfort Nisbet while he set about getting hold of Wee Hammy. At least if he wasn't a divorce lawyer, he'd know somebody. Meanwhile, the papers that Rob, Steel an Cheat 'Em had just served on him lay on Angela's desk like some kind of heavier-than-air, dark cloud, a dark cloud foretelling a tempest followed by a maelstrom. Through the door, from his workstation, it kept drawing his eye like an executioner's axe. It seemed to be growing in size until it looked like a manila shipping container.

After some forensic work and several calls to Wee Hammy's office, he got a reply and arranged to meet him in the pub at five. It suited Wee Hammy, he was needing to get out of the office early to get a couple of pints down him before circuit training.

"*What an animal,*" thought Nisbet. "*Pints before rugby training.*"

Even Nisbet wouldn't do that. He'd puke during the warm-up. Stomach crunches in the rain with a couple of pints in you was not an attractive proposition; he'd tried it once. But Wee Hammy thought nothing of it. For a second row forward, the required personality traits were: a) hard as nails, and b) thick as mince. But was it a good combination for a lawyer? Maybe the hard-as-nails part would help.

--------o0o--------

Matheson

"You look like shite Boss," said Bryson when Matheson got back from court late the following morning. "Did ye no sleep last night?"

Matheson looked up at Bryson, he was gaunt, grey.

"Naw, me neither," said Bryson.

"It's a lot of money to lose Alec. An awful lot of money."

Bryson had never seen Matheson wring his hands like that. He felt an uncharacteristic rush of sympathy for his boss, but stopped it in its tracks. What his boss needed wasn't sympathy, it was a faithful hard-bastard. Matheson was far from poor, a millionaire, probably several times over. Old money, from a long Edinburgh dynasty of advocates, not to mention pots of money from his own endeavours, meant that he was 'comfortably off'. To say the least. But even for a wealthy man like Matheson, four hundred-odd thousand was indeed an awful lot of money.

To Bryson, it was more than he could picture in his mind's eye. He always spent all of his own money. He had only seen the boss's squirreled-away cash wrapped in brown paper when Julian had finished packing it into the boss's old 17" MacBook Pro laptop bag, the only bag Julian could find big enough after carefully designing and wrapping the slabs of money. As it went into the big laptop bag, Bryson had commented that he'd forgotten the ribbon.

"We'll get it back boss," he said. "*Ah'll* get it back. Huv ye heard ony mair frae yon wee Sassenach creep?"

"No, I think we'll need to track him down physically. Do some forensic work. I called my friend in London last night, the one who, indirectly, put us in touch in the first place. To be frank, he said he couldn't help, it was out of his hands he said. He said that if I'd encountered organised criminals, those kind of people are too dangerous to go messing around with. He was quite, … uncharacteristically impatient with me."

Indeed, Rogoff had told him, in the most gentlemanly terms, to piss right off. He'd given him a route to a contact and if the deal had gone sour, it was nothing to do with him.

"I'm only the marriage broker in this instance Roddy, not the divorce lawyer," he'd said, in his usual friendly, but patronising tone.

"Aye, track him doon … *physically*," said Bryson.

Cinematic pictures were colouring the sadistic TV screen of Bryson's imagination. The starring role was Bryson with the little shit, under a spotlight, *physically* tied to a Mastermind chair in a basement, and Bryson making enquiries, *physically*, refusing to take *"Pass"* as an acceptable answer.

"And whit aboot yon motur boss? Ony news frae yon wee turd Moss?"

"Not yet, I'll try him again."

But just then his phone rang and he picked it up.

"He-llo? Ah, Mr Moss, do you have something for me?"

He listened for half a minute, just nodding and making affirmative noises.

"Excellent. Thank you Mossy ... yes, a BMW, quite old, bit of a collector's item you say?" He made notes as he listened. "No, that's all I need for now, thank you very much indeed. We'll sort you out for that."

He put the phone down slowly and gently on the desk, held delicately between his finger and thumb as if it was fine bone china. He was wondering if the police at Fettes kept records of their outgoing calls. He assumed that they didn't on the grounds that they were meant to be morally pristine. They were also, from a data point of view technically bereft. This meant that on-the-make bent cops like Detective Constable Moss were less criminally endangered, but it was wise to use burner phones. Moss would call him from police HQ from somebody else's desk.

"He's unearthed only one car that fits the bill: a red 1989 BMW Alpina, N15 BET."

"Auld motur." said Bryson. "Private number maybe. Bit o' jalopy if it's that auld?"

"No. According to Moss, if the car's in good order, it would be bit of a collector's item."

"Like the one Ah seen the boy take aff in," nodded Bryson.

"Indeed. And surprisingly, under these circumstances, you'd think the number would be fake. But it's not fake even if it sounds it, N15 BET, registered to someone called Sangster, in Balerno. Only one red BMW registered with a number anything like that."

"Ah thought it wid be a fake number ana'," said Bryson. "But a private number? That's a real wanker's number by the way. Maybes the motor wis hot."

"No, it's not listed as stolen. Weird. And whether he's a sole trader, or this is gang related, it was a tiny bit cheeky to use his own car."

"And schoopit, if it wis the owner that done the deed," said Bryson.

"Stupid indeed, and we shall find out in the long run, assuming that we're not barking up the wrong tree here. The owner of this car could have nothing to do with it, just a coincidence that he was there at the same time as you, dressed a bit like you."

"Nae coincidence boss, same time, mair or less, same place, mair or less, dressed like me, mair or less and runnin' like fuck when Ah went efter 'im."

Bryson was used to people running away from him, and it never entered his head that people run for other reasons - like expired parking permits. But he was right nevertheless: N15 BET was his target.

His boss looked at him over his spectacles again. He could see that his favourite operator was writhing internally from the shame of this cock-up and aside from an undoubted determination to get the stuff back, was plotting a horrible revenge. He didn't need Bryson taking horrible revenge; it was something he had a flair for.

His relationship with Bryson had begun when he'd got him off of a culpable homicide charge after he'd been attacked outside a Leith pub by a couple of small-time hoodlums. They were no match for Bryson's size and martial arts skill and each took a single blow to the head. One of them never got up again.

Already 'known to the police', in fact known to the police since his teens, the police had, on the grounds of probability, charged him with murder. The procurator fiscal had offered culpable homicide on the basis of expediency, but with the input of several witnesses - truthful witnesses, but also with an eye to their own well-being, Matheson had got Bryson off clean as a whistle with self defence.

Having, been in danger of a fifteen-year sentence, and for the first time in his life, feeling truly innocent of all wrongdoing, Bryson had sworn undying gratitude and life-long loyalty.

For all the differences in their social backgrounds, he and Matheson had a lot in common: they were both shifty and they both liked more money than you could earn legitimately. With Matheson's ex-hippy wife owning an under-glass, "recreational" skunk factory farm on her family's farm in rural Fife, Matheson saw Bryson's potential as his wife's interface with the underworld. Business had expanded into other recreational and disco drugs and branched out into the performance enhancers and steroids which Bryson himself had been taking occasionally to enhance his naturally powerful physique. He'd always been big, but intense work on the weights now had him looking like a bull cape buffalo. A cape buffalo with bad skin and expensive taste in clothes.

Matheson's batty wife had lost interest in the skunk farm, mainly on the basis that it was now commercial, and no longer the break-even, charitable herbal remedy operation, proselytising the karmic benefits of being half-stoned half of the time. She now grew orchids under glass and gave yoga classes in the kirk hall. Half stoned. Matheson entertained tarts in his town flat or on his yacht on the Forth. The money rolled in. Everything was hunky dory. Until this first disastrous attempt at secluding a large chunk of his hard-earned, ill-gotten gains.

"Let's think about this Alec. Some wise guy finds out about our deal. He intercepts it but doesn't have the nous to cover his tracks. So he's either an idiot, new to bad behaviour, or there's much more to this than meets the eye."

"Aye," said Bryson, brows furrowed. "Maybes aye, maybes naw. But who the fuck is he? Of course, maybes it's no him, just a coincidence like ye say. He wis just there at the same time."

"Maybe just a coincidence but we'll check the car, and the address, out," said Matheson. "Coincidences never happen by coincidence."

"Aye, so assumin' it's no a coincidence, there's naeb'dy roon' here wid dare get involved, even if they ken't whit we wur daein'. They'd huv tae be a professional operation tae pull that aff at baith ends. Couldnae be Weegies could it?"

"Hmm ... Glaswegians," pondered the boss. "Well, that would be a battle we couldn't afford. I mean, I am owed a few favours in Glasgow – for successful verdicts, so to speak. But if it was any of my former clients moving in on us, I'd be deeply disappointed. And apart from anything else, as we discussed, how could they possibly know anything? We're a stand-alone operation."

"Let's think about this," continued Matheson. "Who knew about this? You, me, Julian and only the one of your 'eejits' as you call them: Mackenzie."

"Aye, Mackenzie. But he just ken't we had a swop tae make."

"And he's very loyal. I'm topping up his grandparent's pension. Apart from that, he's too dull-witted to think something up," said Matheson.

"Well, that would only leave Julian."

Alec let the boss's son's name hang in the air for a moment, then tranquillised that line of thinking before the boss could react in his son's defence.

"Naw," continued Bryson. "Julian wid be as discrete as the rest of us."

But it depended on your definition of discretion. Bryson was culturally suspicious of, and slightly nauseated by Julian's commitment to the bachelor life. He didn't have a girlfriend and plainly would never meet one considering the company he kept. He was aware, however, that Julian didn't give a toss what anybody thought about his "bachelor" lifestyle.

"Some o' yon Weegies pit theirsels aboot. Could still be Weegies."

Alec hated Weegies, they were all soap-dodging bastards as far as he was concerned. It made him tense just thinking about them.

"I don't see how it could be Glaswegians," said Matheson. " They wouldn't be interested in us anyway. We're a small-time operation compared with them. There are two Glasgow organised crime families, the Dawsons and the McElbies. They basically run the drug trade in west Central Scotland, and are in cahoots with Belfast and Dublin mafia, respectively. They hate each other, been at war for years. Besides, I'd consider it something a betrayal of trust. I've been defence council for people from both of their organisations you know," he said proudly, as if it was like dealing with crime royalty. "So I think we have a sort-of understanding."

"Aw really?" exclaimed Bryson, he felt a little betrayed. He hated

Weegies even more now. "Did ye get them aff?"

"Yes, in both cases ... or was it three?"

"Were they guilty?"

"Awash with guilt. They're bad people. Anyway, it wasn't that difficult, they're professionals, they let the munchkins do all the dirty work. The trouble for the big boys, and us, is hiding the money. The police are always ill-prepared in these cases, they think they'll get a conviction simply because the accused is a serial naughty boy. It's all about preparation Alec. Preparation, preparation, preparation; the watchword of good ... ehm ..."

"Preparation?" said Bryson.

Matheson smiled at him.

This was followed by a few seconds silence while they both pondered the complete overload of preparation that Julian had applied to this relatively simple swop of goods for money.

"Anyway, I don't think it'll be Weegies, I mean Glaswegians."

"Ah widnae bet on that boss. Could be newcomers rather than the Dawsons or McElbies. Onyweys, what if it is Weegies though?" persisted Bryson, his prejudice still every bit as clenched as his fists.

"But apparently it's not," said Matheson, interrupting Alec's obvious kill-all-Glaswegians train of thought. "From the look of this."

From his notepad he tore the address to which the car was registered and handed it to Bryson.

"Sangster, registered to an N. Sangster, Balerno."

"Ah'll get it checked oot."

"I think you should. But don't go yourself."

He knew that Alec Bryson would be unable to contain himself if he came face to face with the car's owner. He only had one method of enquiry and it rarely even started with a question. This person might be completely innocent of any involvement and still get thrown around like a rag doll.

"Send Mackenzie, just for a look round. Oh, and it wouldn't do any harm for Julian to go too. He needs the mileage. And this was partly his fault. Too much subterfuge, too much underhand dealing and not enough straight business. I think we should give him some achievable objectives. His confidence has taken a bit of a knock. If that car's at that address we've got something to work on."

Bryson resisted the impulse to observe that too much subterfuge and underhand dealing, and not enough "straight" anything was what the Boss's son was all about. He nodded. The boss's son needed more than mileage; he needed a bloody good reaming. Except that he was probably getting that anyway from his stuck-up public school chums.

Bryson was instinctively homophobic: he resented gay people, not because he particularly disliked them, or their lifestyle. It was just that he was quite good at resentment and any excuse would do.

"OK boss, Ah'll send Mackenzie and Julian. They're sittin' aboot daein' naethin'. It'll keep the baith o' them oot o' bother."

----------oOo--------

The Patullos

Moira Patullo pulled up outside the barber's shop where Greg was waiting on the pavement. In the back of the car, Gary, their German Shepherd went mental, leaping onto the back seat barking savagely at this apparent stranger that was approaching the car. Greg climbed into the Toyota estate, the dog recognised him by smell, calmed down, wagged its tail and licked his ear.

"One thing," said Greg Patullo as he pulled on his seatbelt, "nobody's ever going to get into this car with the show of teeth that Gary put on if he doesn't like the look of you."

Moira smiled at him. "Well, I like the look of you," she said.

He looked great, his bald head was shining, the barber had given him a nice modern, short, very short back and sides and he actually resembled the man she had married: taking the comb-over off had taken twenty years off him. Well, ten at least. She stuck the car in gear and headed west, for the Livingston shopping mall. All she needed to do now was get him fitted out with clothes from the twentieth century and she'd have a new man. Clothes from the twenty-first century might be too big a culture shock.

"Can we nip back into the house on the way past? I've forgotten my credit cards."

Back at the house he went into the drawer, opened the laptop bag, pulled out a decent wedge of fifties and stuffed them into his wallet. It barely folded shut as he slipped it into the inside pocket of his anorak. The coat he'd been wearing yesterday was never, ever coming out of the cloakroom again unless it was on its way to the dump. His wife had already decided that it was on its way to the dump. It was too dull, even for a charity shop.

In the outdoors shop in Livingston shopping centre, Moira got him fitted out with a new pair of slacks, jeans, a couple of new shirts, a new casual jacket and a pair of outdoorsy walking shoes. She didn't care about the expense, she was modernising her man.

Greg Patullo didn't care about the expense either. He was modernizing his spending habits. He got up and followed the assistant to the till while Moira looked at women's outdoor clothes. At the till, he lifted a pair of Aviator-type sunglasses from the display. He paid in cash. Fifties and pocketed the change. He put on the new jacket, dumping the old one in the plastic carrier bag, then went to the men's changing room and put on the new slacks and shoes. He looked in the mirror: no moustache, no trilby, no comb-over, short haircut, baldy head, new outdoor clothes. He wouldn't have recognised the figure in the mirror himself. He was utterly unrecognisable: Greg Patullo, ex-university lecturer, man of mystery, master of disguise!

"Hey, you look pretty smart!" exclaimed Moira when he caught up with her. Actually, she'd nearly missed him, she had instinctively looked around for a dowdy university lecturer. Instead, he looked like a nice looking bloke.

"I didn't expect you to put it all on straight away. Did you put it on the credit card?"

"Aye," he lied. "I'll pay it off on line before we get charged interest. Shall we go for a bar lunch?"

He took the sunglasses from the jacket top pocket, put them on and gave her a big grin.

"Wow!" said his wife. "You look like Tom Cruise in Top Gun."

But she didn't say, "Except for the bald head," in case it had him longing for his comb-over.

They went for a nice lunch. He paid cash. Then they went to the caravan shop and bought some nice gadgets for the caravan. He paid cash. They bought two refill gas bottles for the caravan: twenty-four quid each. He paid with a fifty. Keep the change. He'd never said that in his life before. It felt good. Then they filled the car's tank to the brim. He paid cash.

"We'd better pay that credit card off pronto," said Moira. "We've kind-of gone a bit mental with it today."

"Och, you're only young once," replied her husband.

--------oOo--------

Bryson

"How's yer nose?," inquired Bryson of Mackenzie.

He wasn't troubled by any sense of guilt at having smashed the kid's nose into his face. Nor, indeed, was he encumbered by sympathy. For purely practical purposes, he didn't need an invalid on the job, even, or for that matter, especially if the invalidity was his own doing.

"You broke my fucking nose," said Mackenzie, resentful but afraid. He had two black eyes into the bargain. He looked like a resentful panda.

"Look on the bright side," said Bryson. "Yer nose is still approximately in the middle o' yer puss." He tossed the Mercedes keys to Mackenzie. "It's in the car park gettin' valeted, ye bled oan the upholstery. Dinnae bash it."

"Whit dae ye want me tae dae?" asked Mackenzie, his spirits lifted. Like any snivelling little cur, he would take any amount of abuse for the odd morsel of trust. Getting to drive Bryson's Mercedes again always felt like a promotion.

Bryson handed him the note with Nisbet's address. "Go and see whit ye can see. Is there a red Beamer there? Is the owner there? Who the fuck is he? Stuff like that, but keep yer heid doon, dinnae hing aboot. We need tae ken whae the fuck this is, whit he does and how the fuck he ken't whit we were daein', if he did ken. Oh, and by the wey, the boss says tae take that wee p … take Julian wi' ye. Then there'll be twa useless bastards in the motor."

"Ok Alec," said Mackenzie, "Balernae."

"Get whatever information ye can oan him."

Mackenzie headed for the door.

"Oh and Mackenzie."

"Aye?"

"Dinnae fuck up."

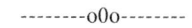

--------o0o--------

Hermens

The stress and humiliation were getting to Hermens. He'd barely slept a wink, thrashing the hotel bed to a foam in his angst. He had always prided himself on his icy coolness, or rather, had prided himself on the screen of icy coolness that he'd erected about himself. But now it had completely collapsed.

His phone rang and he grabbed at it, knocking it from the bedside cabinet. It slithered across the bedroom floor with him after it. With his head under the hotel desk he answered it,

"Eric?" said his cousin's patronizing voice. "I have a contact for you. Phone this number and they'll give you a local contact in Glasgow. Do you have a pen and paper?"

Hermens climbed onto his knees and scrabbled on top of the desk for the hotel notepad and wrote the number down.

"Thank you Aaron, thank you, I won't forget this."

"Forget it is exactly what we'll both do Eric. Good luck." And the phone went silent.

Before the hour was out Hermens had a contact in Glasgow. He checked out of the hotel, nothing more to pay, no extras, no bar bill.

Across from the hotel, a man in a business suit cut in front of Mackenzie who almost fell over the wheeled suit case.

"Wanker!" said Mackenzie in his best wee hardman voice. "Watch where ye're gawn!"

In return he got a look of such malevolence that he almost thought the man would turn on him. And indeed, such was Hermens' frame of mind that he almost did. But it looked like somebody had got there before him as Mackenzie's two black eyes looked away nervously. Instead Hermens strode in the direction of Haymarket Station enjoying a little frisson of pleasure that at least he'd spooked one of these Scottish Neanderthals.

"Fuckin' arsehole," said Mackenzie to the guy's back, this time under his breath and when Hermens was out of earshot.

"The next Scottish bastard that screws with me," thought Hermens, as he dragged his roller case towards the railway station, *"is getting it."*

In fact, all Scottish bastards were going to get it if he had anything to do with it.

Heading into the carpark outside Bryson's top floor executive apartment, Mackenzie slid between a Ford and a Jag, nonchalantly scraping Bryson's front door key down the length of the Jag as he headed for Bryson's Merc.

"That'll be three or four grand tae fix," he said to himself.

Bryson's S-class Merc was gleaming. He had it valeted once a week. Mackenzie got in and marveled once more at how quiet the engine was as he revved it up. The rev counter needle waved at him but there was barely a whisper from under the bonnet. He slipped it into drive, slid out of the parking space and schmoozed towards the West Approach. He opened the glove box and took out Bryson's Ray Bans. No point in not looking the part and besides, he had two black eyes. On Angle Park he floored it past a pickup truck and cut in front, almost clipping the front wing. The pickup's horn blared.

"Wanker!" said Wee Mackenzie, making a wanker gesture in the mirror, something Bryson would never have done. But in Alec's car, Mackenzie felt well hard.

He peeled off onto Angle Park, turned up towards Polwarth and wound his way back through Edinburgh's poshest streets to The Grange and Julian's apartment.

-------o0o-------

Glasgow

Hermens, still fermenting his hatred of Scotland and all of its ingrate inhabitants, seethed his way along to Haymarket station, dragging his wheeled case behind him. He bought a ticket to Glasgow. An hour and a half later he was outside Glasgow's Central Station queueing impatiently for a black cab.

When his turn came he leant into the cab window and said, "The ehm ... Barrow Lands?"

"Aye, raBarras, hop in."

"No, the Barrow Lands."

"Aye, raBarras, hop in."

Hermens hesitated. There were at least twenty people behind him wanting a cab.

"Jim, dae ye wahnt a hurl or no?"

Hermens hesitated just a split second too long. Somebody else got into the cab and shut the door. The cab drove off.

"*What a shithole of a country,*" he thought. "*They're savages, they don't even speak English or have half the brains of a Romanian social worker.*"

He went to the next taxi, and bent down to the window.

"Whit wis 'at a' aboot?" said the driver.

"*Jesus bloody Christ,*" thought Hermens, "*The taxi drivers actually are Romanians.*"

"Eh? I, ehm..."

"How come ye never ta'en yon cab in front?"

"Oh, I, he..."

"See pal, in Glezgy, ye get in, then ye tell the driver where ye're gawn. Get in."

He got in.

"The Barrow Lands, if you please."

"If you please is it? Aye. Polite! Ye'll be English?" He didn't wait for an answer. "Ra Barras. It's cried Ra Barras, Ra Barras aye. We cry Barrowland, Ra Barras," said the taxi driver, helpfully, over his fat shoulder. "No mony folk go there nooadays Jim, speshly no ootsiders."

Hermens' wonder what 'no-money folk' were. Typical Scots perhaps, never had any money. Spent it on drink and drugs, probably. His hatred of the Scots deepened every time the taxi driver's sing-songy, nasal Glaswegian voice twanged and wittered through the glass divide.

"Have ye no goat an address?"

"Yes, but it's ok, just drop me in the middle of The Barrow Land and I'll walk."

He didn't want even the smallest chink of evidence trailing him to where he was going.

"Ye'll no be a Gers fan then Jim? Wan o' they Arse-anal fans eh? Orraspurs?"

"Pardon..."

"Dinnae foelay fitba? Mair a rugby man eh, mibby?"

He did his best to make conversationally appreciative *Yes* and *Really*? remarks as the driver traversed Glasgow speaking some kind of cross between Serbo Croat and gibberish.

At last the cab arrived in what looked like a particularly shabby part of Beirut, turned up a side street and pulled up.

"Will this dae ye Jim?"

"Eh, my names not Jim," said Hermens, indignantly.

"Sorry Jim."

He fished out the fare and climbed out of the taxi. The place looked desolate. Wheelie bins and snowdrifts of litter occupying the gutter. Town planners could have a field day here - with nuclear weapons.

Glasgow's Barrowland, 'The Barras', has been there a thousand years and in all that time it has been the shopping mall of choice for those looking for a bargain, junk or bootleg anything from DVDs to counterfeit designer clothes and counterfeit fags. You could, it was said, even be sold bootleg counterfeit junk. Or even fake, bootleg counterfeit junk.

Hermens knew nothing of this, but he was starting to put it all together: the atmosphere was similar to that of the old London street markets like Leather Lane, not far from his uncle's place in Hatton Garden. But much scruffier. Glasgow hitherto had simply been a name on the map to him. But he had been told that there were people here who could either help him get his goods back, or his money, or revenge and by now, he didn't much care which, as long as he got one of them.

He followed the directions on the phone app, around a corner to be told by a comfortingly English voice on his phone that he had arrived at his destination. Above the entrance to a close, a dark close, which looked like a rectangular troll cave, was a neon sign proclaiming the existence of a pool hall. A dog-legged neon arrow indicated that it was down the close and upstairs. He seemed to be in the right place.

The troll cave entrance was blocked by a man, troll-fat, and troll tall. Tall enough to fill the bottom two thirds of the aperture. Hermens asked for his contact and simply replied, "*Yes,*" to the fat man's question, was he the Londoner? It seemed that he was expected.

"Hey Tam!" cried the fat man, as far over his fat shoulder as he could turn his fat head, considering that his fat head seemed to be neckless, attached directly to his fat shoulders and hence, immovable. Another shorter, but equally fat man appeared to guide Hermens to his rendezvous. He squeezed past the cave troll and got a whiff of unwashed armpit so foul that he nearly threw up.

On the way up the stairs, each landing was narrowed by stacks of boxes so that his fat guide turned sideways to squeeze past, his huge belly making him not the least bit narrower. The fat belly skimmed over boxes and boxes of Armani shirts, Dolce & Gabanna handbags and shoes. It made no sense. Why, would criminals anywhere near the top of the criminal heap have a counterfeit clothing business? Only in Glasgow could small-time fraud be a front for big-time organised crime? And why would they all be fat? It was an alien culture.

Bloody Jocks, he hated their guts more intensely with every step up the dim stairs. They arrived at the pool hall and passed inward, past many pool tables, some with men playing pool or snooker, all either chalking their cues or clunking balls down holes, half of them smoking despite the ban on smoking in public places.

This was Glasgow: no mean city. If the cops came in here, the last thing on their minds would be illicit indoor smokers. And if the council men came in to inspect such a recreational premises, the last thing they would do would be make any demands about smoking, if they wanted to *walk* out.

Hermens had never been in a pool hall before, or Barrowland, or Glasgow or, for that matter, ripped off, ever, not even for a sum of money a thousandth of what he'd just been screwed for. Four lifetime firsts in two days. And he seemed to have gone through a chink in the space-time continuum and landed on the planet Fatbastard. For pity's sake! Why are they all so fat?

He was ushered into an office at the far side of the network of pool tables.

Fat wasn't in it. Billy Bryce was massive, about the size and shape of an upright sperm whale and with an equally well defined neck. He was sitting with his back to the light, behind a desk about the size of a snooker table which, with him behind it, looked like a normal-sized office desk. On the desk were scattered the empty wrappers of what had plainly been a major raid on MacDonald's. And clearly, by the look of the half gallon coke cartons and litter of burger wrappers and cartons, they had '*gone large*'. Twice. Each. There were no leftovers.

The scale was all wrong. Had he gone down the rabbit hole? Had the hotel's coffee been spiked with "Drink Me"? Before him sat the real Humpty Dumpty. Except he was unfeasibly huge. The King's horses and King's men would have their work cut out for them if he fell off the wall and shattered. Assuming fat could shatter.

Bryce didn't get up from behind his desk to welcome the newcomer. He simply leant forward and swept the junk on the desk onto the floor with a left arm the size of a sumo wrestler's leg, the leg of a sumo wrestler who had spent too much time in the tattoo studio. The arm was almost completely blue from the injection of many pints of tattoo ink. Even accounting for fat, it was a massive forearm; obviously Bryce's lard was underpinned by muscle. Underpinned by muscle, and overpainted with Reflex Blue.

And there seemed not a hint of embarrassment from Bryce at having been interrupted with a ton of junk food wrappers on his desk, or having cleared his desk in that unconventional manner. Plainly, the man was an utter barbarian.

The room was almost dark, the royal blue walls trimmed with red reflected very little of the glow that came from the Union Jack lampshades on the wall. But it blended well with the blue of Bryce's forearms. On the wall, was a huge Rangers FC plaque.

As his eyes became accustomed to the poor light, Hermens made out Bryce's three chins and pock marked face, the moonscape skin of teenage acne supplemented by adult steroids. With shoulders that intersected his neck just below the ears there was little room afforded for even a double chin let alone a treble, but a treble chin was there, not three distinct rolls of fat, but one, slightly creased, extra-large, XXXL lump of lard. As Hermens' pupils dilated further, he saw in the shade either side of the window, two stooges each of a size only slightly more diminutive than their boss: mere hump-backed whales.

It made sense now: three fat cetaceans and the trash from six Big Mac meals gone large. Perhaps in Glasgow, fat was de rigueur for the criminal classes. You get large by *going large*. In London, a gangster boss might be "Mister Big"; in Glasgow it would be "Mister Bumper-sized".

Hermens leant forward and offered his hand to what might be the most disgusting creature he had ever seen in his life, let alone met.

"I'm Eric Hermens, we spoke on the phone."

"Aye," said Bryce, without offering his gigot-of-ham fist in return, something which, despite the poor manners, was no disappointment to Hermens, considering the greasy muck that had just been casually swept onto the floor. The light from the window was bouncing off the oily sheen on Bryce's fingers, illuminating the out-of-focus hand-done, probably prison tattoos on his fingers.

"Sit doon big man."

Unfamiliar with Glasgow etiquette, this sounded at best like irony and at worst like sarcasm. Not off to a good start. Hermens looked around nervously. For criminals, allegedly near the top of the Glasgow heap, there wasn't much sign of success: the place was foul. Perhaps Glasgow's organised crime was just poorly organised.

Bryce smiled, "Ah ken whit ye're thinkin' pal."

He paused to let Hermens' eyebrows rise quizzically, then tapped his oily nose with a greasy finger the size of a Cumberland sausage.

"Hide in plain sight, ken. Nod's as guid as a wink, ken."

Hermens made an appreciative and positive 'Ah' reply with his eyebrows. To the fastidious Hermens, this made no sense at all, they looked like scum, dirty, filthy scum. Only scum would choose filth for their 'plain sight' in which to hide. He was in the wrong place. He simply nodded and corrected Bryce, "It's Hermens, Eric Hermens."

"Ken," replied Bryce, wondering if Hermens was short of a few slates.

Hermens wondered the same about him. As for himself, as of yesterday, in a laptop bag, he'd acquired all the slate he'd ever need.

"Afore we proceed wi' onyhing, wid ye like a cuppytea?"

This took Hermens aback. He wasn't expecting any domestic niceties.

"Oh, oh, yes, yes please." Might as well break the ice.

Bryce turned his head the full two degrees of which his sperm-whale neck was capable and completed the rotation with the aid of his swivel chair – a swivel chair the size of a railway turntable.

He spoke to the goon on the left of the window, "Wull. Awa and pit the kettle oan."

"OK boss," said Humpback Wull.

Then on his way out, to Hermens, Wull said, "Haw Jim, dae ye tek mulk and sugar?"

Hermens winced at the familiarity.

"Yes please. Ehm, it's not Jim, it's Eric."

"Ken."

"So … *Eric* …," said Bryce, with sarcastic emphasis. "Whit can we dae fur ye?"

Well at least he'd stopped calling him Ken.

"Well, Mister Bryce, as I explained on the phone..."

"Oh by the wey, we need tae get some protocol oot the wey, ken."

"Oh, of course," replied Hermens, glad that some sign of normal business practice and manners might be emerging. "But please, just call me Eric."

"Aye, ... Eric... Ye're no a Tim ur ye, ken?"

Not another first name! thought Hermens.

So far he'd been called Jim and Ken. Now it was Tim. What the hell was wrong with these people?

A "Tim" was the local, deeply unflattering and pejorative slang for a Catholic, particularly one of Irish descent. Hermens, of course, knew nothing of Glasgow's fascination with sectarianism and religious prejudice.

"I beg your pardon," was all he could muster. "Tim? No, it's Eric ... Eric Hermens."

"Ken. But ur ye a *Tim*? As in Fenian, ken. A left fitter, a *Tim*!" Bryce clocked the look of consternation on Hermens' face. "As opposed tae a Proddy."

Like many of its native ethnic types, it did not occur to Bryce that the weird sectarian lexicon of Glaswegians should be unique to Glasgow. For many Glaswegians, sectarianism and religious prejudice wasn't just a lifestyle, it was their hobby.

Hermens' blank look hid a rapid thought process: perhaps a Tim was some kind of social group. If he was a Tim, he'd have known that he was a Tim. He concluded that he wasn't.

"No, I'm not a Tim."

"Proddy then? English Proddy?" The tone was lighter.

The penny dropped, "No, I'm not a church goer. I'm from a Jewish background."

He immediately regretted saying that because it could mean he'd be classed as yet another target for prejudice.

"Fair enough," the voice was patient, patronising. Then slowly, as if speaking to an idiot, Bryce asked, "But ur ye a Proddy Jew or a Cafflick Jew?"

"No, neither, I'm not really religious at all."

"Whit the fuck's that goat tae dae wi' it?" Bryce exclaimed in astonishment.

He sighed sarcastically, then looked the swivel chair to the left to get agreement that he was dealing with a dunderhead. The fat thing on his left rolled his eyes and wobbled his flabby cheeks in sarcastic disbelief.

"Ok, proceed … Oh, apairt frae that, ye came weel recommended, ken."

Hermens decided to give in on the names front.

"Thank you, as did you."

It was of little comfort that the disgusting Bryce had been highly recommended as a fixer by his contact in London. But Hermens was here now, so he might as well get on with it. The white heat of his rage had dimmed but little and any dimming had simply been his rage distilling down into determination.

"Well as I explained to your London, ehm, agent, I've had some dealings with some people in Edinburgh and, well, to put it bluntly, I've been swindled out of a substantial amount of money. Now I have neither the money nor my goods."

"Edinburgers eh? They Embra folk ur a' bastards, they're a' …" He shook his head, pursed his lips and seethed for a moment. "See Glesca, see Embra… Dinnae stert me." He sat shaking his head for a few seconds.

"So thur Embra boys ripped ye aff and ye want yer money back?" He pronounced *want* like *scant*. It was taking Hermens a while to tune into their scant knowledge of English.

"Yes, or the goods."

"Whit were the goods? Oot o' interest, ken," asked Bryce. "Smack? Coke?"

Puzzled silence from Hermens.

"Jellies? Swedgers?" All local jargon for hard drugs.

He hadn't heard of these either, it was all new to Hermens.

"No, nothing like that. Diamonds," he said quietly.

"Fuck sake!" said Bryce. This was new to him. "Diamonds! Dae ye hear that boys? Fuckin' diamonds! Whae the fuck buys diamonds? Whit dae they buy they fur?" He swiveled round to get supportive astonishment from the fat goon on the left. The cheeks wobbled supportively.

"Well, they're a hedge against hard times," explained Hermens. "They keep their value as well as, or better than anything else, other than gold. But they're much more portable and it takes the money out of circulation - as far as those who inspect the proceeds of crime and money laundering are concerned. But it's not my business why people want them. I just sell them."

"Aye, Ah suppose," said Bryce, thoughtfully, his fat eyebrows pushing some other fat further up his fat forehead..

He swiveled back to the other fat thug who had come back with a beautiful, but probably fake, very genteel and delicate Wedgewood tea set.

"Maybes we should buy diamonds boys." He turned back to Hermens. "Sharely it's no illegal tae trade in diamonds?"

"No, not specifically. What I do is source them and move the money around. And, of course, I pull a modest commission on the transactions."

"Whit aboot the proceeds-y crime? Ken?"

The fat goon with the tea set began to lay it out on the desk and then, with the precision and delicacy of a royal footman, to pour cups of tea from the matching teapot. Unbelievably, he had a crisp white tea towel over his arm like a real footman.

"There's, a lot of ... slack in the system ... in the diamond market."

"Right, maybes we *should* dae diamonds. Oneyweys, hoo much did ye get skelped fur?"

"Nearly half a million pounds' worth."

No harm in egging up the pudding slightly, to account for shrinkage.

"Fuck me pink!" said Bryce, starting to sit up. "Hauf a fuckin' grip! Hauf a fuckin' grip! Nae wunner ye're cheesed aff."

"Indeed," said Hermens, "Cheesed ... aff ... hardly comes close."

"Sugur?" said the fat royal footman to Hermens.

"Pardon?" said Hermens, not expecting any interruptions from the hired help.

"Sugur? Does wan tek sugur in wan's tea?"

"Oh, ehm, yes please, thank you," replied Hermens. "Two please."

Two cubes of sugar were delicately dropped into the delicate china with delicate sugar tongs that looked about the size of a hairpin in the fat fingers. Hermens felt he had entered some kind of Salvador Dali-esque or Lewis Carroll parallel reality. He definitely had gone down the rabbit hole.

"Mulk?" said the goon, holding up a delicate little milk jug.

"Oh … yes please," replied Hermens and was handed his cup and saucer.

Like an automaton at his grandmother's for afternoon tea, he took the delicate little spoon and stirred his tea. He looked at the spoon. Blimey! It was hallmarked silver. He lifted the cup to his lips and quickly spun the saucer, to look underneath; it was real Wedgewood. He thought it had looked too good to be fake.

"Fuckin' nice gear eh?" said Bryce. "Ah'm a stickler furra relaxin' cuppy tea. It aye tastes better in braw china."

"Yes it does," said Hermens, truthfully, still swaying in the distorted reality. The tea was very good indeed, assuming the bacterial count was low.

"So, ye goat hit fur hauf a grip an' a's ye goat wis a whit?"

He translated that successfully in his head.

"Some stone tiles, two cheese rolls, a paperback book, two sheik kebabs and a copy of the Koran."

Immediately he said it, he wished he hadn't.

Sarcastic silence for several seconds as Bryce choked off a snigger.

"No a very guid trade right enough," said Bryce, only his shoulders sniggering.

"The Koran? Ah could hae gied ye wannay thame. Ah've twa boxes in the lockup. Why wid they gie ye the Koran? And Kebabs? That's pure weird so it is."

"Hey Boss! Mibbies it's some kindae Muslim code," suggested one of his fat goons.

"Aye, maybes. Mibbies some kindae Embra Muslim code."

"Aye, a antimiseptic Embra Muslim coded message," said the other fat one. "Like in the Goadfaither. Mind? *Luca Brazzi sleeps wi' ra fishes* ... 'n' 'at, ken."

Puzzled silence.

"Ken ... like in the Goadfaither ... Deid gangster, big fish wrapped in newspaper ... ken?"

"Whit? Fish? In newspaper? That's just a normal fish supper. Oneyweys ... It wis a horse's heid in the bed, wis it no?" replied Bryce. He turned to Hermens, "Were yer contacts Muslims? Pakistani or Bangladeshis?"

"No, they were white, at least the one I met was white."

"Whit else wis there?"

Hermens filled him in on some more detail.

"A rid beamer, suhum, suhum, suhum B.E.T. and a big boy wi' a leather jaikit?

"Yes," said Hermens.

"Is that it? Is that aw ye've goat?"

It wasn't. Hermens explained the background, the buildup, the overly complicated, spy-versus-spy handover, the contact's phone number, the fact that there seemed to have been two, similarly leather-jacketed men.

"Did ye no smell a rat efter ye heard the plan? Yon's a pish handower by the wey," said Bryce. "A's ye needed tae dae is fuckin' turn up in Embra and dae the trade in the fuckin' pub car park. It's no as if the Embra cops has goat ony idea aboot London diamond dealers meetin' up wi shady fuckers. They'll be jist like Glesca cops, lazy bastards, arrestin' recreational dope smokers tae get their stats up. If the cops hud ony brains, we'd a' be fucked."

He thought for a minute.

"So why wid they wahnt tae hide hauf a grip? Whae's goat hauf a grip they dinnae wahnt naeb'dy tae ken aboot? It'll be drug money, sure as Frank Haffey let in nine. Embra drug money."

Hermens already knew this would likely be the case. It was a lot of money to want to hide, if that's what they'd really wanted to do and not simply screw him for the diamonds.

"Yes. It could be drug money – I suppose."

"Then we just need tae ken which operation we're dealin' wi' and then get intae swing. This is no gawny be cheap by the wey. It means grabbin' this boy, whoever he is, extractin' the facts, disposin' o' him, gettin' tae the tap o' the heap and then, weel, we see whit develops efter."

"Can you do it?" said Hermens, not quite sure why he was asking, because they didn't look like they could. They didn't look like they could do anything except eat junk food by the hundredweight.

"Oh aye, we can dae it. Weel, no us, but we can expedite it fur ye. Can ye pey?"

"How much?" said Hermens. He might as well get down to the hard facts.

"Fur mere revenge, a disposal, a Clydesdale."

"Pardon?"

"A *Clyde*sdale. Like a *pony*. Only a big yin, ken."

Hermens was still none the wiser.

Bryce continued, "Fifty K. tae find the boy, an' that'll probably involve dealin' wi' 'im efter. It's no likely he'll simply hand ower the goods wi'oot bein' … asked nicely, ken. So he'd need tae be dealt wi'. If we retrieve the goods, it's ten percent o' the hauf million street value."

"Actually, it was closer to four hundred and fifty thousand," said Hermens, now regretting he had upped the figure.

"Same difference, Eric. We're dealin' in roond figures tae make the arithmetic easier. So, fifty K tae dispose o' ony combatants - ye're looking' at better than a hunner grande total. But everything left a' neat and tidy efterwards, nae forensic pish furra cops tae work wi'."

Hermens swayed. The proposition, killing a man, was being talked about as if it was a deal for landscape gardening. And a hundred grand was a lot of money,

"And what if you don't get the goods back?"

"Well, yer man needs tae be managed oot the game, rid cairdeed."

Hermens looked blank.

"Aff the park. Early bath - in the Clyde. Permanent like. Concrete wellies, ken. So the fifty grand sticks. Ony detritus in the wey o' other disposals is included."

"Good grief!" thought Hermens. *"He's talking about possible multiple killings as if it was a trip to the shops."*

Out loud, he said, "I don't want anybody killed."

"See here Eric, that might be an inevitable side effect. Naeb'dy's gawny hand ower goods worth that kind o' money wi'oot being asked nicely. Ye're dealin' wi' bad people here Eric. If we dinnae get the goods then we still need tae pey fur time and materials, say twenty-five grande."

Hermens nodded and thought for a while.

"So, in summary, we're looking at fifty thousand for the return of the goods, and another fifty for any casualties incurred along the way?"

"Aye. The fifty could include, say two casualties. Just as a wee kind o' loss-leader, a wee discount."

"That's very considerate of you," replied Hermens, somewhat lightheaded at the thought of murder being offered on a supermarket-type buy-one-get-one-free basis. Would he get a loyalty card?

"And the terms?" he asked.

"Pey in stages, twenty-five up front. We need tae get wur subcontractor's attention. Then twenty-five, then the balance efter we deliver, dependin' on casualties."

"How do I know you'll deliver?"

"Ye dinnae, and naithur dae we, that's why ye pey up front."

Hermens looked blank again. He was weighing up the chances of getting shat on again.

"See Eric," continued Bryce, detecting his trepidation.

He leant forward, clasping his Cumberland sausages on the desk like a headmaster speaking to a wayward pupil.

"It's like this: when the coal man came up oor hoose an' ma mammy asked fur credit, he wid just go, *'Sorry, cannae dae it doll.*

Nae money, nae coal.' That's life. But ye'll get yer coal if there's the least chance that we can dae it, or ye'll see that we gie'd it wur best shot. Besides, it widnae dae ony herm tae create a gap in the supply chain in Embra. We'll see if we can get Wee Shady oantae it."

"Wee Shady?"

"Aye, ye'll like Wee Shady, he's smert and gets things din."

"Din?"

"Aye din, as in soarteed, feenished. Ken?"

"*Jesus Christ,*" thought Hermens, "*I'm screwed whatever I do.*"

But he was bent on some kind of recompense for yesterday's disastrous loss, and he also wanted revenge for the way he'd been treated – the humiliating, piss-taking goods in the laptop bag.

"We'll let ye ken when Wee Shady's available."

"I'll text you it." He took out his iPhone.

"Is that yer Ain phone? Fucksake! Wull, awa an get Eric here wan o' they pey-as-ye-go phones. There's boaxes in the pool hall oaffice."

A few minutes later, a cheap, Chinese pay-as-you-go mobile phone was handed to Hermens.

"There's a few bob in it tae get ye stertit. Dinnae chairge up the credit wi' yer bank caird."

"I am aware of the process with mobile phone anonymity," said Hermens.

"*Stuck-up wee Sassenach shite,*" thought Wull.

Hermens phoned the hotel which Bryce had recommended as a good place to meet Wee Shady. One of Bryce's goons ordered him a taxi.

"Ye'll like this hotel, Jim," said the driver. "It's pure dead modern. Funky. Ken?"

Hermens didn't like funky. Inside the hotel, it was too funky, far too pure-dead-modern. There was no proper hotel reception, just some computers attended by what looked like a pre-pubescent child. An androgynous child at that, with facial jewelry and the blue of too much tattoo ink creeping out of the collar of his or her funky, hotel-logoed shirt. The child walked him through the check-in process on one of the computers. The process was cryptic, annoying and demeaning. Add it to the list of reasons why Scotland should be nuked.

He took the elevator and let himself into his room to discover that literally half the room, at the far end, was entirely taken up with a wall-to-wall bed big enough for a game of five-a-sides. A quarter of the room was occupied by a giant, translucent plastic pod containing a toilet and shower, and the quarter left had just enough space for a wash basin the size of a soap dish. You could bang your elbow just brushing your teeth. But, it was under a hundred quid and it had been recommended as a good place to meet this person called Wee Shady.

After meeting Bryce in the squalor of his Barrowland headquarters, he couldn't imagine what somebody with a name like Wee Shady would look like, but he was prepared for somebody equally disgusting. He went down to the main concourse to find that at least the hotel seemed to be inhabited by humans rather than the bloated, Star-Wars-Bar genetic mishaps he'd met so far. The public area was sprinkled with people, mainly young businessmen and women, apparently having meetings.

Not wishing to encounter even the civilised-looking inhabitants of this deeply irritating funky landscape, he decided to eat out. He chose Chinese. At least he wouldn't have to navigate a native menu full of Scottish muck like haggis. The first thing to catch his eye on the Chinese menu was "Sweet and Sour Battered Haggis Balls". He nearly threw up. He didn't know what kind of creature a haggis was, but he certainly wasn't going to eat its balls.

His appetite long departed, he left and got a bag of chips. At least there wasn't going to be any of the local roadkill in a bag of chips. He snuck it back to his funky hotel room, ate about six chips and retired to spend another sleepless night.

--------oOo--------

Julian

Mackenzie banged on the door of the converted mansion which contained Julian's apartment. After an impatient half minute, he banged again, this time harder. At the third time of hard and persistent banging a window above him slid upwards and an elderly lady's head popped out.

"What do you want?"

"Is Julian no in?" enquired Mackenzie.

"I might have known. What are you?" asked the very posh Edinburgh accent, emitting from a wrinkled face. "Another bloody rent boy? Why don't you try ringing your fellow bender's bell on the intercom?"

The window slammed shut.

"Rent boy!?" thought Mackenzie. "*Bender*?"

He checked himself over to see if he looked slightly gay. Even the homophobic Mackenzie could be shocked by such a foul-tempered and unfashionably homophobic tirade. He checked the door, and sure enough, there was an intercom panel screwed to the inside of the sandstone portal. He scrutinised the list of names on the panel and leant his finger on the button marked "J Matheson Esquire".

"J Matheson Esq. Bender." he thought, keeping his finger in place.

At last Julian's put-on posh Edinburgh accent crackled out of the grill on the panel, "Yes, Julian Matheson here, who's calling?"

"Rent Boys Are Us, at your service," said Mackenzie. "Yer faither says ye're needed fur a joab."

"Oh, it's you Mackenzie. Don't push your luck you little cretin. And keep your voice down. What is it?"

"Well Ah'm no gawny shout it up the fuckin' intercom am Ah? Bryson says we've tae get a move on."

After several seconds while Julian presumably gathered his wits and his underwear, he said, "I'll be down shortly, wait in the car."

Half an hour later and dressed in a blazer, slacks and cravat, looking like a nineteen sixties bookmaker, Julian opened the back door of the Merc and his boyfriend got in.

"You can give Nigel a lift to Waverley station," said Julian as he climbed into the passenger seat of the Merc.

"Whit am I? A fuckin' taxi service?"

"Nigel, meet Mackenzie, he's a homophobic little shit and he works for my dad."

"How do you do," said Nigel from the back seat and proffered a hand for Mackenzie to shake. "Nice car."

"Eh, hello," said Mackenzie, somewhat off his guard. He'd never, as far as he knew, shaken the hand of a gay person before. He reached his left hand back and Nigel took it and shook it and Mackenzie was surprised to find that the hand was calloused and hard. He drove off, eyes bulging.

"It's not Mackenzie's car, it belongs to one of my dad's other employees."

"Your dad obviously looks after his employees," said Nigel, the accent wasn't Edinburgh, it was from the rougher parts of North Lanarkshire.

After a few seconds, while Mackenzie gathered his composure, and getting back into full homophobic mode, he said, "That auld wummin that lives in the flat above your front door's got some mouth oan 'er."

"She's an old bag," said Julian. "A nosey old bitch."

"She said you were a really, really nice young man."

"Really?" said Julian, surprised.

"Aye, something like that. Yer dad says we've tae go and check oot that red Beamer. Balernae."

He handed Julian the notepaper with the address and car number on it.

"Your dad looking for a new car Julian?" asked Nigel.

"Ehm, yes, sort of," replied Julian looking at the notepaper. "Neat number plate," he said, raising one buttock to adjust his underwear.

"It's a total' wanker's number plate," replied Mackenzie, in the sort of tone Bryson would use. He looked at Julian. "Ah bet they thongs can get right up the sheugh o' yer erse. Right - up - yer - erse." And he lewdly pointed his middle finger in the air, twisting his wrist.

"You watch it Mackenzie, or my father will give *you* one up the arse."

"Wid he no delegate that tae you?"

"You'll get yours one day Mackenzie, mark my words."

"Happy to oblige on your behalf Julian," said Nigel from the back seat. He leaned forward and whispered in Mackenzie's ear in a very husky voice. "Happy to oblige Mister Mackenzie."

Mackenzie looked in the rear view mirror, Nigel was quite a big bloke.

"Nothing I like better than converting a homophobic little tosser like you to the true gospel."

"Eh … eh … Aye, right … nae offence," cringed Mackenzie.

"None taken," said Nigel.

They dropped Nigel off at Waverly Station and Julian got out and kissed his boyfriend on the lips.

"Jesus fuckin' Christ," said Mackenzie. "That's fuckin' well oot the park."

"Shut your face you little piece of shite," said Julian.

Nigel put his hand in the car window, grabbed Mackenzie by the collar and hauled his head and shoulders out of the car.

"Here was me wondering how you got the two black eyes wee man."

Julian grabbed his wrist to stop him from reinforcing the work done by Bryson's fist.

"Just forget it Nigel. He'll get it big time one day."

"Thanks for the lift," said Nigel, and hanging onto Mackenzie's collar, gave him a big smacker on the lips. He let him go and Mackenzie banged his head on his speedy retreat back inside the car. He sat rubbing his mouth with his sleeve as if he was trying to sandpaper any trace of Nigel off.

"Byee!" said Nigel, waving to Mackenzie.

Mackenzie kept rubbing.

Julian got back in the car and sat while Mackenzie gathered enough composure to drive the car.

"Why do you have to be such a nasty little shit Mackenzie?"

"Goes wi' the territory," said Mackenzie, trying to sound like a hard-man. "You need tae toughen up Julian."

"Ever heard of Walter Mitty? That's you."

"Did he no play fur the Jambos?" said Mackenzie.

--------oOo--------

Gym

Nisbet sat at his desk and worried. It seemed to be the only thing these days that he was any good at. He wondered if there was a department at the university where he could get some part time work lecturing carefree students on how to become overburdened by care and woe when you reach the job market, and then get married to the wrong person and get even more messed up.

He called through to Angela. "I'm starting to stiffen up Ange, I think I'll piss off to the gym to loosen up for half an hour and do a bit of stretching out before I go and see Wee Hammy,"

"That's what you need to do Nisbet, chill out."

"I said *stretch* out."

"Is that not the same thing?"

Angela had no idea what went on in a gym. Stretching out for her involved a settee, a box of chocolates and Eastenders omnibus.

"Kind of. I'll see you in the morning," he said, on the way past her desk.

She looked up at him. "Nisbet, don't worry. Millions of people have got divorced. It'll work out fine. Most people get divorced on good terms. Brenda doesn't want a fuss."

"Most people don't have Joseph Stalin for a father in law."

In the car, he spotted that his sweat-soaked kit was still lying there on the passenger seat, he'd forgotten to swop it out last night. His brain was mince.

In the gym, he shivered his way into his wet gear, warmed up and loosened off on a cross trainer for half an hour, did some gentle crunches then laid the contents of the portable puddle of his sweat-soaked tee-shirt and shorts on one of the mats and did some gentle stretching, some disguised yoga (you don't want other blokes to see you doing yoga), meanwhile making sure that his wedding tackle didn't flop out of his shorts when he sat in his best effort at the lotus position.

The only good thing he'd ever got out of Brenda's communing with the astral plain was that yoga was a good way to stretch out for competitive sport, even if it was a sissy, earth-mother thing to do.

She'd made him attend yoga classes with her once. He was the only guy there, but it wasn't so bad: some of the women were pretty fit ... those that weren't fat and over fifty.

Satisfied that he might have staved off a little of the ghastly, day-three, post-training stiffness that he'd surely get, he fetched some paper towels to wipe down the matt.

"Don't bother with that," said a female voice from behind him.

He stood up, it was a twenty-something fitness trainer. What a wee cutie!

"I'll need to get a bucket and mop."

"Eh?"

She smiled sarcastically at him.

"*Oh well*," he thought. "*It's hard to impress a young cutie when you're dripping with sweat and have just flushed half the gym down with it.*"

"Are you sure?" he said.

"Well, it'll be cheaper than a whole pack of paper towels."

Cheeky little shit. He showered and headed off to the pub to meet Wee Hammy. At the pub, he parked in his usual spot next to the wall and went inside.

--------oOo--------

Grand Theft Auto

Mackenzie, with the reluctant Julian in the passenger seat, headed off in the direction of Balerno, out the West Approach and onto the Lang Whang, the long road to Lanark.

Even though he'd driven it many times, the Merc still felt to Mackenzie like a very big car to squeeze through the traffic in the narrowness of Juniper Green. But being the nasty little shit that he was, he had no fear of aiming the car ever so slightly towards oncoming cars to get them to move over a bit more. One thing Mackenzie could do was drive and a big black car like Bryson's Merc was the perfect weapon for intimidating other road users, especially the Renault Cleo- and Fiat Five Hundred-driving retirees of daytime west Edinburgh.

Another mile up the road, he slowed down as the car two ahead of them signaled to turn right into a pub car park. The traffic freed up, the car, a red Beamer turned into the pub car park and the car behind it pulled away. As the Merc surged forward, Mackenzie glanced to the right and nearly jumped out of his skin.

"Fuck me Jools, a red Beamer, N15 somethin'! That's the motur! That's fuckin' it!"

But he couldn't stamp on the brakes, he was already past the pub and a row of cars and buses was behind him.

"What? Are you sure?" said Julian.

He'd been texting his boyfriend Nigel, and occasionally fidgeting in the car seat, something Mackenzie secretly put down to Julian's love life.

"Fuckin' looked like it. There's no that many red Beamers like that gawn aboot."

He signaled right and u-turned at the next side street.

In the pub car park the red BMW was parked up against the wall at the far end. There was a bloke just approaching the back door of the pub, tall, brownish hair, leather jacket.

"Maybes that's him," said Mackenzie as the pub door closed behind Nisbet.

"Aye that'll be him, same description Alec gied us. Same kindae leather jaikit. Dae ye think that's him Jools? Maybes we should grab him." Mackenzie was trying to sound hard.

"It's *Julian*!" He hated to be called Jools. "There must be ten other cars here, it might be somebody else entirely. Maybe we should just wait and see who comes and drives off in it. After all, we've got the address."

Mackenzie looked at the car; that was it alright, N15 BET.

"Ya beauty!" said Mackenzie. "Grab the motor."

He checked for CCTV cameras. Only one, pointing at the pub, away from the cars.

Then he turned to Julian, "Naw, that's definitely the motor and that was definitely him. He'll hae went in fur a pint, he'll be ages yet. Gie me two meenutes."

He reversed the Merc into a vacant space, got out, opened the boot and removed his kit bag. This would be a dawdle. Like any self-respecting small-time felon, he went, as the police termed it, "equipped to commit crime".

He stuck his head in the Merc's window, "You take the Merc, and if ye see that Beamer move, fuck off pronto."

"What are going to do." Julian was new at this.

"Lift the boy's' motor."

"What for?"

"Well it's only been a few 'oors. The bastard's maybes still got the stuff in the boot."

"Can't you just look in the boot then?" asked Julian, never having been involved before in car crime.

"Aye, spend ten meenutes searchin' a motor in a fuckin' pub car park. You're no cut oot fur a life o' crime Jools."

Julian nodded in agreement. That was becoming plainer by the day.

Mackenzie walked towards the BMW. It was a nice car, umpteen years old but an absolute beaut, a collector's item. And old cars were a piece of piss to nick. He lifted a thin strip of metal from his bag, slid it down the glass of driver's door, and popped up the lock. Inside the car, he thumbed through his huge collection of car keys and selected two or three old-style BMW keys to try. The third fitted.

Julian had barely climbed into the driver's seat of the Merc and started the engine when Mackenzie drove past him in Nisbet's Beamer, grinning like a Cheshire cat. A cat with a missing front tooth.

Julian had the sense to sit there for several seconds so that it wouldn't look like they'd left together. He would never have had the nerve to do that: steal a car, in broad daylight, even if he knew how. That was the difference between ordinary people and criminals: criminals think they'll get away with it, so they do the crime, and by and large they get away with it. Julian knew already that Mackenzie was right: it definitely seemed that he wasn't cut out for a life of crime. Well, not this kind of crime. He didn't scruple to do crime. But crime where you didn't get caught would suit him better. Such as financial services, or politics.

He drove back to his father's office, left the Mercedes keys on his dad's desk and went home. He had no interest whatsoever in what Mackenzie was up to.

--------oOo--------

Wee Hammy

"Niz!" said Wee Hammy, walking up to him in the pub. He gave Nisbet his usual car-crusher handshake, which popped some sweat out of Nisbet's forehead, and some wax out of his ears.

"Good to see you. I heard you were at the rugby club the other night."

Nisbet massaged his newly deformed hand.

"Don't mention it Hammy. We ended up …"

"Aye, I heard you were totally hammered. Doing the one-legged walk. Tommy said he was just about as bad."

"Tommy? Was he there? … Aye, I suppose he was." Nisbet couldn't really remember much about the night. "Honestly, I'd no idea how I got home."

"You drove, apparently."

"Yes, it looked that way, but I made it."

They both pondered, silently for a moment, the mentalness of driving as pissed as that. Full board and lodgings at Her Majesty's Hotel and Mail Bag Factory, Saughton, a criminal record and no driving license for decades afterwards could have been the outcome.

"Oh well, stuff it Niz, you survived. Glad you've resurfaced anyway, you've been missed, we could do with you back on the wing, the young lads are all shagged out by half time. Ye've got to be thirty before you can do self-harm with real conviction.

"So anyway, what can I do for you? Bit out of the blue, getting a call from the frequently reported-missing Nisbet Sangster?"

Nisbet explained the situation with Brenda, how she'd flown the nest along with their daughter.

"Divorce? Ho, ho Niz! Good effort!" he raised his pint in salute and took two inches off the top. "*Good eff*ort!" he said again, slapping Nisbet on the shoulder as if he had just put down a winning try. "You and ehm ... whatsername ...?"

"Brenda."

"Brenda, aye, Brenda." He paused as if recalling Nisbet's soon-to-be ex-wife. "You and her were never a good match Niz. Too precious, spoilt. Too many hang-ups. That kind of burd will keep a man from his rugby. Nice tits though!"

Hammy's pulverised and pock-marked face broke into a big grin. Flat nose, cauliflower ear, missing front tooth, the perfect advert for how sport can improve your health and well-being.

"No, actually, it's her that's divorcing me."

"Same difference Niz, you'll get humped either way. Middle class white men you and me. Every bastard in the land hates us, especially if there's a wailing wife and a child involved. Are those the papers?"

"Aye," Nisbet slid the fat envelope across the table to Hammy.

He looked at the branding on the envelope.

"Jesus Niz! Robb, Steal and Cheatem? They're a blood-thirsty bunch of barbarians. Just plead guilty, ye'll get a reduced sentence."

"Aye, very funny. So anyway Hammy, can you help?"

Hammy didn't reply at first, he was thumbing through the papers one by one.

"No," he said at last, poured another three inches of his pint down his throat, wiped his mouth with the heel of his hand, then wiped his nose with the back of his hand. What an ape: typical second row.

"Divorce isn't really my line, I do commercial litigation mainly. I just turn up and look deranged and they run for it," he joked.

But by the look of him, it could easily be true. He read on for a minute or so.

"This is pretty-much standard, boilerplate stuff Niz." Hammy was some kind of speed reader. "But they're going for your throat. Mental cruelty? What's that all about?"

"I refused to go vegan, eat health food and watch Strictly Come Dancing every weekend. It drove Brenda crazy."

"Nut cutlets?"

"Aye, and tiramisu. Vegetarian sausages."

"Jesus! Insane psychopathic bitch! That'll do it every time:

husband refuses to eat lesbian vegan health food, eats pies and chips; wife has nervous breakdown; man-hating feminist sheriff sentences husband to death. You heartless bastard Niz. Plus you're a rugby player so they'll say you were beating the shite out of her."

Nisbet's heart jumped and his stomach sank.

"They're not saying that are they?" he asked.

He had only flicked through the papers on the basis that he wouldn't understand it even if he read it thoroughly.

"No, but they will if and when it gets dirty. 'Hashtag MeToo', Niz. All white men are woman-mutilating bastards."

He raised his pint and removed another inch from it. Hammy was twenty nine or thirty and already divorced. His ex-wife was a lawyer too. She'd been shagging one of the partners at her practice on the side. But then, so had Hammy. So they called it quits.

Hammy's new steady date was a second row forward too. They'd been shagging each other on and off since school. Hammy had even given her one up against the toilet washbasins at his own stag party. But then, so had Nisbet at his. And half the first fifteen, allegedly. And half the women's first fifteen too, probably. She was an energetic young woman. She and Wee Hammy made an attractive couple - if you were a Neanderthal.

"So what do you think?" asked Nisbet.

"Basically, Nisbet, ye're screwed."

"How do you make that out?"

"Well, it would be ok if you did what me and Linda did: split up on good terms and remain pals. But this is standard, adversarial, total-hatred, we-get-everything divorce stuff. Brenda's lawyers will be ringing up the till big time. Does she have money?"

"Her ape of a father does, and it'll be him behind this."

"Well there you go …"

"So what do I do? Should I speak to Brenda?"

"Christ no! They'll simply bring out the big artillery. They'll say you're trying to intimidate her, more bullying etc. Then the bairn gets used as weaponry: bad parent and all that. Have you got much to lose if you were to walk away without contesting all of this?"

Nisbet thought for a minute. He didn't really have much to lose.

"Well, just my share of the equity in the house, all the stuff ... and of course, our daughter, Samantha."

"Samantha Sangster? It's got a ring to it," said Hammy, slowly, pensively and with deliberate irony. He smiled at Nisbet. "Sammy Sangster for short."

"I know," replied Nisbet, with no irony whatsoever.

"Anything else?"

"Well, I've still got my flat, it's a two-bedder in Dalry.

"Well, there'll have been some growth in that, I suppose - a bargaining chip. Look, you really need a family law specialist. We've got a nice lass in the practice, she's shit hot."

"What kind of hot?" asked Nisbet.

"Both, and it always looks better if a husband's got a nice looking woman representing him in court, it means that your safe around women."

"What if the sheriff's a woman?"

"Even better, she might fancy you." He laughed and took the last half inch out of his pint. "I can speak to her in the morning if you like. Do you want me to pass these on?" He waved the papers at him.

"Aye, Hammy, that would be fine. How much is this going to cost?"

"If you dig your heels in? Everything you've got. Me, I'd just walk off the park. You could come out of it where you were before you got married. All you've got to negotiate is access to ... Samantha. You'll get that no bother."

That didn't sound so bad to Nisbet, just three and a half years of his life down the drain.

"Pint?" said Hammy, rising to his feet and heading for the bar without waiting for an answer.

Nisbet lifted his half-finished pint and necked it to catch up with Hammy. At least Hammy's off-hand attitude was calming him down. He needed a big brother sort to take care of him. Even if this particular big brother was a complete animal.

Hammy had two more pints and lifted Nisbet's envelope.

"Right, off to training, when are you going to turn up?"

"When I'm not quite fit enough I'll show up. At the moment, I'm not fit enough even to start getting fit. But like I said, I've started back at the gym. Properly."

"Good effort Niz." He stood up, towering over Nisbet, who himself was a little over six feet. "I'll have my people to speak to your people."

He stuck out a hand the size of a bread board. Nisbet held out his hand to have it crushed again.

"See when you're through with this divorce Niz?"

"Aye?"

"Can I ask wee Brenda out?" He smiled a lascivious, gap-tooth smile at Nisbet.

"Be my guest Hammy, but she comes with some heavy baggage?"

"She's mental?"

"She's just a bit anal Hammy. But her father's a basket case, and he's part of the whole package."

"Shame. Nice tits though ... Brenda, not her father."

He shone his missing tooth at Nisbet again and poured the last half of his final pint down his throat.

"They're all mental – women - you know that, don't you? If you want to know where you're at with a woman - pick one up that's just come out of the funny farm. At least you'll know from the start that she's mental. They even get a certificate. Gimme a call tomorrow. Good to see you Niz."

He crushed Nisbet's hand again and headed out the door.

Nisbet sat down and stared at the pint in front of him. It was more than he should drink what with the car outside but, to hell with it. It didn't bother Hammy: three pints and off to circuit training. Nisbet liked his beer but that would have had him chucking all over the park.

--------oOo--------

Robbed

Mackenzie looked around the inside of the Beamer as he drove towards the city centre.

"Bloody nice motor," he said to himself. "Leather upholstery, turbo, goes like a cat wi a dug up its erse." He looked at the dial. "Full tank! Ya beauty!"

So instead of going directly back to show off his loot, he took it for a drive around the back roads of Midlothian and down the A68, heedless of speed cameras. Two hours later he parked it up in the Boss's lock-up garage behind the office and went to the pub.

Nisbet stepped out of the side door, his habit when walking home from the pub. He usually walked home when he'd had a few, more afraid of losing his license than killing someone. And now he was especially chastened having driven home totally pissed a couple of nights ago. Fifty yards up the street he spotted his mistake. Shit, he'd meant to drive home, he'd only had two and a half pints, it wasn't exactly wife beater strength, he'd be ok to drive. Probably.

Back in the pub car park he scanned it to see where he'd left the car. No car. Shit, he must have left it on the street, what a dork. Out on the street his car was nowhere to be seen, but he met another of the boys from the rugby club turning into the pub car park.

The window of his transit van came down. "Hi, Niz. I could have sworn I passed you on my way through Colinton. Your car, your number. On the way back into town."

"No, not me, Alan." But the reality was beginning to dawn. "Aw Jesus!"

He ran back up to the car park, clear in his mind now about where he'd left the car. Alan passed him and reversed into the very space his Beamer had been in.

He got out and looked at Nisbet's face, "Who stole your scone?"

"More like, Who stole my car?" said Nisbet.

"So it *was* your car I saw in Colinton?"

"Looks like it."

"Well I did say it looked like it," said Alan.

Nisbet fished his phone out of his pocket, "Better call the cops."

"Aye," said Alan. "C'mon Niz, I'll buy you a pint while you're waitin' for the polis."

"Naw, no thanks, I'm drivi..."

"Doesnae look like it Niz." Alan put his hand on Nisbet's shoulder. "C'mon, ye can have a pint while ye're waitin'. The polis will be ages. Besides, maybe somebody in the pub saw something."

"Aye. Jesus Christ!" said Nisbet, furrowing his brows, rummaging through the clutter in his head to see if he'd renewed his insurance.

He knew that he would have, or rather, Angela would have, but life was such a pisser right now that it could easily have un-renewed itself out of spite.

He sat and had another pint and put in a call to the police to report the car being stolen. It only took an hour for a police car with two uniformed cops to turn up in the pub. They both looked to be about sixteen years old.

"Hello, I'm WPC Redmond," said the apparently sixteen-year-old WPC after asking for Nisbet by name, to the amusement of the whole pub. She seemed quite nice. A friendly smile.

"And I'm PC Thom," said her pencil-necked companion who seemed to be taking charge, presumably on the basis that his colleague was a woman and consequently incapable of managing this sort of high level criminal investigation.

"Right Mister Nesbit," continued PC Pencilneck, "shall we go out and have a look at the scene of the crime?"

"My name's Sangster, Nisbet Sangster, Nisbet's my Christian name."

"We don't talk about Christian names these days," said the pompous pencilneck, It's *first* names. The police are too inclusive to use divisive expressions like that."

"Like what?" said Nisbet.

"Like religiously divisive words like *Christian*." He took out his notebook. "So your full name is what?"

"Nisbet ...,"

"Nisbet what?"

"Nisbet ... Christian ...," said Nisbet, deliberately, about to give his full name.

"You just said it was Sangster."

"No, my middle name is …"

"What? Sangster?"

"No, Christian."

"Are you trying to be difficult? Giving a false name to a policeman is an offence."

"Just put Nisbet C Sangster," suggested Nisbet.

"Second name? Your actual second name, not your, ehm Christian, ehm, second, ehm, middle name"

"My full name is Nisbet … Christian … Sangster."

It was noted down. The WPC smiled knowingly up at Nisbet. The poor girl had to share a car with this dimwit.

Nisbet took them out to the car park to show them a Ford Transit van sitting where his car had been.

"So this is where you left it?" asked the cop.

"Yes."

"What right here?"

It seemed to perplex the young constable that there could have been a BMW also parked where a Ford Transit was currently parked.

"Yes," said Nisbet, "I got here before the van."

Despite himself, the policeman stooped very slightly to look under the van, then piped up, "So tell me Mr Nisbet, had you been drinking before you allegedly parked your car here?"

"Well, I didn't allegedly park it here, I *actually* parked it here, and no, I came to the pub more or less direct from the office, for a meeting with my lawyer."

This was approximately the whole truth nor nothing faintly like the truth.

"But you did have something to drink? I can smell drink on your breath. You do know that drink driving is against the law?"

"Yes, I had a brief drink - *after* I got here. Then I had another couple while I was waiting for you."

"And you were planning on driving home afterwards? In that state?"

"Oh, for pity's sake!" said Nisbet. "No, I was going to walk home."

"Well, you'd certainly have to walk home if your car had been stolen. But what if it hadn't been stolen eh? Were you planning on driving home if it hadn't been stolen?"

"I wasn't simply going to walk home because it had been stolen."

"So you *were* going to drive it home in that state," said the inquisitorial pencilneck."

"I live just up the road, I quite often walk home from the pub." This was only mostly true. "Look, can we get on with the stolen car thing please?"

The cop gave him his best intimidating-a-suspected-drunk-driver look.

"I think you were planning on driving home after you had a drink. Would that not be your usual modus operandi?"

"Modus what?"

He looked at the female cop. She smiled and shrugged sympathetically.

"Look, I haven't been drink driving! I don't have a car! It's been bloody-well stolen!"

Even the highly stressed Nisbet noticed his voice almost peaking at soprano.

"Sir, I have to warn you that if you get any more abusive I'll arrest you for drunken disorderly."

"*Jesus Christ!*" thought Nisbet. "*Better cool it.*"

"Look," he said, "I apologise, I've had my car stolen, it's a stressful business. Yes I had a pint, while waiting for you. No, I wasn't planning on drink driving, I've simply added to my collection of pints since calling you. I am not drunk, nor have I driven since drinking, nor do I, or did I, intend to drive after drinking."

"Very well then, apology accepted," said the mentally deficient policeman to the not-entirely truthful Nisbet. "Can I suggest you calm down now? Please give me some details about your car. Make?"

"Yes, it's a red BMW, Alpina B10…"

"BMW," said the cop, writing it down with his tongue out, "Model?"

"Alpina B10"

"Colour?"

Nisbet wanted to say, "It's fucking red, like most red cars are! You fuckwit!" But instead simply reiterated the car's colour.

"What shade of red?"

"Oh, I don't know, pillar box red."

The cop wrote that down.

"Registration?"

"En, one, three, Bee, Ee, Tee,"

He wrote it down.

"Is that a private number plate?"

"Yes, it's my very, very own."

Pint-laden sarcasm was in danger of taking him towards a drunken and disorderly arrest.

The policeman sighed, "Year of manufacture?"

"Nineteen ninety four."

"Date purchased?"

"Eh? Ehm … I'm not sure, sometime in January the year before last."

"What? You don't know when you bought it?" He looked at his colleague for confirmation that the accused was drunk. "Value?"

"I dunno," said Nisbet, "it's a nice one, low mileage, maybe twenty grande."

"Twenty grande for a twenty-year-old BMW!" exclaimed the cop, and he shook his head in disbelief at the fiscal fecklessness of alcoholics such as the accused.

--------oOo--------

4

Wee Shady

Hermens breakfasted in what looked like a funky cross between a coffee bar and a school dinners canteen. He chose the healthiest things he could see from the buffet-style offering and with his tray in one hand and the Times in the other he wandered around until he found a vacant "funky", "hot-desk" area to eat the overcooked food he'd collected.

There were no vacant stools so he ate standing up at some kind of breakfast bar. Gradually his hatred of Scots, Glasgow and Edinburgh in particular, rose into the red again. After breakfast he checked out at reception, which was attended by a different tattooed, pierced, androgynous twenty-something, and took his wheeled overnight bag to the break-out zone of this annoyingly funky boutique hotel. He sat discretely in a booth with his back to the lobby area. It was populated by a sprinkling of young business types, all with laptops, all tapping away at the keyboard or staring at their phones or talking too loudly into them.

At the agreed time of ten o'clock, he went to the seated lobby area and wandered around looking for somebody with a similar mutant genetic physiology to Bryce. Nobody fit the bill. He got a coffee and sat at one of the many meeting tables that were spread about the lobby.

After a couple of minutes a small man, well dressed in an immaculate 3-piece business suit seemed to materialise beside him.

"You'll be Eric Hermens."

The voice was cultured, educated. The accent was west of Scotland but plainly of a different sort from Bryce. Hermens almost leapt to his feet, relieved at last to meet a Scot who sounded, and looked as if he could join two thoughts together, and speak English.

"Yes, yes," said Hermens rising to his feet. "Eric Hermens. How did you know?"

"Takes one to know one," said the small man.

"Are you …?

"Just call me Mister McShaed."

He held out his hand but didn't offer a first name.

"Oh, so it's not a nickname?"

"Yes, it is, in a way. My family is in the domestic lighting business."

"Ah, so Wee Sh…"

"I think we can dispense with the *Wee*."

But the double entendre was obvious. Shady is as shady does.

"Bryce will have told you a little about me."

"Well, yes, a very little," said Hermens, it was obvious why Bryce had referred to him as 'Wee Shady' but he hoped that Mr McShaed would turn out to be deeply shady and deeply helpful.

"He told me a little, but not much. He said you could … organise … getting my goods back."

"Well, we'll need to see, but we can't discuss it here, can you come with me please?"

He turned and Hermens followed him, pursued by his wheeled overnight bag, out of the hotel and onto the pavement where McShaed hailed an apparently passing black cab. A black cab with its yellow "For Hire" sign unlit.

"We can talk in here," said McShaed, opening the door for Hermens.

"I was thinking of somewhere more discrete," said Hermens.

"Oh this is discrete," replied McShaed. "Isn't it Malcy?"

"Aye," said the taxi driver over his shoulder. His voice sounded exactly like the Piltdown primate that had driven him from the station to Ra Barras.

"Just drive around Malcy." He turned to Hermens. "This is my office, so to speak, occasionally. Now, tell me everything from start to finish. Leave nothing out."

McShaed listened carefully to everything that Hermens told him as the taxi toured Glasgow city centre. He went through the whole meeting scenario: the overly complicated, somewhat theatrical swop; the laptop bag; the weird stone samples; the books. Then the chase up the Mound, and finally, how the big man in the leather jacket seemed to be trying to catch a red car. He gave McShaed the part of the number plate he remembered: something, something, something, B-E-T. McShaed wrote it down.

McShaed enquired about the swop. How much money, for what in the way of goods? He raised his eyebrows when Hermens described the goods.

"OK, thank you Eric. Tell me, why would somebody in Edinburgh want to buy almost half a million pounds-worth of diamonds?"

Hermens went through the possible reasons. "Well, diamonds are a good hedge against inflation, in difficult economic times they grow in value, or at least keep their value and they're more portable than gold."

"But then stocks and shares," said Mr Shade, "would be a more traditional way to invest your hard-earned money. Could it be that this money was being ... salted away in the form of diamonds?"

"It could be."

"In other words, money that would be an embarrassment if it were to come to the attention of the authorities, say, the Inland Revenue, or the police?"

"Well, it's none of my business," said Hermens. "I merely sell the goods."

"But it would more than likely be spare cash from some kind of illegal trade." This was a statement, not a question.

"I suppose it could be," said Hermens.

"So do I," said McShaed. Then he leaned forward and spoke to the taxi driver, "Malcy? Who do we know in the pharmaceuticals business in Edinburgh?"

"Ah'll make enquiries, an' speak tae Brycey ana'," said the driver. "Gie me a minute." He picked up his phone.

McShaed leant back and turned in his seat. "Now, we need to talk money, what did Mister Bryce tell you about costs?"

Hermens repeated what Bryce had said about costs and McShaed nodded. "And you're happy with that? Excuse me." He leant forward again. "Malcy, take us back to the hotel, we're nearly finished here."

"I want my stuff back, or if I can't get it back, I want …"

"Some payback," said McShaed, his voice matter of fact.

"Yes," replied Hermens.

"OK. Now, I need to stay in touch with you while I do some background work. Malcy, can I have two phones please?"

Two 'burner' phones, cheap, virtually disposable Chinese phones were passed through the glass divider of the taxi. McShaed handed one to Hermens. "This is yours, the only number on it is the number for *this* phone."

He held the other phone up and wiggled it.

"But don't call me, I'll call you, and it won't be today, and possibly not tomorrow."

The taxi drew up, back at Hermens' hotel.

"I already have a phone, Bryce gave me a phone. Plus I have my own, so I don't need another."

"Yes, you can use that to contact Bryce if you need to, but you don't need to, you'll be dealing with me exclusively. Use this for contact with me, I'll manage Mister Bryce."

Hermens sighed, he was used to using 'burner' phones for off-limits reasons but now he had four phones in his case, his own personal phone, his own discrete pay-as-you-go, Bryce's and now McShaed's, he'd better not mix them up.

"What should I do?" he asked.

"You need to get the down payment to Billy Bryce. I'm working for him on this one, he's my agent in this case. Cash. How you source it is your affair but he'll need it all before I start work."

"How do I know I can trust you … or Mister Bryce?" said Hermens.

The ironic tone was not lost on Mr McShaed. 'Mister' seemed too respectful an epithet to use on a savage like Bryce.

"You see Eric," said Wee Shady, putting his hand on Hermens' arm, "in this line of business, as I'm sure you know, you don't stay in this line of business, if you don't deliver. It'll be the same in your line of business. And that's why I find the sort of treachery you've experienced quite disturbing."

He smiled one of those smiles that emphasise the undeniability of what has just been said. He opened the taxi door. Hermens got out immediately, feeling out of his depth.

McShaed leant forward, still holding the door open, "And failing to deliver, is the cardinal sin that your Edinburgh friends have committed."

"Should I stay in Glasgow?"

"Well, you have to raise some cash," said McShaed. "But after that, I can keep in touch with you wherever you are."

He smiled a reassuring nod and closed the door. The taxi drove off leaving Hermens on the pavement, feeling only slightly less desolate than before. At least McShaed seemed intelligent and capable.

The taxi driver, Malcy, drove on, one-handed as he finished his call. He stopped at the lights on West Nile Street.

"There's only three, maybe four serious operators in Edinburgh boss. The Colqhouns are the main desperados in Embra. Causin' some friction wi' them, there's the clans, the Dawson and McElbie clans, same as here, but they're overstretched. Plus there's the Chinese and yon new arrivals frae London: darkies frae Tottenham apparently. County lines boys.

"It's no the Colqhouns because, well because it's no. They widnae have wanted tae meet in a busy public park. They'd have wanted tae meet oot in the countryside. Where they might simply have shot the boy and ta'en the goods. It's no the Dawsons or McElbies because they're no well-enough connected in the east. It's no the Chinese because they're mainly production and wholesale, and it's no the darkies because they've no got enough traction up here yet, an' onwey, they'd kinday stick oot like a sair thumb."

"So who else is there?"

"Well, apparently there's this operation that mainly does skunk, resin, cocaine and smack. Oh, and steroids - the stuff Brycey and his mates use. It's a small time, wee, sort-of faimly-run-type operation."

"Tinks? Travelers?"

"Naw, just a kind-of faimly business."

"So how come they're still in business?" asked McShaed. "The big boys would shut them down."

"Ower wee, no intae too much o' the big money stuff, white stuff like coke, crack or the synthetics. Dinnae tread on ower mony taes, Ah suppose. They're probably buyin' frae the big boys onywey. Dinnae ken if they dae the low-level stuff like swedgers or jellies. But they get left tae theirsel's. Plus the Chinese are a bigger annoyance everywhere when it comes tae the weed. Same everywhere, they rent a flat, install a' the horticultural equipment, grow it in the flat for a few months then disappear. They can make about fifty K a month frae wan rented hoose. And they supply tae the clans. If the clans were gawny shut onybody doon they'd go for the darkies first.

"In fact, the darkies huv a'readies hud a wee sermon, a wee dressin' doon ower here. Wan o' them wis washed up oan the beach at Barassie, in his underpants. Droon't. Absolutely fu' o' whisky. The polis pit it doon tae some nameless African seaman fa'in aff a freighter comin' oot the container terminal."

"Thins it down a bit Malcy. Does that lad of yours want to earn some pocket money? Get him over to Edinburgh, act like a student and source some skunk and we'll work our way up the supply chain."

"He's a'ready a student in Edinburgh," said the driver.

"Really?"

"Aye. He's studyin' law."

"Funny old world," said McShaed.

Hermens caught a flight back to London, he had to get some money together. The flight, at such short notice, had cost him a fortune, adding to his losses and his hate-all-Scottish people frame of mind.

--------oOo--------

The Car

Alec Bryson had Mackenzie pinned against the wall in the passage of the boss's "other" office.

"Are you a total fuckin' imbecile?" he yelled, stooping to get his face right in the terrified, post-, and now possibly pre-re-assaulted face of Mackenzie.

"Did you hear me say tae steal his fuckin' motor, ya useless wee prick?"

"Ye says tae get everything Ah could. So Julian says we should take the motor. He thought the stuff might be in it."

"Did he fuck! He's a fuckin' wee public school prick. It widnae cross his mind tae steal a motur!"

Bryson was coming to the boil.

"But the stuff could hae been in the motur Alec," pleaded Mackenzie.

"Aye, that's right, this guy is every bit as fuckin' daft as you and Julian, so he leaves a king's fuckin' ransom in swag in the motor ootside the pub and goes in fur a pint. Get fuckin' rid ae that motor!" He paused for a moment. "Naw. On second thoughts, keep the motor fur a bit, we'll need tae go through it wi' a fine tooth comb, forensic-like. Where is it?"

"It's in the boss's lock-up."

"Jesus bloody Christ!" Bryson's eyes closed in disbelief.

The boss's lock-up was in the mews behind his law offices. Now the biggest criminal law practices in Edinburgh had a stolen car on the property: a possibly twice-stolen car, in its private garage.

"Ya fuckin' wee moron, whit the fuck possessed ye tae day that?"

"H, h, hide in plain sight Alec," stammered Mackenzie, starting to crap himself from the murderous look on Bryson's face. "Like ye'r aye sayin'."

"Aye, but there's a clue in the word *hide*."

He thought for a minute.

"Look, ya wee fuckwit, get that fuckin' motor the fuck oot o' the boss's fuckin' garage, go through it wi' a fine tooth comb, let me ken if ye fun' onything."

"Ok Alec."

"Then take it somewhere and torch it. Then efter ye've feenished wi' the motor, get yer arse up tae Balernae and check oot that address. We need tae fun' oot whae these bastards are, whae this Balernae bastard is an' if he's involved at a'. If Ah could get ma haunds oan him Ah'd fuckin'…" Bryson's fists bunched up again.

"Ok Alec, Ah'll get right oan it," said the trembling Mackenzie, turning to go. Then at the door he turned. "Whit wull Ah dae wi' the motur?"

"Fucksake!" said Bryson, exasperated, "Torch it!"

"Aye. Ok Alec."

"Torch yersel while ye're at it. And take that Julian and torch him ana'. And dinnae forget tae check oot that address!"

Mackenzie went into the kitchen where Julian was leaning on the sink, on the phone to his boyfriend.

"Right Jools," said Mackenzie in his most dynamic tone. "We've tae get oan wi the next phase."

Julian excused himself from his phone conversation and responded impatiently, "My name is *Julian*! And what, does *next phase* mean, pray tell?"

"Pray tell?" said Mackenzie. "Pray that Alec and yer faither dinnae kick the shite oot o' us. We've tae check oot the Beamer, then check oot the hoose in Balernae, then ditch the Beamer. Or wis it the other wey roond?"

"Where is it?"

"In the garage ahent yer faither's office." Mackenzie headed for the door.

"What! Oh Jesus!" said Julian. He followed that in a daze of incomprehension with, "We … no, *you* stole a car for, it turns out, nothing! And now it's in my father's garage! And how are we - no you - going to get rid of a stolen car?"

"Dinnae worry Jules,…"

"It's *Julian*!"

"… Ah've got this totally under control."

They walked the two hundred yards along the lane from the boss's 'other' office to the garage behind his law offices. Mackenzie opened the side door of the garage and switched on the light. The red BMW looked superb sitting there in the bright fluorescent lights of the garage.

"Right, we've tae check oot his hoose, you get the garage door."

"What? Go to his house, in his own car? Shouldn't we - no *you* - ditch it? It'll have been reported stolen!"

"Naw, he's a crook, he's no gawny phone the polis an' report a stolen car stolen is he? Alec says tae check the hoose oot and then torch the motor. Ah think that's whit he says oneyweys."

He pushed past the stunned Julian, grabbed the handle of the lock-up door, rolled it up over their heads and climbed back into Nisbet's BMW.

"This is all going to end very bad indeed," said Julian, getting into the passenger seat.

"Hey Jools," said Mackenzie in his best Bryson voice, "where are *you* gawn? Get oot and shut the garage door efter Ah back oot. Then lock up. C'mon Jools, hurry the fuck up!"

Julian gave his best attempt at the evil eye at Mackenzie but saw the futility in continuing to protest that his name was Julian. He dealt with the door as Mackenzie fired up the engine and slid the car out of the garage.

--------oOo--------

Shopping

The carless Nisbet took the bus into the office. He dressed a little more casually. There was no way he was going to sit on some manky bus seat in the Hugo Boss slacks that had cost him an arm and a leg, so he wore his comfortable, cargo-type chinos. They had pockets everywhere, but were new-ish and not intolerably scruffy.

Luckily, a Number Forty-four bus went all the way from Balerno almost to the office door. It had taken him half an hour of investigation and deciphering Lothian Buses' cryptic app to discover that his worst fears were unfounded. If he'd known that the bus went straight there, maybe he wouldn't always have driven to the office and wouldn't have moaned so much about being forced into renting an office on the wrong side of town. What a dunderhead!

On the other hand, the damned bus had taken about an hour. An hour sitting there in a bus full of elderly people and students, all with bus passes. And crammed into a seat with enough leg-room for a short-arsed Hobbit.

Nope. On reflection, now that he'd given the bus a go, the car was the answer: private, your own music, no smelly people. But it was still a bitch of a commute when he could be working from home. But then, he wouldn't have Angela, and he really wasn't sure he trusted himself to work from a home office. Angela was a grafter, when she had enough work to keep her busy, and being the sort she was, she had a knack of keeping Nisbet on the straight and narrow and shaming him into grafting in the same way that she could.

He called her from the bus and explained the situation about his car.

"I take it my insurance is up to date?" he asked, after she'd calmed down.

Angela was so honest that she couldn't imagine why somebody would even take paperclips from the office let alone steal something like a car.

"Of course it's up to date. Have you reported it to the police?"

"Yes, of course, immediately. They were pretty decent – apart from asking if I'd been drinking before or after I'd parked it. Idiots."

He even managed to get into the office a little early, having left early to compensate for potential bus-travel cock-ups. Early, but still not early enough to get in before Angela.

"You'll not believe this Angela," he said. "The forty-four from Balerno stops on the main road there, a hundred yards away!" he said, as he headed for his desk.

"I've been telling you that for two and a half years."

Nisbet pretended not to hear. Pretending not to hear was entirely excusable in people who were congenitally incapable of listening.

"Well I'm still gonna drive in when I get my car back," he said. Then glumly, "*If* I get my car back."

The day passed and Nisbet worked at his desk for as long as he could bear it. He felt awful. Life was pure shite: impending divorce, car stolen, probably going to lose the house, alimony, child support. He had a permanent pain in his guts which felt like a belch which wouldn't come. He tried belching but that didn't help and the way his luck was running he didn't dare try farting. All he needed was to have to go home from work on a public bus with a giant skid-mark the size of a Calzone in his underpants.

Nervous tension was doing his head in. Mounting problems made you insecure and worrisome which gave you a pain in the guts, which felt like a bad fright, which made you tense and nervous. What did they call that? A positive feedback loop? Or was it a negative feedback loop? Negative feedback of a totally negative pile of crap?

In the afternoon, he got up from his desk and said, "I'm off Angela, I'll probably just work from home tomorrow, until I find out what the sketch is with my car. Besides, getting the bus is a major drag."

"Have you thought that your insurance might entitle you to a rent-a-car while this is being sorted out?"

"Really?"

"I'll check."

Nisbet left for the bus stop.

He got off the bus two stops early, and wandered around the Co-op like an automaton until he eventually remembered what he'd come in for: some potatoes, butter, milk and a few other things which, up until now, he'd have relied upon Brenda to get, such as toothpaste and razorblades. At the check-out, he stood in the usual ten-mile queue at the only one of four tills that had an attendant. All the other staff were probably round the back smoking dope. Bloody students.

Having your laptop bag nicked was more than a little annoying, but then having your car nicked was a pure pile of crap - as if he didn't have enough to worry about with Brenda about to sue his arse off.

When his turn came at the checkout, he let the young idiot get on with scanning his stuff at a snail's pace. Nisbet never went shopping - except for clothes or the odd thing that Brenda might have asked him to get on his way home - so he didn't have a shopping bag. He didn't need one, he usually just chucked the few things he'd bought on the back seat of the car. What bloody car?

He paid for his stuff, then stood in the most sarcastic posture he could muster. After a minute or so, just as the attendant was starting on the next customer

He said, "Can I have a carrier bag please?"

"Oh. Yes," said the little git. "They're a pound each."

He had an earring in his nose and a thing in his earlobe that looked like a piece of garden hose. Nisbet could see through the idiot's ear to the cigarette rack on the wall behind.

"A quid for a plastic bag?" said Nisbet, withholding the part about *ya wee prick,* which both of them knew he wanted to say.

"Yes, it's part of the Co-op's environmental campaign," he simpered. "Plus the Scottish government probably wants half of it. Or would you like one of our fair-trade hessian "bags for life"? They're made from recycled sugar sacks from Venezuela: handmade by … ehm Venezuelans. They're three quid."

"*Three quid for a bag made out of a bit of bug-ridden old sack that was too shagged out to use for sugar anymore? Call that fair trade? No chance. Don't get me' started!*" he thought.

He sighed in resignation. "Gimme a plastic bag," and he chucked a pound coin down on the counter.

He packed everything that would fit into the plastic bag until it was near to bursting, lifted the two-litre carton of milk and left. Outside, he realised that he'd been all round the supermarket and aside from potatoes he still hadn't actually bought anything decent for his dinner. He went back in to see what he could get for dinner.

It seemed that all they had was ready-meals of one sort or another. A choice between Linda McCartney vegetarian lasagna rubbish, the sort his wife would buy, and cheap pizzas. It was a choice between quasi healthy eating or the ultimate in supermarket junk food. He wandered along the aisle a bit and came to some fresh butcher meat.

He stared at it.

Staring back at him was a shrink-wrapped pack of beef mince. It dawned on him. Mince and tatties! Bloody great idea! He hadn't had mince and tatties since before he got married to Brenda the food Nazi. He knew how to make it well enough, he'd helped his mum with it often enough when he was little, and he had the tatties in his extortionate plastic bag. He lifted the mince and headed back to the check-out queue where he began to review his recent culinary past.

It seemed like it had been years since he'd eaten a proper meat-and-two-veg meal at home, like his mum used to cook. But now that Brenda was out the house, he could eat what he damned-well pleased. The wholefood, health food, Nisbet-moral-improvement scenario of the last few years ran a slide show in his head:

Slide 1:- Brenda was so screwed up about what amounted to a healthy diet, that all she ever ate was lettuce and low-fat crap. In the fridge there was always a tub or two of some "healthy" vegetarian, whole-food sludge, all of which seemed to have names like tiramisu or taramasalata which may, as far as Nisbet was concerned, have been the same thing because they looked like somebody had already eaten them. Or couscous. Which sounded like it was made of ground up dried dormice. These things were described as being "good for you".

Slide 2:- Ludicrously expensive pre-packs of "healthy" crap, like mung beans and pea pods with no peas in them. Or anything with sun-dried tomatoes in it. Sun dried tomatoes for pity's sake! The Italians were great marketeers: a surplus of over-ripe tomatoes that nobody wants, left in the sun to dry. Then some hairy-arsed Louigie comes up with the bright idea of selling them to the Brits as a fashion health food. Then he phoned the French about their pea pods with no peas in them. With the bit between their marketing teeth, the French then persuaded the Brits to buy Beaujolais Nouveau for decades until somebody pointed out that it was complete cat's piss that the French wouldn't take in a gift.

Slide 3:- Brenda had forced that type of faddy, health food diet shite on Nisbet for the last three and a half years. Everything she served up was described as, "They're really good for you" or, "they're organic".

Silly woman even used to do it in restaurants. Out with friends, everybody would order up the best scran on the menu except for Brenda. She'd order a bloody salad! A salad that would cost Nisbet fifty quid when the bill was split. Fifty quid for a designer plate of rocket, pea pods with no peas, two tomatoes the size of a rat's gonads and a "drizzle" of some dark brown stuff that looked like it had leaked out of a gearbox.

Slide 4:- Rocket? What the bloody hell's that all about? Intercontinental ballistic docken leaves? It was called rocket because it was so disgusting it should be put on one and fired into outer space.

Thank God for lunchtime pies and after-work pints and crisps or he'd have died of health-food-induced malnutrition.

Coming back to his senses in the queue for the single functioning check-out he shuffled along, the only bloke in a row of old ladies. When it came to his turn, Nose-ring had been replaced by a flaccid looking young woman with about eight gold studs in each ear and a ring in her nostril. What was it with rings in noses? What happened if she got the cold? How did she de-snot her nose without serious injury. Or, if she took it out to blow her nose, did snot shoot out the side of her nostril and hit some poor bastard in the face?

He plopped the mince down on the checkout and laid the milk on the floor at his feet.

"Is that it?" she said, looking into Nisbet's full shopping bag suspiciously.

He was looking in her slightly gaping mouth to see she had a shining gold stud through her tongue.

"That must hurt like shit getting that done. You'd be getting tube fed for a week while it healed," he thought.

Then aloud, he said, "Yes, that's the lot."

He wondered what else had been pierced. He'd read about some teenager going down on his girlfriend's pierced fanny and getting his dental braces caught in her gold pussy ring. He smiled, imagining the girl's male parent having to turn up with a pair of wire cutters. What would get cut in order to free the embarrassed young lovers from their coytus interruptus, cunnilingual, dental attachment? Would it be the pussy piercing, or the boyfriend's four-grande dental wiring?

The check-out girl interrupted this reverie.

"What about the milk? Ye've got milk there."

She leant over the counter and pointed at the milk.

"I paid for that already," replied Nisbet.

"Aw aye?"

Nisbet fished his receipt out of the bag. She looked at it and shrugged, "Do you need a bag for that? We've got a choice of ..."

"No, no thanks," said Nisbet, reluctant to fork out another quid. And before he was told about the bug-ridden sacks from the bug-ridden failed state of Venezuela, he said, "I'll make do with this one."

He paid, and balanced the mince on top of his near-to-bursting bag of provender, lifted his carton of milk, and left.

Outside the Co-op, the mince fell off and landed on the pavement. He put it back. It fell off again so he picked it up and with nowhere else to put it, exasperatedly shoved it in the thigh pocket of his cargo pants and walked off, the mince swinging around in the loose fabric.

It started to drizzle and of course, he wasn't wearing anything remotely waterproof. Well, you don't need such things when you've got a car do you? But then, you do when you don't.

Nothing was going right: it was bad enough feeling bad about himself all the time, but now he looked like some weird leper with a giant bulging growth on the side of his thigh and a homeless person's bag of stuff hanging from his arm. As he headed up the street to cross over for the bus back to Balerno, he swore he could hear a couple of schoolgirls sniggering at him behind his back. Prats and losers were easily identified: they were insecure, had nervous tension, broken marriages, over-filled plastic bags and giant growths on their legs.

His self-esteem took another dive to hitherto unplumbed levels and the insecure, nervous feeling returned. He caught his reflection in the supermarket window as he walked by. The pack of mince swaying around against his thigh and his heavy posture made him look, and consequently feel, more like a total loser. He knew he had plenty of things to be nervous about and that the huge leaden weight in the pit of his stomach was because of them. But this ache in his belly and in his heart was now so overwhelming it was as if it was the root of all his worries. It had taken on a life of its own; it had become such a solid, objectionable object in his life that he almost wondered if it could be surgically removed - like a tumour. Like the apparent tumour on his leg, the mince in his thigh pocket, it could simply be grabbed and hurled across the street. Then the worries would go too. Perhaps Alka Seltzer would get rid of the ache in his guts and all the worries would just piss off. Perhaps cyanide would work too.

In his present slough of despond, it felt that the leaden weight in the pit of his stomach had always been there. It seemed that he couldn't really remember a time without it. It had been making him nervous, deliberately giving him worries on and off for the last Christ knows how long. It had probably moved in on the run-up to sitting his GCSE exams. Decades of things to worry about all caused by a leaden weight in the pit of his stomach.

He came to his senses just in time to see the bus slowing down for the stop across the street. He let a transit van pass him and then hurriedly stepped off the kerb, heading for the bus stop.

--------oOo--------

Impact

Mackenzie drove Nisbet's BMW through the city and along Edinburgh's West Approach to a supermarket car park on the edge of the town. Parking up on the fringes of the car park, he and Julian got out to search the car.

"This is insane," said Julian. "We'll be seen, the car will be recognised, it's not exactly a Ford Focus!"

"Well, Alec says we've tae go through it "forensic like" and then check the boy's hoose, then torch the motur."

He went through the instructions in his head again, counting them out on his fingers.

"Aye. Then we've tae torch the motor." he said, "Ah think. Right, better forensic the motor Jools.

"Forensic is an adjective, not a verb," replied Julian to a blank look from the sub-literate Mackenzie who had just opened the boot and was rummaging around.

"You forensic the front Jules, Ah'll forensic the boot."

"I'll get Nigel to forensic your boot," replied Julian, beginning to look under the seats.

After two minutes of cursory forensic inspection, Mackenzie

stood up with a large nylon sports bag, "Got it Jools, got the stuff!" he crowed, holding it aloft.

"Never! Wow!" said Julian, backing out of the back passenger door. "That's a score, let's see it."

They both leant over the car's boot, hearts pounding with excitement at having saved the day. Mackenzie unzipped the bag.

"Whit's this?"

Mackenzie pulled out a wet towel. Then Nisbet's cold and sweaty gym kit, a pair of old and smelly trainers with a wet sock stuck inside each of them, and a wash bag.

"Not exactly a treasure trove," said the dismally disappointed and slightly nauseated Julian.

"Naw. And it's mingin' forbye," replied Mackenzie, also disappointed. If it hadn't been mingin', he'd have taken it for his own. "C'mon Jules, there's nothin' here, he must hae it in the hoose. Get in."

"I think we should get rid of this car."

"Aye," said Mackenzie, "but we'll definitely huv tae torch it noo, it's covered in oor fingerprints."

Julian looked at the palms of his hands as Mackenzie started the engine.

"Oh Jesus."

He got in, pulled his handkerchief from his top pocket and began to wipe down everything on his side of the car that he might have touched. He wound the window down and wiped the outer door handle, then headed for the back seat to erase any fingerprints he might have left there.

"Ye neednae bother wi' that," said Mackenzie, "the polis will get wur D an' A. We'll still need tae torch it. Onyweys, it's a'right fur you, you've no got a record, Ah huv, Ahm NTP."

"NTP?" enquired Julian. He was still learning about crime, and coming to the conclusion that Mackenzie was right, he just wasn't cut out for it. "What's NTP?"

"Known Tae the Polis," replied Mackenzie with an air of pride.

Julian closed his eyes. Mackenzie was literally illiterately beyond redemption.

"Right Jools, we'll check the hoose first then dump the motor. Get in."

"Actually," said Julian, under his breath, "I think I should be getting *out*."

But he got in, resigned to his fate and wishing he'd got a nine-to-five job in some shitty accountancy practice. Mackenzie turned back onto the Lanark Road and booted the BMW.

"Bloody nice motur, fur an auld yin, like."

He passed a few cars and jumped the lights at Chesser.

"For heaven's sake Mackenzie, you'll get us killed. And you'll draw attention to us. What if the police see us? There are police around Asda all the time, it's where the riffraff shop! What if we get got by a mobile speed trap?"

"Well, it'll no be me that gets booked, it'll be the motor's owner," said Mackenzie. "So, fuck'im! Ya beauty!"

Heading towards Currie, they slowed down for the usual gaggle of small cars, buses and shoppers in the bottleneck of Lanark Road with Mackenzie impatiently terrorizing oncoming road users. Julian kept his eyes on his iPhone, too nervous to look out the windscreen. In Currie, about to boot the BMW past the cars in front as the traffic freed up, out of the corner of his eye, Mackenzie saw a man in a leather jacket on the pavement on the other side of the road.

"Fuck me Jools, that's him again! We just passed him!"

Julian was texting Nigel, but he woke up immediately and looked out of the back window as Mackenzie booted the car up the road looking for a place to turn.

"What the hell are you doing?"

"Gawnae get the bastard."

"Are you crazy? What do you mean "Get him"? This is his car! It's broad daylight! He's a big guy! Mackenzie! What do you think you're doing? It's the middle of the afternoon!"

But Mackenzie was on a mission. In his fecund imagination, he was a hardman like Bryson and awash with brainless criminal zeal.

"Let me out! Let - me - out!" demanded Julian.

But Mackenzie didn't hear him. He U-turned at the next junction, booting the Beamer to spin the tail end round with white smoke coming from the tyres, and pulled back onto the main road.

"Fuckin' nice motor," he said as he straightened the car up in the opposite direction.

He roared back down towards the spot where he'd seen the guy in the leather jacket, scanning the pavement while Julian sank deeper into the passenger seat.

"Aye, braw motor. It can shift when ye boot it, eh?" said Mackenzie as he overtook, and tucked in front of a small Renault. He hammered up towards the next vehicle, a white transit van a hundred yards ahead. Travelling at about sixty miles an hour, he took his foot off the throttle. Now only twenty-five yards away, the van was level with the shops. Mackenzie saw his quarry, the man in the leather jacket, come into view, heading for the kerb. Just as the white van passed him, the man in the leather jacket stepped out onto the road. Mackenzie hit the brakes and the ABS vibrated into action, twelve-inch discs working overtime.

"Jesus!" screamed Julian as he slammed forward into his seatbelt.

Out of the corner of his eye Nisbet saw a red car bearing down on him at speed. Too late to check his forward stride, he managed instinctively to jump a little and curl up, his years of taking tackles from giant second-row forwards like Wee Hammy instinctively kicking into play.

Wham! The red car, now down to a mere fifteen or twenty miles per hour, scooped him up onto the edge of its bonnet and tossed him over its shoulder. He spun a couple of times in the air like an ice skater doing a horizontal triple Axel, and landed on his side on the wet tarmac. Taking some of the impact, his bag of groceries burst in all directions and the milk carton gave the red BMW a fairly decent respray so that as it screeched off down the road, smoke pouring from the tyres, it was mostly now a pinkish red, not that the airborne Nisbet had noticed.

"Fuck me pink," said Mackenzie, groping for the windscreen

washers.

He floored the throttle, passed the white transit van and sped east down Lanark Road, cutting up other cars as he went. A mile or so down the road, going twice the speed limit, he took a red light at the crossroads and drifted the car, tail-out around the left hand turn, tyres screeching, headed for the city bypass.

Mackenzie certainly could drive, a natural. But it was small consolation to Julian. He was now practically hiding in the footwell on the passenger side.

"You stupid imbecile, my father is going to kill you. You've just killed a man! Oh Jesus."

Now he would definitely go to prison. In Julian's mind's eye he had visions of rows of hairy arsed HMP Saughton inmates queueing up to enjoy his youthful physique.

"That'll make three when Bryson funds oot," said Mackenzie, already fearing the worst. "We better dump this motor."

"Dump me Mackenzie, let me out!"

"Naw, naw, you're in it up tae yer neck pal, you're impricated. Ye'll huv tae help me dump this motor."

"Where for Christ's sake? Where can we get rid of a car like this?"

"Ah ken a place," said Mackenzie, although he only had a vague notion. "Oot in the country where it'll no be noticed."

"Are you mental? Everybody notices everything in the countryside. Let me out!"

--------oOo--------

Conscious

Nisbet came round very slowly. At first it felt strangely peaceful lying serenely on the road. There seemed nothing unusual about inspecting tarmac this close up. He could see the different colours and textures of the damp stones embedded in the tarry mix as the soft, late-afternoon sunlight glanced little rainbows off their rain-wetted sheen. He'd never noticed before that it was anything other than dark grey and black. But then, he'd never looked closely before.

In the far distance, or so it seemed, there were voices, but they were not relevant to him, so transfixed, so mesmerised was he by the attractive texture of the road. It was quite beautiful.

The light began to dim around him and the shade spoiled the close-up picture of the road surface, de-saturating the colours, robbing them of their vibrancy. He wanted the light to come back.

As the light around him dimmed a little more, he became aware of faces crowding around him. He also became more aware of himself. As consciousness made its unwelcome return, suddenly, he was being swamped by an incoming tidal wave of unspeakable agony. He couldn't stifle the squeal as the new, even more vibrant colours and textures of intense and acute pain slammed through his body. The whole of his right side was so painful it felt as if it had been hit by a car. A fierce burning pain consumed the side of his head and even as his head swam and was compressed by the iron band of concussion he knew from past experience on the rugby park that he had taken a very bad blow to the head. He could feel warm fluid running from his scalp.

"That'll be blood or I'm a monkey's uncle," he mumbled to himself.

He tried to move and a shot of sheer undiluted agony ran through his whole body, so intense that it gagged in his throat, leaving him mouthing like an escapee goldfish on the carpet. Fortunately, concussed as he was, he passed out for a few seconds.

Painless seconds of unconsciousness went by and then pain returned as he came to. Nisbet squinted his eyes to see a circle of inquisitive faces crowding round. He daren't move his head for fear of discovering that it was no longer attached to his neck. His swiveling eyes scanned the faces in the hope of seeing one that was concerned as well as merely curious. He was badly hurt, this much was obvious, but he couldn't really understand why. Nor could he understand why the onlookers didn't do anything to help him.

The fact was that he had been unconscious for a minute or so, looked so badly hurt and was bleeding so badly from the head that they were all terrified to touch him. After a moment, in the corner of his eye, he caught sight of a dark figure pressing its way between the bodies. It stooped over him like the angel of death. Nisbet closed his eyes on the basis that if he couldn't see it, it couldn't see him.

Sadly, it wasn't any kind of angel. It was a first-aid enthusiast who had legged it a hundred yards to the scene of the accident hoping to get first aid brownie points. Diving down like a religious zealot on a backsliding sinner he took Nisbet by the wrist to take his pulse.

The nosey bastard's disgusting breath flushed over Nisbet's face like an olfactory nerve agent and hit the big green button of his gagging reflex. He shuddered a small convulsion of revulsion.

"Stand back everyone! He needs to breathe."

"*I don't need to breathe that shit*," thought Nisbet. "*What luck! A first aider with the oral hygiene of a dung beetle.*"

"Stand back! While I put him in the coma position."

"Ye neednae bother pitting him in a coma sonny," said an old lady. 'He's in a coma already."

"*I wish I was,*" thought Nisbet.

"No, coma *position*," emphasised the first aider. "So he doesn't swallow his tongue."

"Why wid ye swally yer tongue?" asked a slurred and slightly sozzled voice that had just transported itself from the pub's outdoor ashtray.

"That's not possible," said the old lady. "Leave him where he is."

"*I agree,*" said Nisbet's brain, attempting to make radio contact with his mouth. But his mouth simply made a bubbling noise.

"He's foamin' at the mouth," said the drunk.

The first-aider maneuvered Nisbet into the coma position while Nisbet screamed. He was not keen on lying on his right side. Plainly, it was bashed to bits.

"Loosen his tie, sonny," said the old lady.

"He's not wearing one," said the first-aider.

"I've got a tie," said someone, helpfully.

"Loosen his trousers then."

Nisbet didn't like the sound of that.

"His head's bleeding something awful," said a sympathetic female voice. "Maybe he's got a head injury."

"Aye. Brain damage," volunteered somebody else.

"He had that already," he heard the drink-slurred voice say. "He just walked oot in front of that car, deliberate like."

"*Deliberate*ly!" mouthed Nisbet, strangely exasperated at the poor grammar. "*And it wasn't deliberate!*" he mouthed, but nobody heard him. The carpeted goldfish impersonation was back.

"He's trying to say something. I don't think he's too badly hurt."

"*That's what you think!*" thought Nisbet.

Nisbet turned his attention back to the only thing he felt he could trust: the tarmac. At least that wouldn't let him down.

For a time he floated in and out of consciousness while the first-aid person fiddled around with him. He bobbed around in his sea of pain like a dayglow fishing float on a windy pond, hoping that he *would* choke on his own tongue just to spite the smug, goody-two-shoes, first-aid proficiency-badge, foul-breath bastard.

"I think he's having difficulty breathing," said the first aider. "I may have to do some CPR."

"Eh?" and "Whit's that?" enquired a few of the bystanders.

"Cardiopulmonary Resuscitation, The Kiss of Life, Mouth to Mouth Resuscitation," explained first aider.

"Rather you than me," commented somebody.

Nisbet did his best to take in a lungful of air to prove him wrong. There was always the danger, worried Nisbet, that if he passed out, the first-aider would try to give him the kiss of life. That would be unspeakable. Even if he passed out again, having somebody, with such putrescent breath that smelled like a long-dead badger, clamp his bacteria-festooned gob over Nisbet's like some kind of face-hugger from the Alien movies. It would be too awful to bear. He decided to make an unconscious effort to bite the bastard's bottom lip off. Even if he was unconscious. And then die out of spite.

The first aider's face came uncomfortably, noxiously close to Nisbet's face along with its putrescent breath. A warm fetid miasma flowed over Nisbet's face. It seemed to stick to his skin. This guy didn't just have poor oral hygiene, he'd been eating roadkill. Out of date roadkill.

"*Jesus bloody Christ,*" he thought. "*He's actually going to do it.*"

Then the drunk guy came to his rescue.

"Wid ye no be better phonin' an ambliance instead of tryin' tae snog the poor bastard."

"Yes," said the lady, "That's not natural."

"*Bloody right it's not,*" thought Nisbet.

"It's the prescribed method," said foulmouth.

"That can't be right. It's dirty," said the lady. "Dirty, dirty, dirty."

"*Bloody right it is,*" thought Nisbet and tried to lapse back into his coma, the only place he felt safe.

Fortunately, a second or so later, which felt like two years of abject, orally-induced horror, two policemen turned up and took over.

"Just lie still sonny the ambulance is comin'," said one of them.

"*Sonny indeed! Even when you're semi-cadaverous, you get no respect,*" thought Nisbet.

"He deliberately ran oot in front o' yon motor," said the drunk. "Suicide if ye ask me."

"Nobody asked you," said the cop, squatting down to check Nisbet over. He seemed like a decent bloke, which in Nisbet's experience of cops, was out of the ordinary.

"You in pain?"

Nisbet managed an almost imperceptible nod.

"There's an ambulance on its way, mate, just lie still. It won't be five minutes."

The voice was sympathetic, caring, entirely unlike the psychopathic village cop where he'd grown up. Maybe he should reassess his lifelong impression of the police as dangerous psychopaths that take your ball off you for playing in the street. Or wallop you round the ear for no apparent reason.

Meanwhile, as this nice cop began to check Nisbet over, his partner began to collect some information.

"What kind of car? Did anyone get the number?"

"It was a red BMW," said the death-breath first-aider, still kneeling beside, and breathing over Nisbet. "Registration number

Enn fifteen, Bee, Ee Tee. It passed me down there as I was coming to the rescue."

"Very observant," said the policeman writing it down.

Red BMW, Enn fifteen, Bee, Ee Tee rang some very loud bells with Nisbet but the effort of puzzlement made his head hurt like shit so he tried to slip back into unconsciousness. At least the fretful pain in his guts had gone. But considering the agony in the whole of the rest of his body, it wasn't much of a trade-off. In the distance he could hear the unmistakable siren of an ambulance. Nisbet prayed that the paramedic's bag was full of morphine: to give an overdose to the foul-breathed first aider. He tried to pass out again, but it didn't happen. He just lay there, glad that the cop had diverted first-aider's attention from snogging road traffic victims.

Most of the crowd of the merely curious dispersed and the extra light made the tarmac glisten like a kaleidoscope again. It was quite beautiful: restful, and yet intriguing.

The policeman began to take a brief statement from the first-aider. It was crisp, informative, and extremely pompous, but the policeman made all the right noises. As he noted the salient points from the witness, Nisbet became aware that the policeman was reversing around Nisbet's head, pursued by the now-vertical hyena-breath first aider.

To the first-aider, the policeman said, "I'll need your name sir. You are?"

"John Galbraith."

"Junglebreath?" thought Nisbet. *"The name suits him!"*

The cop seemed to agree because he reversed back from Junglebreath a little more.

"By the way sir, could you stand back a bit, your breath is making my eyes water," said the policeman.

"I don't think that's very helpful, or polite, or respectful. Coming from an on-duty police officer."

"Perhaps not," said the cop. "I apologise, just doing my job. But I could give you a bit of advice about your ehm … halitosis."

"Oh really!" replied first-aider, his hurt feelings bringing out the sarcasm in him.

"Yes. When you get up in the morning sir, take a spoonful of dog shite."

"Very funny. I suppose that'll cure it, will it?"

"No sir. It won't cure it, but it'll tone it down a bit."

The policeman went off to interview a few other witnesses.

Magically, so it seemed, Nisbet found himself in the ambulance, although he wasn't quite sure where he was. It felt like it was moving. It made him nervous. He looked around for some comforting tarmac but there was none. At least the first-aid bastard wasn't there. Instead, a green uniform came into view and a hand took his hand.

"Hello," said the kind face of the paramedic. She looked nice. Nisbet did his best to smile. "Do you know where you are?"

He nodded. Then shook his head.

"You're in an ambulance and we're taking you to hospital. You've been hit by a car."

He smiled and nodded, that was fine with him.

"I need to get some idea of what sort of damage has been done, if any, and pain is a good indicator, do you have any pain?"

Nisbet nodded.

The paramedic began to quiz Nisbet gently about his pain, "Try to quantify it," she said.

It meant nothing to him, you couldn't quantify infinity. He did carpeted goldfish for a bit, then said, "Big?"

"O.k. You got hit by a car. Where did it hit you?"

He got some saliva circulating in his mouth. "Currie Main Street, near the chippy," said Nisbet.

Then he worked it out. "On my right side."

This seemed to stimulate a need-to-know in Nisbet's head. Despite requests from the paramedic not to bother, and since it was the topic for discussion, he thought that he had better check out the epicentre of agony. It seemed to be around about his right calf, right knee, right thigh, right hip, right arm and the right side of his head. It was a right-of-centre epicentre.

Obviously an inventory of broken and missing bodily parts was in order. While the medic was occupied with substances to squirt into a dagger that had mysteriously appeared in the back of his hand, he agonised himself up onto his left elbow and peered down the length of his body.

What he saw, to his horror, was much worse than even the pain had indicated. There was a sea of red gore where his right thigh and hip should have been. Pulsating raw flesh was oozing from the torn fabric of his cargo pants. White, blood-streaked tissue of some sort could be seen protruding through the carnage virtually from his knee to his trouser belt. Plainly, the impact from whatever had hit him had ripped open his leg and exposed the bruised, pulped flesh and subcutaneous fat below. He was sure that what he saw was the white of bone protruding from the gore.

"Oh Jesus Christ!" he groaned and gagging down his own vomit fell into a dead faint.

The paramedic checked out his pulse, then did Nisbet the favour of wiping the Co-op's Best Steak Mince off his trousers for him, wrapped it in what remained of its white polystyrene and shrink-wrap packaging, and dumped it the bin. Then she put on fresh surgical gloves and began to clean Nisbet's actual own blood from his head to get a better look.

--------o0o--------

McShaed

McShaed's phone rang, his own phone.

"Malcy, what have you got for me?" He listened to his driver. "Interesting. Look, thank you for that. I think I can use that."

He hung up the call and picked up the cheap pay-as-you-go mobile, the twin of the burner he'd given Hermens and dialed the only number in the memory. It was answered almost immediately.

"O.K. Eric, we have something on these people, we know roughly who and what they are, or might be. The big gangs have left them untouched in Edinburgh, the reasons for which are, so far, unclear, possibly because they're in cahoots with one of the big operators. ...

"No, I need to give this some thought but I'm just letting you know that we have made some small progress already. Now, the money? ... Oh, you're in London already! ... a day or two? Eric, you need to get a down-payment to Bryce *now*. I already have people on the move, the clock is ticking ... Ten now? No Eric, twenty-five ... no twenty-five ... thousand. O.K ... No, just post it, to be signed for ... it'll be fine ... it's the best way with small amounts ... O.K, you're right, it's not all that small. Oh by the way, not too many fifties please, the money needs to be easily distributed." He reminded him of Bryce's address. "And we'll see the balance when? ... O.K."

He hung up. So did Hermens, his arsehole twitching with anguish: He was a control freak and he seemed to have no control over what was happening.

He got on the London underground. He had five bank accounts, each reasonably well stacked with his hard-earned money. He'd have to go round each of them and withdraw a chunk of the fifty grand to pay for the services of McShaed, Bryce and whoever else they'd engage. Relatively small cash withdrawals wouldn't catch the eye of anybody that might want to scrutinise his finances.

He felt ill. He'd expected to make a nice profit of nearly two hundred grand by shifting some diamonds of questionable quality to a bunch of third-world hicks. Now he was out of pocket to the tune of what seemed like an unending amount. Right now he should be walking around London sticking cash *into* these banks. He walked into the Bank of Canada and withdrew ten grand, losing a chunk on the exchange rate: the Canadian Dollar had slumped a bit.

He headed for the Bank Leumi and got a little lift: the rise in the shekel meant that he was quids in. But he was still depressed, and more than a little on edge. Walking around London with tens of thousands of pounds in a briefcase looking like a very tempting mugging target. He couldn't dress in his drab, old-loser garb, or he'd have been refused entry to the banks. He took a taxi to the Europe Arab Bank.

--------oOo--------

Countryside

Mackenzie hammered the BMW round the Edinburgh City Bypass, weaving between cars and lorries like slalom poles. Julian, still so low in the seat he was almost in the footwell, continued to demand to be dropped off. Mackenzie turned off the bypass and headed south out the A68. There was a flash as he set off a speed camera.

"Oh Jesus, you've just been clocked by a speed camera!" exclaimed Julian, climbing back into the seat and putting on his seatbelt.

"Doesnae matter," giggled Mackenzie. "It's a stolen motor, the owner will get fined. Aye, he'll get points oan his license. Ho Ho!"

"Do you not think that it might be evidence or something like that? Or somebody will report us going at this kind of speed?"

"Naw."

The car headed out through Pathhead up onto the higher ground with Mackenzie's foot still on the floor.

"Where are you taking us?" said Julian.

"Gawny dump this oot here somewhere, up a quiet road and torch it. Shame though, nice motor, goes like shite aff a shiny shovel."

He kept his foot to the floor and passed a giant articulated wagon without looking for oncoming traffic.

Julian's white knuckles clamped himself down into the bucket seat.

"Let me out! I don't want anything more to do with this!"

"Shut the fuck up Jools, ye're in up tae yer neck. Ye're an accomplish."

"Jesus," said Julian, his face now in his hands, afraid to look out of the windscreen. "I'm in a stolen car with a cast-iron bloody blockhead!"

"Blockhead? Naw. If it was an American motor, mibbe. But Ah think ye'll find," said Mackenzie knowledgeably, "that it's a fuel-injected, straight six-cylinder, like maist sporty Beamers."

Hammering through a spring downpour, several miles out into the countryside south of Edinburgh, Mackenzie turned off the main road and drove two hundred yards up a remote, tree-lined farm track and stopped at a farm gate opposite a large break of sitka spruce plantation. They got out and stood in the steady rain while Mackenzie unlocked the petrol cap then threw the key into the wood.

"We'll no be needin' *that*. Widnae think. Ah'll no be nickin' nae mair ancient Beamers like this. Right Julian, gie me yer lighter."

"I don't smoke."

"Ah thought you smoked a wee joint noo and then."

"I don't exactly carry it around with me do I?"

"Shite!" said Mackenzie. "We'll use the cigar lighter in the car."

The rain got heavier.

"It won't work without the car key you idiot. Don't you have another key – for stealing BMWs? In your 'going equipped' toolkit?"

"They're in the boot of Alec's Merc."

"Oh, for pity's sake! And you think *I'm* not cut out for crime!"

"Well, too bad Jools. We'd better leg it."

"In this rain? We're miles from anywhere. I'll phone Nigel for a lift."

"Who the fuck's Nigel?"

"My boyfriend. Remember?" said Julian. "You already met him."

"Him? Yer boyfriend? We're daein' crime here Jools, ye cannae just phone yer pals."

"He's more than a friend, we're …"

"Dinnae bother. Ah dinnae want tae ken whit you and him get up tae. Ah'll phone Bryson."

"He'll kill us! I'll phone Nigel." Julian got back in the BMW. "Anyway, I'm not walking anywhere in this rain, I'm soaked already."

Mackenzie got in too.

"Aye, ye dinnae want tae get yer D&Gs wet. Gie me the phone when ye get yer pal, he'll need directions."

"I can't phone him. There's no phone coverage out here."

Julian got out and walked around in the rain until he could get enough bars on his phone to make a call. When he got back to the car he was drenched to the skin. He got in and removed his jacket, opened up his shirt and loosened his trousers to try and dry off. The windows were already starting to steam up.

"Nigel's leaving work early to come and get us. He'll be an hour and a half at least."

"Aw aye? Whit does he dae for a living? Hairdresser?"

"You *would* think that, wouldn't you, you homophobic little prick! No, he's got a scaffolding business."

Mackenzie's eyebrows went up.

"A fuckin' gay scaffolder? Ah hope at least his planks are straight."

"You're going get yours one day Mackenzie, you homophobic little misfit. Mark my words."

Half an hour later, the farmer, Jim Nichol, drove his aged pickup around the unusual looking red BMW.

"Nice car dad," said his son.

"Windaes are all steamed up. Winchers likely. And in broad daylight! They young folk have nae shame," said Jim. He got out. "You wait here son, it's just some young couple. I'll need to chase them."

He walked up to the BMW and knocked on the driver's window. The window came down two inches.

"Look son, ye'll need tae find somewhere else tae take your girlfriend, this is a busy farm road."

He looked further into the car. In the passenger seat was a young man with his shirt wide open and his trousers unbuttoned.

"Whit the hell are you twa up tae in there? And me wi' a young laddie in the motor. Right, I'm phonin' the polis, ya ... ya... Jesus Christ Almighty!"

Both car doors opened, Mackenzie nearly knocking the farmer from his feet, and the two of them legged it into the sitka spruce plantation.

"Dirty bastards!" said Jim Nichol, angry, perplexed and slightly nauseous.

The farming community wasn't one where you were likely to run into many gay people, let alone catch them enjoying one another's company. Most farmers would be happier being called a sheep shagger than, well, it wasn't worth thinking about. Jim Nichol took out his mobile phone to call the cops. Shit! No signal, it would have to wait, he had ewes and lambs to feed. He'd call the cops from the house when he got back, but no doubt the car would be long gone. They'd probably leave as soon as he was out of sight. He got back in the pickup.

"What were they doing dad?" asked the little boy.

"You don't want to know son. You just don't want to know. It disnae bear thinkin' aboot."

Julian and Mackenzie climbed the rusty barbed wire fence on the far side of the sitka plantation and stepped out onto the road. They were drenched, covered in green slime and needles from the spruce trees and Julian had scratched his face.

"You're going to pay for this cock-up Mackenzie."

"There isnae gawny be a cock-up Jools. Well, there might be when yer gay pal get his mits on ye," sniggered Mackenzie with his forefinger in the air.

"He's a big lad Mackenzie," said Julian. "I'll ask him to start on you. Give you a good reaming. I think you'd like it."

He mimicked Mackenzie with his forefinger twisting its way up towards Mackenzie's nose. Mackenzie just stood there, glazing over at the unwelcome image it conjured in his feeble brain. His arsehole was pulsing at the horrible thought.

"That shut you up didn't it? You nasty little creep," triumphed Julian. "Meanwhile, I'll need to decide what to tell Nigel when he asks how we got here."

"Just shut yer puss aboot stolen motors. Just say we broke doon. And as faur as Bryson and yer faither is concerned, a's we did was dispose o' the motur. C'mon, let's get a cuppa."

"Where are we going to get a …?" said Julian.

But Mackenzie pointed. There was a bacon roll van in a layby a mile or so further along the highway. They set off.

"Right Jools. Phone yer pal Nigel and tell him we're at the first bacon roll van on the A68 aboot five miles past Pathheid. Dae ye want a roll and … *sausage* … while we're waitin'?" he asked with the usual lascivious, homophobic and sarcastic undertone, screwing his forefinger up into the air in front of Julian's face.

"I'm a vegetarian," said Julian, dialing Nigel's number again.

"Does Nigel eat meat?" The double entendre didn't go past Julian, but Mackenzie was on a roll. "Or a bit o' white puddin' eh?"

"One day Mackenzie, you'll get it, you homophobic little maggot," said Julian, coming to the boil. "In fact, now that I think of it!"

He swung a punch at Mackenzie, a well telegraphed punch. Mackenzie swayed back out of the way.

"Aye, ye'll need tae dae better than that Jools. Ah grew up in a hard part o' Edinburgh. Ah've got some slick moves."

Julian kicked him in the balls and Mackenzie moved slickly onto his knees, clutching at his groin, and making strange animal grunts.

Julian walked off towards the bacon roll van.

By the time Mackenzie caught up with him, he was ordering two bacon rolls and two cups of tea.

"Thanks," said Mackenzie. "But there wisnae nae need fur that Jools. Ah wis only jokin'. Ah couldnae staun' up fur five meenutes."

"You were needing it," said Julian, handing him his tea.

"Thanks," said Mackenzie, accepting the polystyrene cup. "But ye need tae learn tae take a joke Jools. Mah baws are killin' me," he said, turning to accept the bacon roll handed to him by the bacon roll man.

"Brown sauce?" said the bacon roll guy, waving a big squeezey sauce bottle. "You could rub it into your balls wee man. Get your buddy to do it for you."

They shivered under the bacon roll van's canopy for two more cups of tea and another bacon roll each. Trucks came and went.

"Ah thought you were a vegetrainian Jools," said Mackenzie, pointing to his second bacon roll.

"He didn't have anything healthy," said Julian. "Besides, bacon doesn't count."

Mackenzie refrained from another homophobic meat joke for fear of another kick in his homophobic goolies.

At long last, Nigel turned up in his car. It was a two-seater Mazda sports car. Soaked to the skin as Julian was, the cups of tea had done little to raise his core temperature and he was shaking like a leaf.

"Thank you Nigel," said Julian, when Nigel got out the car. He kissed him on the lips.

"Aw get tae fuck!" said Mackenzie. "Gawny no dae that? That's fuckin' disgustin' so it is. It's no natural."

"Listen you homophobic wee microbe," said Nigel, his big scaffolder's hand taking hold of Mackenzie by the throat. "I'll beat the crap out of you and leave you in a ditch."

Then he turned to Julian, "Come on, Julian, let's get you home and get you warmed up."

They both got into Nigel's two-seater.

"Hey, whit aboot me? Ah need a lift a'na'! Ah'll get in the back."

"There isn't a back, you revolting little pussnodule," said Nigel. "You can hitchhike back to town, get a lift from a lorry driver."

"Yes," said Julian from the passenger seat. "Just offer the next lorry driver that stops a cup of tea and a blow job for a lift into town."

Nigel and Julian drove off.

"Ya, ya … fuckin' … fuckin' … BASTARDS!" yelled Mackenzie at Nigel's disappearing exhaust pipe.

"Hey, you, ya wee poof," shouted bacon roll guy. "Shut it! Less of the language."

After about an hour, with cramp in his arm from holding his thumb out, a sixteen-wheeler stopped for him.

"Where are you going bud?" said the gruff Yorkshire accent, as Mackenzie climbed up onto the cab's step.

"Edinburgh," said Mackenzie, peering over the passenger door.

"That's exactly where I'm going. Climb in."

After a mile or so the driver patted the seat with his left hand and invited Mackenzie to sit a little closer.

"You'll need to sit here and put your seat belt on."

Mackenzie did as he was told, it seemed reasonable. He responded to the driver's small talk in as friendly a way as possible with his limited grasp on current affairs. He laughed at the guy's jokes. They were vulgar, even for Mackenzie's taste, and they weren't funny. The driver was a bit of a creep, but he was obliged for the lift, so he tried to be nice, and friendly.

A few more miles passed, and the driver put his hand on

Mackenzie's knee just as he turned into a layby. Mackenzie broke out in a cold sweat. As the cab slowed to a walking pace, Mackenzie clicked his way out of his seat belt, jumped down out of the cab and ran for it.

--------oOo--------

"Aye," said the local bobby to the farmer. "If they've no come back for it, it'll be because it's stolen. Joyriders probably."

"Aye Mark," replied Jim Nichol. "More than likely, joyridin' wis what they were up tae if the steamed-up windaes an' unzipped troosers were anything to go by. Pair o' dirty wee Edinburgh ..." His son was standing next to him, "horses hoofs."

"Awfy," said the policeman shaking his head, "But ye canna say that sort of thing these days Jim. It's no politically correct. The polis cannae allow that kind of talk. Ye canna say poof. It's hate speech. Ah'd hae tae arrest ye fur a non-crime hate incident. Besides, mah sister's laddie's just come oot as a bender ... Ah mean, as gay." He took a few more notes. "Is the car in the way where it is?" asked Mark the policeman.

"No really," said Jim. "It's just annoyin' me."

"Well, if you don't mind, I'm goin' off duty and it's getting dark. Can it wait 'til the morning? It's only car theft, we get joyriders frae Dalkeith and Bonnyrig dumpin' motors out here now and again. The paperwork's a pain. And I expect your two ... boyfriends had somebody waiting to pick them up."

"Aye, Ah suppose."

"OK, I'll come up first thing and get it checked out. Did you see where the two, ehm, young gentlemen went?"

"Intae the forestry plantation. And Ah'm no goin' in there tae look for them."

"Fair enough," said the cop. "Just don't mess about with the car. The fingerprint boys will want to go over it."

He stuck a "Police Aware" sticker on the side window and they went their separate ways.

--------oOo--------

179

Hospital

Nisbet came to his senses slowly, alone in a strange room. He hadn't been completely unconscious, but he'd given himself over entirely to the shot of morphine he'd had and as a result, was having what felt like some kind of out-of-body experience. He looked around. It looked institutional. It smelt like a hospital maybe. Was he in a hospital? Or was it just hospital smell?

"*Bloody hell!*" he thought, as he looked up at the square, institutional ceiling tiles, "*Did I bang a nurse last night?*"

He looked to see if anybody was in the bed with him. He'd had that exact experience as a twenty-year-old: waking up, hungover, to a strange ceiling in strange girl's bedroom.

Nope, it couldn't be a score like that, not the way his luck was running.

It took him a few more groggy minutes before he could even begin to get his bearings, but vague recollections of being transported to the hospital in an ambulance appeared in his head and floated around: random snapshots from a movie trailer. This was followed by a foggy period with several people fussing over him, some in green hospital garb and some in blue hospital garb. Was this a Rangers and Celtic Old Firm hospital?

It could all have been a dream and he lay for a while trying to discern what was real and what was imaginary; when it had happened, when was the present? Was it now or was this a dream? It was all a bit strange, but slowly his consciousness returned to something vaguely resembling compos mentis.

Concentrating as hard as he could, he made a mental grasp for reality. Sadly, with the current state of his mental wiring, his mental grasp turned out to be an actual physical grasp and the waving hand that sought reality came to a sudden halt when it reached the limit of the tube that stretched from his hand to a bag of clear fluid. It hurt like shit. He groaned out loud. A nurse came in, put his hand back down by his side, re-taped the needle in place, checked him over and left. That all seemed real enough: he was in hospital for sure, and began to get a grasp on reality. Reality included the raw realisation of the pain he was in. Reality was crap.

He lay still for what seemed like an age, terrified to move. The ceiling tiles moved in and out of focus. Then slowly, the ceiling tiles began some strange anti-clockwise movement. He tried to focus on them as they spun. Did he have the whirly pits from being on the piss? The ceiling tiles stopped rotating then slipped back over his head. It wasn't the whirly pits, he was definitely moving. He accelerated, the ceiling was going past at a good rate of knots. Holy shit! He had no controls! He was in a run-away bed! And not only that, he was heading somewhere feet first. Had he snuffed it while his attention was otherwise distracted? But no, still alive: he felt the mild G-force of a corner and the ceiling turned round ninety degrees. Watching the ceiling tiles rotate gave him more of the whirly pits. Surely you don't get the whirly pits if you're dead? Dead drunk maybe. One second later, he was wheeled into a metal box.

The fluorescent ceiling of the box wasn't moving; it felt a little safer, so he raised his head and looked around. There was a clip board lying on his chest and there were two men, in green uniforms. They spoke to one another in a foreign tongue. It sounded East European. Shite! He'd been kidnapped by the KGB! He looked at the name badge on one of them: Krzystoff. The other was Wieslav. He *had* been kidnapped by the KGB! He looked both of them in the eye and they smiled their sympathetic, institutional smiles back at him.

There was a gentle jolt and the metal box ejected him. More ceiling tiles, a slightly different colour of ceiling tiles. They spun around a few times more and then it stopped. The two east European hospital orderlies departed. Nearby, somebody was snoring, loudly.

A young woman in a nurse's uniform came in, spoke to him, looked at something behind him on the wall, and went away. He lay there for a bit, hoping he'd get the hang of the pain, like you do when you get slammed on the rugby park: you lie there until the pain subsides a bit then you do a quick inventory of moving and broken parts, get up, run it off and rejoin the game.

But the pain didn't subside. He couldn't run it off, and he wasn't going to rejoin the game. He hit rewind in his feeble memory cells.

Once again, little flickers of recall overlaid the ceiling tiles, like the incoherent rapid-fire flashes of action in a blockbuster movie trailer: tyres screeching, ghoulish faces peering, first-aid guy, putrescent breath. The comforting sparkle of the tarmacadam road surface came into view, the ambulance, the nice policeman, and not necessarily in that order. It all seemed very surreal: a Dali-esque, soft-clocks landscape of distorted time and events. Then he got a shocking jolt of adrenalin as he remembered the gore down his right thigh.

Glad to be the centre of attention once more, his right side reminded him that it was still the ocean of pain it deserved to be considering it had body-checked a car and most of the inside of his thigh had fallen out of a hole that stretched from his knee to his pelvis. He didn't dare try to move his leg in case it wasn't there. Horrible sick-joke scenarios flitted through his befuddled, bandaged head preparing him for the bad news: *"Doctor, doctor, I can't feel my leg."*... *"I'm not surprised, we've cut your hands off. Ha ha ha!"*

The nurse came in again, put something in his mouth, gave him a sip of water and left. Soon after, he fell asleep.

--------oOo--------

5

Hospital

In the morning, after a very fitful night, as slow as a winter sunrise, wakefulness slid over his brain. The little sleep he'd had was limited by pain and a lot of worry. He was good at worry nowadays, and it seemed to take his mind off the pain. Who'd ever have guessed that dread, foreboding and trepidation would have analgesic properties? And underpinning the eye-widening stimulus from the whirling fog of negativity inside his head, was the loud snoring of his neighbour in the next bed.

Nisbet had a look around to get his bearings. A bulky young nurse came in with a cup of tea for him, and left it out of reach on the bedside cabinet. Then she came back and topped up a glass of water which she also left out of reach. He fell asleep for a little while when the snoring from the next bed stopped.

Some clanking of trolleys and busy nurses woke him: the day shift was in full swing. The man in the bed next to him was sitting up in his dressing gown and slippers reading a paperback through glasses that were held together at the corners with sticking plaster. There was no sign of anything wrong with him except that he looked like a complete nurd.

"What are you in for pal?"

He'd been poised, ready for Nisbet to rouse.

After a minute of searching for saliva in the Namib desert of his mouth, Nisbet replied muddily, "I got knocked down by a car. I think."

At least, that's how he remembered things so far.

"What kind of car?"

This wasn't what Nisbet was expecting.

"Don't know. A motor car."

Nisbet moved and it hurt like hell. He lay still.

"Aye, a motor car." His neighbour nodded and gave it a little more thought. "Aye, that would be right, a motor car. Did ye get its number?"

"Yes, I wrote it down as it drove over me."

Sarcasm was the highest form of wit that Nisbet could muster right now.

"That was quick thinkin'. They should get the bastard then. I'm in wi' my leg. "

"With your leg," replied Nisbet, matter-of-factly. "Of course you are."

To be fair, it wasn't necessarily obvious that his neighbour would be in with either of his legs - it was a hospital after all. He still wasn't sure whether he was in with both of his. He hadn't dared look. But it was probably still there because it hurt like hell. Maybe it was phantom pain in the missing limb. That would be typical - getting fake pain instead of the real stuff. Which was worse?

"Aye its pure murder so it is. They dinnae ken what's causing it. They've brought me in for observation, but Ah've no seen onything yet. I can barely stand it. I've been aff my work for months with my back too. You get nae sympathy ye ken."

"I know." He was right there.

"Whit's your name?"

"Shite," thought Nisbet. *"Here we go again."*

"Nisbet," he said, aloud, in the usual forlorn and resigned tone, he reserved for social introductions.

"Aye, Nisbet. Whit's yer first name?"

"Shite," thought Nisbet. *"Here we go again,"*

"Nisbet. Nisbet's my first name."

"Aye. Nisbet. Right enough. Ah'm Willie, Willie Boak."

"How do you do Willie."

"No that great. I've had tests and everything ye ken. Have ye ever had a lumber puncture?"

A lumber puncture? What was that? How to deflate a tree trunk?

"A what puncture?" Nisbet could barely be arsed. "No, I don't have tyres anymore, or a car."

He stared at the random texture of the polystyrene ceiling tile directly above him. At least it was stationary now. Suddenly, a face materialised in the pattern. It looked familiar but he couldn't place it. It wasn't a nice face; he looked away, it gave him the creeps.

"They stick this needle in yer back and draw oot the fluid. Then they pit it back in again. Then ye usually faint. Pure murder so it is. It gie's ye the dry boak."

"Dry boak?"

That was a new one on Nisbet. And plainly, Willie Boak didn't see the irony in being called Boak and having the 'dry boak'.

"Aye, dry boak. That was the day afore yesterday. Ah've no had a shite since then. Murder so it is. Ye can aye no get a shite efter an operation."

"No shit?" said Nisbet.

Something to look forward to: a Long John Silver wooden leg and constipation would brighten things up no end.

"Sometimes ye canny get a pee neither."

That would finish it, if he had to go the rest of his life with a colostomy bag hanging from his belt. Try picking up women at a disco with a colostomy bag and a wooden leg. Every time you shook your booty to the music, your wooden leg would creak and your colostomy bag would slosh. Nisbet couldn't even see the funny side.

The pain in the right side of his body was so fierce that apart from the fact that he knew it was in his right side, he had no clear picture of where the main source of pain was. He tried to move again to get just a little relief and another bullet of agony ran up the full length of his right side and ricocheted off the inside of his skull. He took the hint: move and you're dead. But at least he'd found the source of his misery: it was him.

His neighbour driveled on incessantly about absolutely nothing worth hearing for what seemed like a geological epoch while Nisbet did his best not to tell the silly bugger to shut up and give him peace. He stared at the ceiling tiles again but couldn't find the face. That was ok, he hadn't liked that face one little bit. He had enough shite going on in his life without being stared down by a supercilious ceiling tile.

By and by a nurse came in, an extremely attractive nurse with short, fairish brown hair. She was dragging a strange looking trolley, festooned with gadgets.

"Good morning, I'm Staff Nurse McMartin. How are you feeling this morning?"

Staff Nurse McMartin had a lovely soft Irish accent and a gentle manner which had an immediately soothing effect on the troubled Nisbet. Edinburgh hospitals, so it seemed to Nisbet, had millions of Irish nurses. However, Nisbet had the impression that most of them worked in the Simpson's maternity unit, which was where he had first encountered them. Nisbet supposed that since (so he'd heard) the Irish (being Catholics), didn't use contraception, they (he had concluded) must have greater need for skill in delivering babies. Then, once trained at the expense of Ireland, they left their turf huts for the big money offered by Lothian Health Board who needed their calm Irish natures when it came to hauling squawking brats like Samantha out of the arses of precious parturients like Brenda. He had still been in love with Brenda at that time, mostly, but the Irish nurses had won him over there and then. And some of them had been quite cute into the bargain.

This Irish Staff Nurse's voice fitted the bill in the soothing department. *And* ... she had such an unabashed way of looking Nisbet in the eye that it quite took hold of him. It seemed that he'd never seen such direct, cornflower-blue eye contact before. And strangely, this obvious intrusion into his soul didn't make him feel uncomfortable. Obligingly, however, having noticed it and being the person he was, he felt uncomfortable.

And it was just as well she had him by the eye because she had a very nice figure did Staff Nurse McMartin, as far as you could tell under the blue uniform. And her figure would normally be where his eyes would have lingered, being the sort of ordinary bloke that he was. She had a nice top deck as far as he could see, desperately trying not to stare, what with its upside-down watch and name badge: a nice cute, polite, modest, manageable, sexy top deck: the top deck of a frigate, rather than Brenda's Battleship Potemkin. And already she compared well with Brenda in another department: with her direct eye contact and soft smile, she didn't look like she'd be awash with hang-ups.

The name badge, for he at least he managed to read it, rather than contemplate its anatomical substructure, read, "Staff Nurse Deirdre McMartin."

He couldn't remember ever meeting a Deirdre before. He'd been missing out. Staff Nurse Deirdre McMartin was very pretty.

Nisbet tried to reply, but his mouth had dried up again, so that only a guttural, muddy grunt came out.

Staff Nurse McMartin was used to this so she gave him another sympathetic smile, and couple of seconds to get some saliva circulating in his mouth. She held the plastic tumbler of water to his lips and he took a sip.

She started again, with a cheeky smile, "Good morning, I'm Staff Nurse McMartin. How are you this morning?"

"Fine, thank you."

Why did he say that? What a wanker. He wasn't fine. He was far from fine. He was a totally unfine person. He had a broken marriage, and a broken body. He'd lost his car, and as far as he could tell from his foggy recollection of events, a leg too. He needed all the sympathy he could get. He was not fine.

"Do you have any pain?"

The tone seemed genuinely, rather than merely professionally curious, and all the more so for the accent.

"No, I'm fine, thank you," he grunted and the effort of taking in air almost made him pass out with the pain. When he recovered he felt like an idiot for saying that. He was not fine. He was in a lot of pain.

Staff Nurse McMartin gave him another smile, one which said, "Yes you do." She could see it in his face. At least he wasn't going to be a whinger.

Nisbet struggled to keep his eyes off the location of Staff Nurse McMartin's name badge. What a little honey. She looked to be about twenty eight or so did the lovely Irish Staff Nurse McMartin. She explained, when Nisbet got enough saliva into his mouth to enquire politely, that soon a doctor would be round to speak to him. Nisbet worried a little that this might be to tell him that the pain in his leg was phantom pain and that they'd removed the mangled limb and thrown it in the hospital skip.

The nurse checked his pulse and his bandaged head and then, instead of kissing him, which was what he was half hoping for, said, "I'll get you some pain relief in a minute but we need to know your name. When you came up here from A&E last night you weren't being very coherent and you'd no I.D. on you. I'm sure your family will be absolutely distraught wondering where you are."

"I don't feel very coherent now," mumbled Nisbet. "You're Irish."

"So are my tits," thought the nurse as she spotted Nisbet instinctively checking where she kept her badge. She waited until he looked back at her face.

"Ah, so you'll be Mister Sherlock Holmes then."

She pretended to write it down.

Nisbet tried for an appreciative smile but it turned into a grimace. His face wasn't responding to central expression control.

"It's Sangster. Sangster," he grimaced.

"Good, you're Mister Sangster Sangster. Now, do you have a first name or could your ma' and da' not be bothered and they just gave you the same name twice?"

The cornflower blue eyes locked onto his ill-focused, concussed eyes. It made Nisbet blush.

"Sarcy bitch," he thought, despite her overall attractiveness. This was the bit Nisbet hated about introductions. Why couldn't his parents have called him Jim or Rab? Bloody Nisbet for God's sake!

"It's Nisbet."

"Nisbet Sangster," said Staff Nurse McMartin without flinching. She entered it into some kind of computer thing on the trolley.

"Still two second names, any advance on that?"

"Eh, no, that's it, apart from my middle name, that's a surname too, I have three second names. Everybody calls me Niz."

"Heavens! Tree second names, must be a world record. Ok, Niz it is," she quipped.

Nisbet just scowled. "Aye, Niz it is."

Her tone softened; she could see the joviality was glancing off him.

"Sure is there not anybody we should notify about your admission? Your wife maybe? Mrs Nisbet Second Name Sangster Sangster?" she asked, not too cockily.

She looked like she was quite fun did Staff Nurse McMartin. And she had a nice place to keep her name badge.

But the thought of the hospital notifying Brenda and her baboon of a father cascading off the sofa in helpless mirth at Nisbet's predicament was too horrible to contemplate.

"No, no thanks, just the office. Maybe I'll phone them later."

Angela would probably think he had been out on the piss again. Maybe he had. He couldn't remember.

"How long have I been here?" he asked, his voice a little shaky. "Where am I?"

"Well, you're in hospital, see? The beds and me nurse's uniform, they're a clue."

It didn't sound sarcastic, just witty, and cute. He liked it.

"You're in the general medical ward at the infirmary. It seems you were admitted in the late afternoon or early evening. You're me first RTA this month. You got hit by a car, apparently, well definitely, 'cos you look it. You've had a nasty bang on the head and the rest of you ain't so pretty neither. Once they checked you over at A&E they sent you up here. You weren't very responsive but you don't check out for any serious damage so far, except you've suffered a pretty bad concussion."

Nisbet thought for a minute. "I got hit by a car didn't I?"

"Yes," she said, "you got hit by a car."

One thing about concussion, you could have these conversations with both of the victim's personalities.

"You're Irish, aren't you?"

She thickened the accent up. "Begorra! Oi didn't tink it would be dat obvious."

"I got hit by a car didn't I?"

Staff Nurse McMartin smiled to herself. Concussion. "Yep. Hit by a car," she said.

"Which part?"

"I imagine it was the front of the car that hit you." The cheeky smile again.

"No ..."

"Ah," she said with her cute smile. "More or less the whole of your right side. And a few other bits."

"No, which part of Ireland?"

"Ah ... Donegal."

"That's in Ireland," Nisbet heard himself say, then spotted he was being dim. Plainly, concussion had dropped his IQ thirty points.

"Yes it is," said the nurse, smiling her cute and sympathetic smile at the plainly concussed Niz.

Not knowing where-about in Ireland Donegal was, Nisbet decided not to pursue it in case he looked even more of a twat, and anyway, furrowing his brows thoughtfully hurt his head.

She seemed to see what he was thinking. "It's up the top left hand side of Ireland. Next stop Canada."

Nisbet made an "Ah" face, and left it at that.

"About your accident," continued Staff Nurse McMartin. "It seems that the driver didn't stop, as far as we understand. The police came in just after you were admitted. They've been told to come back later."

"The police?" What did they want? He hadn't done anything illegal that he could remember. "Oh, right, my parking tickets. Oh dear."

More shite to worry about. It would be hundreds of pounds by now. He wished he'd paid them.

"I don't tink they're after you as the head of an illicit parking cartel," quipped witty Staff Nurse McMartin. "It was a hit and run, apparently. That'll be quite a serious offence so it will."

"Yes. A hit and run? Blimey."

He remembered his intimate acquaintance with the tarmac; it was the only nice memory he had of this part of his life. Then the faces of the people standing round him popped into his mind's eye, then a flash of the first aider, a whiff of his rotting corpse breath, then the ambulance lady.

He looked up at her, "I got hit by a car."

"Yep," thought the nurse. *"A nice dose of concussion."* Then, she said, "Yep, That's why you're in here, in hospital, remember?"

Nisbet could tell he was being patronised, but she was so cute, he'd take as much patronizing as she wanted to give.

"Look, are you sure you don't want us to contact somebody for you? Your wife? By the way," she pointed at her face, "This is me face, up here."

He'd been staring at the substructure of her badge again. You'd think she'd be used to it; she had lovely figure.

"We should let your wife know."

Nisbet shook his head slowly and let a long stuttering thread of air through his lips.

"Wrong thing to ask," thought the nurse. "Girlfriend?" she asked.

A brief but solemn look of resignation rippled over his otherwise blank face. "Nope."

"Boyfriend?" said the nurse.

Nothing was out of the question even if he looked too much like an ordinary bloke-ish bloke. But you never can tell. Nisbet's head flopped back and hit the pillow with a thud. Pain twisted its way through him like a corkscrew and his face showed it.

"No," she said, he didn't look gay. "Just joking. What about your parents? Siblings?"

"Jesus!" thought Nisbet. If they phoned his dad and told him he'd been hit by a car his dad would freak out. Nisbet hadn't spoken to him for a fortnight at least. If he phoned his sister he'd get the Green Cross Code recited to him. He'd phone them later. Probably.

"How come you didn't know my name," asked Nisbet, "didn't anybody check my wallet? My cards and my driving license are in it."

"I don't think you had any I.D. on you when you came in."

"My wallet's in my hip pocket."

"Well I'm sure they checked."

"Jesus! I've been identity thieved by the NHS," he thought, and

groaned.

"Listen," she said, and patted his hand. "I'll go and ask, but if it's missing, your wallet maybe fell out of your pocket when you got hit. It'll get handed in to the police, so it will."

"Yeh. So it will," said Nisbet, knowing she didn't believe it either.

"So who do you want to contact?"

"Ohhh, nobody, really. Just the office. What time is it?" He looked at his wrist; no watch. Where was his Omega?

She flipped up her upside-down watch. "It's five past eleven."

She pointed at her watch, then at her face. His eyes went back up from her extremely beguiling name badge location to catch her eyebrows authoritatively and insistently on the way up. He took the hint and blushed. But she didn't seem to mind too much. He was just a normal, deeply concussed bloke.

"Five past eleven! Bloody hell, I've been conked out for eighteen hours?"

"Mostly, yes, but not totally conked out. Sleeping mostly. You had a wee sedative too. Probably why you feel groggy. We've been keeping an eye on you."

Nisbet couldn't figure it out.

"OK, if you're sure all you want to do is phone the office, I'll get you the telephone trolley."

"It's ok," said Nisbet, "I'll use my mobile."

"Don't think so," said the nurse.

"Oh yeh, they're not allowed in hospitals."

"Well, nobody bothers with that anymore. In the cabinet, there, they're all in there."

"They?" asked Nisbet, "I've only got one pho..."

"The pieces," said the nurse, "of your phone, they're in the cabinet, in a poly bag."

Nisbet gave the bedside cabinet one of his total-hatred looks. He felt completely and utterly defeated. Worse than that time they'd gone down twenty-seven, three to Burghmuir and he'd come off in the second half with a broken nose and a dead-leg.

"Shite," he added.

"Yup. That about sums it up," said the nurse.

He looked back up at Staff Nurse McMartin.

"Is it ok if I stay here for a while?"

"I tink it'll be perfectly alright, you're not going anywhere for a while. Look at you, you're all bashed up."

"Is that the official diagnosis?" he asked. "All bashed up."

"Pretty-much sums it up," she said. "Listen, the duty doctor will be along later. You'll probly get no lunch I'm afraid."

"What about breakfast?"

"You've missed that. We woke you up for a cup of tea but you went back to sleep. So we just left you."

"I don't remember that. What time is it?" He looked at his empty wrist again."

"It's just after five past eleven. Remember?"

Concussion; he'll ask again in a minute.

"I could go a roll 'n' squarey wi' broon sauce an' a tattie scone."

"Naw, nae roll 'n' squarey fur you," she said. She was rubbish at putting on a Scots accent. "Nope, no roll and squarey, just in case they want to do some x-rays. Besides, you'd likely chuck on it. We'll get you a cup of tea and a digestive biscuit. It won't make such a mess if you do chuck."

"Ok, thanks."

That would do. He felt like he could chuck buckets. The bathroom scenario of the other day, whenever that was, flashed across his field of view. He didn't have the moral fibre right now for another episode like that.

The nurse rolled up the loose sleeve of his hospital-issue gown, lifted the blood pressure gadget from the gadget trolley, wrapped the broad Velcro strap around his upper arm and pressed a button. The pressure went up until it felt as if his fingernails were going to ping off and then it let itself down. The digital display beeped the results and presumably logged it somewhere in its robot memory.

"Well you're not going to explode by the look of it," she said, "You have abnormal blood pressure - for Scotland."

"Eh?" said Nisbet.

"Yes, it's normal."

She lifted another gadget from the trolley. It looked like a pastel-coloured electric screwdriver. She poked the screwdriver bit in his ear. Obviously, it wasn't a screwdriver. Or maybe he actually did have a few screws loose.

"Can you see anything needing tightened?" asked Nisbet.

"It's a thermometer. Your temperature is normal too."

"A thermometer? Well I'm glad you didn't want to stick it up my bum like the vet does!" said Nisbet.

She laughed. "What are you like?"

She already had his pulse from the blood pressure doofur, but she took hold of his wrist anyway. Her fingers were cool on his skin and a substantial amount of the latent tension in his pulverised muscles relaxed. Old fashioned nursing. Hands-on healing. Much more personal than a Star Trek robot trolley.

"I'll get you some pain relief in a little while, but I see here that you've already had some," she said.

She gave him another cute smile and trotted out of the ward with her gadget trolley.

Gorgeous. Nice lady, neat little figure, good legs, nice bum, mousey fair hair, cornflower-blue eyes, warm heart, cool hands, and an exceptionally nice location where she kept her badge. Nisbet wasn't so badly hurt that he couldn't fancy a nice looking little colleen. He would marry her in his hospital bed, they would honeymoon in a health farm and she would nurse him back to health until he learned to use his wheelchair.

He lifted his head and tried to get another look at her backside through the ward window as she strode down the passage. A Mexican wave of pain washed up through him again. Jee-zus! And he'd had some pain killers already? God knows what it would be like when it wore off.

Strangely, despite his pain and his angst, he felt slightly cocooned from all of the crap that was going on in his life. At long last, somebody was taking care of him, and nobody else knew where he was or could get to him: not Brenda nor her anthropoid ape male parent, nor their grouperfish lawyer. Nor even Angela, nor clients. Nobody, presumably, knew he was here. He was marooned, isolated from the world and it felt ok, even though it was for a crap reason. But he'd have to call somebody soon - Angela probably. He fell asleep, still dopey and drugged to the eyeballs.

--------oOo--------

Bryson

"Did ye dump that motor?" said Bryson, when he eventually found Mackenzie the following day. "And where the hell have ye been?"

"Aye Alec, we dumped it oot the Jedburgh road. Aye, Ah think it was the Jedburgh road."

"And did ye torch it?"

"Eh, naw, we had tae leg it."

"So where huv ye been? And where's Julian?"

"Well, we baith hud tae go hame and get dried oot. We got a soakin' efter we dumped the Beamer."

Mackenzie gave him some sketchy details.

"So, ye went and dumped the motor, wi'oot thinking' tae take another motor wi' ye tae get back in? Ye only had wan job for Christ sake! Dump the Beamer and check oot the boy's address. Is there somethin' ye're no tellin' me?"

Julian wandered in, saw the two of them and turned around to go out again. Bryson grabbed him.

"Come here ya wee shite." Bryson was coming to the boil. "Right, baith o' ye, gie me the details."

Mackenzie, shaking in his shoes, gave a description of how the guy with the leather jacket had, by pure coincidence, simply walked out in front of the BMW and Mackenzie had no chance to avoid him.

"Ye accidentally ran him ower? Jesus Christ! Then what?"

"Well, we had tae get away fast, so we booted it, then went and dumped the Beamer."

"Is that right?" barked Bryson at Julian.

"Ehm, more or less," replied Julian, starting to tremble like Mackenzie. Even though Julian was the boss's son, and theoretically untouchable, Bryson was still pretty scary.

"And did ye kill him? This guy ye ran ower? Assuming it wisnae an innocent bystander."

"It wis definitely him," said Mackenzie. "The same guy that got oot the Beamer in the pub car park, wasn't it Jools?"

"Well, it certainly looked like the same guy, and it wasn't far from the pub where we saw him the first time," said Julian.

"Do you think you killed him?"

"We don't know. Mackenzie just got us out of there as fast as possible."

"Jesus bloody Christ!" exclaimed Bryson. "Well, ye were meant tae torch the car first. But thank fuck ye never ran the poor bastard ower wi' mah motor!"

He calmed down.

"But noo we've got a potentially deceased contact that we needed tae speak tae, a hit and run RTA, so the cops could be looking' tae arrest somebody on a manslaughter, or even a murder charge, a car in the countryside that wisnae torched and is covered in your fingerprints nae doubt. Did ye wipe it doon?"

"Aye. Jools wiped it doon."

"I only did my side."

"Bastard!" said Mackenzie. "Ah'm NTP!"

"He means KTP," said Julian to Bryson's puzzled look.

"Aye, that's it," said Mackenzie, "Ken't tae the polis."

"Shut it!" said Bryson. "Ye ran him ower wi his ain motor. And we're still nane the wiser as tae whether the guy was involved at all. Look, Ah'll speak tae the boss. You two idiots, get oot mah sight."

--------oOo--------

Hospital

Lunch arrived at an unnaturally early time of day and it looked ghastly. Everything was a cooked-to-saturation palette of de-saturated colour: the butterbeans an unappetising shade of pale beige; the sausage, a darker shade of beige; the potato, a whiter shade of pale … beige. Nisbet played with it for a while, left handed, pushing it around the plate, looking for his appetite. It didn't show up. What was that colour called nowadays? Taupe? He ate the half-melted ice cream - left handed. At least it wasn't beige.

All during lunch, the man in the next bed hadn't even found it in him to shut up, even when his mouth was full. Fortunately for Nisbet, his concussed attention span was an even shorter period than his usual fleeting attention span, and all the poor man managed was background noise. He didn't even seem to require any response and was happy to burble away unheeded.

Lunch was cleared away, and Staff Nurse McMartin returned with a chap, plainly a doctor because he wore a white coat and had a stethoscope looped around his scrawny neck. But he could easily have been on work experience from high school because he looked about fourteen years old and was about the right height too. Nisbet looked to see if he had short trousers on under the white coat. He didn't, but he had the look of a tawny-haired school swot, and had what must be his first moustache. It looked like a stick-on, joke-shop moustache: furry rather than bristly. It must have taken him weeks to grow it - hiding for a month until it reached maturity. His bottom lip was poised beneath this hairy canopy like a little pink shiny slug. Nisbet didn't fancy the look of him at all.

Staff Nurse whatsit McMartin pulled the screens around the bed and stood beside the doctor who was looking at Nisbet's clipboard.

"This is Doctor Rutherford," she said.

Nisbet groaned inwardly. It had to be Rutherford, not Smith, or Wilson or Mitchell. Rutherford. A good serviceable, in-charge sort of name. A middle-class name. A hereditary name.

"Well ... ." Doctor Rutherford looked again at the clipboard, "Mister Nezbit, you've hed a bit of an eccident."

The doctor had a stick-on bedside manner as well as a stick-on moustache. And a genuine Edinburgh private school accent which, like all Edinburgh private school accents, sounded, and was, put on. As deep as possible, sounding through a hollow mouth and pursed lips, and emanating from a birdcage chest so that the good doctor sounded like the principal boy in a pantomime. Nisbet wondered if he was wearing tights and buckle shoes beneath the white coat, but couldn't be arsed looking.

"Its Sangster, Sangster," croaked Nisbet, painfully, belligerently but incoherently.

Nurse McMartin held up two fingers and mouthed, "Two surnames," and smiled cheekily at Nisbet. Nisbet smiled back at her name badge.

"I expect it is Mister Nezbit, but we'll get you some pain relief. Now ... " He pronounced the two syllables "Nez-bit", like the sort of hyphenated names he'd probably been at school with.

Nurse McMartin came to the rescue. "The gentleman's name is *Nis*bet Sangster."

The poor lad obviously was on his first day on the job. Or even the first day out without his mum.

"Yes. Well, anyway, we don't think that there isn't much damage done beyond a fairly severe concussion and some very severe bruising. However, we're looking out for possible internal damage."

When Doctor Rutherford spoke his fluffy brown moustache and his shiny pink bottom lip reciprocated eagerly. A brown mouse was shagging a pink slug on the lower half of Doctor Rutherford's face.

"What will probably heppen is thet we'll keep you in for a whale, take some ferther eggs-rays when the swelling gows dine and you'll be howme in now time, I expect."

This was news to Nisbet. What about the pain, what about the open wound on his thigh, what about all that blood.

He said, "What about all that blood?"

Doctor Rutherford looked at Nisbet's notes. "Well you hed a nesty cut on your head Mister Nezbit. You've hed a few stitches in thet. It would have been bleeding quate bedly."

"But my hip and thigh were covered in blood and ... stuff."

"I don't know about thet Mister Nezbit. No mention of that has come up from A&E. They'll have eggs-rayed you. What you seem to hev is mainly very severe bruising and severe concussion. If there are any frectures they'll show up on the eggs-rays. You've been very lucky Mister Nesbit."

"Yep. Lucky old me," thought Nisbet

All of this started Nisbet thinking about his gore festooned hip and the gaping flesh. He looked down for the first time at what he was wearing. A white gown tied at the neck and nothing else. Hells teeth! Where were his clothes? He gathered his wits about him again and got back to the identity crisis he'd acquired since he'd woken up.

"By the way, it's *Nisbet Sangster*!" croaked the man of that name.

But the young doctor was off to the idiot with the lumbar puncture and dry boak, while Sister McMartin opened up Nisbet's screens again.

Trying not to sound confused and idiotic, which he certainly felt, he asked, "Where are my clothes?"

"Oh they'll be in your locker, so they will. Wit the bits of your phone. Do you want them?"

She pulled a polythene bag from the base of the bedside locker, and laid it gently on Nisbet's knees. She smiled a kind, smile at him with those blue eyes. It was half a nanosecond longer than it needed to be, and went straight in through his eyeballs to the middle of his head, banged his amygdala together and made him blush. Why the bloody hell was he reacting like this? Must have been the bang on the head. He'd only been a hospital hostage for a day, and already he had Stockholm Syndrome!

Nevertheless, when his captor turned and went over to the doctor's side to help with Mister Dry-Boak, and draw his curtains, Nisbet calmed his eyes on her backside for a second or two. She disappeared behind Mister Boak's curtains.

He reached and opened the polybag with his clothes in it. This was the first time that he had really used his hands and his right arm wasn't for moving. Left-handed, he groped in the bag. Inside, on the top was another, smaller polly bag and inside that were the bits of his phone and his Omega. The glass was cracked but it seemed ok. Maybe he could claim it on his insurance. He put it on, dropped the bits of his phone back in the bag and wincing with the effort, rummaged, left-handed through his bag of clothes. More pain. His left shoulder and upper arm were groaning every time he moved them. While lying still he hadn't noticed them quite so much for the dominant pain in his right side and the pounding headache, but now he realised that there was hardly a part of his body that hadn't taken a hammering.

Finding his cargo pants at the bottom of the bag he slowly pulled them out with his left hand, wincing all the while. He laid them on the bed. They were filthy, covered in dirt from the tarmac and greasy all down the right thigh. The right-hand pocket was torn open. But no gore. He went through the other pockets. Nothing in the left, a tenner in the hip pocket. At the bottom of the ripped right thigh pocket his fingers felt something soft, cold and damp. Something slimy. Out came his hand while his stomach churned and looked at the contents. Horrible realisation.

Nisbet groaned out loud. "Mince!"

He slumped back in the bed dying of internal embarrassment and feeling like a complete idiot, he let out an airy gasp of pain. And a sigh of relief.

The nurse came over. "Are you all right Mister Sangster?"

"I'm fine," he said, a bit too sharply, wiping his embarrassed hand on his trousers and trying to stuff them back in the bag to hide the evidence. He wanted to stuff his head in the bag too.

"I'll leave you alone then. Grumpy."

"Yes. Sorry."

They were having their first tiff already.

Nurses came and went as the ward went about its business. Later on, Nisbet was pleased to see Staff Nurse McMartin return, with another, slightly younger and somewhat chubby nurse pushing a trolley.

"We're going to give you an injection to ease the swelling Mister Nisbet," said the chubby nurse. "And then we'll give you some pain relief."

They pulled the screens around him once more and rolled him onto his left side.

"In the bum no doubt. Can't I have it in the other side?"

"Sure then you'd have two sore bums instead of one," she answered, "Besides, you've got a hole in the other bum from a previous incident."

Bloody hell! The Paco Rabanne, toilet bowl incision incident! Had they been looking at his arse when he was unconscious? Obviously they had. At least she didn't know how he got it. Being the sort of twat that cuts his arse on the toilet seat while puking on his pubes probably wouldn't impress any woman.

From the way her shoulders chuckled, the plump nurse seemed to find that funny. Did she know? Had he babbled in his semi-comatose sleep about his cut-arse hangover incident?

She had a nice smiley, round face and he felt she was enjoying his embarrassment as she untied his hospital-issue gown at the back and let it fall off him, leaving his thigh and bare bum on view. His embarrassment was quelled immediately by the shock of the first sight of his real injuries. His whole leg, his calf, his knee, his thigh and hip were a glorious balloon-swollen, Technicolor display of black, yellow, blue and purple flesh. His knee looked like a mandrill baboon's arse: all blue and red and a bit too in-your-face. And his thigh looked like a baboon's face: full of mischievous intent. It was that livid, it looked pleased with itself, and it had no right to be. What he could see of his arse was no better; it was an eight-inch tomato and black olive pizza with mushrooms and pepperoni. And anchovies, probably. He hated anchovies.

"Nice mess," said Staff Nurse McMartin producing a hypodermic and studying it against the light. "The rest of you, your arm and your ribs are a good colour match, and your shoulder, and your back and your napper."

The other nurse nodded. "Yep, it's a nice picture, so it is."

She gave him a cheeky look out the corner of her eyes.

Shit, they'd had a look at his whole bare body. He felt violated.

Still holding the hypodermic up to the light, the staff nurse squeezed a drop of whatever it was out of the tip of the needle. She was dead bloody cute with her freckles and all and her nice everything. She was dead bloody cute, but she was going to stab him.

"How are you with needles?"

"Never mind me," said Nisbet. "How are you with them?"

"An absolute expert," she said. "Look the other way Mister Sangster, this won't hurt a bit. Just lie still for a minute."

"You think so?" he said. *"Lie still?"* he thought. *"I daren't bloody move a muscle."*

He braced himself for the stab of the needle. Nothing happened.

"Well it didn't, did it?" said the Staff Nurse.

She dropped the syringe in the plastic bin on the trolley. Nisbet unbraced himself. Then he felt a slight sting in his backside.

"That was the sore one. What a big toughie you are."

"You didn't seriously jag me in that bruising did you?"

"No," said the podgy nurse. "She wasn't being serious, she just jagged you for a laugh. Boom, boom!".

The Staff Nurse rolled her eyes.

The plump nurse tied his gown again at the back and they rolled him gently onto his back again. He watched the staff nurse retreat with the trolley out of the door as the other nurse tucked him in. Nice bum, he thought once more.

The nurse saw his eyes follow the staff nurse out of the ward.

"What are you like? Oi'll get ye a bucket of cold water," she said and trotted off. He watched her bum too as she retreated. It was a different kettle of fish altogether. A kettle for large fish.

"How come you're getting all the attention?" sparked up his neighbour. "I expect you'll be gawn for yer lumber puncture soon."

"X-rays, I think," said Nisbet, being friendly now that the cool breeze of the painkillers was flowing through him.

"X-rays, and a lumber puncture! Ya beauty!"

There was nothing to do now, except lie there and not listen to Willie Boak, so he studied the ceiling tiles again. Thankfully, he couldn't find the ceiling tile face. He dosed off, but a little later he was wheeled from the ward in his bed by the two KGB spies, who still chatted away in whatever language it was, while Nisbet gazed up at passing ceiling, ready to catch the eye of any ceiling tile faces, if one should pass by. In Radiography, he was X-rayed from various different angles, the move for each of which was done gently by cool hands. But not quite gently enough. This was followed by an insertion into a giant plastic tube, and being told to lie still while it made loud grinding noises as if it was still digesting a previous patient and going to eat him next. Bedded again, he was ceiling-tiled back to the ward, where he enquired what was next. One of the nurses predicted that he'd probably be kept in for a day or two for observation. Observation would be fine with him because he would be working hard on the observation of cute Staff Nurse McMartin and her fit little figure.

--------oOo--------

Angela

After lunch, Nisbet asked one of the nurses if there was a phone he could borrow. A trolley was rolled in with a pay phone. It only took debit cards or coins. The plump nurse trotted off with his tenner to get him some change. He phoned Angela at the office.

"Well hello stranger," she said. "Where have you been all day? Are you planning on coming in today?

Nisbet immediately felt like a wayward schoolboy. How come, even though it was him that employed Angela, it always felt like the other way around?

"Well, I couldn't come in, I got hit by a car yesterday on my way home."

"Yeh, right." There was a pause, then Angela said, "Seriously?"

She'd been weighing the news up for its joke coefficient. Her employer was always joking about stuff. Despite his current inner turmoil, her employer was outwardly a happy-go-lucky, likeable guy.

"No, seriously Angela, I got hit by a car. I'm in hospital."

Angela almost had hysterics.

"Run over by a car? In hospital?" she shrieked.

"No, it was me that went over the car," he joked.

But Angela missed it and carried on, on the fringe of hysterics.

"Oh, oh! Are you ok? Are you hurt?"

"Well you don't end up in hospital if you're in the peak of health. But I think I'm ok."

"You *think* you're ok?"

She continued to throw a wobbler for a bit, but eventually he managed to calm her down.

"Look, I'm fine, just a bit bashed up that's all. I'm fine, honest." Jesus, he felt far from fine. "They've x-rayed me, and CAT scanned me, or dog scanned me. To see if any bones are broken, or internal injuries. I think."

"X-rays? Broken bones? Internal injuries?! I'll come in. Do you need anything?" Her voice was still at panic pitch. "What ward are you in?"

That was a good question, he had no idea what ward he was in. It hadn't occurred to him to ask. He ran it round in his head for a second. He didn't think Angela would get it if he said, "I'm in the ward with the cute Irish nurse with the nice arse."

"Good question," he replied. "I don't know what ward I'm in, I'll need to ask. I'll phone you back. Look, in the meantime, I could do with a few things."

"Pyjamas, you'll need pyjamas, I'll go round to your house and get some. You'll need pyjamas. And your toothbrush."

It took Nisbet a while to get her to understand that he didn't possess a pair of pyjamas. Determined to help, she said she'd bring a pair of Colin's pyjamas, they'd fit. Besides, she didn't have time to go across Edinburgh to Nisbet's house and he couldn't stay in hospital for any length of time without pyjamas.

Colin's pyjamas would fit alright, where they touched. Colin was a podgy little short-arse - near-enough a head shorter than Nisbet, and a foot wider. It was all too depressing. Marooned in a hospital, in dire pain, probably maimed for life and trying to impress a sexy nurse while wearing a short, fat civil servant's pyjamas.

"Tell you what Angela…"

"Soap, you'll need soap … and a face cloth … "

"A phone, I could do with a new iPhone, my phone got smashed."

"That's ok, it's insured," said Angela. "Never mind the phone … underpants, you'll need underpants."

Good heavens, she was acting like his mum instead of her usual big sister.

"Ok, but can you nip into town and get me a new iPhone please?"

The conversation ended with Angela dithering: oscillating between pyjamas and phones. This was very unlike her usual calm and competent self, but eventually, with a list of things that she thought Nisbet needed, she got back to normal. Nisbet hung up the phone and wondered who else to call. Certainly not Brenda.

But unbeknownst to Nisbet, and always one to do the right thing, Angela had a sudden notion that Brenda should know that her husband was in hospital. She picked up the phone.

Nisbet's bedside neighbour, Mister Boak, started up again over dinner, which consisted of butterbeans: pale grey this time and greyish brown stewed beef – well, it looked like beef. Butterbeans obsessed Mr Boak for a little while, then football took over. As a rugby person, football was as interesting for Nisbet as a lumbar puncture. Heart of Midlothian, "The Jambos", need look no further for their next manager. Mister Boak was a lifelong fan, a season ticket holder and deeply in love. The only thing that Nisbet knew about football was that Scottish football was rubbish and Hearts among the rubbishest.

The prattling went on and on, and Nisbet was just getting used to it, like he had the petrol driven cement mixer which the workmen had running at the back of the office. Then, like the cement mixer, he became aware of it again only when it stopped. Midway through a sentence Mister Boak just dropped off to sleep. In a minute so did Nisbet but was woken up again twenty minutes later when Mister Boak's sentence started again, where he'd left off.

At the end of his shift, P.C. Mark Borthwick suddenly realised that he'd yet to deal with the stolen car half way up Jim Nichol's farm drive. He got into his car and drove round, checked that he had the registration number correct, and with an eye untutored in the mystical business of classic cars, made a note that it was some kind of old BMW and went home. He'd sort it in the morning.

--------oOo--------

6

Hospital

After no sleep whatsoever until the crack of dawn, Nisbet was woken five minutes after falling asleep, to be given some pills to wash down with some tepid water. He would have taken strychnine if he'd been offered it because the ferocious headache and the network of departmental pain that was his body had operated a rota system to maximise wakefulness. Then, heedless of his groans, the night staff propped him up and gave him a cup of tea with no sugar. He watched it go cold, out of reach of his immobilised right side, not that he would have drunk it: tea without sugar was about as appetising to Nisbet as strychnine.

Staff Nurse McMartin's bright smile didn't so much light the room up when she came on shift, it lit Nisbet up. The smile she gave him sent a buzz through him as she whizzed round the room checking on the other inhabitants and left. Nisbet smiled back at her, and disappointed that she'd missed him out on her inspection, he smiled at her backside on its way out of the door. At least it relieved the tedium. He'd had hours and hours last evening before lights out, of inane prattle from the fuck-wit in the next bed, apart from a short break in the early evening when Angela and Colin visited him. Mrs Boak came in to take over the post of locum tenens drivel listener. Later, after Mister Boak's wife left, Nisbet got more lumbar puncture drivel, football, then his wife's prolapse and he had the full low-down on all the gory details. The mystery pain in the leg featured regularly.

Later, Angela arrived with a bag of stuff for Nisbet, including a pair of Colin's pyjamas. Horrifyingly, and yet somehow unsurprisingly, the pyjamas had racing cars all over them. 1950s Ferraris, Porsches and Jaguars with speed whooshes and puffs of exhaust smoke. Colin obviously was as embarrassed as Nisbet was horrified. But Angela had made up her mind: Nisbet needed pyjamas, and pyjamas he would get. Knowing Angela, she had picked the pyjamas for Colin. Colin was a dork but he wasn't so much of a dork that he'd buy pyjamas with racing cars on them. His wife, however, was the sort of uncomplicated lady who thought that all men, regardless of their reading age, liked cars of any sort, in any form. With no VAT on kids' clothing, she'd probably got them in the 'fat kids' section of Matalan (there had to be one). Angela managed her own money as well as she tried to do Nisbet's.

Mister Boak in the next bed prattled on. About midway through the morning, midway through a sentence, once again Mister Boak dropped obligingly off to sleep: "You know, one of the problems wi' a bad back is ... Zzz ... "

Two minutes later, Staff Nurse McMartin came in with another nurse and said, "Well we'd better be getting you out of that gown, cleaned up and into your jimjams."

Nisbet's face was a picture. She wasn't really suggesting stripping him off and helping him put on those ridiculous pyjamas was she? He could feel his face glow like a brake light.

"Ok," she said, seeing the embarrassed panic in his face. "We'll get two of the guys up to help you, get you cleaned up, and into your racing cars."

That made it worse, getting bathed by two male, possibly KGB nursing assistants and then helped into pyjamas designed for a size triple-XL twelve-year-old would be the pits. But it turned out it wasn't so bad. The guys might not have been KGB for all he knew, they just spoke some weird East European gobbledygook. But they were calm, friendly, professional and didn't mention anything remotely connected with automotive male night attire. They'd probably seen it all.

Back in a freshly-made bed he felt refreshed and more relaxed and with the sheet pulled up to his chin, the racing cars were hidden.

Nisbet was just enjoying the relative peace of, for once, a non-snoring Willie Boak when a nurse came in and announced that there were two policemen outside to see him. Once again the screens were pulled around Nisbet and two CID men were shown in, accompanied by the young, upper-class, but classless Doctor Rutherford with the rodent-like mouse-tache.

"Good morning Mister Nez-bit," said the doctor, carefully hyphenating Nisbet's name. "These gentlemen would like a werd with you abite your eccident."

"*What a ridiculous bloody accent,*" thought Nisbet. "It's Mister Sangster, Nisbet Sangster," said the man of the very same name.

"How do you do Mister Nezbit. I'm Detective Sergeant Fleming and this is Detective Constable Gorman."

"It's Sang-ster, Nis-bet Sang-ster."

"Got that," said Detective Sergeant Fleming. "Always good to have the full name."

The tone was bored and Nisbet got the feeling that he was hindering them in their work, keeping them from cracking a major crime, like social media non-hate crime speech. Detective Sergeant Fleming had big bushy eyebrows which joined in the middle. They were off the same joke-shop production line as Doctor Rutherford's moustache.

"We'd like to ask you a few questions about your accident. You see, it was, technically, a hit-and-run, which is quite a serious offence."

"You're not kidding it's serious. I'm seriously in hospital. Did anybody get the number of the car?" asked Nisbet intensely, deciding to look vibrant and interested, helped on by the last dose of painkillers.

Cops made him nervous even when he was the victim. This probably went back to the time when he was about twelve years old and P.C. Rooney, the town policeman and possibly its only psychopath, had walloped him round the ear, knocking him to the ground, and for no reason at all other than he was in range. Even in a small town, with the police, it was possible to be the victim and the accused simultaneously. Accordingly, Nisbet had grown up under the indelible impression that cops were mostly bigger thugs than the thugs, and to be avoided at all costs.

"As a matter of fact, somebody did get the number, but it doesn't help much with identifying the driver as the car was reported stolen a couple of days ago. Did you, by any chance, get a look at the people in the car? Apparently there were two men in it."

Doctor Rutherford had stepped a little closer. Nisbet wondered what it had to do with him and gave him one of his withering looks. He didn't wither. Too thick to wither.

"Well no," said Nisbet slightly sarcastically. "My photographic memory let me down just as I flew over the windscreen."

"Mister Sangster,"

"It's Mister Nez-bit," interjected Dr Rutherford.

"Oh for fucksake!" said Nisbet.

"Mister Nezbit!" said the sergeant, having been in-corrected. "We're only trying to help here."

"It's Sangster! My name is Nis-bet Sang-ster!"

"Yes, so it is," said the sergeant looking back at his notebook. "I do beg your pardon." He gave the wither-proof doctor a withering look which went clean over his head.

"I beg your pardon," repeated Nisbet, suitably contrite. "It's Sangster, Nisbet Sangster. I don't think I really saw the car at all. It all happened a bit quick." Then he remembered his Beamer. "Weird co-incidence though, my car was stolen the other day."

Nisbet wasn't sure just when that was exactly. The other day could have been yesterday, or the day before yesterday, or a year ago. He was caught in a warp in the space-time continuum. Time had a way of being inestimable when you had Mister Boak for company.

"You know, you really shouldn't step off the kerb without looking," said Detective Constable Gorman, who hadn't really been listening, but wanted to make a contribution nevertheless. He went back to not listening.

"No indeed," said Doctor Rutherford.

He was grasping his stethoscope with both hands at the ear pieces as if he was about to start listening to the conversation through it. Nosey little squirt.

"I'll try to remember that. Green Cross Code and all that," said Nisbet sarcastically, remembering the ageing road safety poster on the walls at his school.

"Green Cross Code. That's right," said the good doctor.

He was young enough to know about the Green Cross Code and looked young enough still to be in The Tufty Club. Basically, he was too young.

"Oh for pity's sake!" said Nisbet.

"We think it was probably two joy-riders in a stolen car and they just got unlucky," said the Sergeant said, taking over again.

"*They* got unlucky!?" said Nisbet, his bruised ribs and his exasperation making the words wheeze out of him.

"Yes. They probably dumped the car somewhere and legged it. Bit of an open and shut case. The car will turn up sooner or later ..."

"Oh goody," said Nisbet, wishing *his* car would also turn up - sooner *rather* than later.

"It'll probably get found abandoned up some farm track, burnt out."

"Whose car was it?" asked Doctor Rutherford, now taking even more of an interest in none of his business.

"Oh ... " Sergeant Fleming gave Doctor Rutherford the same look he had earlier but looked at his notes anyway.

"Ehm, it was reported stolen the day before yesterday, November one five, Bravo, Echo, Tango."

Nisbet thought about that. It had a familiar feel to it.

"... by a ... Mister ..."

Sergeant Fleming consulted his notebook two pages back. He paused for a moment. Then he shifted his weight to the other foot and paused for a very long moment, staring down at the page. His eyebrows came down to meet the top of his nose and he looked directly at Nisbet.

"... by a Mister, Nisbet Sangster."

The two policemen looked at one another in silence. Sergeant Fleming's eyebrows went back up where they belonged for a moment then went up behind the fringe of his hair. They looked at Nisbet.

"Is there something you want to tell us Mister Sangster?" asked the Sergeant

"Yes?" said Detective Constable Gorman, who was as mystified as he looked.

Nisbet was staring at the ceiling. There was that creepy face in the pattern of the ceiling tile again, sneering at him. His reason at last had left him. He had been run over by his own car.

"*How do you do that?*" he thought, "*Get run over by your own car? A day after it was stolen?*"

This was taking bad luck into the realms of an art form.

In the background he heard Mister Boak start up again. "Ye get nae sympathy ye ken. When did they screens go up? Hey Nurse!"

"I think we have to assume that that's a paperwork error, and in the meantime carry on with the hit and run incident," said Fleming.

The Sergeant continued to question Nisbet about his movements prior to the accident. He got very little help from the extremely confused hit and run victim.

Nisbet began answering everything with either, "Yes I think so," or, "I don't know," alternately, interspersed with short strings of just the one or the other. The rhythm of it was comforting and the Sergeant seemed to be satisfied because he wrote them all down.

In the main, when Nisbet said, "I don't know," what he meant was, "What's it all about? What does it all mean?"

Eventually, it got boring enough for Doctor Rutherford to leave, no doubt to spread the word round the canteen that he had a patient called Mister Nez-bit who had got run over by a Mister Sangster.

Eventually, Staff Nurse McMartin came in, and spotting Nisbet's deranged expression, asked the two policemen to leave. Which they did, Sergeant Fleming intrigued and Constable Gorman in the same boat as Nisbet: completely bamboozled.

Nisbet's deranged expression remained. He wasn't thinking anymore. His life had collapsed and his brain had imploded. Drawn in on itself like a dying star it lay in the bottom of his cranium about the size of a marble. It was a black hole, adrift in cranial space: immense gravity was sucking in perplexed misery from the far reaches of the galaxy. He rocked his head from side to side a little and was sure he could hear his brain swirling around the bottom like a ball bearing in a cereal bowl.

Staff Nurse McMartin came back in and tucked him in again. She was lovely. Nisbet decided he didn't want her for a lover, he wanted her to be his mum. Irish girls made good mums - well they had to, what with there being no contraception in Ireland, still, probably. He pondered that for a while because it was less challenging than thinking about how he'd got himself run over by his own car and taken to hospital. He dozed off for an hour or so.

The moment Nisbet woke up, Mister Boak wasted no time in coming to some pretty preposterous conclusions about Nisbet and the police. Nisbet went into cement mixer mode and stared at the ceiling, letting Mister Boak churn away. Eventually Mister Boak eased off a bit after realising that his only listener was past caring. Lunch came and went. Nisbet's lunch went back uneaten. Tired, cheeseless macaroni cheese with some strange white (with a hint of beige) pudding. Was it semolina, or tapioca? He hadn't seen anything like that since school dinners.

"You're no a very happy wee Hector are ye?" said Mister Boak

"Pardon?"

"Well, see son, Ah go on a bit, but I'm no schoopit. There's mair botherin' you than a wee whack wi' a motor."

"Wee whack?"

"See what you need is yer wife tae come and visit ye. See my Nancy, ye couldnae ask for better. She just tells me tae shut up."

"Shut up," said Nisbet, concurring in full with Nancy Boak.

"Aye. Ah go oan a wee bit Nisbet, but it's just nerves. Hospitals make ye nervous. And ma sair leg. Did Ah tell ye aboot ma sair leg?"

"Did Ah tell ye aboot mine?" said Nisbet.

"See, dinnae you worry yersel' aboot onything ither than getting well. That's what Ah'm goany dae. Everything will work oot for the best Nisbet."

This was a new side to Mister Boak and Nisbet chatted to him for most of the afternoon. He was really quite a nice man. He was just nervous and talked a lot of crap. The early afternoon slid by with the help of Mister Boak. About halfway through the afternoon Mister

Boak went to sleep again in the middle of the conversation. A nurse came and woke him for his supper and he said, "Christ is it tea time already? When did it go dark Nisbet?"

"You went to sleep. "

"I don't remember that. "

"Well you were asleep weren't you?"

"The nights are fair drawin' in."

"Out actually, its Spring. "

"So it is Nisbet."

Mrs Boak arrived soon after with a bag of things for her husband.

"This is Nisbet pet, he got run doon wi' car."

Mrs Boak said hello. She was a nice prim little lady and seemed bright as a button, not an exact match for Willie Boak. She sat beside Willie and hardly said a word while he rabbited on. Nisbet didn't have the strength to hold up a copy of Hello magazine so he read a two-year old copy of Private Eye.

--------oOo--------

Hermens

Eric Hermens collected the money together on his dining room table and sorted it into bundles. It was mixed denominations as McShaed had requested, mainly twenties and fifties. To be on the safe side, he counted it out again into bundles of a thousand and put a rubber band round each. It was making him sick doing this. Just the thought of parting with twenty-five grand when he had already lost three hundred-odd grand's-worth of diamonds and the four hundred-odd grand he expected to get for them. It would make anybody's head spin. And there was another twenty-five to go.

Satisfied that the numbers were right, he packed it into the reinforced mailing mag that he'd bought and stuck on the Royal Mail mailing label he'd printed on his bubble jet printer. He'd chosen the option to insure the parcel - for a mere two thousand five hundred. What a joke! Insuring twenty-five grand for two and a half grand. And the postage had cost him twenty-nine pounds and sixty pence. He agonised some more but it did not dent his resolve to pursue those

Scottish bastards, either for the money or for some kind of payback.

He headed for the post office, his stomach churning at the thought of entrusting twenty-five thousand pounds to the Royal Mail. Maybe he should get on the train and hand deliver it to Bryce. No, maybe he'd get mugged in Glasgow Central Station. Should he fly up? No, his overnight bag would get x-rayed and some nosey bastard would want to see whether the bundles of notes were explosives. He thought about it. No, it would be ok. Diamonds were regularly shipped by ordinary post, at least inside the UK, so why not bundles of money. He stepped into the post office.

At the post office desk he said that he'd like to hand over his parcel, he'd bought the postage on line.

"That's fine," said the can't-be-arsed voice behind the counter and she took the parcel and weighed it. "You're over weight for the amount you've paid, you've put the wrong weight on your label. It'll cost you another, ehm, four pound eighty. Do you want it insured?"

He said yes, for the maximum, "That'll be thirty-four pound forty please." She ripped off his nicely printed label.

"You just said it would be four pounds-odd!"

"Yes, that's the difference, but I can't sell you the difference, only a new label, you'll need to get a refund on line for your first purchase."

Hermens' normal ice cool demeanor was about to explode in the way it had done in the Edinburgh toilet cubicle. He calmed himself and fished out his debit card. Seconds later his twenty-five grand was casually thrown into a large canvas bag, half full with other parcels. He went home and failed to get a refund on line.

--------oOo--------

Brenda

Brenda Sangster put the phone down and stood ashen-faced as her daughter Samantha tugged at her sleeve, girning for attention.

"For goodness sake Samantha! Will you please just shut up for once!" she yelled, and immediately the child started to howl like a banshee. Samantha didn't like being ignored and had never been shouted at.

From the sitting room, Brenda's father's gruff voice irked its way into her consciousness.

"Who was that pet? Was it bad news ... or whit?"

"It was Angela, Nisbet's secretary. Apparently Nisbet's been knocked down by a car and he's in hospital."

"Whit?" cried her father, leaping from the settee and striding out into the hall. "He's no deid then is he?" he asked, only just managing to keep his tone merely sanguine rather than euphoric.

"Oh daddy," sniffled his daughter. "No, but he's very badly hurt. I think Angela said he was in intensive care."

Angela had over-egged the diagnosis, and the prognosis.

"He'll be in hospital for quite a while, weeks maybe. But she thinks he's going to be ok eventually."

"So it's neither good news nor bad news then. But at least he's in hospital," he said. rubbing his hands together.

"Yes, Angela said it was a hit and run. They haven't got the driver."

Brenda sensed by the smug expression on her father's pock-marked face that he was enjoying the news and got her suspicions confirmed when he followed up with, "In hospital for weeks ye say? Hit and run ye say? The bastard was probably askin' for it. Hit and run eh. Aye, somebody that kens him nae doubt. Oot fur revenge."

"Oh daddy," said Brenda, hoping he didn't mean it. "What should I do?"

"Nothing!" he barked. "You an' him huv separated. It's nane o' your business noo. Ye're gawny make a clean break. Remember?" And then in a more matter-of fact tone, "In fact, the sooner the hoose is sell't the better."

He sloped off, his ugly brain going up through the gears from callous to its normal vindictive cruising speed.

Brenda went through to the kitchen to tell her mother while Lockerbie sat in the dining room to eat his lunch. He was quiet now, concentrating. He sat chewing, his mouth open, like a bullfrog eating a songbird, his pitiless mind working in time with his reptilian jaw.

After he cleared his plate, he went back to the sitting room, sat and thought for a while longer, then through to the kitchen, he shouted, "Hey, is Sangster really hurt that bad?"

Brenda came through from the kitchen, wiping her hands on a dish towel.

"I think so daddy. Angela sounded really worried. They're going to x-ray him to see what's broken. He might have internal injuries and he's been knocked out. He's very badly concussed, unconscious for several hours. He might have serious head injuries."

"So he'll definitely be in the hospital for a while?"

"Angela said he could be in for a couple of weeks. Several weeks maybe."

"Oh dear, whit a pity," replied her father, his voice showing all the empathy of a hyena salivating at a dead baby gazelle.

"Best place for him then," he continued. "They'll look efter him pet. Ah widnae worry. If he's brain-damaged, he'll just get pit in an institution. So he'll be looked efter. You'll no need tae bother wi' him ever again."

Brenda went back to the kitchen, once again disappointed by her male parent's psychopathy.

With her out of the room, Lockerbie took his mobile phone out of his pocket and dialed the office. It rang, and rang. He pursed his irate lips and fumed. At last it answered.

"Hello! Aye, it's me, pit me through tae the warehoose."

He waited several more seconds while the warehouse phone rang and rang and rang.

"Hullo, Cammy, are ye busy this efternin'? … No a' that busy? Well how can ye no answer a bloody phone when it's ringin'?"

He listened to Cammy's list of duties for the afternoon.

"Look, never mind they deliveries. Just tell the customers there's been a wee delay, ye're waitin' fur parts or the like. The usual excuses. Listen, Ah've got a wee removal job fur ye - well, no that wee, actually. It needs done pronto. Ye'll need baith the big vans with the tail lifts. Just postpone a' the deliveries fur the day. Ah'll be back in the office shortly. Ye'll need a hand, some o' the furniture's quite big. Get Wull and the other installation crew - there's fifty quid each in it fur them."

He spoke for a few minutes more, killed the call and went through to the kitchen.

"Isn't it terrible about Nisbet? He's been run over by a car and he's very badly hurt," said Mrs Lockerbie with the usual apologetic, trepidatious tone she used when speaking to her ogre of a husband.

"Aye, too bad eh, whit a shame. In hospital eh. Never mind. Every cloud has a silver lining. Something good will come out of it."

He put his hands in his trouser pockets and rocked contentedly backwards and forwards from heel to toe. Neither of the women enjoyed the self-satisfied look on his smug moon-scape face. His mobile phone rang so he left for the sitting room.

--------oOo--------

Removal

"We've emptied the vans boss," said Cammy.

"Aye, gie me five minutes and Ah'll come roond wi' the keys for the house."

"Whit's the joab," asked Cammy.

"Ah'll tell ye when Ah get there."

He went back into the kitchen.

"Who was that dad?" asked Brenda Sangster.

"Aw, naeb'dy pet, just business."

But she noticed he was looking very pleased with himself.

Lockerby finished his coffee and left. Half an hour later his Mercedes SL spun into the warehouse car park. Cammy and Wull, his warehousemen and two of the other crew were waiting inside. The vans were empty and Cammy had packed extra padding, blankets, tape dispensers, cardboard boxes and bubble wrap, the usual when they got a house removal job on the side.

Lockerbie got Cammy round the back of the vans and spoke in hushed tones.

"See, what Ah want ye tae dae, is empty wee Brenda's hoose. She's gettin' a divorce frae yon prick o' a husband o' hers and Ah'm sellin' the hoose."

"Aye, whit a prick. Stuck up rugby-playing prick." Cammy was happy to adopt his boss's opinions. "So they're gettin' divorced?"

"Aye, so go roond tae Brenda's and empty it. Everything. A' the furniture, beds, carpets, fridge, cooker, the lot, even the ketchup and bring everything back here 'til we fund somewhere tae store it. Make sure ye bubble wrap a' the china and the breakables."

"Whit about his stuff? Leave that?"

"Naw everything, the lot, dinnae leave nowt. He's no got nowt onyweys. Bloody waster. He widnae hae nowt if it wisnae fur me."

"Are ye sure he'll no be there?" Cammy wore size M shirts and Nisbet was an XL, a substantial size difference.

"Naw, ye'll no hae nae bother, there'll be naeb'dy hame, he's in hospital."

"Hospital? Ya beauty!"

"Aye. Now, away ye go and get started. When ye've finished, just bring the stuff back here an' stack it a' thegither up the back. Careful mind, it's a' Wee Brenda's furniture. Aye, it'll likely take ye a couple or three hours, but just make sure it's done right. I'll see ye when ye get back. You and Wull will get a wee bonus, just make sure they ither twa keep quiet. Dinnae tell them it's wee Brenda's hoose. They'll get peyed when ye've finished."

Forty minutes later, the first of two large, red Luton vans with the livery of Tom Lockerbie's company, Castlerock Systems emblazoned across their panels pulled up outside the Sangster house and the overall-clad passenger got out to direct the driver as he reversed into the drive. Not far behind them was the second van. In swift order, cardboard boxes, bubble wrap and polystyrene beans were taken into the house.

By midafternoon, Tom Lockerbie's two warehouse crews had virtually stripped the house bare. They were used to this kind of removal work. The boss was quite capable of diversifying to keep the vans and the crew busy when business was slack. Anything from light haulage to house removals could be the order of the day.

Almost finished, from the master bedroom, the foreman, Cammy, dialed Lockerbie on his mobile phone.

"That's it boss. ... Aye, the lot, mair or less, aye except the stair carpet and a couple of bedroom carpets – nae room left in the vans. Plus a couple of things in the utility room like the washing machine. We've no got room for them either, it'll take another trip."

He listened to Lockerbie rant for a bit.

"Aye, the lot, apart frae whit looks like his claes, hangin' in the built-in wardrobe ... Eh? ... Naw naeb'dy seen us, dinnae think sae onyweys. The hooses is a' deserted. They're a' at work."

"Aye, right enough, Balerno's the spam belt. It'll be a ghost toon durin' the day: just wives at hame wi' the bairns, and auld wimmin. They'll a' be watchin' the soaps."

"So whit should Ah dae wi' his claes? Just leave them?"

"Aye," said Lockerbie.

Then, after a second or two while the spite synapses of his brain kicked in, he said, "Naw, hang on a minute Cammy. The hoose is gettin' sell't. He disnae live there onymair. It's no even his hoose. Just chuck his claes oot the windae."

"Oh ya beauty! Bloody' great idea. Ok boss, oot the windae it is."

Cammy killed the call and sniggered as he opened the window and turned to the built-in wardrobe. His boss could be a right bastard when he wanted to be, but Cammy didn't feel sorry on this occasion.

"Effin' rugby playing, stuck up architect prick," he muttered to himself, scooped an armful of clothes from the wardrobe and headed for the bedroom window. "Oh, what a shame, it's rainin'."

The first armful of Nisbet's clothes went out the window to land in a pile on the flower bed. Then the next armful, until the contents of the wardrobe were all out in the garden. With the wardrobe empty, he turned to the pile of Nisbet's underwear and socks which had been discharged onto the floor from the chest of drawers. Gathering up an armful, he threw them out of the window. On the way down, to meet Nisbet's jackets, trousers, shirts and pullovers, the breeze caught a pair of underpants and some socks, and decorated the birch tree in the garden with them.

With the sum total of Nisbet's clothes outside in the back garden, in the rain, Cammy pulled the front door behind him so hard, it didn't latch. He ignored it, closed up the tail lift of the van and both vehicles headed off out of the housing estate.

Approaching the road junction on the A70, Cammy pulled in tight to the kerb and waved forward a big black S-Class Mercedes which had just turned into the estate.

"That's a *real* Mercedes that is Wull. Nane o' yer silly wee two-seaters like the boss's."

"Aye, right enough," said Wull, nodding. "Ye couldnae get a shag in the back o' the boss's SL."

"The boss couldnae get a shag naewhere," cracked Cammy and they laughed as they watched the front of the S-Class lift slightly as it surged past them without a wave of acknowledgement.

As it passed, Cammy caught a glimpse of Mackenzie in the driver's seat, complete with Alec Bryson's Rae Ban sunglasses hiding his black eyes.

"Jeez! How can a wee twat like that afford a motor like that?"

"Bet he's just the mechanic takin' it fur a hurl," said his passenger. "This isnae an S-Class Mercedes street, it's the spam belt, it's a' Skodas and Mazdas."

"Aye," said Cammy, flooring the throttle and hearing a crash of collapsing furniture from the back of the van. "Oops."

--------oOo--------

"Do you really think so daddy?" asked Brenda Sangster.

"Aye," replied Tom Lockerbie. "Ye cannae go back there while he's still livin' there and when he's eventually oot the hospital and oot the picture, ye dinnae want tae go back and be rattlin' aboot in that big hoose on yer ain. Ye're faur better back here wi' us. And yer mammy can help ye wi' the bairn. And when yer divorce is a' sorted oot and ye've settled doon, we can look fur a nice wee place fur you and the bairn, maybes something in the village here. A nice wee flat."

The truth was that although the house was in his daughter and son-in-law's names, he had stumped up half of the total purchase price as the deposit, his daughter's share of the purchase. He could well do without a hundred and fifty grand sitting doing nothing, tied up in an empty house.

"But what about Nisbet's share? What if he doesn't want to sell?"

"He doesn't have a share, just a mortgage. He'll just hae tae buy ye oot and Ah dinnae think he's got the money, no wi' that pissy wee business o' his. Onywey, he'll hae enough tae worry aboot wi' lawyer's fees."

"I don't think it's such a bad business," put in his daughter. "After all, he designed and built this extension, and did all the planning. ... And your warehouse extension and ..."

"Yon's just draughtsmanship at best, the rest's just a case o' gettin brickies an' joiners in. Besides, he's in hospital, he's no earnin' nowt, he cannae pay the mortgage, Ah widnae think. He'll likely go bust. Bankrupt. Oot oan the street. Selling' The Big Issue."

He dusted his hands together as if it was mission accomplished.

Brenda Sangster knew there wasn't much point in arguing when her father was in this sort of mood: completely in awe of himself. She decided to change tack.

"Daddy ... about getting the lawyers. ... Nisbet and I decided we were just going to make a clean break, we don't need to get lawyers involved. We can just tell the lawyers not to ... ."

"Aye, that's whit he wid say, the cheapskate bloody ... arse. See pet, ye cannae dissolve a marriage wi'oot a reason, ye need grunds fur a divorce. Onyweys, the lawyers huv ta'en yer instructions and is a'ready oan the case. He'll a'ready hae been served wi' ... wi' whatever it is ye get served wi'."

He rocked back and forward from toe to heel again, hands in his pockets, face smug.

"Irretrievable brekdoon o' the marriage. Due tae mental cruelty, probably. That's whit they'll be gawn fur."

"But it's not like that daddy, we just ..."

"Well then, was there another woman?"

"No, we just haven't been getting along. Nisbet's so ... it's just the way he is ... he's just ..."

"An arse," interjected her father. "And if he's been an arse then it's mental cruelty. Did he ever knock ye aboot?"

"No!" she said, emphatically. "Nisbet's not like that!"

She didn't mention that she'd decked her husband a few times.

"Coz if Ah thought he'd ever laid a hand oan ye, Ah'd ... ." His fists were bunched up inside his trouser pockets.

"No Daddy, Nisbet's not like that!"

"Then it's mental cruelty. I'll phone the lawyer fur ye, add that tae the list. We'll hae the bastard's troosers at his ankles in minutes."

Brenda Sangster sighed. There was no arguing with her father when he'd made up his mind. He'd never liked her choice of husband. They had never been on good terms, her father continually making remarks, sniping, pointing out that he'd stumped up for half the house *and* the extension *and* half the furniture. Then once, after Nisbet had politely asked to be paid for the umpteenth job that he was being asked to do for her father, or one of his pals, her father had gone completely apeshit, yelling in Nisbet's face, calling him an ungrateful bastard. Things hadn't been going well in the marital front, but after that, the downhill slope became a precipice with Brenda's loyalties to her father growing with every marital spat.

Lockerbie left for the warehouse.

"Aye, that's braw Cammy," said Tom Lockerbie as the last of the furniture was stacked in the warehouse extension. "The morn Ah'll find somewhere tae get it stored: wan o' yon storage places doon in Leith or the like."

Tom Lockerbie smiled to think of the horrible irony that all of this furniture was being stacked in the very warehouse extension that Nisbet had designed and built for him - without being paid a penny for his work. All Lockerbie had to pay was the bricks and mortar. He pulled the warehouse door closed as Cammy drew the last of the two vans out of the warehouse.

Lockerbie pulled his wallet out of his pocket and gave the crew a hundred quid each.

"Well done boys, good job, good job."

He got back in his Mercedes.

--------oOo--------

Julian and Mackenzie

"Right, you pair," said Bryson. "Me and the boss are tryin' tae get in touch wi' yon London weirdo. You twa, take the Merc and have another go at checkin' that boy's hoose in Balerno," .

"Whit if he's there?" said Mackenzie.

"How's *he* gonna be there ya dopy wee twat? Ye ran him doon wi his ain motor! Fuck sake! He's probably in the bloody morgue! Look, just try tae no fuck it up this time, it's no exactly that hard! Go up tae Balernae, check the hoose oot, see if onyhing looks weird, or dodgy, if there's folk there. Then fuck off back here again."

He tossed Mackenzie the keys to the Merc.

"Dinnae bash it."

The Merc's satnav took Mackenzie and Julian right to the door of Nisbet's house.

Eighty-five-year-old Mrs Hamilton was watching from her sitting room window across the road. First two furniture vans emptying that young couple's house and then a big black limousine, like one of those wedding cars.

Mackenzie looked around furtively as he knocked on the door. To his surprise, it creaked open an inch. He turned and looked toward Julian who was still sitting in the passenger seat playing with his phone. He gesticulated impatiently, caught Julian's eye then cocked his head in the direction of the house. Julian got out with a sullen look on his face. He was way too important for this sort of work and besides, it was raining. He'd had enough of being soaked. The two of them walked into the echoing hall.

"It's totally empty," said Julian. "I think this must be the wrong house. Obviously nobody lives here."

"Naw," said Mackenzie. "The address has been checked oot. This is the right hoose, the Beamer's registered tae here. Must be just a dummy address, tae pit folk aff the trail."

He walked up the stairs, "Empty up here ana'," he called from the landing.

Coming down the stairs he said, "Come oan, I think we need tae get oot o' here, there's a wee wummin' watchin' us frae ower the street. She'll hae ta'en the Merc's number."

"That'll be Bryson's problem then," sneered Julian. "Wait a minute. I'll bet she misses nothing around here, I'll speak to her."

"Ye'd better no," said Mackenzie. "She'll be able tae identify us. Yer faither will go spare."

But he was more afraid of Alec Bryson than he was of Matheson.

"You're too furtive," said Julian. "There's nae herm in it, we're no brekin' nae laws," he said, mimicking wee Mackenzie's working class accent. "Besides, hide in plain sight, that's the trick."

"I'd like to see ye try that accent on Bryson," said Mackenzie, mimicking Julian's up-his-own-arse Fettes accent. "He'd deck ye."

"Very amusing," said Julian, ushering Mackenzie out the door.

But he knew Mackenzie was right, and pulling the door closed behind him, he made as if to lock it to give their visit some air of legitimacy. Then he walked across the street and knocked on the old lady's door. She answered it almost immediately, one eye peering through the links of the security chain.

"Hello," said Julian in his best posh Edinburgh accent, and with his most engaging smile. "We're from the estate agent's and we're just doing a valuation on the property across the street and ..."

He quizzed the nosey old bag for a few minutes. Happy that he'd allayed any suspicions, he went back to the car and they drove off.

Just as Julian and Mackenzie turned onto the main road, they failed to notice a disheveled and well-worn Ford Focus with a middle-aged couple in the front, turn into the housing estate. It was Angela's car with her husband at the wheel, Angela intent on fetching a selection of Nisbet's clothes to the hospital.

"This is it," said Angela, fishing in her handbag for Nisbet's house keys. "It's a nice house isn't it?"

"How will you know which clothes are Nisbet's?" asked Colin.

Angela rolled her eyes. "They're a heterosexual couple with a little girl," she said patiently.

Angela had long ago given up on sarcasm with her husband and simply explained things to him as she would the children.

"So I think we can assume that all of the men's clothes in the wardrobe will be Nisbet's clothes. Mmm?"

"Aye, right enough," said Colin. "Unless they've a lodger."

Angela sighed, got out of the car and headed for the front door.

--------oOo--------

Matheson

"So whoever it was in yon hoose, they just seem tae huv evaporated," said Alec Bryson. "It was totally empty was it?"

"Well," said Julian, "the lady across the street said we'd only just missed the removal vans."

"By how much?" said Sanderson.

Sanderson was an old hand. He'd been at the game as long as Bryson and although equally, criminally ruthless, he could keep his head, and he had to, he was in charge of distribution. He didn't have Bryson's colossal physical presence but at least he was a thinker. It was an unusual combination: cerebrally capable and criminally competent.

The boss watched the conversation play out, disappointed with his son's immaturity, intellectually intrigued as to where this would lead, and angry and frustrated at the fiscal damage that the whole incident had done him.

"She couldn't say exactly," said Julian. "She seemed a bit senile."

"Well, that's cleared things up an' nae mistake," said Bryson. He was having trouble keeping his hands off the effete little git.

"How many other geriatrics did ye quiz?" he barked.

"Look," put in Sanderson, "we're clearly dealing with a strange class of operator. They move into our operation at two levels, manage to swank the money *and* the goods and piss off into the blue yonder, so far without a trace." He paused. "Who owns the house?"

"Aye," said Mackenzie. "Good point. Maist hooses is owned by somebody. If we ken wha owns this yin we'll be near enough tae kennin' wha we're dealin' wi."

"Well done Mac," said the boss, intervening at last. "Tell you what, can you put the kettle on please, I'd love a cup of tea."

"Aye boss," said Mackenzie, proud to have been selected for this important mission.

"He's a good lad," said Matheson, when Mackenzie was out the door. "Fiercely loyal."

"And thick as two short planks," said Julian.

"At least he pits in the effort," said Bryson. He continued, "Yon hoose'll just be rented, pound tae a pinch of shite, it'll be rented. Ye widnae use yer ain hoose as a base fur a sting like this."

"Well, we'll see who owns it," said Sanderson, lifting the phone. "And whether it's let. At all events, the car was registered to that address."

He dialed a contact in a conveyancing practice. When the call answered he held out his hand to Julian for the address of the house, enjoyed a few pleasantries with the person at the other end, read out the address, closed off the conversation and hung up.

"I'll get billed for that. Lawyers are all bastards," he said and all present nodded sagely in agreement, including Matheson. As a barrister, he knew exactly what lawyers were like.

Sanderson looked at Matheson apologetically.

"None taken," said Matheson.

There was a long pause, while Mackenzie came back with the tea and handed the mugs round.

"So, where are we wi' the removal vans?" said Bryson.

"There wis twa big Luton vans at the road junction when we drove intae the estate," said Mackenzie. "Yin o' them had tae stop tae let us by, and the ither wisnae faur ahent it."

"So after the old lady mentioned removal vans Julian," said his father, "you didn't think that might relate to the vans that passed you on the way in?"

"He wis oan his iPhone tae his bum chums," said Mackenzie, not in the least sensible of Matheson's sensitivity about the company that his son kept.

Julian looked daggers at Mackenzie.

"I wasn't exactly there to monitor traffic."

"Well wee Mac saw them ... ," said Bryson, the unsaid, "*ya wee prick*," plain for all to hear in his tone.

Mackenzie gloated at Julian, "Aye, they were red vans. Big red vans, Luton-type vans, like furniture vans but no sae big," he said.

"Red vans?" said the boss. "Like the old Tunnock's Caramel Wafer vans?"

Everybody looked at him as if he had lost the plot.

"You know ... ?" he said. "They used to have Tunnock's on the side and Tea Cakes on the back and it said, 'Now a fleet of ... well, however many Tunnock's vans they had."

He looked around for some help with the reminiscence. Blank stares. He spread his hands as if it was obvious. "Tunnock's, Glasgow biscuit company? Tea Cakes? Carmel Wafers? Remember?"

"Tunnock's Caramel Wafers is Weegie biscuits?" said Bryson with a mixture of surprise and disgust. "Fucksake, Ah didnae ken that." He liked them but he would never eat another.

"Like post office vans? Royal Mail?" asked Sanderson.

"Aye," replied Mackenzie. "But it widnae be post office vans in a hoosin' scheme wid it?" He paused, then helpfully, "Unless maybes somebody wis gettin' a great big giant load o' parcels frae Ebay or Amazon. A birthday maybe. That could be it."

"Two big vans full of presents?" The boss's head headed for his hands again.

"Aye, like twa tons o' books an' records, three tumble dryers, five fridges, fuckin' twenty eight air fryers, four kettles an' a toaster? All by Royal Mail fuckin' Parcel Post?"

Bryson's sarcastic tone of voice was little different from his pre-assault tone of voice.

"How no?" said Mackenzie, ready to duck.

"Ye've done a'right wi' the thinkin' so faur wee man. Dinnae ower stretch yersel'," said Bryson.

"Onywey, ye see they vans gawn aboot the toon. Deliverin' stuff," said Mackenzie.

"Ye dae? I mean, you do?" said the boss. He didn't get around town much these days.

"Well stuff my fuckin' chicken!" said Bryson. "Imagine that. Vans deliverin' stuff, in a city. Whitever next."

"And there's that catering company," said Mackenzie.

"They're green," chorused everybody, except Matheson.

"And that double glazing company," offered Julian. "Could have been a double glazing company."

"That's right," said Bryson, getting into the swing with sarcasm. "They got contractors in tae replace the fuckin' windaes afore they done a moonlight flit in broad daylight."

"Alec!" said Matheson with a cautionary tone. But Bryson didn't apologise.

"And yon other lot. They others, wi the rid vans. Ye ken?" said Mackenzie helpfully. The boss put his head back in his hands. "Computers and stuff," continued Mackenzie. Nobody listened.

After a short period of more intrigue, Sanderson heard the fax machine whine to a start in the next door office. He got up from the corner of the boss's desk and came back squinting at a sheet of paper. The fax was of a handwritten note.

"The house is owned jointly by a Mister N. and Mrs B. Sangster; changed hands over two years ago, previously in the name of Thomas Lockerbie who bought it the year before." Sanderson passed the fax across the desk to the boss. "No way of knowing whether it's let or not."

"Sangster. That's the name the car is registered to. I don't suppose we know who these Sangster people are, do we?" asked the boss.

"Don't know any Sangsters, but Thomas Lockerbie rings a bell. There's a Tom Lockerbie," said Sanderson. "He's running for Trinity ward in the council elections. Owns an office equipment and computer company. Rags to riches socialist."

"Red vans," said Mackenzie. "Aye! It's them that services yon lazyprinter," said Mackenzie. "Their sticker's oan the front,"

They all looked at him.

"Castlerock Systems," added Julian.

"And they dae computers an' stuff. Office equipment. Furniture. Ah ken't it wis them," said the triumphant Mackenzie.

"Result!" said Matheson, trying to sound streetwise. "Now what?"

Silence.

Matheson continued, "So, vans owned by Castlerock Systems, which is owned by a Tom Lockerbie, appear to have emptied a house. A house which was previously owned by a Tom Lockerbie, and which is now owned by somebody called Sangster who owns a car that was at, or near the scene of the crime."

"That's mair than a coincidence dae ye no think?" suggested Mackenzie.

"Shut it," said Bryson. "And go and make fresh tea."

Mackenzie collected the mugs and scuttle off to the kitchen.

"Actually," said Matheson, "Wee Mac was more help there than the rest of you put together. He must be due a raise."

"Platform shoes?" said Julian.

He was sick of the sight of wee Mackenzie.

--------oOo--------

Hospital

In the morning, after sleeping in five- and ten-minute sprints, then slogging through longer periods of wakefulness, Nisbet absolutely wolfed down his breakfast while Mister Boak droned away in the background with his mouth full of toast, to the echo of Nisbet occasionally saying, "Aye," or "Really?" with a full mouth.

This tactic seemed to work every bit as well with Willie Boak as it had done with the police. After breakfast, the nursing shift changed, and Nisbet lay in bed keeping a weather eye open for a glimpse of any of Staff Nurse Macmillan's attractive features. She had a neat little figure, but now, equally attractive to Nisbet, were her smile and her cornflower blue eyes. And her ... something that she had about her that he couldn't pin down.

It was all he had to look forward to. Normally, he would have gone stir crazy in hospital. Nothing happened other than, if you were lucky, you healed up. And if you didn't you got four or five hospital-acquired infections, went into a death spiral and came out in a hearse. But he was enjoying the rhythm of it. All you really had to do was lie in bed and watch it get light outside the window, and then get dark, and then light again. You didn't need a watch in hospital, just a calendar.

Lunch came and went. Willie Boak driveled on for a bit but then shut up suddenly in his usual manner and went to sleep. Then, ten minutes later, he woke up. In the afternoon he went to sleep again and this time there was no snoring.

When the duty nurse came in she couldn't wake him.

"Mister Boak! Mister Boak! Willie!" she said, getting louder each time, her hand on his wrist searching for a pulse.

She turned and ran from the ward. Nisbet was transfixed as Staff Nurse McMartin, Doctor Rutherford and two other nurses came in. They couldn't wake him either so they wheeled Willie Boak and his bed out of the ward in very quick time.

A little while later, Nancy Boak came into the ward to visit her husband, she saw the empty space where his bed had been and asked Nisbet where Willie had gone. Nisbet could see she was very anxious when he told her he'd gone to sleep and then they'd wheeled him out, probably for tests or something. He wanted to help calm the poor lady, but he knew from the faces of the nurses that had wheeled Willie Boak out, that something dire was in store for Mrs Boak. A nurse came in and led Mrs Boak to the office.

Instinctively, Nisbet knew what had happened. He'd seen faces like that on the staff when his mum had died in hospital. He dragged himself upright in bed and swung his mooring rope legs off the bed, and in waves of pain tried to stand up. Pain shot through every square inch of him as he steadied himself on his feet and tried to take a step forward with his right leg. It almost buckled underneath him and he only just saved himself from tumbling to the floor by grabbing for the bed. He knew that feeling of old: although this was in a class of its own. Through the pain he could feel the numbness and vagueness of a dead leg. He'd had a few in his rugby career. But this was the best yet.

Standing again he swayed for a moment and crept, shuffling his racing cars a few inches at a time, slowly toward the ward office, clinging to door jambs and walls as he went.

Mrs Boak was sitting down in the passage on one of a row of four plastic chairs. Nurse McMartin was down on her hunkers holding the poor lady's hand. She wasn't weeping, she just looked stunned, white as newspaper, utterly aghast.

She looked up at Nisbet, "He was only in with pains in his leg Mister Nisbet."

Nisbet collapsed onto the chair beside her and put his good arm, his less bad arm, around her thin shoulders. Immediately she put her face against him and wept long, deep tears into his chest. That got Nisbet going so he dripped a few tears onto her woolly hat. Poor old lady. He held her tight for ages until the deep cries of grief and shock and the tears slowed and her thin shoulders began to stop shuddering.

Weeping, thought Nisbet, was just like laughing: you can't keep it up for long no matter how bad the grief or funny the joke.

After a while, and seeing that Mrs Boak was in a safe pair of hands the staff nurse got up and left them alone. In a little while she came in with a mug of tea for Mrs Boak and told her that the doctor would speak to her in a minute. Mrs Boak didn't take sugar so Nisbet drank it and topped it up with the odd tear dripping from his nose. It needed topped up because he could barely hold it level with that shaky right hand and he spilled a fair bit. He tried to wipe his nose with his sleeve and got more tea on his racing cars.

Looking down he could see that the red Ferraris and yellow Porsches on his pyjamas were soaking with a mixture of Mrs Boak's tears and hospital tea. It crossed his mind, as it always did when he saw one, that a Porsche was a real tosser's car. Colin's pyjamas were a tosser's pyjamas.

He held onto Mrs Boak for a little while longer until young Doctor Rutherford arrived with Staff Nurse McMartin and asked her if she'd like to come with him. He'd take her to see her husband. Doctor Rutherford's face was pretty grave too: he didn't look like a jumped-up little squirt any more, he was a bit red in the eyes, as if he might have been weeping too.

"I don't know what to do," said Mrs Boak, hanging on tight to a handful of Nisbet's racing cars. "I don't know what to do."

She didn't like the look of Doctor Rutherford, he looked like a wee boy. She looked up at Nisbet, "What do I say to Tommy and Evie? And Tommy's in New Zealand too."

These must be her children. Nisbet knew how they would feel, he remembered how it was when he'd lost his mum.

"They'll not understand."

"No, they won't, not to begin with," said Nisbet.

"What will they do with Willie Mister Nisbet?"

"They'll look after him," said Nisbet.

The staff nurse turned up.

"What will he do without me Mister Nesbit? He's no use on his own. I don't know what to do either Mister Nesbit.

"Nobody ever does," said Nisbet.

The nurse held her hand out for Nancy Boak.

"Away ye go and see Willie," said Nisbet. "He needs you now." And he held her hand up for Staff Nurse McMartin to take.

Mrs Boak was led away to see Willie, wherever he was now, and Nisbet watched her go, the odd tear still dribbling down his face. She looked even smaller now, crushed down to nothing, smashed to pieces, run down like him, but by stone-hearted providence.

Now he didn't feel as bad about himself as he had done. He just wished that Willie could come back and drivel him up the twist for a bit. He sat for what seemed ages, the tea was cold by the time Staff Nurse McMartin came back with the other young nurse.

She took the mug from him and said, "I think we need to get you back to bed Mister Sangster, you shouldn't be up and about. Look at you, your racing cars is all wet."

Together the two nurses helped Nisbet to his feet just enough to be lowered into a wheelchair that had somehow appeared from nowhere. They rolled him back to his bedside.

The two of them gripped him under the armpits and the younger nurse said, "Right Mister Sangster, on the count of tree, ye'll be givin' us a hand wit yer good leg, ye're a big lad, so ye are."

"Christ they're strong," he thought as the two of them hauled him up and spun him round onto the bed.

It was painful to move any muscle let alone a bunch of them. His left leg was stiff and painful too but his dead right leg, although only in periodic radio contact as far as movement was concerned, was armed and fully loaded. How he'd got out of bed under his own steam to go to Mrs Boak he didn't know. He didn't even know why he'd done it. Adrenalin probably: he'd never seen somebody die before, other than his mum. He lay back on the bed and waited for the throbbing in his leg to subside. The other nurse trotted off.

"I'm sorry you got involved in that Mister Sangster," said Deirdre McMartin, "We didn't expect his wife to come in right then."

"You didn't expect Willie to go out either," said Nisbet.

"No."

"I didn't mean to get in the way," said Nisbet.

"You didn't Mister Sangster. She needed somebody to hold her," said the nurse.

"So did I," said Nisbet, matter-of-factly.

The nurse ran her hand over Nisbet's bandaged head.

"Ye're a nice man, so you are Mister Sangster."

She could tell that there was more troubling Nisbet Sangster than a 'wee whack wi' a motor car'.

Nisbet lay back, closed his eyes and sank back into the bed asleep so quickly that the nurse instinctively put her hand on his wrist, feeling his pulse. She didn't check his pulse against her watch. She was just pleased that *he* had a pulse; patients with no pulse had freaked her out enough today. She gave his wrist a squeeze, laid it back on the bed and let her fingers run off it. Then she turned away to the office to help Dr Rutherford with his first sudden death paperwork marathon. For a doctor, he was a useless young eejit.

--------o0o--------

7

Hospital

In the morning, Nisbet felt better for a half decent kip. Poor Willie Boak had snored his last snore, and talked his final drivel, the poor guy. On the upside, with Willie Boak out of the picture, Nisbet had slept most of the night without Willie blasting away like an angry Harley Davidson. He only woke occasionally when he instinctively tried to roll over in bed and the pain roused him. He wondered how poor Nancy Boak had got on for the first time in forty years sleeping without Willie's airways impersonating the battle of El-Alamein all night. Poor old lady. He wished he could give her another cuddle.

At breakfast he kept a sharp eye open for Staff Nurse McMartin. He had to admit it to himself, he fancied her like the clappers. Not only did she have a very nice little bod on her, more to the point, she was just very nice: clever and witty and caring and altogether a deeply attractive person.

When one of the other nurses came round with his medication he asked, "Is Staff Nurse McMartin on duty this morning?"

"Now why would you be asking?" said the nurse, with her hands on her ample hips, her head cocked to one side and a smart, sarcastic look on her face. "Would it not be something I can help you with?"

She sounded even more Irish than the staff nurse.

"*I could be in hospital in Dublin*," thought Nisbet. For all he knew, maybe he was.

Her name badge said Nurse Róisín O'Neal. Róisín, what kind of name is that? She saw him puzzling over it.

"Well ... ehm ...," he muttered, embarrassed.

He really didn't have a plausible reason for asking and it didn't seem the right thing to tell the truth, that he really quite fancied the staff nurse. Nurse O'Neal waited for his reply with a knowing smirk.

"Ehm, she said she'd, ehm, be able to tell me when I'd be getting out," havered Nisbet, looking for a plausible reason.

"Sure, the doctor will tell you that."

"Oh, ok, thanks," he said, looking a bit glum. He had a go at pronouncing her name, "Thanks … Roysin?"

"It's pronounced Rosheen."

Rosheen! It sounded like a brand of Irish furniture polish.

"And you needn't worry, Mister Sangster, Deirdre's on a late. She's at her fitness thing, martial arts or something."

"Yeh, … I thought she looked pretty fit."

"I know ye did," said the nurse, looking him directly in the eye.

He blushed, and she smiled, enjoying his embarrassment. Had it been that bloody obvious that he'd been ogling the staff nurse every chance he got?

"She'll be in about eleven." It was a thick Dublin accent. "And I don't tink she'll be late Mister Sangster. I think ye're her most interesting patient she's had for ages, so ye are."

"Not sure what you mean," said Nisbet.

"You've got the biggest haematoma any of us have ever seen. At least not for some time. Head to foot!"

She patted him on his hip, unnervingly near his wedding tackle.

"Haema...? Oh, very funny,"

In the late morning Doctor Rutherford came round and approached Nisbet. Nisbet's heart sank; he couldn't be arsed with the fatuous young twat. Then behind him, he saw that he was being followed around by Staff Nurse McMartin. He felt better already.

With them, they had another gadget trolley, one with a big computer monitor on it.

Staff Nurse McMartin pulled the curtains around Nisbet's bed once more. Doctor Rutherford was too posh to help with that. He fumbled with the computer, then stared at the screen.

"I hev your eggs-rays hare Mister Nesbit," he said, with his ridiculous accent.

He hit a few keys on the keyboard and the screen went black.

"*Christ,*" thought Nisbet, "*the guy's an idiot, I'm in the hands of a doctor with an IQ in single figures.*"

The Staff Nurse leant forward and switched it on again for him. He started paging through the x-rays, all the while making small, studious, academic, learnéd Hmmm and Ahhhh noises and looked now and again at the radiologist's notes, as he pretended to deduce a diagnosis from what he saw.

"*Jesus,*" thought Nisbet, watching him intently. "*He moves his lips when he reads.*"

Once again, the brown mouse was shagging the pink slug on the bottom half of the noble doctor's face. Despite himself, Nisbet sniggered at his own humour and then, while moving his lips in imitation, he caught Staff Nurse Deirdre McMartin's eye. She'd been watching the young idiot too. She hid her face behind her clip board. It was too much for both of them, but luckily, the burst of laughter from Nisbet caused the usual stun grenade of pain to shoot through him and his laughter was choked off into a loud grunt.

The doctor looked at him without a hint of apprehension that a loud grunt might be an indication of discomfort, and looked at the radiologist's notes again.

After reading through them he said, as if to an assembled class, "The patient presents with multiple deep bruising, severe concussion and ..." on he went.

"*Jesus,*" thought Nisbet again. "*The 'patient presents'. What am I? A game show host? Patronising wee shite.*"

"Well, Mister Nez-bit," said Rutherford.

"It's Sangster," said Nisbet.

"The gentleman's name is *Nis ... bet Sang ... ster,*" said the nurse, leaning forward to emphasise the point as strongly as she could.

"Yes, I *can* read," said the doctor "Did we never get the patient's Christian name?"

"*Fabulous!*" thought Nisbet. "*He's been a doctor for twenty minutes and instinctively he knows how to discuss the patients he's with in the third person, as if they're zoo specimens.*"

He decided to take the piss and let the daft twirp know that his brain still functioned despite the severe concussion.

"I don't have one."

"I'm not a Christian, no Christian name you see, just two second names. And a Middle name. It's a…" He thought for a second, "… a Mormon thing, no Christian names."

The doctor looked surprised. Nurse McMartin made a funny gagging noise through her nose.

"Oh," said the doctor, looking at her disapprovingly, and then surprisingly modestly, "I never knew thet. No, I suppose you wouldn't hev a Christian name. Two surnames, I never knew thet. What was your middle name?"

"Christian," said Nisbet, truthfully. "And it still is."

The staff nurse looked like she might explode.

Seconds passed while the doctor added the middle name to Nisbet's notes, his brows tensed and his lips pursed in thought.

After another moment's apparent thought, trying to work out if he was having the piss taken out of him, the good doctor said, "Well I down't think we need to keep you in hare for very much longer Mister Ehmm …" He looked at Nisbet's notes, "Mister ehm … I think we could think about letting you gow howme arinde midday tomorrow if the swelling's gone dine a bit more and you're mowbile enough to look after yourself, and looking chipper."

"Chipper?" said Nisbet. "Is that a medical term?"

The doctor ignored him.

"Perhaps you should esk your waif to bring in your clowthes when she comes in to visit you again."

"That wasn't my wife, that brought in the pyjamas, that was my secretary," said Nisbet.

"Oh," said the doctor, "Can your wife come …?"

"She used to," said Nisbet, before he could stop himself. "At the touch of a button, as it happens."

The staff nurse tried to stifle a laugh again and nearly choked. This time, stuff came out of her nose and she reached for a paper handkerchief from Nisbet's bedside cabinet. She wasn't meant to appreciate vulgarity. At least, not on duty.

"Bless you," said the doctor. And then after a puzzled moment, "Where was I, oh yes, well, Mister Nez-bit, ehm, it looks as if you hev some very nesty bruising and some quait severe concussion. We also think that you may have what is called a sub-capsular bleed, a fairly minor one. It's just a little haematoma adjacent to the kidney. Minor ones like this are usually left to their own devaces."

"A sub- what?"

"A sub-capsular bleed. It's just a bit of bleeding in your insides - caused by the trauma of you hitting a car."

"It was the damned car that hit me." said Nisbet, indignantly.

"Yes, apparently they got the name of the car's driver too Mister Nez-bit," said the doctor gleefully. He had listened to most of the conversation with the police. "I'm sure they'll treck him dine."

"Christ!" breathed Nisbet.

"Well, that will be all then," and he turned for the next patient looking very puzzled.

"Glad I could help," said Nisbet.

Deirdre McMartin let the doctor get a few paces away, "Behave yourself."

Once she'd disposed of the young doctor, she came back round to Nisbet and leant her hip on the edge of his bed.

"The doctor's decided that if you're doing ok overnight, and you check out ok, you should go home about midday or early afternoon tomorrow."

"Oh goody," said Nisbet without much enthusiasm.

He was starting to enjoy the hospital. Apart from the death toll, things seemed to go quite smoothly and nobody could get to him. It was like being in a big cocoon.

"Can I not stay for an extra week? " he asked, "I like it here. Apart from the butter beans, being injured off the park isn't as bad as it's made out to be."

"Unless you're Mister Boak," she said, a bit glum.

"No. The poor guy, you didn't expect that did you?"

"Nope," she said, "It knocked Doctor Rutherford back a bit. His first stiff. He's just young so he is. This is his first position - registrar."

"He seems a bit of an arrogant little twit."

"Most of them are when they've just qualified."

Without thinking, she pulled a hip up to perch on the edge of Nisbet's bed.

"After a few fatals they learn a bit of humility, until they become consultants and then they mostly go all arrogant again. He's not so bad. There's worse than Doctor Rutherford. He'll make a good doctor. He had a wee bit of a bubble so he did. It wasn't anybody's fault, but he's taking it personally. It's a good sign. Another half dozen fatalities and he'll be spot on."

"That's good to know," said Nisbet. "The more patients that die, the better the doctor gets."

"That's about it," she said, and absentmindedly heaved her other hip onto the bed. They chatted about nothing in particular for a minute or so, with her swinging her legs like a little girl.

"Listen, we better get you fixed up with some clothes, we can't have you going home in an ambulance with mince on your trousers and racing cars all over you. Will I get the phone?"

Then she spotted that she was actually sitting on the patient's bed. She quickly got back on her feet.

"Oops." She smoothed her uniform down. "Anyway, ye'll be needin' some clothes if ye want to go home."

"Yes. Thanks," said Nisbet. "I'll get Angela to go round the house and get some kit."

"Single guy then … ?"

"Yes. Well, I wasn't, but I am now. Pretty much."

"Wouldn't have thought a guy like you would have trouble gettin' a girlfriend."

This was a welcome little indirect compliment. A bit of fishing?

"Well, I haven't exactly been trying. Probably lost the knack."

"Out of practice an' all."

"Yup." Then he thought, "*Bollocks! Might as well give it a go, she's really nice.*"

"Listen, when I get out, could I maybe, take you …"

Her pager went off.

"Oh well, *some*body needs me," she said. And over her shoulder, "I'll get someone to bring you the phone."

239

Róisín brought the phone, Nisbet phoned Angela and asked her to go round to the house and get him some clothes; it turned out she'd already thought of that. But she sounded glum and Nisbet said so.

"No, I'm fine Nisbet, fine, we'll come in with your clothes … and I got you a new iPhone, I've synced it up with all your stuff."

Fantastic, what a star Angela was.

Angela and Colin arrived with a small overnight case containing a selection of Nisbet's clothes. Colin looked a complete dork in his grey, wrinkled, civil servant's two-piece, Marks and Spencer suit, and an ancient baseball cap with "Indianapolis 500, 1992" written on the front. He was in denial about his encroaching baldness.

Nisbet could tell by Angela's face that something was badly wrong.

"Hi," he said, a bit nervously, knowing some bad news was coming. "What's happening?"

"Ehm," she said, "I take it you knew that Brenda was sending somebody round for the furniture?"

"What?!"

"Yes, all the furniture from your house, it's been removed."

"What? My furniture? Out the house? My house?"

"Yes," said Angela

"Shit, you're joking!"

But he knew she wasn't. He got a stomach-churning shot of adrenalin and yet another bolt of pain as his whole body jarred with this mind-altering news.

"I'm afraid so, the furniture's all gone, curtains the lot. The house is empty, apart from one or two bedroom carpets, and the stair carpet."

"What? I've been burgled?"

"Ehm, no, I don't think so, it doesn't look like burglary Nisbet. The doors hadn't been forced, the windows weren't broken. I think whoever it was had a key and just let themselves in and emptied the place. There was bubble wrap and other stuff lying round. I don't think burglars would use bubble wrap."

Nisbet was silent, his head swirling.

"It looks like removal men had been in. There's a few bits and pieces left in the kitchen, the appliances in the utility room: the fridge-freezer and washing machine and tumble dryer."

"Jesus!" said Nisbet. "I never thought she'd do anything like that - we just agreed on a clean break, no divorce-court shite. She could have it all except my stuff when the time came."

"Yup," said Colin, nodding in agreement with himself. "Make a clean break. Best thing, clean break. Aye."

His baseball cap nodded itself down his forehead a bit.

"I'll make a clean break of your neck in a minute," said Angela. She bit her bottom lip and stared at the floor. "Ehm, there's something else …"

"What?" said Nisbet, knowing there was even more bad news to come. She was starting to mist up. "What is it Angela?"

"Well, the bedroom window was open so I went to close it. … Your clothes: they were all dumped out of the bedroom window. In a pile in the back garden. In the rain."

"What?" exclaimed Nisbet.

"Whoever emptied the house threw all *your* clothes out of the bedroom window."

There was now no doubt who was at the back of this.

"Fucking evil old bastard!" exclaimed Nisbet and winced from the effort as anger and indignation ignited every muscle fibre in his body.

Angela winced at Nisbet's language. He never dared swear in the office. He lay there wringing his hands for a minute or so. Brenda could be a petty little shite when she wanted to but she wouldn't stoop to anything nasty like this. It was plainly her bastard of a father at the root of it.

"He must have known I was in here and the house was going to be empty for long enough to pull that off. How did he know I was in here?" asked Nisbet, incredulous. He'd thought he was safe in hospital.

"Well, ehm," said Angela, "I phoned Brenda, I thought she should know you were in an accident … and in hospital. I mean, for

Samantha's sake. I mean, you're her dad."

Nisbet felt like he was being dragged down, as if the hospital bed was quicksand. He hoped it would swallow him whole.

"Aw .. Angela..." he groaned.

"I'm sorry Nisbet. I thought it would be the right thing to do," she replied, biting her lip.

Angela always wanted to do the right thing. It was just that sometimes it could also be not the right thing.

"Uhu, it was the right thing - I suppose," said Nisbet. "If Brenda's male parent wasn't the arsehole of the millennium. Unbelievable! Is everything gone?"

Angela nodded contritely. "Looks like it. The house has been stripped. But not the kitchen or the utility room … the washing machine and tumble dryer … and the fridge, they're still there."

"Aye, and the light bulbs," put in Colin helpfully. "The light bulbs are still there."

"Thanks Colin," said Nisbet. "I won't bang into the missing furniture at night."

"Aye, right enough," replied Colin, nodding his eyebrows up in stoic agreement. "You'll be fine there, they left the bulbs. Aye, and the shades, so you'll be fine for lights. Aye."

"Oh well, it's not so bad then," said Nisbet. "I've got light fittings and a fridge."

"Aye," continued Colin, helpfully. "All ye'll need to get by will be a bed and a television, and ehm, a kettle maybe. … Maybe a microwave … or an air fryer …"

At this Angela got hold of Colin's jacket collar and marched him out of the room like a springer spaniel that had just shat on the floor. She sat him down on a chair in the passage and Nisbet saw her elevated index-finger indicating in no uncertain terms that he should sit and stay. He sat looking glum and wronged - a springer spaniel unable to comprehend having done anything wrong.

"So they've even taken the bed?" asked Nisbet when she came back.

Angela nodded. "All the beds. Including the child's bed."

It was just too much. He wanted the hospital bed to swallow him whole. Then he thought about all of his own stuff, his Bose stereo, his CDs, his Fender Stratocaster.

"What about all my stuff? And my clothes? What about my clothes? They must be totally fu… " His voice trailed away hopelessly. Then he said, "…fucked." He couldn't be arsed worrying whether bad language annoyed Angela.

Angela started to cry.

"I'm awful sorry Nisbet, we've gathered them all up, Colin and me, and they're in the car - except for the things we've got here. I put them through the tumble drier. It's still in the utility room. Unless you need them now, I'll take them home and iron them."

Colin was at the ward door holding up the overnight bag for Nisbet to see.

"I'm sure everything will work out for the best," he said, helpfully, from a safe distance.

"Ohh, you be quiet!" said Angela and bent and gave Nisbet a cuddle.

"Eeeech!" gasped Nisbet as she cuddled some pain up from his shoulders.

She let go fast. Colin took a step back into the passage, out of the firing line.

Nisbet continued, in fits and confused starts, to try to deal with this mind-numbing situation until his mind was numbed up like a gum at the dentist. He couldn't process thought at all, other than to be staggered at the depths of nastiness to which his detestable father-in-law was capable of sinking.

Angela eased off trying to comfort her boss. She could see that words like "awfully sorry", "it's really dreadful" and "but I'm sure it's all a misunderstanding", were going to make Nisbet explode. Or cave in.

Just at the flashpoint of being unable to take any more sympathy from Angela, the staff nurse came in and Angela took that as a signal to leave. She was happy to go. The nurse politely accompanied the two visitors out of the ward and spent a few minutes with Angela out of Nisbet's earshot. She came back in to speak to Nisbet.

"Your secretary? She's very nice. She's very worried about you."

"Yes, Angela. She's fabulous. I couldn't get by without her. Three kids, her husband's a bit of a dork."

"Yup, snappy dresser. So is that your clothes there in the bag?"

"Yes. Well, I suppose I need to get home anyway, sort things out."

"Not much to sort out really. Just go home and rest in bed for a few days."

"What bed?" he said. "Did Angela not say anything about the house?"

He explained how his house had been ransacked while he'd been in hospital and all his furniture was gone. He didn't go into the bizarre detail of who was responsible.

"Oh my God," she said. "What will you do? You'll be gettin' the police round again."

He hadn't thought about the police because he knew it was Brenda's bastard father that was behind it: suspect number one. However, there wasn't necessarily any way he could know that for a fact, not at this stage, necessarily. What with being in hospital.

"Yes," he said, seeing the potential for some pay-back. "You're right, I think I might need to phone the police."

"You're not exactly mister lucky are you?" she said, leaning her hip up on the bed. She laid her hand on Nisbet's and gave it a squeeze. "Well, we'll need to get you fixed up ready to go home tomorrow. We'll get an ambulance to take you."

"No, it's ok, I'll get a taxi."

"And pay for it with … ?"

"Oh bugger!" He'd forgotten that his wallet had gone missing.

"I could lend you a few quid, so I could."

He looked at her. "Seriously?" She nodded a tiny affirmative. "Oh, I couldn't, said Nisbet. "It's very kind of you, but I couldn't. I'll get Angela to fetch me in some cash in the meantime."

"Sure it's no bother, just a couple of quid for a taxi an' all. Ye can pay me back."

She leant on the bed again. "It's no bother. A couple of quid for a taxi and stuff."

"A bit above and beyond the call of duty for the average nurse," he said. "Honestly, I can get Angela to get some cash from the bank, she's got access to my accounts, and she's ordered a new debit card for me."

"Sure, then she'd have to come back in here in the morning. I'll get you some cash from the machine down at the hospital shop. It's no bother."

There was a long pause. It wasn't an awkward pause, the nurse just stood there with her hand absentmindedly on Nisbet's, her hip leaning on the bed. Then she spotted it and whipped it away, suddenly aware that leaning on the patient's bed, holding his hand certainly was not normal nursing best practice. She stepped back from the bed, and had a quick look round to see if anybody had spotted it.

He looked up at her again, "You're very nice."

She let that hang in the air for a second, then smiled, "It's in me job description so it is. Under the heading, *Be noice to the patients.*"

"Can I see you again? You know, after I'm out."

She looked at him again, softly, her blue eyes almost through him, looking inside his head through his eyes.

After a few seconds she said, slowly and firmly, unequivocally, "Yes. I'd like that."

For a minute, everything that was bothering Nisbet evaporated. She smoothed down her uniform bashfully, blushing a little.

"Besides," she said, over her shoulder as she headed for the door, "you'll be giving me me money back, so you will."

In the ward office her colleague Róisín was doing paperwork.

"It's a very dedicated nurse you are Staff Nurse Deirdre McMartin," she said with smirk.

"That would be me, dedicated Deirdre."

"You're meant to nurse them, not romance them."

"What?!"

"That chap in room four, you fancy him."

"Oi do not fancy him!"

"He's quite good looking," said Róisín.

"You think so?" said Deirdre.

"So do you, by the look of it."

"No. Just being noice, he's had a tough time."

But she was blushing like a rear fog light now.

"Everybody in here's had a tough time," said Róisín smirking. "It's a ho-spi-tal. It's full of sick people ye know."

"Honestly Róisín, you can be a roight shoite. I'll put that in your review."

Her colleague laughed, "What, that I said you fancy a patient? That'll look better on my review than it will on yours. How I'm good at psychoanalysin' horny nurses. Ye fancy him so you do."

"Oi do *not* fancy him!"

"Yes you do. Sittin' on his bed and all. I bet your knickers is fookin' wet through roight now."

"You're disgusting."

"Yep. Bet you shag 'im."

"Fook off Róisín."

She lifted her coat and headed off to the hospital concourse to get some cash for that patient that she didn't fancy. But a few seconds later she put her head back round the office door.

"Is it that obvious?"

"Yep."

"Jeez."

"Bet you shag him."

"I will not!"

"Well I certainly would. Where are you goin' anyway? You're not off shift for ages yet."

"Back in a minute." She headed for the hospital cash machine.

Ten minutes later she came back into the office, took off her coat, took an envelope from the desk drawer and slipped a hundred pounds in twenties into it.

"What's that for?" asked Róisín.

"None of your business!" she said, a bit too sharply. She folded the envelope and put it in her pocket.

"Ok, don't get your knickers in a twist. Besides ... ."

"Besides what?"

"... they'll be needin' to dry out."

"Honestly Róisín, you're disgusting. Ye've a mind like sewer."

"Yep."

Deirdre went through to Nisbet and as he lowered his magazine, she laid the envelope on his chest, as if it was no big deal. She looked less confident than normal, bashful.

"I got you a hundred."

"A hundred? Pounds?"

"Yep, you'll be needin' a taxi, and to buy stuff, dinner, and things."

"Oh, you shouldn't really. ... But thank you. You're very kind."

He wasn't so concussed that he didn't get the message: it was a retainer. He opened the envelope. In with the money was a piece of paper. He pulled it out, glanced at it and then slipped it back into the envelope.

"That's me home phone number ... so you can pay me back an' all. Plus me mobile number. Plus me email address."

He smiled, "National Insurance number? Even a bloke with a bleeding submarine capsule..."

"Sub-capsular bleed."

"... should be able to find you. Thank you. Can I ... ehm, maybe buy you ... ehm, take you, out? Or something."

"You don't have to do that, just pay me back the money is all. But, yes, that'd be nice."

"Ok, it's a deal. Your boyfriend won't mind?" It was a bit late to ask her whether there was a boyfriend.

"Nope, no boyfriend."

"Girlfriend?" She just cocked her head and looked at him.

"Got you back for that one!" thought Nisbet, but at least it cleared the path for progress.

"Look, Oi'll probably not come on shift by the time you leave tomorrow – so. Oi hope it goes well, wit the house an' all." She was still blushing a bit, looking inward, her accent getting more Donegal.

"Is that you finished your shift?" asked Nisbet.

"Yep. Training."

"What? More nursing training?"

"No. It's me Muay Thai night."

Nisbet was none the wiser. It sounded like something on a Thai restaurant menu. He didn't bother to make the joke.

"Muay Thai. It's like kick boxing, kind-of."

"Wow! Kick boxing? I thought you looked pretty fit." The compliment wasn't missed. "Martial arts? Blimey."

"Well, I'm not that good. Only been doing it a couple of years."

"Self defence?"

"Well, you know … once bitten … "

"*Oh dear,*" thought Nisbet but he didn't pursue it.

She continued, "It's mainly a way to keep in shape really."

"Well, it seems to be working," said Nisbet.

She blushed a bit more. "Plus you get to, you know, get stuff out of your system."

"Well, kicking folk would certainly do that," observed Nisbet. He imagined himself expertly kicking the shite out of his father-in-law. He might take up Mooy Tie, or whatever it was called.

"No. You don't actually kick people. Much. You mainly practice on dummies and stuff."

"I know a few dummies you could practice on," quipped Nisbet. "I'll give you their names."

She smiled. "Oh well, better get on wit looking after sick people,"

"Listen … Deirdre …"

It was the first time he'd called her by her name and it seemed to clang like the bell for the start of round two.

"… thanks again for the loan."

She stood up. "Well, that's the thing. It's a loan. You'll be payin' me back, so you will." This was said with a cheeky smile and a nod.

"I certainly will."

She patted his hand. "Right, I'm off to tend the sick," she said and turned away.

"*Jesus!*" thought Nisbet. "*What a nice thing to do.*" He watched her turn out of the door. "*And what a nice arse. Kick boxing? Bloody hell!"*

Some kind of karate-type thing, he supposed. But it wasn't doing her figure any harm. She looked as fit as butcher's whippet. Not skinny, just slim, and fit, and generally gorgeous.

He lifted his new phone and entered her contact details into his address book. He felt a million times better than he had twenty minutes ago. Better than he had for weeks. Being the victim of a road traffic accident and having your house stripped at least had some wholly unforeseen side benefits.

Back in the office Róisín was leaning on the filing cabinet with a mug of coffee in her hand. "That's a thing you don't see every day."

"What?" asked Deirdre, on her guard already.

"We ... ll." Róisín was grinning from ear to ear. "Oi was pretty sure you wanted to shag him, but obviously he doesn't feel the same. Otherwise, why would ye have to bribe him?"

She laughed like a drain. Pleased with her own joke.

"You're a bad, bad wummin Róisín O'Neal," replied the staff nurse, blushing anew. "And a nosey bitch."

"But Oi'm right, am I not?"

"Well ..." she decided to give in and stop denying it. "Ye're partly right, the money's just a deposit, to kind-of, secure the goods. He'll be paying me back, so he will."

"How much did ye give him?"

"A couple of quid."

"It was a fookin' sight more dan a coople of quid!"

Deirdre hesitated, then confessed, "A hundred."

"Fook sake Deirdre. A hundred? Ye'll fookin' kill him makin' him pay dat back."

"Eh? How?"

"Well he's not fit for it yet in his present condition."

"How's that?" said Deirdre.

"Well yooz Donegal girls is only a pound a go, he'll hurt himself working off a hundred, so he will."

"Fook off."

--------oOo--------

Bryce

Billy Bryce opened the package. He already knew what it was. He didn't need to count it but he did anyway. He liked counting money, sorting it into denominations as he went, his fat, greasy, tattooed Cumberland sausages delicately laying the money out on his desk. It was all Bank of England money, all used, but relatively new notes.

Satisfied with the loot, he picked up the burner phone that was paired with the one he'd given Hermens and dialed the only number in its memory.

"Hello, Eric? Aye it is. Yer package has arrived safely. ... No, no, we're making some progress. Wee Shady is on the case. But these things take time. ... Yes, ye'll be the first tae ken, ken. ... Naw, there's nae need tae call. If Wee Shady husnae called ye for a day or twa, it's simply because there's naethin' tae report. The fewer calls ye make, the mair secure we'll be."

At the other end, Hermens put the phone down and wrung his hands. He felt helpless. It was the worst possible state to be in: to be a victim and now to have set something in motion over which he had no real control.

He thought about whether he'd made a mistake, starting something that could easily end in somebody being killed. He mulled it over, then discarded the notion. Eric Hermens was not a very nice person and he really didn't mind if Bryce and McShaed killed twenty people - he just wanted pay-back.

--------oOo--------

The Car

A vehicle recovery truck, on behalf of Lothian and Borders Police, made its way up Jim Nichol's farm drive. The flat-bed was lowered to meet the rear of Nisbet Sangster's BMW. Hawsers were attached to the transmission. One of the breakdown crew got into the unlocked car, let off the handbrake, knocked it into neutral and the car was unceremoniously hauled up onto the back of the truck. Forty minutes later the car was dropped off at the police car compound and parked up with several other cars, most impounded for parking offences. The

BMW was signed for and the crew left for another job.

In the office, no information had percolated through from headquarters yet that a car with that number had been reported stolen. All they knew was that the car was associated with a hit and run in Currie, so it would be impounded until that case was closed. Lothian and Borders police admin would have to be in touch with the owner - obviously a potential suspect in the hit and run. A police car would eventually be dispatched to visit the address where the car was registered. The mill stones of criminal investigation ground very slowly indeed, especially with police time taken up with more serious matters: tracking down the perpetrators of "non-crime hate speech".

--------oOo--------

Lockerbie

Tom Lockerby, MD of Castlerock Systems sat back as his desk, admiring his new Investors in People accreditation certificate: the more the merrier when it came to awards and plaudits on his way up the ladder of recognition. As for investing in people? He couldn't really give much of a toss. Aside from a few key members of staff, his employees were just units, particularly the sales staff. He'd already barked at them in the showroom this morning, getting into his usual mindless, Basil Fawlty rant about individual sales performance, lack of loyalty, endeavour, bellowing into fearful faces.

He was reasonably heavily built and could be physically intimidating, and would have been more so if he'd been fit. He wasn't. But as a boss, he was still intimidating when in a rage, which he frequently was, ranting away about how badly let down he was by his salesforce, and his admin, and his service crew, and almost everybody but a few brown-noses

Barely a week went by when Tom Lockerbie hadn't made one of the girls in the office cry. Barely a fortnight went by when he hadn't made one of the men cry. Barely a month went by when he didn't sack somebody in a fit of pique.

Lockerbie could be, in fact he was, a complete bastard, and only a few missed junctions in the switchback road of life had kept him from a career path similar to Alec Bryson's. Neither was he above criminal behaviour, he just kept his nose clean. At least Bryson had one or two of the common traits of decency, like loyalty and respect for his peers. Lockerbie didn't have any peers, not as far as he was concerned.

He sat and wrung his hands, picked his fingernails and simmered internally, thumbing through the index cards in his head of all of the things in life that disappointed him, angered him, frustrated him or simply got on his tits a wee bit. A well-thumbed mental index card popped into view: the Nisbet Sangster index card. That made his temper effervesce enough to pop his cork.

With nothing better to occupy his psychopathically furtive mind, it scrutinised the business of his daughter's broken marriage and the house, for which he'd forked out a substantial lump sum.

She, according to his thinking, would no longer need the house if she was, in all likelihood, moving permanently back home. So the house might as well be sold. He'd screw his noxious, soon-to-be ex-son-in-law, get his money back for the house - kill two birds with one stone. In fact it was three birds, he'd already killed one by stripping the house of its furniture. That made him smirk. He would have laughed, but he didn't have the right chromosomes for mirth. In fact, it might have been years since he'd laughed at anything other than misfortune: somebody else's.

Nevertheless, he wished he could be a fly on the wall when his son-in-law found out that the house had been stripped - and his shitty clothes dumped out in the rain. Come to think of it, he could screw him even more with some brutal and uncompromising legal shit to run up Sangster's divorce proceedings legal bill – leave the bastard destitute if he could.

He lifted the phone and called his lawyer, Berwick, his perpetual dirty deeds, legal hatchet man. No sense in hanging around.

Berwick updated him on the serving of divorce papers and Lockerbie updated Berwick to the effect that his prick of a son-in-law had deserted the family home, neglecting to mention that his son-in-law had only vacated the premises because he was in hospital, or that Lockerbie had, to all intents and purposes, stolen all the contents.

This would not have bothered Berwick, indeed it would have spurred him on after the disrespectful way he felt he'd been treated by Sangster in his office. So, Berwick was happy to be assured by his client's father, that his client's husband had deserted the family home and had subsequently agreed to sell, more or less, kind-of.

"How fast can we move, get him to sign yon papers you sent him and then get the hoose sold?"

"Well," said Berwick, "assuming he wants a quick settlement, there's no reason to think that it would take more than a few days, assuming we can get court time. The divorce is a little tricky but if he agrees to hand his share of the equity of the house over to your daughter and any borrowing is settled, then we can put it on the market straight away."

"Aye. Make sure that wee Brenda gets everything: custody of the bairn, alimony, everything. Leave him wi' nowt."

"Does he have money?" asked Berwick.

"No."

"Then if he contests anything, we'll take his trousers down."

"Well, in that case we might as well get the house valued and ready tae put on the market immediately the divorce is finalised."

Lockerbie thought for a moment. If his son-in-law merely acquiesced to everything that was demanded by Berwick, he wouldn't get the opportunity to skin the bastard alive in court. Still, can't have everything. On balance, he'd rather sell the house and bank the cash.

"I'll put you through to our property department," said Berwick.

After a ten-minute, humourless and demanding chat with the property department, they promised that as soon as one of their property valuation people was available tomorrow, they'd send someone round to have a look at the place.

--------o0o--------

Visitors

Just when Nisbet was about to nod off in the early evening, a tall dark figure appeared at the bedside. He nearly shat himself. It took him a minute to regain his composure, but blinking against the lights he saw that it wasn't the Ghost of Christmas Yet To Come, it was the huge silhouette of Wee Hammy. Behind him were Tam Gibb and Beastie Saunders from the rugby club. They had a box of chocolates for him. It had already been opened. But Nisbet was really, really pleased to see them.

"Aw, gee whizz guys, thanks for coming in to see me. How did you find out I was in here?"

"I phoned your office looking for you," said Wee Hammy. "Your secretary told me."

"So tell us what happened," said Tam Gibb.

"Nothin' at all," said Beastie, a tight-, occasional loose-head prop. Either side of his head was decorated with cauliflower ears like pink Yorkshire puddings.

"He's a winger," continued Beastie. "Cannae take a tackle."

"Aye, ye're right there," said Nisbet. "Ah saw this tight-head motor car coming, so I thought, well, it's him or me …"

"And it was you," said Tam, and they all laughed.

"Aye," said Hammy, "no sooner back at the rugby club than he's off the park wi' a wee bruise."

"Anyway," said Tam, "He's no a winger, he's whinger."

"Wrong!" said Beastie, opening the chocolates and helping himself to four. "If I recall, he's actually an offside-centre."

"Aye, right enough. A penalty machine," said Wee Hammy.

"You can talk," said Nisbet.

"Aye, but at least with me, it's deliberate."

Nisbet just smiled. He'd almost forgotten how good it was to have the piss ripped out of him by his pals.

They chatted away for a while and Nisbet was reminded what real mates were all about. He hadn't seen much of them for what felt like half a millennium, pretty-much since he got married and they were still there for him. Mind you, his mates had been there for him a few nights ago when they'd got him hammered beyond comprehension.

"Did you tell the lads about the divorce?" asked Nisbet of Wee Hammy.

"No. Client confidentiality. Didn't say a word," he lied.

Nisbet updated them about the divorce and although it was an emotional struggle, he told them about how the house had been emptied by Brenda's father.

"Jesus!" said Beastie. "Wid ye like us tae go round and kick 'is melt in?"

"Noooo!" chorused the other three.

Beastie Saunders was a nice lad from the wildest family in a socially dysfunctional part of the same town as Nisbet. It was a background that had brought him up as hard as nails. Both of his brothers were occasionally not in jail. He was well capable of simply going round to Nisbet's father-in-law's place and giving him a hammering. It was rugby that had got him on the straight and narrow: he could do his violence on the park.

"Ah don't think so Beastie," said Hammy. "Poor Nizzy here needs to keep on the straight and narrow if he's not going to come out of this divorce with only his pants on fire."

"Ah had that once ," exclaimed Beastie proudly.

"Eh?" said everybody.

"Pants on fire. Ah set mah Y-fronts on fire. Did Ah never tell ye aboot this? Ah won this fart lighting contest when Ah was in Polmont young offenders'. Anyway, on mah victory lap Ah went for a world record. I lit a beauty and got blow back. Ah'll never wear nylon Y-fronts again. They caught fire, melted with the flames and stuck tae mah arse. The hairs on my arse were burnt clean aff, except them that were tangled up wi melted pants."

This caused Nisbet to laugh himself into spasms.

"But looking on the bright side Beastie," said Tam, "If you'd got a proper back draft up yer bum, with all the remaining farts still up there, your arse would have been blown clean off."

Nisbet went into paroxysms of pain.

"Aye," said Hammy. "An explosion in Beastie's colon. A turd blown out both his ears."

More pain for Nisbet.

"Ah think it was the skid marks tae blame," said Beastie. "They must be flammable because that was the epicentre of the inferno and there wisnae a trace efter the fire went oot."

Raucous rugby club laughter.

A nurse came in and told them loudly and sternly to make less noise or get out. They calmed down.

"Anyway," said Wee Hammy, wiping the tears from his face, "we'll need to hope Niz heals up in time for next season or he'll be sitting on the bench with the other hypochondriac wingers."

"Did you say, wankers?" said Tam.

"Aye, not half. I'm gagging to get back on the park," said Nisbet. "If the coach will have me." He changed the subject. "Did you get a chance to speak to your colleague, Hammy?"

"Wingers are all pansies," interrupted Tam Gibb.

"He'll no come back as a winger," said Beastie. "He'll be too slow. He can play his favourite position."

"What's that?" asked Tam.

"Water boy."

Nisbet persisted on the divorce topic, "Did you get a chance to speak to your colleague Hammy?"

"Indeed I did," replied Hammy, looking pleased with himself. "She's looked your stuff over and she says that the divorce will be an absolute cinch and she'll see you when you get out of prison."

Tam and Beastie sniggered.

"No really, did she say anything about it, after she read those papers?" asked Nisbet.

"Nope, just give her a call. She'll see you as soon as she can. She knows you're in hospital. She's a smart cookie, you'll be in good hands."

"I hope so," said Nisbet, starting to worry again, his recent default frame of mind.

"When are you getting out?" asked Gibby. "

"With luck, maybe tomorrow, lunchtime-ish. If I pass the fitness test, and once I've got myself sorted out with a bed to sleep in. Can you believe it, I don't even have a bed? I've got nowhere to sleep."

"Ah ken where ye can doss," said Beastie. "Mind that time on the school trip, when we all got pished and fell asleep in Princes Street

Gairdens? Ye could bide there, summer's comin', ye'll be fine."

"Good idea. If it's no windy he can cover himself with his Big Issues to keep warm," added Tam.

Nisbet's pals were a load of bastards.

"Were those your mates?" asked the Staff Nurse, after Nurse O'Neal had ejected them. "They seem like a nice bunch."

"They're animals," said Nisbet. "Complete animals."

"Yep, cauliflower ears everywhere."

"Tight five," said Nisbet, by way of explanation. "Front and second row," But he didn't expect she'd know what that meant.

"Me dad played rugby," she said.

"Oh yeh? Where'd he play?

"Stand-off, mainly." Then she worked it out. "He played for Connacht for a good bit."

"Connacht! Blimey! He must have been pretty good."

"Oi tink so." She got a bit more Irish reminiscing about home. "He was still playing when Oi was a wee girl but he had to give it up. He got blind-sided in the liver."

"Blimey! That must have been some tackle!" said Nisbet. "I got blind-sided by a car and I only got a bleeding submarine capsule.

"Sub-capsular bleed," she corrected. "Anyway, Oi tink it was a dirtier game in those days."

"Oh, I don't know," said Nisbet. "Guys like Wee Hammy and Beastie still take a pride in causing life-changing injuries."

"Exactly. Me mam made him give it up after that, but I think he'd kind-of had enough of spending his life healing up by then. He's still rugby mad though. He comes over here wit his Ballyshannon pals for the Six Nations. He always gets me a ticket for Murrayfield."

"You like watching Scotland getting stuffed by Ireland then?"

"Of course. Anyway, must get on with me job," she said, and trotted lightly off with Nisbet watching the whole picture rather than just her backside.

"*Bloody Hell!*" he thought. "*Grew up in a rugby family!.*"

She got more attractive by the minute: a woman you didn't have to explain the concept of offside to - repeatedly.

Back in the ward office, Nurse Róisín O'Neal said, "That Mister Sangster can have no complaints whatsoever about the levels of medical and financial assistance he is receiving from the NHS. Are ye tinkin' of gettin' in beside him and shaggin' him back to health?"

"Fook off Róisín! Just leave it!"

"Sorry."

--------oOo--------

Ash's flat

Angela appeared again shortly after Nisbet's pals had left. She was dragging the wheelie overnight bag. She'd taken a selection of Nisbet's clothes that hadn't suffered too badly from being out in the rain, and dried and ironed them. The rest would be washed or sent to the dry cleaners. She opened it and let him see. Everything had been ironed and was neatly folded. She lifted out a pair of jeans. They had been pressed like the trousers of a business suit, with creases in them. He'd never seen jeans ironed like that, but then, her Colin didn't wear jeans, he had no casual clothes whatsoever, just ghastly anoraks and slacks, or the grubby suit that he wore to work. It was a complete mystery to Nisbet why even senior civil servants always dress like skint Russians.

"Thanks Angela," he said. "Dunno where I'm going to stay when I get out. I'll give Ashad a phone and see if he's got anything. Otherwise I'll need to rent somewhere, or get a B&B somewhere. I can't exactly move in with my dad, I'd have to sleep on the couch."

"Actually, I phoned Ashad already," said Angela. "Just in case. He said he can probably fix you up with something. Just give him a buzz."

With his new iPhone, Nisbet rang Ashad at the letting agency to see if he had a place where he could crash until his flat was available.

"Hello Nisbet," said Ash. "Angela tell me about your accident. Very bad thing, very sorry. Very sorry about Brenda." Ash had a very calming, sing-song Lahore accent.

"Yes, thank you Ash, it's all a bit of a nightmare."

"Yes, total nightmare Nisbet. Let me see what I can do. I phone you back. Bye bye!"

"*What a nice man,*" thought Nisbet.

Sitting up in bed now, he contemplated getting out of hospital. Actually, he didn't much want to. Except for having good friends, everything in his life outside the hospital was total pants. He had nowhere to stay yet, and not only did he feel nice and cocooned in hospital, he was rather enjoying the occasional contact with the lovely Staff Nurse McMartin. He felt he'd very much enjoy regular, even closer contact with her.

According to Angela, the house had been emptied even down to the removal of stuff that was unequivocally his - such as the Bose stereo and his Fender Stratocaster. He didn't expect ever to see the Strat again. Now he regretted hardly ever playing it.

However, it seemed that they hadn't touched the garage for some reason, so his tools and his fitness gear would still be there. Not much hope of sleeping comfortably on that lot. Trying to stretch out and sleep on his bench-press gear wouldn't be all that comfy. Plus there would be all the other crap like barbecues and Samantha's old pram which Brenda had kept in the hope that she might give birth to another squawking, spoilt, extortion racketeer. Thank God she hadn't.

There was some good news from Ashad though. While Nisbet had been languishing in hospital, worrying, fascinated by Deirdre McMartin's neat little body, and groaning about his own, it transpired that the tenant in his old flat had called to say that he'd got a job in Newcastle and would like to quit as soon as possible. Ashad had been round to the flat to check it over. It was manky and full to the brim with old newspapers and magazines - two years-worth. Apparently his tenant never threw anything out or cleaned the kitchen or the bathroom. Ashad would get the cleaners in and repaint the things that needed it. In a panic, Nisbet asked how much that would cost.

"No, no, no Nisbet," said Ashad. "No cost. Tenant is a complete idiot. Dirty man. Dirty, dirty man! He lose his deposit, eight hundred pounds. Plenty left for new mattress and sheets, no problem."

Ashad had access to wholesale everything.

"Eight hundred quid?" thought Nisbet. He never even knew that there had been a deposit.

Well, at least he now had a place to stay - eventually, or would have when Ashad's team had sorted it out and made it habitable. But that would be another eight hundred quid a month in rent not coming in to pay the mortgage on the flat. He resolved to stop paying the mortgage on the house - a two-edged sword. He had a nice new contract with the council with staged payments so there would be steady money coming in, and if Lockerbie didn't pick up the mortgage on his daughter's and Nisbet's house, it would get repo-ed. Fuck 'em.

At least, that's how it might work, he hoped. And with the mortgage payments stopped, even though there was no rent coming in from that, he'd be able to afford the mortgage on the flat, which was way less than half what he was paying on the house. He'd lose any equity that the house had earned on Edinburgh's ballooning house prices, but never mind, he'd be better off financially. Except for alimony. And child support. And legal fees. And community charge ... Bloody hell!

He looked at the small suitcase of newly cleaned clothes that Angela had brought. She'd washed and ironed everything that she could. Now he just needed somewhere to doss after he got out until he could get into his flat. But a few minutes later, his new mobile phone rang, it was Mahmoud.

"Is that you big man?" he said, keeping up his authentic Glaswegian. "Aye, mah da's got ye a place tae bide for a couple of weeks. A wee one-bedroom place in Leith."

"Really? Fantastic Mahmoud, how much is the rent?"

"We ... ell, it's actually one of my dad's flats." The "authentic" Weegie accent got dropped to be replaced by his real Bearsden accent.

"He's not long had it. It's an Airbnb flat. But it really needs a wall knocked through to make it a kitchen-living room. Nice wee flat. We can talk about it."

This was code: Nisbet would draw up the modifications for Planning Department and stick in the application. It would only take him an hour or so to measure the place up whilst he was ensconced in it, and a couple of hours to do the planning paperwork in the evening. Then all he had to do was expedite it with his trusted contacts in the building trade.

"It's a deal, it's just until my own flat frees up."

"Well your tenant just walked out already. But my dad says the place is absolutely mingin'. It needs a good clean. Dad's dealing with it as we speak. Just come down to the shop when you get a minute and I'll give you the keys for the Leith flat."

"Thanks Mahmoud, and tell your dad thanks."

"Tell 'im yersel' when ye see him Niz. How's yer body by the way? How are ye daein'?" The Weegie dialect was back now that the business negotiations were over. "Ye've no hud nae luck big man! Stolen motor, ran ower, divorce, hoose ransacked, a' in wan week. Must be a record."

"Aye, a record. Oh well, never mind that Mahmoud, at least I've got good friends. Thanks for all the help."

"Nae bother big man, just keep me posted when ye're gettin' oot."

"Will do Mahmoud, I'll get Angela to sort some sheets and towels and stuff."

"Dinnae bother, the flat's been made ready fur Airbnb, fully self-catering: except for wee packs of sugar, coffee, milk. The bed will be made up. Ye dinnae need nowt. When ye come by for the keys, wid ye like tae stay fur yer denner?"

"Aw man, that would be fantastic!"

And it would be. Mrs Khan was a fabulous cook.

"Just gie me a buzz and Ah'll tell ma mah tae make extra. Ye can turn up aboot whit, hauf six, efter prayers."

"Fantastic!" said Nisbet, at least some things were falling into place.

"Or ye could come fur prayers, ya Proddy eejit. Huv ye read yer Koran?"

"No. It got stolen the other day, along with the rest of the contents of my laptop bag: my kebabs and cheese rolls. And a proposal for a job. It was lucky it didn't have my laptop in it."

Silence for a moment. Nisbet could tell that Mahmoud was weighing up the conundrum of whether or not a stolen Koran was a suitable subject for mickey taking. Plainly, he'd concluded that it wasn't. He'd have been relieved to know that the Koran had been rescued by a Malaysian tourist. Nisbet, however, would have been a little put out to know the tourist had wiped his arse with his proposal.

Nisbet interrupted Mahmoud's thinking, and filled him in on the Princes Street Gardens weirdo.

"Sounds like he got the best part of the deal, Niz: my mum's kebabs and the Koran. Hope he reads it."

"He might read my proposal instead."

"You're gettin' on my nerves, Niz," said Mahmoud. "See you later."

A moment later, Nisbet's phone rang again. It was Angela, "Your car's been found. The police have got it."

"Wow! Is it ok? Has it been trashed?"

"No. The bonnet's a bit dented, but other than that, it's ok."

"That would be me hitting the bonnet. Or the bonnet hitting me. Can I get it back?"

"No, apparently not, not yet. I would think they'll want to do police stuff to it, fingerprint it and so on. Evidence. It'll be a week. Plus, they won't let it go yet because it's been involved in a hit and run. It's a serious crime."

"It certainly is, especially since it was me that got hitted and runded," said Nisbet.

He went on to describe his lifelong misgivings concerning the IQ of the average police officer.

"The two CID cops that came to the hospital were a bit dim."

"Oh, I think the police know what they're doing," replied Angela.

Angela had a naive belief that those in authority could always be relied upon to do things right.

Nisbet didn't.

--------o0o--------

8

Hospital

Nurse Róisín O'Neal drew the curtains around Nisbet as he sat on the edge of the bed and watched. He was comparing her extravagant rump with his mental picture of Staff Nurse McMartin's neatly package bottom. She turned and he looked away but she gave him a look and laughed. Plainly she couldn't give an arse what he thought of her arse.

"Right. Now Mister Nisbet…"

"It's Sangster."

"…Sangster. It's too quick off the mark are you Mister Nisbet Sangster. Are these some of your clothes?" She gave the suitcase that Angela had brought a gentle tap with her foot.

"No, that's my entire wardrobe for the time being."

"Roight, we need to get you on yer feet and dressed - get ye out of yer racing cars. But first we need to go for walkies to make sure you can manage."

She held out her hand, then hauled him onto his feet. Surprisingly, he didn't feel too bad. He must have done some healing up overnight. He could stand quite steadily. She pulled his left arm around her shoulder and put her arm about his waist.

"Come on then big fella," she said. She stepped forward and Nisbet went too. They got to the ward door with Nisbet stifling groans with every step of his dead right leg, and she turned and took him down the passage. It was pretty painful but he could do it and the more he moved his leg the easier it got, as he knew it would, having had to play through plenty of lingering injuries in his day.

She let him take himself back to his bed as she watched from behind.

"Now, can ye get yourself dressed or will ye be needin' a hand?"

There seemed to be a note of optimism in her voice. He declined the offer and she disappeared. Five minutes later she came back to find him sitting on the chair next to his bed with his jeans half on, and a shirt mostly on. He was staring at his bare feet with his socks in his hand. He'd had plenty of bother with his underpants.

She took the socks from him, turned them half inside out, shoved them on his feet and pulled them up his ankles with slick expertise.

"Done that a million times for me little brothers and sisters."

She pulled his shirt on over his stiff right arm, then she reached for his trainers and in a minute she had hauled him back onto his feet.

"Roight, better get your jeans up round your backside. Ye can't go home wit them round your knees."

She bent down, grabbed the waistband of his jeans and gave his underpants a good look as she heaved his jeans up, swatting his hands out of the way to do up his zip and buckle his belt for him.

He stood there like a three-year-old as she finished dressing him, apparently not seeming to mind a bit. Nisbet could imagine her in later life, half-again as plump, getting five squawking kids ready for school.

"Ok, another couple of victory laps of the stadium and we'll let ye go," said the nurse.

As he hobbled around, he got a bit looser. It began to feel like he could move quite adequately under his own steam, so he kept it up, wandering around. A little while later, he was taken aside and the bandage on his head was removed, his stitches checked, and a smaller dressing replaced it. He hadn't really realised it, but looking in the mirror afterwards, he saw that his head had been shaved. He looked like a prison inmate: one that had been hit by a car.

Lunch came and Nisbet gave it a miss. He had an eye on a Big Mac, or fish and chips, or anything else unhealthy. After days of wholesome but nevertheless tedious and spectacularly bland hospital food, he needed a health-giving E-number and saturated-fat infusion.

"This is Codeine Mister Sangster," said Nurse Róisín O'Neal. "You take no more than two every four hours. Mind you, if you do that, you'll be constipated, so you'd be better not taking them at all if you don't feel you need them. If you know what I mean. If you do take them, eat plenty of high-fibre food: wholemeal bread, AllBran, fresh vegetables, bits of old carpet, stuff like that."

Recalling the bathroom experience of a few days ago, Nisbet thought he preferred the idea of constipation to another dose of Gandhi's revenge. At least is would mitigate the danger of Cornish pasty-sized skid marks.

"And if ye do take them, don't drive," continued Róisín. "They'll make you light-headed and it's a driving ban if you're caught with opiates inside you."

Again, the chastening memory of having driven home totally shit-face flitted through his head.

"These are anti-inflammatories. Ye take two every four hours. Make sure ye take them on a full stomach. And if ye're also taking the codeine, that'll be wit yer stomach full of All Bran. These are antibiotics, just to be on the safe side. Tree times a day and make sure ye finish the course.

"Ye've an appointment to see yer GP. Here it is. And this is a letter for your GP: what ye have wrong wit ye, what we've done to ye and what ye've been given. C'mon, I'll walk ye to the elevator."

She hooked his good arm over her shoulder and put hers round his waist, not that he needed the help now that he'd done some walking on his own, but it felt nice to have an arm round him. The nurse pressed the elevator button and they heard it whine into action.

"Thank you," said Nisbet. "Thanks for everything, and tell Staff Nurse McMartin thanks too."

"Oh, Oi tink ye'll be telling' her that your very self, so I do." She poked him in the chest. "I believe you have her number. She'll be wanting her money back."

She looked up at him with a big, tight-lipped, cheeky smile. Nisbet blushed like a brake light.

"Aye, ye can blush away Mister Sangster. I'd give you me own phone number, but I don't fancy you. But Oi tink she definitely does."

There was a pause, and then she poked him in the chest with her finger a couple of times.

"And you be noice to her Mister Sangster, d'ye hear? She's a real diamond, so she is."

A nod was all Nisbet could manage. He couldn't think of a fitting superlative for Staff Nurse McMartin. Diamond didn't come close.

Róisín wasn't done there. She was holding his arm quite firmly.

"She's had some bad luck wit the boyfriends. So you be noice to her Mister Sangster. D'ye hear me?"

Nisbet blushed some more and nodded. That bit about bad luck with boyfriends made his head spin. He looked the nurse in the eye.

"I'll be nice to her," he said. "I can't imagine who wouldn't."

"I'm sure ye will Mister Sangster," she said, squeezing his arm hard. "I'm sure ye will, ye seem like a nice fella."

She let go his arm. The elevator door slid open. The nurse patted his blushing cheek.

"Off ye go then," she said, and turned on her heel.

Nisbet watched her broad beam retreat back towards the ward. "*Blimey*," he thought. But he wanted to give her a big hug anyway.

He pressed the ground floor button and a few stiff, slightly unsteady minutes later, he was out in the fresh air.

He got a taxi to the office, but had the driver stop off at a butcher's shop to get two Scotch pies. The driver went. At the office, he paid the driver with some of Nurse McMartin's money, took a few seconds to ache himself out of the cab and hobbled into the office.

Angela was at her desk, on Facebook. With Nisbet off sick, she didn't have as much to do, other than keep clients at bay.

"Goodness," she said, "I didn't expect to see you. I thought you'd go straight ho…" But she spotted that that might not be the best destination.

"Home? Aye, that would do: lie down on the carpet and heal up. They did leave the carpets didn't they?"

"The stair carpet."

"Fine. I'll sleep on the stairs."

"And a couple of the bedroom carpets," said Angela, sounding as if that might help a bit.

"Superb Angela! I'm sorted!" said Nisbet, crabbily. "I'll just roll myself up in the bedroom carpet. A deep-pile Axminster sleeping bag."

Angela looked at him, her bottom lip quivering. She'd never seen him get angry before. But then, she'd never seen him on the rugby park.

"I'm sorry Angela. I'm not angry with you. It's just all so ... unbelievably ... shite. Anyway, I'm fixed up with somewhere to stay for the time being. Mahmoud's dad's fixed me up with a flat. Now all I need is a car."

"It's ok," said Angela. "Your car insurance entitles you to a hire car. It's all sorted. All you have to do is take your driving license over to the car hire place and pick up your car, it's all booked."

"Blimey Angela, that's fantastic! I'll just need to find my driving license."

Angela lifted an envelope and handed it to Nisbet. It contained his driving license and his new bank debit card.

"Aw Angela, I don't know what I'd do without you."

"Me neither. I'll get Colin to drive us over to the car hire place when he picks me up."

She got up and headed for the kitchen. "I'll put the kettle on. You'll be wanting to wash down your pies with something."

"How did you know I'd got pies?"

"I didn't even need to see inside the bag," replied Angela. "I know what a healthy diet you have."

Nisbet perched on Angela's desk, on the basis that he'd have to groan himself out of anything lower when he had to stand up. The pies and a hot cup of sweet tea were pure manna from heaven.

--------oOo--------

Campbell and McColl

Billy Bryce welcomed the two hoodlums into his office. Campbell and McColl were with Bryce to discuss the distribution of contraband cigarettes. However, Bryce took the opportunity to see if they knew about the Edinburgh operation he'd contracted out to McShaed.

"Aye. Ah've heard aboot these Edinburgh folk," said Ed McColl, looking with the same distaste at Bryce's desk that Hermens had done a couple of days earlier.

The vast, neckless, cetaceous bulk of Bryce was beached behind his huge desk, a desk now littered with the remains of a visit from a heavily laden pizza delivery scooter. He was attended, as usual, by his two royal-blue-clad, morbidly obese goons. McColl wondered if the Rangers shop sold their jerseys by size or by the acre, not that he'd ever set foot in the place.

"Aw aye?" said Bryce.

"Well, Ah ken a wee bit aboot their operation, assuming it's the same bunch," continued McColl. "They're small-time, well for these days, they're small time. They'll eventually get ta'en oot, especially if they expand their reach. Either the coonty lines mobs frae doon south, the Jamaicans, or the London darkies, or even us, in wur roll as, the ehm ... diplomatic East-West envoys for the McElbies. It's a wonder they've no been ta'en oot a'ready. There must be somethin' goin' on tae keep the big boys aff their backs.

"Apparently they sterted oot producin' skunk. Growin' it in atween the tomatoes in polytunnels on a ferm oot in the boonies no far frae Edinburgh. But they're apparently daein' a variety of stuff noo. Nothin' major. Coke, speed, disco drugs, stuff like that. And steroids. This could a' be the stert o' them diversifyin' if they're trying' tae stash large amounts of cash. But if this is a sign they've been makin' a bigger mark in the marketplace, they're playing' oot their league."

"Well they seem tae be daein a'right pleyin' in the Premier Division, as faur as things go, according' tae wur client. How come you ken so much aboot them when naeb'dy else does?" asked Bryce.

"That's whit ye'll pey us fur Billy," said Campbell. "Bein' au fait wi' Scotland's criminal underworld."

"Whit dae ye mean "awfy wi' Scotland's criminal underworld?" enquired the aggressive tone of one of Bryce's fat henchmen who had been seething at the presence of two Catholics in the office.

Eyes were rolled on both sides of Bryce's desk.

"No awfy," replied McColl. "Au fait. It's French, fur kennin' aboot stuff. *Au ... fait.*"

"Aw. Right," replied the goon. "French is it? Aye."

Bryce came back into the conversation. "Well, how come ye're au fait wi' this particular pairt o' the criminal underworld?"

"Networkin'," said Campbell smugly. "And mah cousin's in the polis in Embra forbye."

"Perfect. Is he bent"

"Of course he's bent! He's a polis for Christ's sake!"

"Can he lend a haund?" asked Bryce, his sectarian Weegie brain taking a moment to wonder how a Catholic from Springburn in Glasgow could get into any police force, let alone in Edinburgh. That was diversity recruitment for you.

"Maybes aye, maybes naw. Depends. If he's no contracted oot a'readies."

"Well, see if ye can fund oot. There's money in it fur ye."

"Mah cousin wid want peyed ana'."

Bryce leaned forward, "Ye dinnae pey faimily fur favours. Especially no a polis. Ye can hae a wee deposit on account." He opened a desk drawer and navigated an envelope through the pizza cartons.

"Pey him yersel' oot o' that. There's another twa grand if ye get onythin' that produces results. Dinnae hang aboot, we could dae wi' the info sharpish."

"Ye'll get it when we get it," said Campbell, slipping the envelope into his jacket pocket.

"So, whit is it ye're looking for?" asked McColl.

"Well, that's privileged client information. But suffice it tae say, he's been shafted for a good few bob."

"A few grand?"

"A few hunner grand."

Campbell and McColl looked at one another, shrugged, and left to load contraband and fake cigarettes into their van. Bryce picked up the phone and rang McShaed.

"I think we might have something tae go on," he said. "Where this Edinburgh bunch operate from, or hang oot, or used tae operate from. But it's worth checking. I've got two contacts gettin' some info frae the polis in Embra."

"Ok, thank you, I'll stand by for that. By the way, where are you getting this information?" asked McShaed.

"Twa o' the McElbies' eejits. Campbell and McColl. They're just free-lancing a wee bit, shifting' fags fur us. So I asked them."

"They are not the most wholesome of individuals; to say the least." remarked McShaed. "Is that as far as it went?"

"Of course. They've nae interest in onyhing ither than shifting' fags at the moment."

"Ok. If they do come up with something, I'll get the Beatties to check it out. I've got Malcy checking out the retail outlets for steroids in Edinburgh."

--------oOo--------

The Beatties

"It's like this:" explained McShaed, "Our client was expecting to do a trade for a substantial amount of money in Edinburgh. He's been robbed of both the money and the goods, and wants either the goods, or the money, or both returned. Failing that, some pay-back."

He was, as ever, immaculately dressed: three-piece suit, Oxford shoes, silk shirt, and Glasgow High School tie. His shoes were beesed up like mirrors. The contrast with the Beatties' slightly threadbare look was distinct. For hardened, and allegedly successful criminals, they dressed as if they were short of cash. McShaed's shoes were the result of ten minutes buffing to a gleam every morning. The Beatties' shoes looked like they spent ten minutes every morning rubbing them down with emery paper and dusting them with cement.

"Whit were the goods?" asked Rab Beattie. "Just so we ken whit we're looking' for."

"A small brown paper parcel or package containing the best part of half a million pounds in diamonds. He was supposed to be paid in used notes packed in a briefcase or laptop bag. But all he got was roughly the same weight in concrete roofing tiles. Oh, and a cheese roll and some books."

"Hauf a grip's worth o' diamonds fur a roof tile an' a cheese roll!" said Rab Beattie.

"Aye. Nae wunner he's *cheesed* aff," said Andy Beattie, impressed with his own wit.

"Yes," said McShaed. "An expensive lunch."

"Whae in Edinburgh wants tae move that kindae money aroond?" asked Rab Beattie.

"It'll be drug money, for a certainty," replied McShaed, to which the others nodded. Nothing else delivered profit like drugs.

"Now the strange thing, regarding the half million, is this:" continued McShaed. "Our client says that his client is claiming that they got stiffened for the cash at the same time."

"Doesnae sound very likely."

"Well, it doesn't matter to us, we've been charged with the task, either of getting the diamonds back from them, or the money, or failing that, some payback - of a physical nature.

"Maybe they never had the money in the first place," said Andy Beattie.

"I think that's the most likely scenario," said McShaed, patiently. "If you intend to steal something, you don't need to carry its value around in your wallet. Purchasing it isn't what's on your mind. I think that's how robbery usually works, isn't it?"

"Aye, right enough," replied Andy, pensively. He'd never looked at it like that.

"Well, either way, it's diamonds, money, or payback," said McShaed.

"What kind of payback," asked Andy Beattie.

"Yet to be agreed," said McShaed. "But, if you screw people over for that kind of money in diamonds or anything else, then you may have to pay a price."

"Fair enough," said Rab Beattie. "But oor fee will go up considerably if we've tae take somebody oot the gemme."

"There's money in the budget for that," replied McShaed, sounding like a council finance officer. He passed over an envelope.

"Here's a retainer. Depending on results, we'll see if our client is emotionally invested enough in this to push things to that level."

"Fair enough," said Rab, again. "But Ah cannae see whoever it is handin' ower that kind o' loot wi'oot been', ye ken ... asked nicely."

"Actually," said Andy 'The Bat' Beattie. "Ah've just gave it some thought. Ah think we've heard o' this bunch. We dinnae ken onything aboot them, but we've heard of them. On the grapevine. Is that no right Rab?"

"Aye," replied his twin brother, Rab 'Stanley Knife' Beattie. The twin brothers were known career criminals. Although not particularly big men, they were known to be competent, trustworthy, fearless and capable of extreme violence.

"What are they called? Do they have a name?" enquired McShaed.

"Never heard a name, if they've got yin," said Rab. "Dinnae cross borders, dinnae annoy naeb'dy ower much. They just keep theirsel's tae theirsel's by all accoonts."

"So it would seem. How come I've never come across them?" said Wee Shady, puzzled. He prided himself on being well networked. "It's odd that they've not been shut down."

"Aye. Just a wee privately run operation by all accoonts, like a wee corner shop so tae speak, in Embra. They dinnae bother naeb'dy coz they keep tae Embra an' the east. They dinnae come west o' Harthill services. The Dawsons urnay bothered aboot them much 'coz they're ower in the east. For some reason, they just seem tae ignore them."

"Who else is in Edinburgh?"

"Aw … the Colqhuons, they're the main event, then there's the blacks, just stertin' oot up here. They're gawny end up fucked by the Colqhouns like the McElbies dealt wi' them in Glescae. And there's the Chinese, but they're mainly growers. But ye're right, how come they've no been shut doon and ta'en ower, ower there?"

"Could be in cahoots with the Colqhouns?"

"No very likely, but there must be some kind o' understandin', wi' the big boys - or the polis," mused Rab 'Stanley Knife' Beattie.

He was frequently known simply as 'Stanley' because of his method of punishing recalcitrant opposition: two Stanley Knife blades stuck together with a thick piece of cardboard box between. The resulting facial wound was impossible to sew together without removing the neatly sliced, thin strip of flesh. It left a facial scar so ugly that it identified anybody who had crossed the brothers. Rab's brother Andy 'The Bat' Beattie's sobriquet was fairly obvious: he kept a baseball bat in the boot of the car. The damage could be equally permanent but less obvious at first glance: it depended on the message being delivered. And the emphasis.

Neither brother was a stranger to the "Bar-L", Her Majesty's Prison, Barlinnie, but only for small-time offences in their formative years. Nowadays, nobody would ever bear witness against the Beattie twins.

"So onywey, yer client wants 'is stuff back. Or the money. Or some payback," concluded Rab Beattie.

"Correct. That's what we've been contracted to do," explained McShaed. "And what you're telling me lines up with what little I have from Billy Bryce. The Edinburgh operation seems to have no actual premises or address. It seems to be run out of the backs of cars, or something like that. Bryce is working on getting more info.

"Meanwhile," said Malcy, "the only car that remotely matches the details of a red Beamer wi' a number going, somethin', somethin', somethin' B.E.T, seems tae be a red BMW Alpina, N15 BET, registered to a Nisbet Sangster of Balerno."

"Nisbet?" said Andy 'The Bat' Beattie. "That's a shite first name. Emba folk ur a' wankers."

"It's a right wanker's number plate ana'," said his brother, Rab.

"Indeed it is Rab," said McShaed. "At all events, since we now have the address that the car's registered to, it's worth taking a look."

"Aye, we should dae a drive by. Case the joint," said Andy Beattie. "But it's likely the motor was stolen. It wid be a bit mental tae use yer ain motor if ye were gawny shaft somebody."

"Aye, but if they're frae Embra, they'll no be a' that bright," said Malcy, to affirmative nodding from all but McShaed, who did not suffer from any of the mandatory multiple prejudices nursed by the average Glaswegian fuckwit.

"Well, you two check it out anyway," said McShaed. "Meanwhile, we'll try to find out where this cannabis farm is. Billy Bryce is hopefully getting some input from a couple of other contacts."

"Whae?" demanded Andy Beattie. He didn't like the sound of

somebody muscling in on their contract.

"It doesn't matter who they are," replied McShaed. "Billy Bryce is just trying to find out where these Edinburgh people operate from."

"It does bloody matter. Dae ye ken them?"

"Yes I do. But you won't know them, I wouldn't think," said McShaed. "Probably don't mix in your social circles."

"Well, it wid help tae ken whae they are. Just tae be on the safe side.

"Safe from what? It's just two of Bryce's contacts, a fellow named McColl, the other's name is Campbell," replied McShaed.

"Jesus Bloody Christ!" said Andy Beattie. "Ye're jokin! McColl and Campbell are a pair o' total bastards. They dae work for the McElbies. Professional enforcers. It was them that dealt wi' yon Jamaican that washed up on Barassie beach."

"Aye. And they're bloody Cafflicks ana'," said Rab Beattie. "Are you seriously tellin' me that a Hun like Billy Bryce has got Tims that are in cahoots wi' the McElbies working' for him?"

The Beatties were from Protestant stock, and consequently, head-banging Rangers supporters. They did not, would not, could not do work for the McElbies.

"Billy Bryce is a caird cairryin' effin' Orangeman and an independent trader. How can he be workin' wi a pair o' Tims?"

"Because he's a professional criminal," replied McShaed. "And this is business. When push comes to shove, your ingrained social prejudices take second place. In fact, they don't take place at all."

McShaed paused for a response. Nothing.

"Have the two of you got that?" he said, impatiently.

"Well, Aye. But Ah dinnae agree wi' it," said Rab Beattie. "Billy Bryce has just went doon in mah estimation. How can he work wi' a pair o' highly dangerous, treacherous, cheating, two-timin', two-faced, effin' ... effin" ..."

"Tims," said his brother, with an air of disgust and dismay.

"For pity's sake! You won't come into contact with them," said McShaed. "Bryce simply was in contact with them on another subject and happened to ask them if they knew of this Edinburgh operation.

And it turns out that they do happen to know, or know of a few people in Edinburgh who might be able to help."

"Whit if they try tae muscle in?"

"They won't, but if they did, I'm sure you'd all get along famously, you have so much in common with them: sectarianism, violence, thuggery, armed robbery ... murder."

"Ah think ye'll find," said Andy Beattie, interrupting, "that we've no done in ony darkies."

"Well that's comforting," said McShaed. "At least, even if you're head-banging sectarianists, you're not racists. All I'm saying is, you have a lot in common with them."

"Apairt frae fitba," replied Rab.

"Or religion," said Andy. "Whit else is there?"

"Ignorance and stupidity," said McShaed. "Look, for pity's sake, neither of you goes to church. Or to football matches."

"Whit's that goat tae dae wi' it? It's, it's the, the principal," said the genetically sectarian Rab Beattie, confirming that the harbouring of multiple cultural prejudices in Glasgow required no logic or intelligence, only indoctrination and enthusiasm. Anthropologists were completely bemused by Glaswegian sectarianism, to the extent that they almost considered it an endearing cultural art form, like folk music or country dancing.

"Look," continued McShaed, "you won't come into contact with them. They might be able to get us some information. That is all. They have contacts that we don't have. If they can help, they will - and they'll get paid. The idea is to cover the ground more effectively. Once we get any information they might have, they're out of it. They won't even know what we're looking for."

"Aye, well, if they keep oot the road."

"They will," said McShaed. "Can we drop the subject please?"

"Fair enough. By the way, whit dae ye think are the chances o' us gettin' this boy's goods back for him?" asked Andy the Bat.

"Slim. But probably a lot better than getting the equivalent in money. And we need to be careful we don't start a range war with the whole of Edinburgh," said McShaed. "We don't really know anything about these people or who they're connected with. Now, get moving, there's plenty of daylight left to check out that Edinburgh address."

He opened his office door, and ushered the two Beatties out. He'd wait for information coming from McColl and Campbell. They were slightly, but only slightly, more cerebral than the Beatties. Slightly more cerebral, but equally violent.

"*Honestly,*" he thought to himself, "*If the cops weren't twice as thick as the average Glasgow wise guy, we'd all be out of business.*"

On his way to the car, Rab Beattie, with rhetorical sarcasm, asked his brother, "How much is Wee Shady peyin' us fur this joab?"

"Five grand each, for openers. But it's no enough," said Andy. "Findin' oot that Billy Bryce is workin' wi' twa Tims is like, like a…"

"A betrayal. It betrays wur culture, the very fabric o' wur, wur …"

"Proddyness."

"Aye. Exactly," said Rab. He unlocked the blue Ford and got in.

"Onyweys, Ah hope we dinnae run intae they twa Tims. They're a pair o' hard bastards, by the wey. Nasty."

"And big," continued Rab. "Ah widnae trust them tae keep their noses oot. There could be bother. And they twa are *big* bother."

"Bein' a thug these days is no a safe career option," said Andy.

"Aye, that McColl, he's been up on a murder charge."

"So have you!" replied Andy.

"He got aff wi it, the spawny bastard."

"So did you."

"Well, we should go tooled up onywey Andy. Just in case we get bother frae they twa, as well as thur Edinburgh folk."

"Fair enough. But Ah'll take mah bat onywey," said Andy. He liked his bat.

"You should get a catcher's mit and a baseba' oot the sports shop," said his brother.

"How?"

"So if the polis see the bat in the car boot, they'll think ye're awa tae play baseba' insteed o' bashin' somebody tae fuck."

"Aye, Rab. That'll pit them right aff the trail. Whit wi' there being hunners o' baseba' parks in Glesca!" said Andy the Bat. "An' forbye that, they'll no think tae look up mah record for knockin' folk's baws oot the park."

"Just a thought."

"We'll need tae get tooled up onywey. Stop by the storage unit."

The twins headed for a commercial storage unit on the south side.

"By the way," said Andy Beattie. "Wee Shady can get on yer tits sometimes. He talks doon tae ye. He's a nitpickin' wee shite."

"Aye. He tries tae micro-manage everything. He's …"

"Pedantic. Anal."

"Fussy. Shoes are too shiny."

"Aye, fussy. Ah bet he gets oot the shower fur a pish."

At the storage company, they slipped the man at the desk twenty quid to ensure his continued loyalty and silence. And a long, cold smile to ensure his continued anxiety.

They closed the door of their storage unit behind them. From a cardboard box, Andy lifted two Kevlar vests and dropped them into a large hold-all.

"Whit dae ye fancy?" he said, unlocking a metal tool chest. Inside was a selection of hand guns.

"The Desert Eagle fifty caliber."

"The Desert Eagle!? Fucksake Rab!" said his brother. "It's no a big game hunt! The guns is mainly for scarin' the shite oot o' folk! "

"Aye, right enough. But if a hauf-inch muzzle shoved up yer neb disnae scare the shite' oot o' ye, nothin' will."

His brother lifted a short-barreled Sig Sauer. He waved it in his brother's face.

"Mair compact, mair discrete. Easily slipped intae the troosers."

"Mair likely tae blaw yer ain fit aff. They've a reputation fur gawn aff half-cocked."

"Bullshit. Quality German engineering," said Andy, defensively. "Vorchspung durch hingmy."

"See," said Rab, knowledgeably. "It's aboot reliability in combat. The Sig Sauer is a recoil operated semi-automatic. They can easily jam. Whereas, yer Desert Eagle's mechanism is mair like a AK47's: it's gas oaperatit."

"So? Wur Nan's fuckin' cooker is gas oaperatit."

Twenty minutes later, suitably tooled up, they were on the motorway to Edinburgh.

--------oOo--------

Car Higher

Nisbet stood in the car rental office while the gum-chewing lady at the desk, in a less-than apologetic tone explained the situation. He started to feel dizzy with the expectation of more disappointment.

"I'm afraid most of our cars are out today, so I can't give you the level of car your entitled to: a VW Golf or Skoda Octavia."

"Typical," said Nisbet, under his breath. "I'm gonna get offered a whiny wee Korean thing the size of an upholstered roller skate - with a lawnmower engine that wouldn't pull a Sicilian off your sister."

Angela rolled her eyes at Nisbet.

Then to the car hire lady, she said, "Well, what have you got left?"

"I'm afraid all we've got left is a Jaguar SUV." She looked at Nisbet. "It's automatic. Can you drive an automatic?"

Her tone told Nisbet that he didn't look like he could.

"That'll be perfect," intervened Angela, before Nisbet could spoil the cordial atmosphere.

Ten minutes later, uplifted at last by a piece of good fortune, and escorted by Angela and her husband Colin, the dowdy civil servant, Nisbet was climbing gingerly and stiffly into a black Jaguar SUV with tinted rear windows.

"You'll look like a drug dealer driving that," said the professionally socially inept Colin.

"You be quiet," said Angela.

"Right enough Colin. Would you like to buy some cocaine?" asked Nisbet. "Well actually, come to think of it, I *could* sell you some opiates: codeine. I've got a pile in my poke here."

"You can't drive if you're taking those!" said Angela, in full big-sister mode.

"I won't," said Nisbet. But he would.

He looked around the inside of the car. "Bloody nice motor," he said. It still had that new car, leathery smell. Then to Angela and Andy, "Thanks for the lift, and thanks for sorting me out Angela."

He shut the car door, stuck the lever in Drive and schmoozed his way out of the compound

"*It does make you feel like a drug dealer though,*" he said to himself, not that he knew how drug dealers felt. He headed in the direction of Mahmoud's shop to collect the keys to Ash's rental flat.

With the keys, and now some time on his hands, and enjoying the feel of motoring superiority that the Jaguar SUV gave him, he thought he might as well take a spin past the house in Balerno to see the damage, then get moved into Ash's Airbnb flat.

It took him forty minutes to cross Edinburgh and make it to Balerno before rush hour jammed the streets of Edinburgh solid. He made the familiar turn into the housing estate with an apprehensive sinking feeling in his stomach.

--------o0o--------

McShaed

Two hours after the Beattie brothers had driven out of McShaed's yard, his phone rang. It was Billy Bryce.

"We've got something to go on - where they used tae operate frae, or hing oot, but it's worth checking. It's a ferm, or a fermhoose oot in the countryside, somewhere in Fife," said Bryce. He read out the address and McShaed jotted it down.

"They *used* to operate from there? Is that all?"

"Aye, but, it's still worth checkin' oot. The contact reckons they shut doon permanently because they got raided by the polis. But the raid was about a week efter they'd been tipped aff. Possibly an insider in Edinburgh polis HQ. The place had been cleaned oot and the cops reckoned they'd got a bum lead on the address."

"And you got this information from Campbell and McColl?" asked McShaed.

"Aye, but it's absolutely kosher."

"Campbell and McColl are two of the McElbies' goons. Are you sure they're kosher?"

"Aye. Like Ah tel't ye, they're just free-lancing a wee bit, shifting' fags fur me. So I asked them."

"Is that as far as it went?"

"Aye! They've nae interest in onything ither than shifting' fags the now. Besides, they'd be crossing' a line that naeb'dy wants tae cross."

"Very well then. I'll get the Beatties to check it out. They're going to check out an address in Edinburgh anyway. Thank you Billy."

He called the Beatties.

--------oOo--------

Highway Patrol

Two uniformed policemen were whiling away the time in a lay-by in Barnton. The radio sparked into life.

"Guys? Are you anywhere near Balerno? Can you go and check out an address there please? It's linked to a hit and run incident two or three days ago. The car's been recovered and it's registered to the following address."

The address and details were noted down and the police car pulled out, heading for the city bypass, delighted to be dealing with some genuine crime. They put the blue light on. Well, they didn't get excuses to drive like mad bastards all that often.

Nisbet rolled the big Jag into the drive and let himself into the house. It was a shock to see it entirely empty, even though he'd known what to expect. He walked around and sure enough, only the stair carpet and the light fittings were left. He didn't bother to look upstairs. In his present bashed-up condition, the thought of a mountaineering expedition like that without taking enough codeine to float up was too intimidating. He didn't really want to see it anyway.

He carried on, doing a mental inventory of what was left downstairs. The white goods were still in the utility room. He had only a vague idea how to use a washing machine anyway, so that was little consolation. He checked the kitchen cupboards. Empty, except for the only family heirloom he'd ever inherit: his gran's bottle of Worcestershire sauce. He wondered if anybody ever emptied one.

He went to the garage. Nothing in there had been touched. Well, that was splendid! At least he could work out on his bench, or sleep on it! And he could fix things with his tools. And have a barbecue. And mow the grass. Fabulous! Everything the modern single man needs.

He headed back to the house to discover two young, uniformed cops at the front door, one of them middle-sized, and the other, pretty big, a good bit taller than Nisbet - almost Wee Hammy's height.

"Are you Mister Nisbet Sangster? Of ..." and he read out Nisbet's address.

"Yes," replied Nisbet, brightly, thinking that Angela must have reported the house being ransacked to the cops and forgotten to tell him.

"And do you own a BMW registration N15 BET?"

"Yes I do. I hear you've found it." replied Nisbet. He supposed that they must be here to investigate that too - kill two birds with one stone.

"And are you the usual driver of that vehicle?"

"Well, yes, of course, it's my car."

"The car has been reported as having been driven recklessly along the ..." he consulted his notebook, "the A70, in ... ehm ..." He looked again at his notebook. "Currie. The vehicle struck and seriously injured a pedestrian. The driver then failed to stop and left the scene at speed."

The policeman was that tall, he barely had to look up from his notes to look Nisbet in the eye.

Nisbet thought to himself, "*He'd have made a good second row forward if he hadn't been thick as two short planks as well as big.*"

Then out loud, he said, "Yes. That was me."

"So it *was you*, and *your* car that was involved?"

"Well, yes. Bit sort-of, weird, you know. But that about sums it up."

"You don't seem all that bothered," said the astonished cop.

"Well, it could have been a lot worse," replied Nisbet. "But on balance, I've come out of it with very little damage." He pointed to the dressing on his head. "I'm actually more bothered about getting the car fixed and back on the road," he said, trying to make light of the whole thing. "It's a nice car."

The cop turned to his partner, "Bloody psychopath. All he's worried about is a wee bash on the head and a wee bash in his motor!"

"Eh?!" said Nisbet.

The taller of the two cops grabbed Nisbet by the wrist.

"Right! You are under suspicion on arrest of … ehm … under arrest on suspicion of …"

He looked at his partner, struggling to find the right charge.

"Ehm … on suspicion of causing grievous bodily harm due to dangerous driving and leaving the scene of an accident."

"What? Arrest?" cried Nisbet in disbelief. "No, you don't understand. It was me. I was the one who got hurt in that accident."

"What? Your car is the vehicle involved in a hit and run and you're only worried about yourself and your bloody car?"

"Well, I got quite badly hurt. And it's a nice car. Bit of a collector's item actually. I mean, nobody wants their car damaged regardless of who gets run over, do they?" said Nisbet, still trying to make light of it and calm things down.

"Shameless, heartless, selfish bastard! Right! You're under arrest!"

"Look," said Nisbet, astonished at the turn things were taking. "You two have got this arse backwards. Like I said, I got quite badly hurt in that accident."

"Oh you poor bastard," said the cop, sarcastically. "Ehm … where was I? Oh aye … You do not have to say anything, but it may harm your defence if you do not mention when questioned …"

The other officer spun the stunned and perplexed Nisbet around and dragging his right arm behind him, clicked a handcuff onto his wrist.

"… something that you may later rely on in Court. Anything you do say may be given in evidence."

"Oh ya bastard! My arm, mind my bloody arm you big ape," cried Nisbet, struggling to get his arm free of the pain. "Let go my fucking arm, you fucking idiot!"

"Resisting arrest is it? Swearing at the police is it? Any more of that pal, and you'll get tazered."

The cop put a leg behind Nisbet's and judo-dropped him down the two front steps onto his right side on the lawn. His head bounced off the un-mown grass and he grunted in pain as stars whizzed around in the firmament of his recently concussed cranial galaxy as his car-wounded right side exploded in pain.

Both cops were on him now, rolling him face down, burying his face in the grass. His other wrist was handcuffed.

He managed to get his face to the side and spat out some grass. "Get off me you fucking idiots … Aaah! You brainless, ignorant pigs!" he screamed, his voice muffled by un-mown grass.

"Call us pigs wid ye?" said the pig. His full weight went onto Nisbet's right leg and he screamed some more. A fist hit the side of his head a couple of times but withdrew from a third when the pugilistic officer of the law looked up to see a dark blue car turn into the street.

"This'll be the Spam belt," said the driver of the dark blue car, turning into the housing estate somewhere in southwest Edinburgh. "Fur coat an' nae knickers territory."

The satnav's posh English voice interrupted with, "You have reached your destination, on the left."

Rab (Stanley Knife) Beattie slowed the car to a stroll.

"Holy shit, a polis car! Keep drivin'," said the passenger.

"Aye, and that's definitely the hoose there," said Rab, "Accordin' tae the satnav."

"Fuck sake," said Andy (The Bat) Beattie, "Look at that! The cops have got tae him first!"

"Well, at least we ken we're oan the right track. They cops urnae messin' aboot. He must be wanted fur some serious shit."

"Aye. Look at that! That does mah heid in. Polis violence. He's punchin' the shite oot o' yon punter. Ah bloody hate polis violence. Let's take they twa cops oot the gem and grab the boy wursels."

"Naw. Ower many witnesses. Besides, they'll likely hae called for back-up. Better report back tae Wee Shady."

Rab eased the car away from the scene while the two cops waited for it to go before recommencing their police violence.

"Aye. Ah need tae get hame onywey. Got a PTA meetin' at the bairn's school the night."

The cops pulled the stunned and handcuffed Nisbet to his feet.

"Get in the car! Get in the police car!" screamed the two cops in unison. The tone was the usual elevated, aggressive and slightly fearful tone used by police when dealing with seriously violent offenders. Or anybody they wanted to, or had just roughed up.

Nisbet could barely stagger, let alone walk. He was back in sea-of-pain country and still seeing stars. The Pole Star whizzed by, followed by Sirius and Alpha Centauri. The inside of his head looked like a starry-night Van Gogh painting.

"*Jesus Christ*," he thought. "*I'll end up brain damaged. A permanent, swirly, night-sky gibbering wreck.*"

Feeling confused, angry and picked-on to the point of paranoia, his lifelong dislike of cops rose to a new peak and he now reached the sort of full-on anger he'd only rarely succumbed to, even for foul play in a loose ruck. He stood, swaying on his feet.

Over his shoulder, he said, "You bastards are gonna regret this. This is false arrest, you idiots. I'm gonna sue your arses off. I was the one who got injured in that accident."

"Aw, poor thing. Were you not wearing your seatbelt?" said the smaller cop.

"Total bloody psychopath!" said the big cop. "Get in the Police car!" he yelled and kneed Nisbet in the kidney.

"Aaah!" exclaimed Nisbet. "You bastard! That was right on my bleeding submarine capsule … thingy."

"Shut it! Mind your language!" said the big cop.

A size twelve foot was planted in the small of Nisbet's back and it gave him a hard shove. He stumbled forward a couple of pained paces, trying to catch himself up before he fell flat on his face. He caught his balance, then swayed back, put a foot behind and caught himself again. Head spinning in full Van Gogh mode, he righted himself, swayed forward a bit too much and staggered across the lawn on his injured and wobbly legs - away from the two cops.

"He's making a run for it!" said the small cop, and tazered Nisbet between the shoulders. He fell forward, hit his head on the police car and went down for the count.

--------oOo--------

Hospital

Just before she clocked off shift and headed home, Staff Nurse Deirdre McMartin checked back into the ward after her monthly management meeting. She had two days off coming to her and wanted to make sure everything was shipshape.

She was greeted with a heavily weighted, "Good evening," from Nurse O'Neal, also about to head off shift.

"Uhu," said her superior, already on her guard. "What's new?"

"Not much. Except, you know that patient you wanted to shag?"

"Stop it Róisín. It's not funny anymore."

"No seriously. That bloke you were bribing to shag you?"

"You are a nasty piece of work Róisín O'Neal. And ye've a mind like a sewer. Anyway, what about him?"

"Well he must fancy you too. Can't keep away from you."

"What on earth are you on about?"

"He's back in. In the same bed."

"What?"

"Concussion. The stitches in his head burst open, and a new bash on the other side of his head. He's not long come up here from A&E."

"Jesus! What happened?"

"His secretary's just left. According to her, the police went round his house to interview him about his accident and beat the shoite out of him. Then they panicked and brought him straight to A&E.

"A police liaison officer has been on the phone as well. They'll be shiting themselves in case they get their arses sued off, I bet."

The staff nurse took her coat off and turned to head for Nisbet's room.

"Don't panic Deirdre. He's just in with concussion. Ye can shag him when he's fully conscious."

"You're not bloody funny Róisín O'Neal, not funny at all."

Nisbet was sitting up in bed, a new dressing on one side of his head, a large lump on the other.

"Hello soldier," said Staff Nurse McMartin on the way to Nisbet's bedside. "What are you doing back here?"

Nisbet raised a hand and blushed. Why was he always blushing? But he was very, very pleased to see her. And he wasn't even having any lascivious thoughts about where she kept her name badge.

"Och, I was missing you," he said. "So I thought I'd drop by, say hello. Besides, I like it in here. It's a lot safer."

She gave him one of those long, soft, cornflower-blue looks that did it to him every time. For once, he didn't feel the need to stare at her name badge location. She made him feel miles better just by showing up. Probably a thing they taught at nursing school.

She lifted the clip board from the bottom of his bed, had a look, and put it back.

"Back in a minute," she said and trotted off.

Nisbet didn't stare at her backside for once. He just looked at the whole delightful thing turning into the passage.

Five minutes later, she came back.

"Has Doctor Rutherford had a word with you?"

"No."

The Staff Nurse breathed a small sigh. The good doctor was a useless eejit.

"You'll be getting discharged, again, tomorrow, provided you check out ok. They don't think you're all that bad, just a wee bit more concussion. You'll need to go straight home and rest."

Then she remembered that his home was furniture-free.

"Well, rest ... ehm, somewhere ... ye know ... wit furniture."

She smiled at him and shrugged a little embarrassed shrug.

"Well, I do actually have an alternative home to go to," he replied. "I got the keys to a pal's flat yesterday. Or was it today?"

Getting bashed on the head had a way of making time either stop, or whizz by at light speed.

"See. Still a bit woozy," said the nurse. "You'll definitely need somebody to keep an eye on you, what wit your double helping of concussion an' all. Just in case."

"Actually, I feel fine. I've had worse on the rugby park," he said.

It wasn't quite true – he'd had the odd wallop on the head, but he'd never been tazered running down the wide channel. Although, the way things were going with referees, tasers might become standard issue.

"Anyway, if I'm off the park for a Head Injury Assessment, could I not just set up camp in here and you could look after me?"

There was more than a little hint there, from this bloke that she didn't fancy. She blushed so much at the thought, that it made her armpits damp.

To be on the safe side, she chose a nursing-type reply, "Unfortunately, they'll be needing the bed, I would tink. Well, definitely, we're full to the brim. Besides, I'm on a day off tomorrow, I'm afraid. And the day after. So you'd have to make do wit somebody else if you stay in here."

"No. I'd rather it was you. Anyway, I'll be fine on my own - once I get into my pal's flat. Watch the telly, sit and rest, stuff like that. Order take-away dinners. I'll be fine on my own."

He absent-mindedly reached out and took her hand, then let it go. Several seconds' silence.

Then she said, "Look. I'm on a two-day's off starting tonight. Why don't I come by and pick you up? You can call me and let me know when."

She felt her face glowing like her gran's two-bar electric fire. Her pulse was banging in her ears. She'd never asked a bloke out before, she'd only ever been asked. Usually by the wrong kind of bloke.

"Eh?" said Nisbet. If what he thought he'd just heard was right, it was surprising, confusing and extremely welcome, to say the least.

"Are you kidding?"

"No." She was still blushing. "I've nothing better to do. Just, you know, housework and stuff. ... I mean, you'll be needin' somebody like me on hand - what wit me being' good wit the nursing an' all. In case you get all bashed up again."

"Oh, I couldn't mess up your day off," replied Nisbet, doing his best to make it sound like the exact opposite.

"Well, you're in overnight for observation and then to be discharged if you check out ok late morning, early afternoon. Just let me know when and I can meet you outside the main door."

"*What a bloody gorgeous woman*," thought Nisbet. He felt great - apart from the headache. It had almost been worth having the shit beaten out of him by the cops.

He smiled back at her. "Thank you. I'd really like that." This time he took her hand and held it. "You're very nice."

"Right, it's a deal," she said, extracting her hand and stepping back in case anybody, especially nurse O'Neal had seen it. "I'll see you tomorrow."

She kissed the air in his direction and headed for the office.

"You *are* gonna shag him aren't you?" whispered Róisín, out of earshot of the other nursing staff.

For a change, Staff Nurse McMartin didn't quite know how to respond, so she blushed in reply. She felt like a schoolgirl with her first date.

"You are aren't you?" persisted Róisín.

Her boss gulped, then said, "You know Róisín, to be frank, I would not be one tiny bit surprised if I do."

Suddenly, she wasn't in the least perturbed either by the question or the notion.

"It's a bit risky, getting involved wit a patient ye know," said Róisín, for once not taking the piss. "You know, professionally. Plus the police n'all. Every time he's in here, the police come round. You don't really know what he's like, you know, deep down inside."

"I do know what he's like deep down inside," replied Deirdre.

"How's that?"

"I've seen his x-rays." She smiled a sarcastic smile at her colleague. "*And* I've seen him with his kit off."

"Yeh, well I've seen him with his kit off too," replied Róisín. "But he was a bit black and blue under the racing cars for my liking."

Nisbet called Angela.

"They're going to let me out late tomorrow morning. No, I'm fine, I don't need anything. And thanks for sorting out my stuff again. Look, one of the nurses is going to, ehm, make sure I get home ok. ... Yes it is nice of them. ... Yes, the NHS is wonderful. Angela, could you get me something nice for Staff Nurse McMartin please? Just a wee something. I don't know. You know the sort of things girls like."

Two hours later, Angela arrived with a box, very nicely wrapped in posh-looking brown paper with shiny Ralph Loren watermarks.

"It's a set of perfumed candles, in nice glass candle holder thingies. Ralph Lauren. You know - girls like that sort of thing. It was nearly thirty pounds. Was that too much to spend?"

"Thanks Angela. No, no, thirty quid's about right." He took it. It had a nice solid, weighty feel to it.

"I put a gift card in with it."

"What does it say?"

"To Staff Nurse McMartin, with Sincere Thanks and Best Wishes from Nisbet Sangster," replied Angela.

It was a bit formal, but, that was Angela for you.

"So they're sending a nurse to see you get home safely?" remarked Angela. "That's fantastic. I've never heard of that before. Sending a nurse to take you home."

"Concussion. Twice. It's in case I black out - or something like that," he lied. He changed the subject. "They can light those candles in the office."

"Yes, that's what I thought. Here, give me it."

She took it back, opened his case, wrapped a pullover round the parcel and zipped the case shut.

--------oOo--------

9

Lockerbie

In his office at eight o' clock in the morning, Tom Lockerbie picked up the phone and dialed Robb, Styles & Chatham to gee them up about the sale of the house. He hadn't heard from the useless bastards since the day before yesterday. All he got was a recorded message to the effect that the office was closed until 9:00am, followed by some criminally insipid elevator music. He hung up and dialed again, and again. Still no answer. He got up and went to get a coffee, then sat and nursed his wrath, bit his nails and simmered, until eventually, as nine o'clock arrived, his umpteenth call was answered.

"We are very busy at the moment, Mister Lockerbie," said the infuriatingly polite and genteel receptionist in the Conveyancing Department. She'd just taken a broadside from Lockerbie.

"We'll send somebody round as soon as somebody is available. Depend on it, yours will be the first to be attended to when somebody is available, I can assure you."

"Well, make sure it's somebody senior. Ah'm no wanting some jumped up wee squirt of a junior!" replied Tom Lockerbie. "Ah've bought a load of property and sued a good few folk through you people, so a wee bit respect widnae go amiss. You can get me on this number. I'll be over at the property for a look later on."

He killed the call.

"Bloody wasters!" he said out loud and wrung his hands together about how let-down he was by the people around him. He went to the showroom to shout at anybody that wasn't out selling.

After a tour of the premises, barking angrily at his staff, causing disruption in the warehouse, anxiety amongst the technicians, and making one office girl's bottom lip quiver, he went back to his own office and simmered some more.

His febrile, furtive mind turned back to the sale of his daughter's house in Balerno. Well, actually, it was *his* house - definitely -

regardless of whose name it was in. He had stumped up for half of it. So, if it was technically his property, he might as well have another look at it, he'd only ever been there a couple of times. He strode out of the office and headed off to the "former", as he saw it, Sangster residence in his Mercedes SL.

A little while later, driving up to the house, his daughter's house, *his* house, he saw, reversed into the drive, a large, black S-class Mercedes.

"*Pretty bloody flash car for a mere bloody estate agent,*" he thought. "*The bastards must be skinning me. Must be the boss man. At last I'm getting some respect! Must be hungry for business to get here so fast.*"

He got out of the car and walked up the short garden path to the door, to find it ajar. He went in, wondering where the estate agent had got a key. Maybe they kept a spare set of keys on the client's behalf after completing a purchase.

"Hello..o...!" he called, closing the door firmly behind himself.

No answer. He looked around, thinking how strange it looked with no furniture, but was comforted by the thought that a house in "move-in condition" would be a quick sale.

It echoed a little as he walked around downstairs, on the uncarpeted floors. Nothing in the sitting room or the dining room. He checked the kitchen, then the utility room and let out a gasp of exasperation. He'd have to get Cammy and the boys to lift the white goods, there was good money in them on Ebay. Or he'd use them in one of his rented-out flats. No. They were too good for his tenants. He'd sell them on Ebay. He never gave his tenants anything decent, the bastards were too bloody thick to appreciate nice stuff.

With nobody to be seen downstairs, he headed upstairs and went into the master bedroom Not a forensic trace of his daughter's personal effects and furniture remained there either. Smiling to himself he went to the long landscape window and looked out, hoping to see his scumbag son-in-law's clothes lying in a pile outside. Apart from a couple of socks and a pair of underpants hanging on the tree, there was nothing to be seen, no clothes at all. He shrugged. Maybe they'd been stolen. The thought of those clothes being stolen and heaping some more pain on his prick of a son-in-law gave him a warm feeling. He crossed the landing. Nobody in the other bedroom. All that remained there was a large roll of bubble wrap and a packaging tape dispenser with his branded tape, which the boys must have left when they cleared the place out. He would speak to them about that, the slapdash little bastards. Had to keep an eye on costs.

"Hellooo!" he called again. Still no answer.

He went into his granddaughter's bedroom. He'd never been in it before. Well, she was a grand*daughter*, not a grand*son*. It was as empty as the other rooms. All that remained were the carpet, cartoon stickers on the window and a mobile with flying ducks rotating lazily from the lightshade. He looked behind the door and nearly jumped out of his skin. There stood a very big man, immaculately, if casually dressed in an expensive leather jacket, not unlike his own.

"Jesus! Ah nearly jumped oot mah bloody skin! Did ye no hear me shouting?"

The big fellow didn't speak. He just frowned quizzically back at Lockerbie and shrugged a silent 'search me' at Lockerbie.

"Robb, Steel and Cheat'em is it? Which wan are you? Cheat'em eh? The big boss man?"

He sniggered, smiling to demonstrate the intended humour, something he was not good at. A friendly wee snide joke to break the ice. Everybody in Edinburgh knew Robb, Styles and Chatham as Robb, Steel and Cheat'em, even their own staff, probably. In fact, definitely.

"Rob? Steal? And dae whit?"

Bryson's tone and eye contact were his default, not-amused, hard-man style.

"Cheat'em. Robb, Steal and Cheat'em? Get it? Naw forget it."

Bryson wasn't up to speed with the Edinburgh solicitor's nickname. He was only familiar with the city's criminal law practices.

"Is that meant tae be some kind o' joke?" said Bryson.

"Well, maybe no. Nae offence, bad taste eh. Too bad."

It wasn't in Lockerbie's nature to apologise gracefully for a social gaff. He hadn't the vocabulary for it. Or the chromosomes.

He continued: "Anyway, glad somebody turned up at last. Ah take it ye're fully up tae date wi the situation."

"Let's just assume that Ah'm a total newcomer tae "*the situation*" and you tell me whit's at stake," said Bryson impatiently.

He was intrigued to know where this would lead, meanwhile sizing this bulky chap up and down for signs of weaponry or musculature beneath his clothing. He didn't see any.

"Well, tae cut a long story short, we're efter a quick sale," said Lockerbie. "It's up for grabs. The usual thing, for sale to the highest bidder. Or wid a fixed price be a better option?"

"So ye want tae sell it?" said Bryson slowly, trying to keep the note of astonishment from his voice, unable to believe that somebody would want to sell money back to the owner rather than piss off with it. Or was there more to this than met the eye?

"Ah think that's the whole bloody point," said Lockerbie, slowly, and already getting impatient with this big idiot. For a Mercedes-driving senior estate agent/lawyer-type person, the big chap seemed a bit dim.

"So what's the askin' price?" said Bryson.

"Ah think you're supposed tae tell me that are ye no?" replied Lockerbie. "You're meant tae be an expert, are ye no."

Bryson was beginning to heat up. Boiling point and the red mist were only a few degrees away.

"Listen pal," said Bryson, still bamboozled by the weird proposition. "It seems ye've come here tae get a price, but ye must hae a price in yer heid. Everybody wi' something' tae sell has a picture in their heid whit they want for it. Whit they're hopin' for; the least they'd accept. Simple, is it no?"

He leaned forward, his face not far from Lockerbie's. Another cold, hard-man stare.

"Help me oot here," continued Bryson. "You're in possession o' it. So tell me, whit's it worth tae ye? Then Ah'll say whit *Ah* think it's worth, and maybe we can meet in the middle. Is that no how folk normally arrive at a mutually agreeable valuation?"

"Well, Ah've done mah research online, an' going by the current state of the market, Ah would think three hundred thousand."

"Sorry pal?" said Bryson, mystified. "You want three hundred thoosand? You're sittin' on the best part o' hauf a million, and ye want tae sell it fur three hunner grand? Are you takin' the pish?"

"Hauf a million? Eh? Ah dinnae think sae, no even in this part of Edinburgh," said Lockerbie, his own short fuse burning down to flash point. "Listen pal, Ah came here wi' the intention of progressing a sale. Can we get on wi' a valuation? Either way, Ah'm sittin' on a huge pile here and Ah'd like tae cash it in."

This made absolutely no sense to Bryson, and he was in no mood to shillyshally around with this weirdo. He moved a little closer so that Lockerbie was on his left.

"Tell ye whit, here's mah valuation."

"About time," said Lockerbie. "Let me have it."

"O.k. Here it is," said Bryson

Bryson's steam-hammer right fist blurred upwards and hit Lockerbie's jaw. His head snapped back, his brain blacking out instantly. He fell vertically in a crumpled heap.

Bryson stooped to begin going through the victim's pockets, his usual next move. His phone rang. It was Matheson.

"Where are you Alec?" The voice was nervous.

"Ah'm at yon empty hoose boss."

"You never are! What if you get seen?"

"Well, the hoose has been stripped, so I figured they'd done a runner. Onyweys, ye'll no believe this: Ah've got wan o' the bastards here. He turned up while Ah wis here. Unbelievable. Ye'll never believe this."

"What do you mean you've got one of them?"

"Ah went tae recce the hoose, and yon guy, the wan in the leather jaikit turned up while Ah wis here."

"What? ... What happened? Was there any, any trouble?" said the perplexed and worried Matheson. He was afraid that Bryson might use violence. He had a talent for it. And a liking. Bryson had been born with the red mist already half way down. When the midwife had slapped his bottom when he was born, Bryson had probably decked her back.

"Naw, nae bother ata' boss. He's bein' quite the gentleman. But he must have ken't Ah wid be here, he was expecting' me. Somebody's tracking' wur calls, or maybe has the office bugged or something. It's weird."

Matheson asked what the chap was saying now. His fear that Bryson's propensity for violence would ramp up to the point of no return.

"He's no saying' nothin'. He's haein' a wee sleep. Ah've laid him oot cauld," said Bryson. "Honestly, ye'll never believe the conversation Ah just had wi' him."

"Oh dear, what did you do to him? Is he all right?"

"Dinnae worry boss, he'll live, but Ah needed tae deal wi' him."

"Ohhh … oh dear. Well, if you say so. What do you intend doing with him?"

"Well he, or they, have definitely got the money. At least, that's what it looks like. He mair or less said so. And ye'll no believe this boss, he tried tae sell me it! Sell me back wur ain money! He wanted tae negotiate a price fur it. Can ye believe that! Too weird for words. How can ye sell money, why no just keep the lot? It must be some weird scam we've never heard of. A money laundering' scam or somethin'. But it's well fuckin' weird."

At the other end of the line Matheson's hand was on his forehead. What was going on? Had they fallen foul of some high-rolling organised crime syndicate with some weird new racket? If so, he was well out of his league. Selling money made no sense at all.

"Maybe it was the diamonds he was trying to sell. I mean, both parties in the deal got stung simultaneously."

"Could be," replied his faithful servant. "But we've noo got wur hands on wan o' them. Right here. He can help us wi' wur enquiries."

"And has he got the money, or the goods with him?"

"Naw, Ah widnae think sae. They'll no be that daft. But Ah'll check his motor. Onyweys, Ah'll no be long in persuading' him tae tell us whaur it is."

"Look Alec, I, I, … look, don't …"

Matheson wanted his money back but he was terrified that Bryson would take this whole thing a stage further and kill his prisoner.

"Dinnae worry boss. We just need tae get Sanderson and Mackenzie tae rent a van. A Luton van."

"Rent a van in Luton?" asked the mystified lawyer.

"A Luton van is a wee furniture van-type thing. We get Sanderson tae rent wan aff that guy on Seafield. Nae livery, pit fake plates on it and wait for further orders." Then, "Is Francesca at the ferm boss?"

Matheson replied that his wife was away attending a yoga teachers' conference at some earth-mother health farm in Mallorca. She'd be away for another couple of weeks.

"That's fine, we'll use the big tractor shed."

"Oh dear," said Matheson.

He fretted a bit more but at last agreed, there was nothing else to be done, Alec had done what somebody like him was bound to do: take the upper hand. Or upper cut.

Bryson killed the call and went for a look round. He couldn't believe his luck. In another bedroom was a large roll of bubble wrap and a packaging tape dispenser. He took it back to Lockerbie who was just beginning to rouse from his fist-induced slumber. Bryson gave him another gentle sedative on the cheekbone to keep him relaxed for a little longer. He rolled his prisoner face down and stripped off his leather jacket. He taped his wrists behind his back and taped his knees together, then his ankles. A few circuits of tape went around Lockerbie's arms and chest and a few round his face to keep his eyes and gob shut. With the prisoner safely cocooned in tape, he went through the pockets of the leather jacket. A thin wallet with a few hundred in twenties and fifties in it, and some credit cards in the name of Thomas Lockerbie. The name rang a bell. So did the branding on the tape.

Bryson transferred the money to his own wallet, put it back in Lockerbie's jacket and slid Lockerbie's iPhone into his own jacket pocket. Nice new phone: worth a few quid.

Then Lockerbie's phone rang. Bryson took it back out of his pocket and stared at it, then took the call, "Hello."

A female voice said, "Hello Mister Lockerbie, it's about the valuation. Is there a specific time that suits you to meet up? Would ten o'clock tomorrow morning suit you? ... Hello..."

Bryson stared at the phone.

"*Jesus Christ!*" he thought. "*This is too weird for words. He's hawking it around other operations as well. Or is it the diamonds he's selling? What in the name of buggery is going on?*"

"Yes. Ten tomorrow," was all he said, and switched the phone off. He looked at the phone. He had a vague notion that an iPhone's movements could be tracked. Could they be tracked when switched off? Too bad. He switched it off. It was worth a few hundred quid and it might come in handy. He pocketed it. He'd get Wee Mac to fence it in the pub.

With some toilet paper, he wiped down everything he thought he might have touched, but the only things he'd touched so far, were the tape dispenser and Lockerbie's chin. He did a quick wipe down anyway and lifted the seat of the toilet to drop the toilet paper into it. He stared at the toilet bowl. There were traces of dried blood, the blood from the Paco Rabanne hole in Nisbet's arse. It was smeared around one side of the rim of the toilet bowl and down the side. But it looked to Bryson as if somebody had made a pretty poor job of cleaning up the scene of a violent crime. There had plainly been quite a lot of blood. And there were small fragments of glass in the bottom of the toilet bowl. There was definitely some serious shit going on around here. Had somebody been stabbed? Bludgeoned? Taken out permanently? He was dealing with heavies, it was time to get moving.

He called Sanderson and explained the situation, knowing that the boss would probably garble the message.

"We need tae get this boy back tae the ranch. He's no gawn naewhere at the moment. Ah've got him taped up that much he looks like an Egyptian mummy.

"First of all, there's twa motors here: mine's and a Merc SL. We need tae deal wi' the SL. Rent a used Luton van frae yon we shite at Seafield, pit fake plates on it and you and Wee Mackenzie come roond here." He gave him the address. "Get a van wi' nae writing' on it. Come straight roond here. Ah need this done pronto-like. Ah dinnae want tae be here ony longer than Ah need tae.

"Get Mackenzie tae drap ye at the road end and walk in. Come intae the hoose, ye'll see mah motor sittin' there. Then pit oan the boy's leather jaikit, ye're aboot the same size. Efter that, you piss aff wi the SL. Dump it at the airport Long Stay car park, ye'll need tae pit the fake plates oan it aforehand - they've got automatic number plate readers at the car park entrance so it'll read the fake plates. Park it somewhere faur oot in the car park, take the fake plates aff and walk oot. Mackenzie follows ye there and picks ye up ootside the car park in the Luton van. Dinnae let the daft wee bastard come intae the airport car park. Efter that, ye baith come back here pronto. Ye'll need tae be dressed like removal men, scruffy. Overalls if ye've got them. It'll just look like we're finishing the hoose clearance. We load up and take the goods tae the ferm."

--------oOo--------

The Patullos

Greg Patullo backed the Toyota estate out of the garage and his wife, Moira got in.

"Have you got everything?"

"I've got the leisure battery in the boot; it's fully charged. And the tool box. And the air compressor to check the tyres. We don't need much else."

They drove down the hill and turned west onto the Glasgow Road, heading for the farm where the four-berth caravan that they'd owned for fifteen years had spent the winter, stored along with a dozen others. Past the airport, they crossed the main motorway roundabout at Newbridge, and headed south towards the Pentland Hills and the farm where the caravan was stored.

It took all of an hour or two to strip the green caravan cover off their pride and joy, fold it up and put it in the boot of the Toyota. Another hour had the leisure battery installed, the tyre pressures checked and the two new gas bottles slotted into the front compartment. He fitted the towing mirrors to the car and spent some time arguing with his wife until they were lined up properly. At length, with the caravan hitched up, the electrics plugged in, the indicators and lights checked, Greg Patullo slipped the car into gear and eased the caravan out of its winter slot. They pulled out onto the main road, and headed for home.

Turning north once more at the first set of traffic lights on the A71, Tom Lockerbie's Mercedes SL pulled out from behind them and surged past, pulling away at a tremendous speed, heading in the direction of the airport.

"Nice car," said Greg Patullo to his wife, doing some mental arithmetic to see how big a dent in his new-found wealth a Mercedes SL would make.

"Not very practical," replied Moira. "You couldn't tow the caravan with that. No space for stuff, and no space for the dog."

A white Luton van passed them and cut in front of them, nearly taking the nose of the Toyota.

"Arsehole!" cried Greg. "He's surely not racing that Merc in a van is he? Anyway, have you made up your mind where we're taking the caravan?"

"Not really," replied Moira. "How about the East Neuk of Fife?"

"Aye. Or St Andrews. Could get a round of golf."

"You don't play golf."

"I could give it a go." He smiled at her and she rolled her eyes. "Right then, a couple of days in Fife, then head up the east coast?"

Greg Patullo was keen to get well out of Edinburgh. There was bound to be some nuclear heat being generated by those gangsters. They would probably do anything to get their money back. But they weren't going to get it back, he'd made up his mind. All he needed to do, was make himself scarce until the heat had died down, if it ever would. And he certainly did not want ever to run into that big guy again. A year's caravanning around the coast of Scotland would suit him fine.

--------oOo--------

Mackenzie pulled away from Nisbet's house, and followed Sanderson in Lockerbie's Mercedes SL and leather jacket, out of the housing estate. Lockerbie's Mercedes SL was parked somewhere at the far side of the airport long-stay carpark. Sanderson took the shuttle bus and got dropped off at its first stop, the Hilton hotel. He walked out and Mackenzie picked him up at the roadside, still in Lockerbie's leather jacket.

"Dinnae worry aboot the boy's Mercedes," said Bryson, on the phone to Matheson. "It's a flash motor but it's a big car park, it'll no be noticed for months, if no years. Folk wi holiday homes abroad park up for weeks on end and if they go lookin' fur a motor that's been there too long, they'll be lookin' fur wan wi the fake plates."

"You think so?"

"Aye. Mind yon Ferrari at Glasgow Airport? Seven years it sat there afore it was spotted and the polis had tae investigate it. That Merc went in wi wan set o' plates and it's sittin' there wi another so it's no even in their system. Even if the airport car park folk ever spot that there's been a car in the car park wi'oot being removed for months, they'll be wonderin' how it got in wi'oot gettin' logged in the system. That Merc could be there fur years."

Matheson couldn't help but admire Bryson's criminal intelligence, the way he'd dealt with the situation. But he'd moved the whole thing up a grade in criminal activity, he'd kidnapped a man and that was serious, even if the man was a criminal too.

"I'm not worried about the car Alec, but what are you going to do with this, this prisoner?"

"Same as the owner o' the Ferrari. He'll need tae disappear."

"Disappear where?"

"Well, there's really naewhere else other than your ferm."

"Oh, the farm?" said Matheson. "Oh dear." But he was relieved that it was lesser level of 'disappear' than the Firth of Forth.

"It'll be fine boss. Yer wife's no due back for a fortnight. It's the best place, oot in the countryside. Naeb'dy nearby. Quiet."

"Oh dear," said Matheson, his hand on his forehead. "A member of the opposition held hostage at the farm."

"He's no a hostage. He's mair like … a temporary guest."

"How temporary?" Matheson's voice was shrivelled with panic.

"You want yer money back Boss. Ah said Ah'd get it back, and Ah will."

"But, a prisoner? At the farm?"

"Dinnae you worry aboot him Boss, Ah'll deal wi' him, he'll no come tae nae herm - if he cooperates."

"I do hope he cooperates," said Matheson.

"Aye. Me too Boss. For his sake. But if he disnae, well, he'll be a bargaining' chip if things move up a gear."

"Oh dear. Move up a gear, you say? What does that …?

"Actually, Boss, we're already up another gear. We're talkin' aboot gettin screwed for well ower four hunner grand. It was them that moved it up a gear, we're just responding, as we were bound tae dae."

"I suppose so. It is a lot of money. Big-time money," said Matheson, his arsehole clenching and unclenching in time with his pulse. "We need to get it back."

"That's the spirit Boss. Dinnae worry, we've had a lucky break gettin' ho'd o' wan o' them. He'll cough up the goods. Ah'll see ye up at the ferm." He hung up.

At the other end, Matheson was banging his head on the desk rhythmically. His pension-filling criminal enterprise had moved up from medium-sized recreational drug dealing to kidnap, probably torture (Bryson might even be looking forward to that part), extortion, and, if Bryson went too far, possibly even murder. His whole life could collapse around his ears. He could end up being sent down as the ring-leader of a gang of murderous criminals. He pictured himself shut in an eight-by-ten cell in Barlinnie Prison getting rodgered by some seven-foot psychopathic gay bodybuilder. Like the one he'd failed to get off of an attempted murder charge a few weeks ago. He'd heard that prison turns some prisoners a bit gay, even if only for sexually expedient reasons.

He got hold of himself. Maybe he was too old to be attractive to seven-foot gay blokes. He picked up the phone again and asked his secretary to arrange for all his current cases to be postponed due to whatever reason she could conjure up. He got in the car and headed for the family's country retreat, the farmhouse in Fife.

--------oOo--------

Tooled Up

The Beattie twins finished breakfast and got dressed for the forthcoming event.

"Dae ye think these work?" asked Rab Beattie, pulling on the ultra-thin, bullet-proof, wife-beater-style Kevlar vest. "They're gey thin. No much better than a simmet."

"Well, the big yins dinnae fit ablaw yer jaikit. And they're ower warm. They make ye look like a fat bastard."

"Ye a'ready look like a fat bastard."

They pulled polo-neck sweaters on over the Kevlar vests, lifted the hold-all with the guns in it and headed for the car. Twenty minutes later, they were on the motorway, heading east for Edinburgh.

"Ah'd never heard o' Balerno afore. Sounds like it should be in Italy? Or Spain," said Andy Beattie.

"It's that faur east, it might as weel be in Canada," replied his brother.

"That's west, ya eejit."

"Ye could go east. It's longer, but …"

"Ah'll get a nosebleed gawn that faur east.

--------oOo--------

Deirdre

Dragging his wheelie case, Nisbet eased his way along the hospital corridor to the elevator and went down the two floors to the hospital concourse. Deirdre was waiting for him outside the automatic main door. She didn't want to go up to the ward in case Róisín took the piss again.

Nisbet saw her through the glass paneling at the front of the hospital and his heart jumped when he saw her.

"*Blimey!*" he thought. He got a jolt of adrenaline. He'd never had that simply from catching sight of a woman before. "*What an absolute honey!*"

He checked his step just to look at her. Right there and then, he didn't have any pain or discomfort, he just felt superb. This was the best thing that had happened to him since, well, since ever. She looked fabulous. Even better than she did in her nurse's uniform. She was wearing a bomber-style jacket, skin tight blue jeans and neat little, white-leather trainer-style shoes. There was a glow about her, as if she was standing on stage under the spotlights. What a gorgeous woman: pretty, and fit, and well, wow! The automatic door opened, he stepped out and she walked towards him.

They said a bashful hello, neither managing to pluck up the gumption for a kiss, even on the cheek.

"You look *amazing*!" he said, looking her in the eye.

Two seconds' bashful silence. She knew he meant it.

"Thank you."

Another two seconds' bashful silence, then Deirdre took hold of the situation.

"Are you steady on your feet? Here, let me give you a hand."

He held out his arm. She took it, and the wheelie bag. He looked at Deirdre, then looked around, hoping to see envious glances from the few people milling around outside the hospital. He'd never felt this proud to meet a woman before, and have her on his arm. Even when he was in the first flush of love with Brenda, and she was pretty good looking, she'd never made his heart skip like this. He could practically hear his heart thudding in waltz time, skipping beats left right and centre,

"Have you eaten?" asked Deirdre, defibrillating his pulse back to a normal two-four beat.

"Nope."

"Come on, I'll buy you lunch," she said. "What do you fancy?"

"Bag of chips would do me. Anything but hospital food."

They got a bus in towards town. Deirdre got them a burger each at McDonald's and they shared a Coke. He had barely touched her, and here he was sharing a straw with her. It felt even more intimate than if he had kissed her.

They swopped notes: home, school, college. An hour disappeared in a flash.

"I suppose I'd better start sorting myself out, get that hire car back off my drive and get into my digs," he said, eventually. "Thanks for the burger."

A black cab took them to Nisbet's house.

He paid the near-forty-quid fare with the left-over cash from Deirdre's loan.

The rental Jaguar SUV was still parked in the drive.

"Nice car," said Deirdre. "Must cost a bomb to rent that."

"The insurance company's paying. I think I was supposed to get a toy pedal care, but I got lucky, they had nothing else left."

She looked around the houses nearby.

"Nice place to live. Are ye going to show me round your house?"

"There's nothing to see, it's completely empty, apart from a few things like the washing machine and dryer and stuff. Plus they left the stuff in the garage. But go ahead, have a wander."

He unlocked the front door and she stepped in.

"Nice big house," she said, walking around, her voice echoed in the empty rooms. "Nice kitchen. I thought you said they'd left the washing machine?"

"Eh?" He followed her into the kitchen and the utility room. "Holy shit! They've been back since I was here yesterday and lifted the last of the stuff. What a nasty, greedy bastard that man is!"

She put her hand on his arm and his blood pressure dropped immediately.

"Are you going to keep it? The house?"

"I'd need to buy my wife's half, which I can't afford. And anyway, I don't fancy staying here."

"Bad memories, eh?"

"No. Never wanted to live here in the first place - just, you know - took the quiet-life option. I'd rather be in a wee cottage."

"Yeh. In the country somewhere, or a wee village. Can I look upstairs?"

"On you go. I'll wait here, my dead leg isn't up to mountaineering yet. And the altitude might give an embolism. Or a submariner capsule bleed."

He watched Deirdre climb the stairs, her hands in the pockets of her bomber jacket, her jeans tight about her backside.

"*Jesus Christ Almighty!*" he thought, as he watched her jeans go up the stairs and out of sight on the landing. Gorgeous legs.

He adjusted the contents of his underpants, the one area of his body that hadn't, so far, taken a hammering and was still fully on active duty.

She called down from the bedroom, "There's a pair of socks and a pair of underpants hanging in the tree outside the bedroom window."

"Yes, It's a *pair* tree. I'm growing my own smalls."

A little laugh echoed its way out of the empty bedroom and she followed it out onto the landing.

"Nice house all the same. Must have cost a bomb," she said as she came down the stairs.

"Yep, bomb is right. I have a ten-thousand megaton mortgage."

"You're funny," she said.

She stopped on the second bottom step, eye to eye with Nisbet. But not quite close enough. If he leant forward to kiss her, in his present condition, he'd tip over.

After four or five motionless, but easy seconds, she pecked him on the lips, took his hand, and said, "C'mon big fella, let's get you into yer new flat."

He said, "Yes. Not much point in hanging around here. In fact, I'd rather not, in case the cops turn up and give us both a hiding.

Her hand was cool, and strong as she walked him over to the car.

"I'll drive," she said, taking the keys to the Jag out of his other hand.

Just as she piled Nisbet's case into the back of the Jag, a dark blue Ford drove past.

The Beatties turned into the Balerno housing estate. Again, the posh English bint on the satnav proclaimed their arrival.

"That so gets on mah tits," said Andy the Bat.

"How?" asked his brother.

"How can ye no get a Weegie wummin's voice oan yer satnav?"

"Because it would go, *Ye huv just went past yer fuckin' destination ya wanker!* It widnae sell."

"Aye it wid. In Camlachie. Or Springburn."

Just as they approached the house, a couple came out the front door and headed for a huge, black Jaguar SUV.

"Holy shit! it's that poor bastard the cops were kicking' the shite intae. What, in the name o' the wee man, is goin' on here?" said Rab "Stanley Knife" Beattie.

"That could even be the stuff in yon wee suitcase thingy, whatever it is. Either the money or the diamonds." said his brother, Andy "the Bat" Beattie. "Let's grab them."

"No here. Ower mony witnesses. Better tae fun' oot whaur they're gawn. Mibbies lead us tae their HQ. That's a fuck-off big Jag that, by the way. He must be high up in their operation."

They drove past and turned down a side street, then crept back up to the junction to watch the Jag and drive off, the girl at the wheel. The dark blue Ford pulled out of the side street and kept its distance until the two Glaswegians saw which way the Jaguar turned when it got to the main road. They let two cars go past then slotted in behind them on the main road. Two cars back, in a nondescript dark blue Ford, they were virtually invisible.

They followed the Jaguar SUV right across Edinburgh to a quiet street near Leith Docks. It pulled up outside a modern block of flats. They sat in the car, watching while Nisbet and Deirdre parked in one of the reserved, residents' places, took the case from the back of the Jag, and entered the block of flats. The two hoodlums got out of the Ford and Rab got his foot in the door as it slowly swung shut.

Nisbet and Deirdre climbed the two floors to Ash's Airbnb flat. Nisbet clenched his teeth with every step, trying not to look like a complete woos, but with his dead-leg and other bruising actually feeling physically looser the more he moved around. Deirdre followed, dragging the case on its rollers a step at a time up the stairs. This time, she was looking at Nisbet's arse as she went.

"Nice wee flat," she said, as she parked the case in the lobby. She turned to close the door behind her, and nearly jumped out of her skin. There was an ugly bastard of a man standing in the doorway. He stepped in. In his hand was a very large, shiny hand gun. Behind him, was an uncannily similar and equally ugly man removing a baseball bat from underneath his coat. They barged in and closed the door.

"Mother of God! Who the hell are you?" she said, staring at Rab Beattie's Desert Eagle. She'd never seen a real hand gun before. She didn't know they were that big. It looked huge, and shiny, and very scary.

"Shut the fuck up hen," said Rab Beattie, stepping further into the flat and grabbing her by the arm. He pointed the gun at Nisbet's face. "Get the stuff, you're comin' wi' us."

"Who the hell are you? What stuff? What do you want?" said Nisbet, unable to comprehend what was going on, or the level of inexplicable bad luck that was piling in on him over the last few days. He stared down the black hole of the half-inch barrel. It looked like the Clyde Tunnel. But less congested.

"We're just the errand boys," said Rab Beattie. "Just get the stuff and come wi' us."

"What stuff? What are you talking about?"

The gun was pushed up under Nisbet's chin.

"Listen pal, dinnae act the daft laddie. This is the maist powerful handgun in the world," said Rab Beattie. It made him feel like Clint Eastwood in Dirty Harry when he said that. Except Dirty Harry was a polis.

"It can blaw yer brains intae the flat upstairs," he continued.

Nisbet had no reason to doubt this, so he said, "I have no idea what you're on about. What do you want? Money?"

"Aye, ye're on the right track there. Oor boys hus been ontae ye frae the stert. Is this the stuff here?" he said, kicking Nisbet's roller case. It scooted a couple of feet along the uncarpeted compound flooring.

"That's just an overnight bag. It's just some clothes."

"Aye, so it is," said Andy Beattie. "Dae you think mah heid zips up the back? "

"Well if it does, I hope it's zipped up better than your fly," said Nisbet.

The gun-toting hoodlum had a look at his fly. He did it up.

"Fuckin' wise guy, eh?" said Rab Beattie. He moved the gun to Nisbet's forehead and clicked back the hammer. "Is ... this ... the ... fuckin' ... stuff?"

"That's all I've got. Everything in the whole world."

"Everything?"

"Everything," said Nisbet. "The flat's empty, we just took it over. I just got the keys." He held the keys up with the Ash Khan Lettings key ring attached. "See?" He wiggled the keys.

"Temporary' bolt hole is it? Hidin' oot for a wee while wi' the stuff. 'Til the stoor dies doon an' the coast's clear eh?"

"Well, I suppose you could say that," replied Nesbit, trying to remain calm while wondering what the hell was going on.

Deirdre, her pulse rate at two thousand, watched Nisbet with some admiration.

"How is he so calm?" she thought. *"I'm shiting myself and he's so calm,"* unaware of the fact that he'd recently taken two codeine, plus another two for good measure and was ever-so slightly stoned.

But then, the admiration eased off to be replaced by a smidgeon of suspicion. Maybe Róisín had been right. She didn't really know Nisbet Sangster from Adam. Maybe he *was* mixed up in something. These two looked like very bad men. They weren't all that big, but they looked very nasty. The gun looked nasty. And the baseball bat.

She thought about it. Getting arrested and beaten up by the police. That doesn't happen to very many people. And the hit and run. Maybe it was actually a hit. An attempted gangland murder. She gave it a little more thought. No. He couldn't be, he was too nice, witty, and fun. He had a nice secretary. He was just very unlucky. Apparently. She hoped.

Rab wagged the gun again in Nisbet's face.

"Open the bag. Get the stuff oot!"

"There isn't any stuff." said Nisbet. "I have absolutely no idea what you are on about. It's just full of clothes!"

The barrel pushed Nisbet's left nostril up half an inch.

"Open the bag."

"Ok, ok," said Nisbet. He stood on his toes to extricate his nostril from the gun and bent to unzip the bag, happy that there was nothing in there but shirts, underpants and socks.

"Empty it!"

Nisbet flipped the case and emptied the contents onto the floor. His clothes tumbled out, including his pullover, which gracefully unrolled and out popped the Ralph Lauren perfumed candle set, beautifully wrapped in designer brown paper.

"Lyin' bastard!" said Rab, bending to pick up the parcel. He stood and waved it triumphantly in Nisbet's face. "Huvnae got the stuff, eh? Only claes eh? Lyin' bastard."

"Actually, that's just a present," said Nisbet.

"Aye, a present. Five hunner gees. Hauf a grip! A wee present? Dinnae push yer luck pal. Yer nice wee scam has went an' came tae nothin'."

Deirdre stared at Nisbet in horror, and disappointment. Was he some kind of gangster after all? She couldn't believe it. Róisín had been right. This nice man she had fancied had turned out to be involved with some very nasty people in some big-time crime. She felt herself well up, she wanted to burst into tears, but managed to hold it back. Her look of disappointment turned to one of anger directed at Nisbet. He shook his head, trying to deny what he could see she thought.

"That is only a present," said Nisbet, firmly. "Ehm, for, ehm, my girlfriend. Now you've gone and spoilt the surprise."

"Aye, a surprise present. Best part o' hauf a million quid in diamonds! Some fuckin' present."

"Diamonds?" said Deirdre in astonishment, her face full of disgust. "Half a million? In diamonds? "You, you ... bastard!"

"Aw, poor wee thing," said Andy Beattie out the side of his mouth. "He's no exactly gawny tell his fuckin' floozy he's got that much swag on him, is he?"

"Floozy?! Fookin' floozy!?" exclaimed Deirdre, indignantly. That made her even more angry.

"Shut yer Irish puss!" said Andy Beattie. Then he looked hard at her. "Ye're no a Taig ur ye?"

"Oh Taig is it?" said Deirdre, deeply offended by the Irish equivalent of the "N" word. She swung a kick and it made good contact with the bottom of Andy Beattie's kneecap.

"Oh ya fucker!" he cried, hopping around on one foot. "Bitch!"

He swung a slap at her, but she saw it coming a mile away, ducked, and his hand hit the door pillar.

"Oh ya bastard!"

He shook the pain out of his fist and was about to swing another but his brother stepped in.

"Pack it in Andy. Ye can beat the shite oot her efter we're feenished. Here, pit this in the bag and zip it up. We need tae get the fuck oot o' here."

He turned back to Nisbet, as his brother dropped the parcel into the empty case and zipped it up.

"Right. We're leavin'."

Andy's phone rang.

"It's Wee Shady," he said to his brother. "Keep an eye on they twa." He walked to the bathroom.

"Andy, Billy Bryce's contacts have come up with something," said McShaed. "I have an address for you to check out. It's in Fife."

"Where?" replied Andy Beattie, in the sort of puzzled tone you'd expect from a foreign visitor.

"Fife. The Kingdom of Fife. It's a county, it's part of Scotland?" said McShaed.

"Whit the fuck goes on in Fife?"

To be fair, even an educated man like McShaed had difficulty describing what the "Kingdom of Fife" was actually for nowadays. Even those who live there wonder.

"Not much," he said. "They used to mine coal and make linoleum. It's the Scottish equivalent of Yorkshire. Or Texas. But more disaffected – and bitter."

"Good place tae hide oot then. Where is it?"

"Where is Fife? Jesus wept!" said McShaed, astonished at the ignorance of Scottish geography. But to be fair, he'd only ever driven through it on the motorway.

"Look it up on a map," he continued. "The address is a farm, apparently. It might be, or may have been the headquarters of this operation. I've just texted you the address. It's worth a look. Apparently there used to be a skunk farm there at one time."

"Aye, very good. But we've made some progress here an'a'. We've got two o' them. The guy in the leather jaikit that legged it wi' yer client's diamonds. The same boy we seen gettin the shite kicked oot him by the polis at yon hoose in Balerno. He was back at the hoose. We trailed him … Wait, wait, there's mair. He had the goods on him."

"The goods? The Diamonds?"

"Aye, still in the parcel, still wrapped up in fancy broon paper."

"That's fantastic!" said McShaed. "Look, forget about the Fife thing for now, just bring the diamonds back here."

"What aboot the guy? We've got him an' his burd here. We cannae exactly whack them here, oor motor will be on every cctv camera around here."

McShaed thought for a few seconds. He knew the Beatties could be ludicrously rash, and enthusiastically violent.

"Andy, we don't need to escalate this into a multiple disappearance with the police all over it. We're only trying to repossess stolen goods. Look, they could be quite useful. Can you bring them in? They'll be worth having a chat with. Can you restrain them?"

"Ah can restrain them wi' the threat o' gettin' their brains blew oot. Gie me an hour an' a hauf."

He hung up and went back through to the sitting room.

"That was Wee Shady. Ah tel't him we've got the stuff. He says tae bring they twa in."

"Fair enough," said his brother.

He went over to Nisbet and Deirdre. "See, you're coming' wi us. The pair o' ye. Ye'll be in the cawr wi' us. If ye make ony daft moves, make funny faces tae folk, shout for help, the wee Taig gets it. Right?"

"Coming with you?" said Nisbet, calm on the outside but now starting to panic through the painkillers. "I don't think so."

"Wrong!" Beattie pulled back the slider and chambered a bullet. "See, it wisnae even loaded."

Horrible, Hollywood kidnap and murder scenarios flitted through Nisbet's vivid imagination. These thoughts had already flitted across Deirdre's many times.

"Where are you taking us?" said Nisbet.

"Tell ye whit, why don't Ah show ye it oan the map?" said Rab Beattie.

Plainly, sarcasm was alive and well as an art form in the Glasgow criminal underworld.

"Ok," said Nisbet, "Show me."

"Listen pal, dinnae act the smartarse wi' me. Dinnae push yer luck," said Rab Beattie.

But to be fair, now that the subject had come up, he wasn't sure he could find Glasgow on a map.

"Hey Rab," said his brother, "just a minute." Then to Nisbet and Deirdre, "You twa, away and sit on the settee."

He wagged the baseball bat in the direction of the settee, then nodded his brother a little further away in the hall.

"Did Wee Shady no say that this operation turned ower baith parties in this deal? Right? Then there's still the money tae get."

"Sorry," said Nisbet, from the settee. "There isn't any money. I'm skint. Sole trader. Times are hard. Honestly."

"If ye're skint, how come ye can afford a motor like that?"

"It's rented," said Nisbet.

"Aye, rented. Whit? Like yer wee Taig hooker?" said Andy Beattie, pleased with his awesome wit.

He stepped towards her and reached out to grab her by the arm. She parried his hand away with ease and looked up at the ugly bastard.

"You lay a finger on me and I'll ... "

"Ye'll dae whit?" he said. He reached out, grabbed her hair and pulled her forward. He stuck his face in hers, "Wee Taig. Fuckin' wee Tim hoor."

She recoiled from his breath. Exceptionally poor oral hygiene. She'd read a paper on it: "Adult Dental Decay in Scotland, Specifically West of Scotland Working Classes".

He pushed her roughly back into the settee.

She booted him hard in the balls.

"Ooff! Oh ya! Oh ya bastard!" He doubled over, dropping the bat and clutching at his groin.

"*Holy shit!*" thought Nisbet. "*I wouldn't have had the guts to do that!*"

Andy Beattie, ball-ache buzzing up through his body, his knee throbbing, stood up just as Deirdre's foot whizzed past his face for a second kick. Clutching his aching balls, he raised his fist and jabbed one at her. Nisbet's left hand shot out and caught it on its way there. He held it tight, his hand a size bigger than the shorter Glaswegian's. Rab Beattie shoved the gun onto Nisbet's forehead.

"Let go, or Ah promise, Ah'll pit a bullet through the back o' yer heid. Frae the front," said Rab Beattie.

Nisbet let go.

"Touch her again, and you'll have to shoot me to keep me off you," said Nisbet.

Rab Beattie's gun went onto Nisbet's forehead again.

"Dinnae worry pal, Ah'll shoot ye. Andy, ye can dae whit ye like wi' her later. We need tae get them back tae Wee Shady - in wan piece."

"Look," said Nisbet. "Everybody calm down. Let's be reasonable. You've plainly outsmarted me. I give in. You win. You've got your box of diamonds, so why don't you just take them and we'll call it quits."

That was it for Deirdre. Nisbet Sangster had just admitted to having a huge sum of money in diamonds in his possession. He was definitely a gangster.

"No hard feelings," continued Nisbet, his voice calm. "You take that box of diamonds, and we'll all just move on with our lives. Remain friends. Exchange Christmas cards. Post cards from Majorca in the summer."

To Deirdre, instead of sounding brave, now Nisbet just sounded like a hard gangster. His face looked hard. He wasn't scared of these guys, he was their sort.

"Well, why did Ah no think o' that?" said Rab Beattie, airing his knack for dry wit once again. "Nae wonder the cops gied ye a hammerin' pal. Ye're no smert enough - no cut oot fur crime."

Nisbet concurred. He definitely wasn't good at crime. Apart from having the crap beaten out of him by two cops for running himself over with his own car, all he ever did outside the law was park optimistically. And quite a lot of speeding.

Deirdre, on the other hand, was beginning to think that even though he might not be cut out for crime, he was doing it anyway.

"Just a minute Rab," said his brother, and beckoned him over to the hall again. "Listen. Wee Shady's gave me an address in Fife that he wanted checked oot. Might be their headquarters. Plus, as far as Ah can mind, his client says that the other side say they got shafted an'a - for the best part o' hauf a million - in used notes. So this lot definitely, probably lifted the diamonds *and* the money. Might be worth a look."

"Naw, it's no very likely it'll be there. We better get back tae Wee Shady."

"It's a fuckin' lot of money. An' ye cannae exactly bank that amount in used notes. They'll huv stashed it 'til the stoor settles."

Silence, while the wheels of reasoning whirred.

"Aye. Right enough, Andy. Ah mean, it's a long shot, but even if we just came away wi' some o' it, we'd be quids in: gie the diamonds tae Wee Shady, split the loot atween wursel's. That Fife lot dinnae ken we've got their man here, so we can maybe take them by surprise. Auld-fashioned stick-up."

"How faur's Fife frae here?"

"Nae idea." He'd rarely been east of Belshill. He pointed at Nisbet. "But yer man here will ken." He waved the gun at Nisbet and Deirdre, "Right, shift! Baith o' ye's. Ony fancy stuff frae you pal, an' the wee Taig girlfriend gets it."

Deirdre gave him a look of such total malevolence, it surprised all three men.

"I'm not his girlfriend!" she said.

Andy Beattie put his face in hers again, and emphasised, "Naw! Ye're just a wee hoor, a wee fuckin' Taig hoor. Shift!" But he kept his knees together, just in case of another Adidas-testicle encounter.

His brother took hold of her by the arm, put the gun in his coat pocket and stuck the muzzle in the middle of her back.

"*Shit! They actually do that.*" thought Nisbet, looking at the sharp profile of the gun's muzzle poking against the coat like a scene from a gangster movie. But then, he was in a real gangster movie.

The baseball bat was shoved in his back.

"Move it! Ony fancy stuff," said Andy Beattie, "ye get this roond the lug."

"*Fair enough,*" thought Nisbet, "*I can handle that, my head's getting used to it, and I really don't need another dead-leg. Or another submariner's capsule bleed.*"

Down in the car park, Deirdre was assisted into the back seat with some vigour, and followed by Rab, who pushed her along the seat with his Desert Eagle in her ribs. Nisbet was ushered into the front passenger seat of the Ford.

"Try onyhin'," said Rab, "An' yer burd gets it."

"Where are you taking us?" said Nisbet, once more, his voice now a little shaky.

"Just fur a wee look roond yer headquarters."

That was even worse news as far as Deirdre was concerned. Nisbet's headquarters? Criminals big enough to have a headquarters? Nisbet Sangster was definitely involved in organised crime. Her head was spinning. A vortex of fear and disappointment. Another bad choice in men. She started to cry, but choked it back as best she could.

Andy Beattie hit the address McShaed had texted and Maps

opened up on his phone. He started the engine. They drove west out of Leith, following the satnav over the River Forth into the Kingdom of Fife.

--------oOo--------

The Farm

Lockerbie sensed the light come on in the tractor shed. He had spent what felt like a month, pupating like a moth, rolled up in his granddaughter's bedroom carpet, on top of a pile of mouldy old horse blankets. He had not the faintest inkling of where he was, and only the foggiest notion of what had led up to his arrival. Despite his situation, his fear and discomfort were diluted somewhat by the Maslowian narking of his bladder, full to bursting point from too much coffee at the office, many hours ago.

Heavy footsteps approached - the footsteps of a big man wearing heavy, leather-soled shoes.

Bryson bent down towards the end of the carpet. "It'll be quite cosy in there Ah wid think. Snug ... as a bug ... in a rug, ... so tae speak. Did ye enjoy yer wee nap?"

Nothing. It was the wrong end of the carpet. He went the ten feet along to the other end and repeated the enquiry. Lockerbie mumbled some desperate, claustrophobic codswallop through packing tape and three or four layers of carpet.

"Ah think Ah ken whit ye mean," said Bryson. "Wid ye like me tae phone yer partners in crime fur ye? Tell them ye're gawny be a bit *wrapped up* for a while?"

Silence.

"Naw? O.k. Time tae unwrap ye for a wee while."

He bent, gripped the edge of the carpet, heaved it up and rolled the fearful, perplexed, disoriented and now dizzy Lockerbie out onto the floor. Lockerbie felt himself picked up by the armpits, and dragged to a chair. He was too relieved to be out of the carpet's hot, sweaty and claustrophobic confines, and too stiff, to struggle. And this individual was plainly a huge man to be able to lift a big lump like Lockerbie with such apparent ease. Almost elated to be upright and out of the carpet, he could do nothing but sit obediently still while Bryson taped his chest to the upright of the chair with Lockerbie only managing a mumbled, muffled, token protest through the packing tape.

"Dinnae fidget," said Bryson, "Ye'll just fa' ower. Ah'm awa fur somethin' tae eat. Can Ah get ye somethin'?"

Muffled, apoplectic, taped-up gibberish in reply. Lockerbie might be utterly disoriented and shiting himself after hours rolled up in a carpet, but his natural talent for anger shone proudly through.

"Fish supper did ye say? Ah'll see whit Ah can dae," said Bryson.

He went back to the farmhouse where Matheson was frying up a hearty panful of saturated fat, carbohydrate, salt and E-numbers, the only thing he knew how to cook.

"How is our, ehm, visitor now?" asked the nervous Matheson. "Has he said anything?"

Things had taken a thoroughly disturbing turn. Matheson had been benefiting from crime where he didn't ever actually have to get directly involved. Hitherto, it had just been a case of running a clandestine retail operation at arm's length with his troops doing all the dirty work. Like lawyers do.

"Well, he's breathing," said Bryson, with his mouth full of toast. "We'll get the tape aff his mooth efter dinner and he can tell us whit the sketch is. As in, where's the money." He turned to Mackenzie. "Wee Mac. Away and keep an eye on wur guest. We'll need tae kind-of, interrogate him."

"Interrogate!?" said Matheson, his hand shaking nervously as he flipped some square sausage over in the frying pan.

Bryson detected the panic in his master's voice.

"Well, no interrogate – he'll just be helpin' us wi' wur enquiries."

It didn't calm Matheson down much. He had more than a faint idea how his loyal thug of a handyman might make those enquiries.

"Onywey Mac, away and make sure oor guest is in good spirits for …"

"Interrogation," interrupted Mackenzie with his mouth also full of toast. He stood up. "Right Alec. Interrogation, aye."

Buoyed by his selection for this important task, and feeling fully authorised, he headed for the big shed with the zeal of a Spanish Inquisitor.

"Right you! Spill the beans! Tell me everything!" screamed Mackenzie in Lockerbie's ear.

It seemed the right approach because he hadn't actually thought of any questions. As it happened, that would be Bryson's approach too.

The prisoner mumbled and Mackenzie spotted his mistake. He ripped the packing tape off from around Lockerbie's mouth taking a good bunch of moustache hair with it. Lockerbie squawked like an angry baboon, the first meaningful sound that he'd uttered for hours.

"I bet that stung like fuck," said Mackenzie. Then into Lockerbie's face. "Like a wee wax job on yer fanny!"

"Have you got any idea who you're dealing with?" screamed the enraged Lockerbie, the tape no longer stifling his colossal ego.

"Do you know who I am? Untie me or you'll regret it for the rest of your miserable life, you insignificant wee piece of dogshite!"

Lockerbie's superabundance of psychopathic self-esteem wasn't about to let the side down, especially since the small voice indicated a substantial difference in size between this little prick and the powerhouse that had lifted his sixteen stones onto this chair.

Mackenzie's small fist whacked onto the side of Lockerbie's forehead.

"Ooyah bastard!" yelped Lockerbie, more in shock than in pain.

Mackenzie squealed too. He doubled over clutching his hand. He was new at interrogation, and he'd just learned the first lesson: don't punch somebody on the hardest part of their skull. He stood upright, wiggling the pain out of his hand.

"Ye need tae stert talkin' pal," he squeaked through the pain, his voice even smaller, confirming his diminutive stature.

"You must be some kind of retard sonny," said Lockerbie, defaulting to his instinctive bullying tone when dealing with an inferior. Bullying was instinctive to him and, by and large, it worked.

"Ye've no even asked me a question yet ya daft wee shite."

He did some token writhing in his bonds. He'd seen it done in the movies. The chair wobbled onto two legs, hung there for a fretful second, then dropped back down to all fours.

"*Good point*," thought Mackenzie. He yelled, "Just start talkin!" and swung a kick aimed at Lockerbie's ribs.

His foot hit the woodwork of the chair.

"Ooyah bastard!" gasped Mackenzie and hopped around on one foot, clutching the other. Lockerbie roared in anger and did some more energetic writhing, his fury overcoming any lingering fear. He wasn't afraid of this little squirt. He did some more furious and energetic writhing.

"Untie me sonny or I'll, I'll …"

The old mahogany dining chair wobbled onto two legs, and hung there for a second. Lockerbie fidgeted nervously, trying to get it back down on all fours.

"Oooooh shit!" he yelled, and crashed sideways onto the floor.

"Ye'll dae whit?" said Mackenzie, hopping on one foot, adrenalin pumping, foot pounding, knuckles throbbing. It felt like he'd broken something, somewhere. He staggered backwards onto his arse.

The Judas door of the shed squeaked open and in came Matheson, Julian and Bryson to see Mackenzie and Lockerbie both on the floor.

"Jesus bloody Christ!" said Bryson.

He strode forward, grabbed Mackenzie by the collar, hauled him to his feet, walked him to the door of the shed and stood him there like a child on the naughty step. Strolling casually back, he bent, took Lockerbie by the flesh of his flabby lower cheek and raised him upright again as the prisoner squealed.

Matheson winced at the utter brutality of this, but Julian had to admire the raw animal strength that so easily accommodated a one-hand lift of that magnitude: a sixteen-stone man raised upright by one flabby cheek.

Bryson turned and looked at his trembling boss who whispered, "You're not going to … going to …?"

"Whit? Beat him up? Naw, nay need for that."

Matheson breathed a sigh of relief. So did Lockerbie.

"Tell ye whit boss, away and pit the kettle oan please."

Matheson looked at him, surely this wasn't the time for a cup of coffee. He said so.

"Well, a cuppy tea wid dae the trick, noo that ye mention it. But just go and bile the kettle and send Mackenzie back wi' it."

Matheson left, glad to have been deemed surplus to requirements. Mackenzie followed, limping behind, hunched over like a miniature Quasimodo, his hand tucked under his oxter.

Bryson turned to Matheson's son, "Jules, away and get a bucket o' cauld watter. Ah'll need a towel."

On his own now, he turned to Lockerbie. "Remember me?" No answer. "Well, ye will, by and by. In fact, ye'll probably never forget me, for as long as ye live. By the way, ye'll be interested tae ken that Ah'm no gawny hit ye and Ah'm no gawny ask ye nae questions. Ye're simply gawny tell me everything ye think Ah might need tae ken, and even stuff ye dinnae think Ah need tae ken."

"What everything? What am I? An encyclopaedia?"

"Aye, very funny."

"You need to know who you're dealing with here. Do you know who I am!"

Bravado from Lockerbie, silence from Bryson, leaving time for reflection. Lockerbie reflected. His captor was obviously a big bloke.

"Look," said the newly conciliatory Lockerbie. "You've got the wrong person. What is it you want? Money?"

"See, ye're oan the right track a'readies."

Julian returned with a plastic bucket of water and a hand towel from the bathroom. Bryson put his foot in Lockerbie's chest and pushed him gently backwards until he was balanced finely on the back two legs of the chair.

"Time for a wee lie doon," he said softly. Another gentle push.

"Ooooooh!" cried Lockerbie once more and crashed backwards onto the floor. His head smacked the concrete and he seemed to black out for a second or two. He came round gradually, reassembling his compos mentis. He wasn't so much seeing stars as a swarm of fireflies buzzing around inside his head.

"That could easily have killed him," whispered Julian to Bryson: mere prosaic comment.

"Aye," replied Bryson, eyebrows up, acknowledging Julian's matter-of-fact observation with an appreciative, scholarly nod.

He must have been underestimating the lad's potential for violent crime all these years.

While they waited for Lockerbie to recover from the whack to the back of his head, Bryson turned to Julian.

"If ye dinnae want involved Jools, just say, and ye can go and dae yer Facebook updates - and dinnae mention nowt tae ony o' yer ... yer pals, yer ... chums."

Bryson's vocabulary didn't stretch to the in-words for a gay person's circle of friends.

"No, no," said Julian. "I'll, I'll hang around, ehm, Alec. And I prefer Julian, not Jools."

Bryson nodded an apologetic acknowledgement.

Julian was now so deep into crime that he thought he might as well learn the ropes from a master. Besides, he was finding this whole thing a lot more exciting than disposing of stolen cars with Mackenzie, or doing his father's dodgy tax return. Bryson was a monster, but he was the real deal as far as Julian could tell now that things had moved up a level. Besides, his dad was down a colossal sum of money and it was partly Julian's own fault.

"Fair enough, just hing aboot in case ye're needed. This'll no take long. Just keep oot o' his line o' vision when the tape comes aff."

He went back to Lockerbie and ripped the packing tape from across the prisoner's eyes, taking a deal of eyebrow hair with it. Lockerbie squealed and blinked repeatedly while he got used to the dim, fluorescent light in the shed.

Bryson dropped down on his hunkers. "Remember me now?"

Lockerbie stared up at Bryson. "You're the Robb, Steal and Cheat'em guy!"

"Aye, Ah suppose. In a manner o' speakin'," replied Bryson, drawing no inkling from that regarding their conversation at the Sangster house.

"It's a lifestyle choice, robbin' stealin' an' cheatin'. It can be quite exacting work. And there are, well, there are winners and losers. And sometimes, even if there are nae winners, there's still losers."

--------oOo--------

Water

"Ah'm no fear't frae you!" shouted Lockerbie, reverting to his native, working class Edinburgh dialect to match Bryson's. "Let me go or you'll pey fur this. Dae you ken who Ah am?"

"Naw. But by the time Ah'm feenished wi' ye, you'll no ken who ye are either."

Julian passed the towel to Bryson. He'd worked out what was about to happen. The towel went over Lockerbie's face and Bryson stood over the captive with the bucket.

The towel puffed up and down rhythmically as Lockerbie tried to blow it off his face. Julian sniggered at how pathetic it looked. It looked like something on a wildlife program. A puffer fish, maybe.

Lockerbie ran out of puff.

"See, this is quite like gettin' a hot towel efter a shave at the barber's," continued Bryson. "Except it's cauld. Well, it's cauld tae begin wi'. Let me ken if ye like it."

He began to splash water onto the towel from the bucket. Lockerbie screamed, then spluttered. The towel got wetter and wetter. Now he couldn't scream. He tried to breathe in but he couldn't do that either: the wet towel was over his mouth and nose. No air came through it. He tried to breathe in, but only sucked in water. More water, lots more water. Some groaning, gasping, coughing, spluttering. More water, more groaning and writhing. Water was in his mouth, up his nose, in his eyes, running into his ears. He couldn't breathe. He felt as if he was drowning. The feeling of panic, of imminent death was overwhelming.

After a lifetime of only about fifteen seconds, Bryson removed the towel.

Lockerbie breathed in huge lungfuls of air as if he'd just sprinted two hundred yards flat out.

"You bastards! You'll pay for this!" he managed to croak, eventually, and went back to gasping for air.

"Very good!" said Bryson. "Apparently maist folk can only dae ten or fifteen seconds afore they piss their troosers. Ye've no even pissed yersel' yet. Weel done!"

The towel went over Lockerbie's face again. More water, this time for a little longer, little trickles onto the towel, constant wetness, no breathing possible, the feeling of drowning combined with suffocation, combined with claustrophobia. After about twenty seconds, the towel was removed. All Lockerbie could do was breathe as much air as he could get into his lungs. He was given a minute or two to get himself sufficiently ventilated for conversation. It wasn't long enough.

To Bryson's surprise, Julian stepped forward.

"You know, I bet you thought that water boarding didn't sound all that bad when you heard about it on the news. A little water, some cloth, but it's not much fun either," he said, getting down onto his hunkers behind Lockerbie's head, and speaking to him like a patronising school teacher to a recalcitrant child.

Lockerbie croaked but consumed by the need to consume oxygen, he couldn't take the time out to form words.

"Would you like to know how I think this works?" continued Julian. "Yes? No?"

No answer from the hyperventilating Lockerbie.

"Well, I'll tell you anyway. It's quite interesting. You see, there's this thing called the Mammalian Dive Reflex. It turns out that you can hold your breath much longer when you're under water than you can on the surface. Evolution has provided most mammals with this potentially life-saving reflex when immersed in water.

"Well, we've got plenty water here, dribbling onto the towel, so you can't breathe, which, of course, you can't do under water either. But unfortunately, you're not *under* water – at the moment. Not ... yet.

"No, you're lying here on the floor. It means that you get the worst of both worlds: you don't get the underwater benefit of the

Mammalian Dive Reflex. And you have no control. You can't swim to the surface for a gulp of air. But you do get the feeling of drowning, of suffocating. Of dying, potentially. And it's only a towel and a few drops of water! Fascinating stuff, isn't it? Imagine drowning ... Well, I suppose you already have a rough idea how that feels now."

Alec Bryson's eyebrows went up. You learn something new every day. If he'd been asked, he'd have guessed that Mammalian Diving sounded like it might be something Julian and his gay chums were doing to one another. But he beamed with pride at his young apprentice. Who'd have thought that a posh private school would have taught stuff that was useful during interrogation? And the lad seemed to be in his element.

"And you know," continued Julian. "At the moment, you probably can't hold your breath for as long as you could normally, whether underwater or not. Stress, you see. I imagine you're quite excited right now. Your pulse rate is up, your blood pressure is up, your consumption of oxygen, your *need* for oxygen is up. And the corollary to that is that more CO_2 goes into your bloodstream. Your system then detects the need to breathe more urgently. Too much CO_2 in your system makes you gag for breath even more. Not enough breath? Well, it makes you die."

"*Bloody good effort,*" thought Bryson. "*The boy might be gay, but he's a natural nasty bastard.*"

The towel went back onto Lockerbie's face and this time, it was Julian who lifted the bucket. He poured a generous splash onto the towel. Lockerbie gyrated for a bit then went very still and rigid.

"Ah never ken't that, aboot they mammals," said Bryson, coolly, as Lockerbie lay still.

"I was good at Biology," whispered Julian. Then, "I think we've killed him," surprised at himself by how little he cared.

The towel came off and air hissed as it was sucked desperately into Lockerbie's lungs.

"Ah'm all ears," said Bryson, back down on his hunkers.

Lockerbie's chest was hissing in and out like a blacksmith's bellows, rasping with panic.

"What do you want to know?" he gasped after many seconds of continuous gasping.

"Ah did say, Ah wisnae gawny ask nae questions. Plus, Ah'm no gawny answer nae questions neither. Ye're simply gawny be informative, unprompted like."

The towel got wiggled.

Lockerbie's mind was now fully vented of anger and ego, and consumed with fear and despair and a desperate desire for this to stop.

The iron door of the shed opened, and Mackenzie came in with the kettle on a tray with two mugs and a cute little matching milk jug and sugar bowl.

"Ah made the boss a cuppa Alec. He's sittin' in the kitchen worryin' 'is sel' tae fuck." He saw Lockerbie on the floor, soaking wet. "Did he fa' ower again?"

"He felt like a wee lie doon," said Bryson.

Julian smiled. This was better theatre than he ever could have imagined. He wished he could tell his boyfriend Colin all about it. But it wouldn't be fair on a gentle soul like Colin.

They stood around Lockerbie. Mackenzie held the tray while Julian made a big issue of pouring the boiling water into the two mugs, letting Lockerbie see the steam. He handed the kettle back to Mackenzie.

"Two sugars please," said Bryson and accepted a mug of tea from Julian. He lifted the tiny milk jug and raised it in Julian's direction.

"Milk?"

"Naw," said Mackenzie, on Julian's behalf. "He disnae take milk. He's shalactoes intolerate."

"Whit?"

"Lactose intolerant, you illiterate imbecile," said Julian.

"Just shut it, wee man," said Bryson to Mackenzie. "Ye're guid at drivin', leave it at that."

He milked his own tea and put the jug down. He took a few sips. "That's a braw brew, Wee Mac. Add tea tae yer skill set."

Then to Lockerbie, he said, "Right, this is the next level up."

He took a few more sips of his tea, blowing on it theatrically to indicate its temperature. He took a few more sips. After half a minute, he put his mug down.

"Aye. A braw cuppa Wee Mac."

He picked up the kettle and wiggled it over Lockerbie's face.

"There's nothin' Ah like better than a really hot cuppa. Ye'll be the same yersel'. The hotter the better. Noo, where were we?"

Still holding the kettle, he reached for the towel.

"Aaaagh!" screamed Lockerbie, "Please, please! I'll tell you everything."

"And the money?" said Julian. "And the goods?"

Bryson wagged an admonishing finger at Julian. "Nae questions, just let him talk."

Julian took the kettle from Bryson, displayed it flamboyantly around the company like a magician doing a magic trick, making sure that the prisoner's eyes were following its every move. They were: Lockerbie couldn't take his eyes off it. Julian held the towel over Lockerbie's face again.

"Take a deep breath, because your refusal to inform, has landed you in hot water," whispered Julian, as Bryson looked on indulgently. He lowered the towel towards Lockerbie's face.

Lockerbie pissed his pants.

There was a long groan of deep disappointment and shame, as if pissing his pants was the worst thing so far. There seemed to be quite a lot of it as the dark wetness spread across his trousers..

"Fuck sake!" said Mackenzie. "He's pissed 'is troosers. That's pure gross so it is. How many pints is that?"

"Shut it Mac," said Bryson.

Lockerbie croaked, "Anything, anything you want. I just dinnae ken what you want."

"Well, let's see," said Julian. "Our half a million would do it."

"Ok, ok, ok! Half a million."

"Plus expenses. You know, salaries, travel, say, at the HMRC rate of 45p per mile. Plus some compensation, you know, for all the hassle, and the anxiety. Shall we say, fifteen percent? It's all tax deductible you know."

"Good lad!" said Bryson, well impressed with Julian's developing business skills, greed, and criminally creative mind.

"Good lad!" he said again, like a proud parent, his hand on Julian's shoulder. "Ye're good wi' numbers."

"Well I do have a degree in accountancy," said Julian. Then turning to Lockerbie. "Oh, and that'll be in used notes."

"Like the ones you were going to sell me," added Bryson.

"Sell you? Eh? Look, I'll, I'll need time to get it together. Half a million's a lot of money," said the anxious, depressed, but very relieved Lockerbie.

Right now, half a million seemed a small price to pay to stay alive even though, despite himself, his greedy, reptilian brain had done a cost-benefit review of the situation, analyzing the emotional cost-per-minute of hot wet towel against the pain he'd feel if he paid up.

"You're not kidding it's a lot of money," said Julian and he gave Lockerbie a gentle dig in the ribs with his foot.

Bryson wagged a finger at Julian again.

"Nae violence, yer dad disnae like it. The thing is," he said, turning his attention once again to Lockerbie, "hauf a million is just the punch line. Ah want tae hear the stert o' the joke. Get talkin."

Julian gently booted Lockerbie in the ribs once more with the side of his foot. Bryson patted Julian on the shoulder,

"No bad son," he whispered. "But nae violence, yer dad disnae like it. For a gay bloke ye're no bad at bein' a nasty bastard when it's required."

"What makes you think I'm gay?" replied Julian.

The question was rhetorical but Julian gave Bryson a long look. *"Takes one to know one,"* he thought to himself. *"Probably wrong. Bryson's just an animal."*

Julian was as out as out could be everywhere but inside this cute little crime family. As far as he knew, his dad didn't know he was gay - probably. Not that he could give a shit.

His thoughts were rudely interrupted.

"Well, it's no as if ye dinnae *sound* like a bentshot," said the beleaguered, bitter, and belligerently lifelong homophobic Lockerbie, his tone loaded with nasty sarcasm.

He just couldn't help himself. His instinctive psychopathic malice and homophobic prejudices were so embedded that they had momentarily overshot his pants-wetting anxiety.

"Not so much gay," said Julian, "just happy in my work." Then, mimicking Mackenzie, he said, "Ah just dae crime."

Shifting his stance, he booted Lockerbie on the liver. This time the target nearly passed out.

Julian was going way up in Bryson's esteem minute by minute. Any martial arts competitor knows that even a merely half-decent blow to the liver would floor anybody. It sent shock waves through the whole body. Not many people knew that. He was impressed. They must have taught it in biology class at Fettes College along with that mammal-diving stuff.

"That'll dae wee man," he said to Julian, with his hand on his new protégé's shoulder. "We're no interrogatin' naeb'dy here. The gentleman's just gawny tell us a'hing he kens that might be of interest. An' yer dad disnae like physical violence."

"That wasn't part of an interrogation," said Julian. "More of little prod regarding his prejudices."

"I'll get you for that, you wee poof!" croaked Lockerbie as he slowly recovered.

Julian held the towel over Lockerbie's face again.

"Sorry, but I just need to deal with a side issue," he said to Bryson. And then to Lockerbie, "Poof, is such an anachronism, and when used in that pejorative manner, is quite insulting. Try to think of this as therapy. Hypnosis, sort of. Or aversion therapy. With luck we're going to divest you of all of your homophobic attitudes and your whole homophobic lexicon."

He laid the towel gently on Lockerbie's face. Lockerbie lay dead still, holding his breath, waiting for more water.

"Whit the fuck's a lexicon?" said Bryson.

"The boss's wife hud yin," said Mackenzie. "Yon wee sports car."

"That was a Lexus, you dimwit," said Julian.

Lockerbie lay dead still.

"Ye've killed him," said Mackenzie.

"You be quiet!" said Bryson.

The towel came off and Julian waited for Lockerbie to catch his breath. He was plainly at the end of his tether. He couldn't take anymore, even though he'd worked out the routine: towel; water; twenty seconds; towel off. As a checklist, it didn't sound like much but it was absolute torture.

"Well, no water that time," said Julian. "But I can do this all day if you like. It's quite fun."

"Enough, enough! I'll get the money. I'll get the money!"

"We'll get onto the subject of money in a minute, but we're still discussing your attitudes to the LGB community."

"All right, all right, I'm sorry. I've nothing against queers. Sorry! I mean gays, … homo… … people. Ah dinnae ken whit the fuck tae call ye. Whatever Ah say will be wrang! Fuckin' perverts!"

"Pass me that kettle," said Julian, dropping the towel on Lockerbie's face.

He pissed his pants again, emptying his bladder completely.

"Must hae went furra liquid lunch," said Mackenzie. "Yon's at least five pints. An' it's mingin'."

"Asparagus for lunch?" said Julian to Lockerbie.

Bryson shook his head. Julian was an absolute natural at this. But then, his father was a lawyer, so being a nasty bastard when it was required was probably in the genes. He lifted the towel.

"Say you're sorry to my colleague. Properly."

The congenitally unapologetic Lockerbie apologised. It was surprising, especially to him, just how apologetic he could be, and he found all sorts of new ways of expressing sorrow, an emotion that was hitherto completely alien to him.

Julian got down on his hunkers again.

"That's nice," he said. He wrung out the towel and wiped Lockerbie's face gently. "Right. Back to the money."

"Yes, yes," said Lockerbie, enthusiastically. "The money. But no more towel, please."

"Ok, no more towel," said Bryson. "If ye're a good boy."

From behind, he lifted the squealing Lockerbie by both of his flabby cheeks and sat the chair upright again. Lockerbie looked down at himself.

"I've pissed my pants," he said, his tone miserably matter of fact.

"Aye, so ye huv. Always go tae the toilet afore ye act the wise guy," said Bryson. "In case it disnae work oot how ye planned."

He turned to Julian, "He must hae been for a dump afore he came oot. Apparently, they quite often shite theirsels ana'. As far as Ah can make oot."

"How did you learn so much about waterboarding?" asked Julian.

"BBC documentary aboot US troops in Iraq. Ah thought, that'll come in handy wan day. Ah'd raither beat the shite oot the theivin' bastard but yer dad disnae like it when Ah dae that."

Julian beckoned Bryson and they walked out of Lockerbie's earshot.

"I've been thinking," he whispered. "Instead of notes, why don't we get him to pay us in crypto?"

"Crypto?"

Bryson had heard of it, but he wasn't up to speed on modern money trading, let alone anything digital. He was a cash-only person. Other people's cash as often as not. He'd even paid cash for his low-mileage S-Class Mercedes. Thirty-seven thousand pounds in used notes. The car dealer had refused to take such a large sum in cash, in case he attracted attention for money laundering. Eventually, he took it and counted it, which was hard to do with two dislocated fingers.

Julian briefly explained to Bryson how digital currency worked.

"Sounds well dodgy," said Bryson. "Ye cannae beat auld-fashioned cash."

"Well, indeed. But on reflection, it's easier to squirrel away reasonably large sums of money in crypto. And the value can increase as it becomes more of an in-demand thing."

"Why the fuck did we no dae that in the first place?" whispered Mackenzie, who had crept up beside the two. "Ye ken? Pey the man fur the goods in yon cryptle tokens?"

"Because the deal was a swap: money for goods. You can't carry crypto around in a briefcase, now can you?" said Julian.

"How no?" said Mackenzie.

"Shut it!" said Bryson. But, to be fair it didn't seem like an unreasonable question.

Julian went back to Lockerbie, bent and whispered in his ear.

"Do you have a Bitcoin account?"

Lockerbie's non-too flexible negotiating skills were at the end of their stretch and his normal narcissistic social skills were at an all-time low. He was in no mood to argue for fear of more towel.

"Aye. Aye, of course. Of course Ah dae." The angry tone carried only a hint of his natural sarcasm.

"Good. And do you have enough of your ill-gotten gains squirrelled away in Bitcoin to repay this particular debt of yours?"

"Aye. Naw. Well, maybes no enough in Bitcoin. But Ah've got Etherium ana'."

"And you buy and sell through …?"

"Coinbase."

"And do you have your passwords etc in your head?"

"Aye."

"Good. We'll get you a laptop."

--------oOo--------

Payback

Julian sat beside Lockerbie and opened up his digital currency trading account with Lockerbie dictating his log-in.

"Goodness me," said Julian. "You do have a lot of money squirrelled away in here. Nearly four hundred thousand in Bitcoin and, let me see. … Goodness! Seven hundred-odd thousand in Etherium. Plus some other cash in various other accounts."

"Whit!?" exclaimed Lockerbie. "There should be a bloody sight more than that! There wis nearly two million at one point!"

"Seems to have taken quite a hit recently," said Julian. "But if you play the money markets, you know, it goes up and it goes down." He continued, "So you bought, let me see, over the course of this year, about a million in total between Bitcoin and Etherium."

Bryson stepped in. "Ah'll brek mah promise aboot no askin' questions. See here - we're a' criminals here, bad people, right? But that kind-o' makes us brothers in arms, so tae speak. So where did the first million come frae? Just oot o' professional interest, wan crook tae anither."

He casually wiggled the towel to encourage a straightforward reply.

"Just business, just business," said the pitifully stressed Lockerbie, staring at the hated towel.

"Not specific enough," said Julian. "Your day-to-day, legitimate trading will go through your company accounts and banking is done in the normal way and you declare all, or most of your profit on your annual accounts. Of course, you can trade in digital currency perfectly legally. But you look like a very shifty bastard to me, so my guess would be that you're hiding money. Some here, some there, some in digital. Where are you getting this money?"

The towel made a brief fly past like the angel of doom.

"Property!" He almost shouted it. "Ah've a property portfolio - renting oot a few flats and hooses. Hooses in Niddrie, Pilton, ken, places like that."

"And the rent gets peyed weekly - in cash, Ah wid think?" asked Bryson. "A big guy wi' a notebook and a pick-axe hawnle up his jook goes roond and scares the shite oot o' the tenant."

Lockerbie was past lying now.

"No quite like that, but ye have tae be firm wi' these kind of folk. They're idiots when it comes tae managing money, so ye need tae keep on top of them. Cash is preferred, but we insist on on-line access to their bank accounts."

"From which you deduct their rent and any maintenance work and additional upkeep costs? And it's amazing how much those maintenance costs can mount? Especially when these apparently feckless tenants of yours can be very careless." asked Julian.

"Kind-of," said Lockerbie. "but that's just small change."

"If there's wan thing that Ah cannae stand, it's scum like you that prey oan poor folk," said Bryson, putting his hands on Lockerbie's shoulders and leaning him back a little - towards the hated towel-and-bucket position.

"Scuse me a minute," said Mackenzie, stepping into the conversation again. He planted a reasonable good-quality jab right on the end of Lockerbie's nose. It was good shot from such an insignificant wee squirt with a hitherto poor record on successful punching.

"Aaow!" cried Mackenzie and Lockerbie in unison. Lockerbie shook his head and Mackenzie shook his already bruised hand.

"Whit the fuck wis that fur?" chorused Lockerbie and Bryson.

"Ah think mah nan's wan o' his tenants," replied Mackenzie. "Her flat is that damp, even the mould's got asthma."

"Fair enough wee man," said Bryson. "Why don't ye go and boil that kettle again. In case onybody wants a cuppa. Or their face melted. And run that haund under the cauld tap fur a bit afore it swells up."

"Naw, naw! Nae mair towel" cried Lockerbie, tasting the tiny trickle of blood now dribbling from his nose onto his moustache, and desperate to avoid more wet towel treatment, especially boiling-hot wet towel treatment.

"My bloody nose is bleeding!" he said.

"Dinnae you worry aboot a wee nosebleed. Yon blood'll wash aff at the next wet towel interlude," said Bryson helpfully.

"Look, Ah'm trying tae be straight with you."

"Ok," said Julian. "You can be straight with me. And I'll be gay with you."

Lockerbie nodded, choking back the impulse to make another homophobic remark.

"Good," continued Julian. "I can see we're going to get on swimmingly from now on. Now, I don't suppose you let the inland revenue scrutinise this activity. Or Edinburgh City Council, you know, the what's-it-called? The council's Letting Agency," asked Julian.

Bryson looked on indulgently. The boy was a natural.

"Just enough to keep them off our backs. They're quite relaxed."

"And ye hae some guy in the cooncil oan the payroll tae keep them relaxed, Ah wid think," asked Bryson.

"A woman, actually."

"Nice little business model," said Julian, appreciatively. "Anything else?"

Bryson was rocking Lockerbie backwards and forward on the back legs of the chair, to keep him focussed.

"Ah've a building renovations business."

"And your lady friend in the council handles the tenders for mandatory upkeep of tenements and so on?" asked Julian.

"It's a different department. But, they a' need foreign holidays."

"And I expect your buildings renovations company always turns out to be the most competitive?" asked Julian.

A resigned, "Aye," was all they got from Lockerbie.

Julian looked up at Bryson. "Do we have anybody in the council?"

"Aye. We've got a couple or three contacts. Different levels, different departments. But naeb'dy' in properties or the like."

"Nevertheless, continued Julian, "I would think it would be no skin off their noses if this gentleman's Rachmanite landlord practices and extortionist property business, *and* his accomplices came to the attention of say, the Council Chairperson, or the Lord Provost. Or perhaps, the Organised Crime department at Lothian and Borders Police Headquarters."

"Ah think they'd be delighted tae shop wan o' their ain," said Bryson. "They're public employees. They're a' bastards. They'd get a promotion. Better pay."

"Better working conditions, their own office, a better final-salary pension," added Julian. "Or an MBE for services to the community. And simply for humbly doing their civic duty and helping to jail a parasitic piece of human trash like our guest here, along with his people within the council."

"Aw for Christ's sake!" exclaimed Lockerbie. "Yooz are no exactly pillars of the community. Fucking cheap wee drug dealers, that's aw ye's are."

The towel was wiggled again.

"We like to think of it merely as a retail operation," said Julian. "You know, money for goods. Supply and demand, fulfilling a need, that's all. Anyway, let's get our money repaid. Then you're going to write down the names and telephone numbers of everybody involved in your grubby little property business."

"How is it your money?" asked Lockerbie, still completely bamboozled by the whole thing. "It's my bloody hard-earned money!"

"Listen pal, if ye sneak intae anither syndicate's dealings and grab the money and the goods and piss off wi' it, it disnae make it yours."

Lockerbie was none the wiser about that, but he was fully boned-up on wet towel treatment. Julian went back to the laptop.

"Now, there's quite a lot to move so I'll do it in half a dozen transactions to four of my dad's and my own crypto accounts."

"Ye're no gawny take it a' are ye?"

Lockerbie started to weep gently and quietly. Then he got angry.

"Ah've worked mah arse aff for that money! Ah grew up in a single-parent coonsil hoose, ye ken."

"I do not care if your council house only had one parent," said Julian. "Back to this money."

"That's mah money!"

"Not counting the money you stole from us," replied Julian.

"Ah've nae idea whit the fuck you're talkin' aboot, ya wee poo … person."

"Well, I think we're owed it, don't you? And the change, well, it could be redistributed amongst poor people. Like your tenants," said Julian. "Mackenzie's nan, for instance."

"Aw aye!? A gay Robin Hood are ye?" said Lockerbie, the leopard spots of his nasty personality resistant to change.

"Oh dear," said Julian. "And I thought we'd reached some kind of accommodation on your homophobia." Then to Bryson, "Back down on the floor please."

"Naw! Naw! Ah'm sorry, Ah'm sorry. Ah didnae mean it. Ah'm sorry! Just habit."

"Not a nice habit," said Julian.

But to Lockerbie's immense relief, the chair went back down on all fours.

"Just keep him there while I move the money," said Julian to Bryson. "I can continue his homophobia therapy if he shows signs of regressing, or an unwillingness to cooperate."

Ten minutes later, Julian had moved, by various methods, seven hundred thousand in digital currency from Lockerbie's accounts to his own and his father's accounts.

"In lieu of the massive homophobia-deficit you've accrued on your account, I've assumed that you'd like to trade that for two hundred thousand over and above the half million in order to offset any further homophobia-corrective experiences with a towel, cold or hot?," said Julian.

Lockerbie groaned, and wept a little more. "Aye. No more towel."

"No more homophobia towel," continued Julian. "However, now that we've dealt with one of your character issues, on the business front, in exchange for skipping another soaking altogether, both now and henceforth, would you like to give me the names if everybody at Edinburgh City Council with whom you have been conducting your grubby, fraudulent little property business. Plus the names of anybody else that might be involved. You see, we are just honest street traders. We buy and sell pharmaceuticals on an honest wholesale and retail basis. Our customer base is the young, free and single yuppies of Edinburgh. We just help them dispose of their disposable income. And outside of that, none of us likes people who prey on the poor and less well off."

Bryson looked on proudly. He'd never in his life constructed a paragraph that long.

"That's a load of guff. Ye deal drugs. That just makes ye a scumbag drug dealer!"

"Perhaps. But I also like to think of it as being in the leisure industry. Consumption of recreational drugs is a leisurely pastime."

"Aye," said Mackenzie. "He should ken. Him and 'is mates is a' stoned tae buggery hauf the time."

"Shut up Mackenzie," said Bryson. "Away an' heat up the kettle."

"Ah might have known!" said Lockerbie to Julian. "Ye're nothin' but a cheap stoner."

"Well, it's better than being a social parasite," replied Julian.

"Dinnae gie me that moral high ground shite!" said Lockerbie. "Ye's are nae better than me. Cheap drug dealers is a' ye are."

"Be that as it may," said Julian. "But at the moment, we have the upper hand. Anyway, after we get the names of your insiders at the council, we can let you go. And if *you* don't say anything, then neither will we, and we can call it quits – no hard feelings. I'll get a notepad."

Tears of pain, frustration and loss were trickling down Lockerbie's bruised and flabby cheeks. His eyes were glued to the dreaded wet towel as he dictated every molecule of information on his property scam and his council contacts to Julian.

"Thank you," said Julian. "But I'll just need to check out the veracity of all of that."

He took his phone out of his pocket, dialed Edinburgh City Council and after a substantial wait listening to elevator music, asked to be put through to the Properties Department.

Satisfied that at least one of the names that Lockerbie had given was real, Julian said, "Well, that seems to check out. Well done! Now, we need to get you home. We'll drop you off in Pilton or somewhere like that - where your tenants live."

"Aye. Ye'll no look out of place there. There's aye somebody gawn aboot wi' pissed pants an' a black eye in Pilton," said Bryson.

"Aye. Mah grampa for wan," said Mackenzie.

Lockerbie continued to shed tears. This time, as well as tears of pain, frustration and loss, he wept tears of relief.

Bryson turned to Mackenzie, "Away an' make our guest a cuppy tea. Julian, away and tell yer dad that we're nearly done in here. He's got his money back, in spades. Just ask him tae keep tae the fermhoose. Ah'll gie him a shout when we need him."

Mackenzie lifted the kettle and the mugs. "Sugar and milk?" he said, heading for the door.

"Aye. Please. Just one sugar please. And no too much milk," replied Lockerbie, the surreal normality of accepting a cup of tea, and detailing his preferences under these circumstances leaving everybody, including himself, in silence for a few seconds.

Julian left for the farmhouse, behind Mackenzie.

"We've got our money back Dad!" he said to his father. He gave a brief synopsis of what had transpired: how Lockerbie, having had his face washed several times, had happily given the money back and how he was now rather beholden to them on account of confessing his property scams. Julian went back to the shed.

Matheson punched the air, then flopped back into his chair and breathed a long sigh of relief. It took a few minutes to calm down. Had he been a party to a violent interrogation? His son especially. It was a horrible thought. But then, that bastard had robbed him. And after all, water boarding didn't really sound all that bad, on the face of it: just water, on the face. Nope, the end justified the means. Feeling well-disposed to his crew, he decided to make them something to eat.

--------oOo--------

The Stick-up

The Ford rolled past the end of the farm road while its occupants stared up it listening to the satnav lady confirming arrival.

"Is this it?" said Rab Beattie to Nisbet.

"I have no idea," said Nisbet. "Never been here in my life."

"You are so gettin' on my tits, pal. We've got ye bang tae rights in possession o' the goods. Is this it or is it no?"

The cold steel muzzle of the Desert Eagle was pressed against the recently unbandaged, shaven stubble at the back of Nisbet's head.

"Well, since you don't believe me, I suppose you might as well believe your satnav," replied Nisbet, his tone resigned.

He was almost past the point of giving a tuppenny shite about anything. He'd been run down by his own car, beaten up by the cops for the crime of getting run down. Now he'd been kidnapped, and he had lost his new girlfriend only minutes after thinking he'd pulled it off with the most gorgeous woman he'd ever met. But the more he thought about it, the angrier he got inside. He didn't feel any pain anymore, just the constant tingle of adrenaline. He'd already eyed the two of them up. They looked hard, but they weren't all that big. He looked at the driver and eyed him over again. Skinny knees, no big muscle in his thighs. Was the rest of him in the same shape? He looked at the coat. It didn't look all that well filled. Well, not rugby well-filled. Fat-filled, maybe. Was his brother in the same, at best, fair-to-middling physical order?

He turned round to look at Deirdre and only got a fearful, tearful, hateful and steely look in reply.

"Dinnae try onything pal," said Rab Beattie, from the back seat, the half-inch bore of the barrel pointing upwards from his lap.

Nisbet looked down at it. Now it looked like he was peering down a mine shaft instead of a tunnel. He didn't know anything about guns, or calibers, but it certainly didn't look like a slug gun. He looked away. It was creepier than that weird face in the hospital ceiling tile.

Andy Beattie spun the car around at the next road junction and drove back towards the farm. He let the car creep quietly up the farm drive on tick-over. They got within a few yards of the house and farm buildings and stopped.

There was no movement. Then a small man carrying a tray appeared, apparently from the back door of the farmhouse, and disappeared into a Judas door in a big, corrugated iron shed on the other side of the yard.

"There were at least three mugs on that tray, forbye the kettle. So, includin' yon wee guy wi' the tray, there's at least three in that shed," said Andy Beattie. Pulling his Sig Sauer from his belt, he looked at Nisbet.

"Right! Time tae go," he said, wafting the gun up at Nisbet's face.

Nisbet looked down the barrel of the Sig Sauer. It didn't look quite as big a mine shaft as the other gun, but that was no comfort whatsoever.

"Get oot the car," said Andy. "And ye can introduce us tae yer colleagues."

Nisbet and Deirdre climbed out on opposite sides of the car and were manhandled to the front, each with a gun in the small of their back.

"Right, gently does it," said Rab Beattie. "Try onything, and Ah blaw yer brains across the yaird."

"I'm not sure you've thought this through boys," said Nisbet. "I mean, there could be a dozen guys in there, all armed. Maybe only three of them drink tea or coffee. Are you sure the money's worth the risk? No hard feelings, but you've got the diamonds, why not quit while you're ahead?"

This new confession from Nisbet that the package actually did contain diamonds and the shed could be full of his gang was further confirmation for Deirdre, if she needed any, that Nisbet was some kind of gangster, involved in dealing illicit diamonds for drugs, or something. She'd never heard of that sort of trade, but then, she wasn't a professional criminal. Maybe it was payment for drugs.

"Aye, ye'd like that," said Andy Beattie. "Then you and yer wee Taig floozy can shout tae yer pals."

Deirdre was frightened stiff, but she was equally angry. First chance she got, if she got any chance at all, this Glaswegian hoodlum was getting it in his reproductive equipment again.

"I can assure you," said Nisbet. "Whoever is in that shed is no friend of mine. I don't think I've been in Fife more than twice in my whole life."

"Listen pal, you are so full of shite, Ah'd blaw yer brains oot just for a laugh, but we need tae be quiet." said Rab. "Right. Softly, softly, head for the shed door."

Outside, the corrugated iron of the shed did little to deaden the sound of chatter inside.

"It sounds like there's only a handful, four at the most," whispered Andy Beattie.

He reached round Deirdre and turned the handle on the corrugated iron door. It opened outwards, the iron hinges squealing a little. The chatter inside stopped as the door opened and four faces inside turned in surprise.

Into the shed stepped a pretty young woman in a bomber jacket and jeans, firmly held round the throat by a man with a hand gun pressed against her neck.

"Naeb'dy move!" said Andy Beattie, his eyes wide, straining to get used to the dim light inside the shed. "Naeb'dy move, or Ah blaw the burd's brains oot."

The hammer went back on the Sig Sauer.

Bryson, surprised though he was, was enough of a hard bastard not to be anything like as startled as Julian or Mackenzie, both of whom stood rooted to the spot. Lockerbie's bamboozled brain, the ony part of him that was free to move, did some more whirling.

"Blaw her brains oot if ye like pal," said Bryson coolly. "She's a stranger tae me. Who the fuck are you onywey. And whit dae ye want?"

Rab Beattie slammed the door closed behind him and the metal on metal clang rattled around the corrugated iron shed like a gunshot. Everybody, except Bryson, jumped with fright. Andy Beattie instinctively looked at his Sig Saure, as if to confirm that it hadn't gone off half-cocked like his brother said it might. He stuck it back behind Deirdre's ear.

With the open door's shaft of daylight now extinguished, they were left in the dim fluorescent light of the shed. As Deirdre and Nisbet's eyes got used to the dim light, they saw, just behind and to the side of Bryson, a man taped to a chair. He had a little blood trickling from his nose.

"Nisbet!" cried the man in the chair. "Is that you Nisbet?"

Nisbet stared in astonishment to see his soon-to-be ex-father-in-law, taped to a chair. He was almost unrecognizable with a trickle of blood coming from his nose, two faintly blackened eyes from Mackenzie's fist and very florid cheeks. What the bloody hell was going on? It just got weirder and weirder.

Deirdre's gaze darted between Nisbet and the taped-up guy in the chair. More definitive proof, if any was needed, that Nisbet Sangster was involved in organised crime. The guy in the chair was obviously one of his associates. Nisbet was guilty as charged, a career criminal.

"Aw aye," said Rab Beattie, into Nisbet's ear while screwing the Desert Eagle into the back of his neck. "Dinnae ken naeb'dy in the shed? Lyin' bastard. Right you lot! Everybody! Doon! Doon on the flair, cross-legged. The now!"

He waved the enormous handgun in their direction. Julian and Mackenzie dropped vertically to the floor and sat cross-legged like primary school infants at story time.

"Haunds ahint yer heid!"

Bryson remained standing, and said, "Listen wee man. Ah dinnae get doon on the flair for naeb'dy."

"Get ... doon ... oan ... the flair ... pronto!" shouted Andy Beattie, his arm tightening round Deirdre's throat and moving the gun to point directly at Bryson's face. "Oan the flair, or the wee Taig gets it."

""Well, if the lassie's gawny get it, dae ye no need tae point the gun at her?" said Bryson, voice loaded with sarcasm rather than fear. "Forbye that, let's just say that Ah'm no in a position tae get doon oan the flair," said Bryson. "Let's just say Ah'm just physically and emotionally too rigid tae bend. It goes against mah nature. And you look like quite a hard wee bastard yersel'. So Ah'm thinkin', you widnae dae it neither. An' ye're no gawny shoot the lassie, because ye hae tae keep yer wee pop gun pointit at me."

As he spoke, he slowly turned slightly sideways and brought his hands up level with his hips, ever-so-slightly flexing his knees, his weight on the balls of his feet. To Deirdre, it looked like a martial arts stance. Was he going to try and kick the gun out of Andy Beattie's hand. He was a big man, and he looked well fit enough for it. But he was eight feet away, too far from the gun to risk anything.

"You're no gawny shoot me either," continued Bryson. "Because Ah'm the only person here that can help ye wi' what ye want. So let's talk. Let's start wi' a few polite introductions. Mah name's Alec Bryson. Ah run this show. Who the fuck are you, and whit are ye efter?"

Julian was looking up at Bryson with stupefied admiration, wishing he could be that cool under any duress, let alone with a gun in his face. He wasn't very brave. Just doing his father's tax return gave him the willies.

Mackenzie was bug eyed, his gaze darting around between the two hoodlums and their guns, about to crap himself. Earlier on, he'd felt quite well-hard, getting a punch in on Lockerbie's conk. For the moment, he didn't feel hard. He merely felt like he was about to suffer the laxative effects of a handgun-induced, near-death experience. He clenched his buttocks.

Lockerbie was completely bamboozled, but he wasn't going to crap himself. Pissing his pants was enough for one day. He'd been assaulted, kidnapped, water-boarded, assaulted some more; he'd pissed himself, had three-quarters of a million quid stolen from him, was about to lose his highly lucrative, pan-Edinburgh property scam and now his hated son-in-law had turned up, apparently held prisoner by two hoodlums with guns. It was all too weird to take in.

"Get doon oan the flair!" shouted the angry but unnerved Andy Beattie, the Sig Sauer still pointed at Bryson, now with his arm fully extended and his knuckles whitening round the gun's grip. He'd never encountered this kind of sangfroid when he was trying to scare the shite out of people. He was good at scaring the shite out of people. It was his main job description, and he took pride in his work.

"No," said Bryson, calmly and firmly.

Four long seconds of eye contact while he waited for Andy Beattie's response. No response.

"Well?" said Bryson. He waited a second or two.

"If ye shoot me," he continued, "ye get fuck all. And then ye'd need tae shoot everybody and ye'll get bugger all except a lifetime on the run. Or giein' obligatory blow jobs tae some big sweaty Iraqi terrorist in the bad bastard's wing in Barlinnie."

Andy Beattie shuddered. He'd already had that experience in Perth prison.

None of Bryson's admiring spectators liked the sound of anybody getting shot, but Bryson seemed to be as ease with the possibility. He continued.

"So let's talk. Ah take it ye're frae the ither side. The side that got scammed same as us? So this'll be the man ye're efter here," he said, casually indicating Lockerbie with a flick of his thumb.

"He's probably got the diamonds an'a', noo that Ah come tae think on it."

"We've got the diamonds a'readies. Aff his sidekick here," said Rab, tapping Nisbet's head with the barrel of the Desert Eagle, then sticking it back behind his ear. "Ye can see they ken each ither."

"Well, in that case, we're quits," said Bryson. "Ye've got yer diamonds back, and we've got wur money back. So why dae the two o' ye no just content yersels wi' whit ye've got, fuck off and Ah'll no hae tae beat the shite oot o' ye's baith."

Scared shitless, Julian nevertheless continued to look up at Bryson in almost besotted admiration. What a guy! What a monster! What a hero! Indeed, what a hunk. Hitherto, he'd only thought of Bryson as an illiterate thug. Now he seemed like some kind of Odyssean hero.

Mackenzie sat trembling, desperately trying to clench his terror-stricken buttocks. He didn't want to shite his pants. It was amazing how difficult it was to clench buttocks tightly when sitting cross-legged. He rocked from side to side, trying to get his buttocks better clenched.

"Sit still wee man," said Bryson, softly. "Ye'll be fine. Ah'll deal wi' this."

He spoke to Andy Beattie, eyebrows raised, expecting an answer. "Well?"

"Well, Ah think we'll just take the money as well. Tae cover wur expenses," said Andy Beattie. And we'll take the wee Taig hoor here as security."

His hand went down to her breast, the intention behind that move plain for all to see. The move disgusted Bryson. He might be a thug, but ...

The move disgusted Deirdre too, to say the least.

"Get your fookin' hands off me you dirty bastard!" she said, grabbed his wrist and pulled his hand away. He wrenched it free and it went back around her throat.

The gun went back in the back of her neck, "Shut yer Fenian trap, ya wee Taig hoor."

But she kept her hands on his forearm, downward pressure,

keeping it busy resisting her, trying to keep it around her neck.

Seeing Beattie distracted momentarily by the girl, Bryson sidestepped forward, getting within range, just as the click of a door handle and the squeak of iron hinges, blasted cool daylight into the shed.

"Would anybody like a bite to eat?" said Matheson, cheerfully as he stepped in with a tray of sandwiches.

Every face in the place turned to stare at him. He gaped in astonishment at the two guns, the massive Desert Eagle now pointed at him, and the Sig Saure going nervously between Bryson's face, Matheson's torso and Deirdre's ear.

"Mister Matheson?!" cried an astonished Rab Beattie. "Mister Matheson? Whit the fuck?"

"You know each other?" Julian said, in disbelief, and on behalf of everybody else.

-------oOo--------

Deirdre

Time stood still just long enough for Deirdre. For the last few minutes, she had been running in her mind, the moves she'd been perfecting at her kick boxing classes: self defence - what to do if accosted or held by a man. Adrenalin suddenly seemed to be giving her enormous power, concentration and fine motor control.

Andy Beattie was caught completely off guard by Matheson's appearance. Deirdre looked at the open door out the corner of her eye. She was going to run for it. She applied more downward pressure on Beattie's arm, pulling it downward while he resisted. She let go. Beattie's arm flicked upwards and she ducked out from under his loosened grasp. She turned and aimed a kick at the gun in his hand. The gun spun in the air and landed on the concrete floor, barrel up. It went off. The colossal bang rattled round the corrugated iron shed, knocking dust from the steel roof joists. Everybody, except Bryson, jumped in fright, then froze on the spot, momentarily deafened. But Bryson was already on the move, his leg swinging towards Beattie's head as the bullet bounced off a steel joist on the shed roof, ricocheted off the wall and almost spent, hit Bryson on the kneecap. He went down on the floor, clutching at his leg. He barely made more than a grunt.

The gun was on the floor between Beattie and Bryson. Beattie made a lunge for it but Bryson had the nous to kick the Sig Saure four yards away with his good leg.

Deirdre had been going to run for it, but like everybody else, the colossal bang of gunshot had almost shocked her out of her trainers. She gathered herself, on her marks for a dash for freedom and glanced at Andy Beattie. With her reflexes on an adrenaline high, he seemed only to be moving in slow motion, shocked at the sudden turn of events, watching the weapon skitter across the floor. Instead, he lunged at Deirdre, thinking she was going for the gun. She side-stepped him with ease. She was all fired up now, and well, she owed this gangster creep a good one. He turned, making for the gun now.

Running on pure adrenaline, eight-stone Staff Nurse Deirdre McMartin spun around, her foot arcing upwards through 180 degrees, doing what Bryson had been going to do. A perfect spinning hook kick caught the bastard hard on the underside of his jaw with her heel. His head rotated, but his brain didn't follow fast enough. He blacked out for a second, swayed, staggered past her towards the wounded and floored Bryson and fell onto his hands and knees.

"Nice move sweetheart!" commented Bryson through the excruciating pain in his knee.

He tried to get up on his good leg, but fell to the side. Andy Beattie was struggling to get up too, but was obviously badly stunned.

"He's gettin' up, doll!"

Deirdre hesitated, standing behind the groggy, kneeling Andy Beattie. Nobody else could move, frozen, held, or taped to the spot like astonished mannequins.

"Rear naked choke!" suggested Bryson calmly. "It'll quieten him doon."

Somebody who could pull off a kick like that when she was probably shiting herself was bound to know what that was.

Deirdre had only ever seen MMA fighters do it video. But she jumped astride Andy Beattie's back, wrapped her right arm around his neck, hooked her other arm under her wrist and hauled on her arm with all her strength. Now she knew how Khabib felt when he gave it to that Dublin prick McGregor. After five dazed and struggling seconds, Beattie started to drift off to sleep. She held it for a count of five more seconds. She was a nurse, she didn't want to kill him, just put him to sleep. No, on reflection, she kind-of did want to kill the dirty, violent, sexually predatory, sectarianist, criminal piece of shite. So she gave the choke hold another second or two. He collapsed forward, completely unconscious, his forehead hitting the concrete floor with a smack.

"Ah ken how that feels," said Lockerbie.

"Hing on tae him pet," said Bryson. "He'll wake up in a few seconds."

The moment Deirdre kicked Andy Beattie's gun out of his hand, his brother swung the Desert Eagle in her direction. But she was too close to his brother to risk a shot. If he hit her now, the massive bullet would sail straight through her into his brother.

"Oh shit!" said Nisbet. He needed to do something.

He elbowed the distracted Rab Beattie hard in the face, snapping his head back, grabbed his wrist with his right hand, then the gun with his left.

Even stunned, Rab Beattie was stronger than he looked, but the bruised and convalescent Nisbet was not going to let go of that gun. They struggled, kneeing at each other, both hands occupied in the fight for the massive hand gun. It waved around in Tom Lockerbie's direction.

"Aw Jesus Bloody Christ!" exclaimed the distinctly unlucky, self-pitying and now extremely paranoid Lockerbie, flinching every time the gun's muzzle passed him in the frantic, grunting struggle.

The Desert Eagle pointed directly at Lockerbie for a second or so. That was a little intimidating, the black hole of the barrel reminiscent of the black hole that had recently appeared in his crypto account. To his relief, the muzzle went past him. It hovered for a bit, in his hated son-in-law's grasp, pointing now at the door. For once, he wished his son-in-law all the success in the world. The struggle took the Desert Eagle's muzzle past him the other way. Then it went back in line with his face. It went up. It went down. It went off.

Inside the corrugated iron shed, the report from the massive half-inch calibre Desert Eagle, was double that of the Sig Sauer, and deafened everybody.

The half-inch diameter bullet hit the concrete floor a few feet from Lockerbie. It ricocheted off the floor, went past his legs and amputated the bottom half of the back leg of his chair. He wobbled for a split second, ears ringing.

"Aw Jesus Bloody Christ!" he exclaimed again. "No again!"

He tipped back in a north-westerly direction and smacked his head on the floor once more.

"Ah give in! Ah totally fuckin' give in!" he shouted.

Nisbet was getting the better of the out-of-condition gangster, bending his wrist back to prize the gun from his grasp. As Beattie's finger slid off the trigger, he pressed it and the huge handgun went off again, putting every already deafened eardrum in the place, totally out of action for several seconds. A tiny shaft of daylight entered the shed through a half-inch hole in the corrugated iron roof.

They were still grappling furiously, but the adrenaline-saturated, counter-rucking rugby player in Nisbet was getting the upper hand. He did to Beattie what he'd had done to himself (playfully) on the rugby park a few times, only he did it with as much venom as he could muster. Letting go of the hoodlum's wrist, he swung his elbow back, connecting with Beattie's cheek so hard that his head cracked to the side. Nisbet's arm followed through behind him. The Glaswegian hoodlum glazed over for a split second and Nisbet's fist came back from way behind him with a full-on haymaker to the side of the jaw. Rab Beattie went down, and Nisbet staggered back, holding the Desert Eagle loosely in his left hand, shaking his right. As he, and even Mackenzie now knew, hitting solid bone with your knuckles, hurts like hell.

"I'll take that shooter big man," said Bryson, at last standing on one foot. "Good effort, by the way."

"Can I get up now?" said Lockerbie. "Can somebody help me up?"

Mackenzie was on his feet, well-hardness returning like a caffeine hit.

"Shut yer gub!" he said to Lockerbie. "Or ye get mair ... bucket!"

Well used to regular infusions of fear in his diminutive, picked-on little life, he was feeling almost ecstatically well-hard. He was on the winning side, having just watched two Weegie thugs being knocked out, one of them by a girl about the same size as himself. And he'd seen Bryson take a bullet in the kneecap and deal with it as if it was no worse than a skint knee.

Nisbet looked at the gun for a moment, hooked his index finger through the trigger guard and obediently passed it upside down to Bryson. He went over to Deirdre.

"Get away from me!" she said.

It was said with such malevolence that he backed off in case he got the Muay Thai treatment. But it hurt just as much as a kick in the head. Or the goolies.

"Will somebody please tell me what is going on?" said the horror-stricken and perplexed Matheson.

"Aye. Me too," mumbled Lockerbie.

Deafened, and terrified at the first gunshot, Matheson had dropped the tray of sandwiches flat on the floor. Now he was down on his hunkers, absent-mindedly tidying up the triangular escapees, and arranging them neatly back on the ashet.

"Not now Boss," said Bryson. "Julian! Wee Mac! Get the packing tape and disable they twa eejits. Somebody get me a seat for Christ's sake."

"Ye can have mine!" shouted Lockerbie.

Bryson lowered himself to the floor again, tore the blood-soaked fabric of his Boss slacks open and inspected his kneecap. He pointed the gun at Nisbet.

"Dinnae think aboot leggin' it big man. Ah need a word wi' ye."

Deirdre was still holding onto Andy Beattie's neck. She could feel him beginning to wake up. And if he did, she would put him back to sleep.

"I'll deal with him miss. If you can hold him for a few seconds more," said a posh Edinburgh accent beside her.

It was Julian, brandishing Lockerbie's very own Castlerock Systems-branded tape dispenser.

"Sir," he said to Nisbet, "that one's getting up. Can you deal with him please?"

Nisbet turned to find Rab Beattie on his hands and knees, dazed, but trying to get to his feet. He was about to boot him in the side of the head, when Mackenzie nudged past him and did it for him. Beattie fell to the side, out for the count.

"Oh ya bastard!" shouted Mackenzie, and he bounced around on one foot, clutching his other foot, pre-bruised from an earlier encounter with Lockerbie's chair. But he still felt joyfully well hard.

"No bad, wee man!" said a surprised Bryson, always a connoisseur of a well-placed stupor-inducing blow to the head - somebody else's head.

Mackenzie hopped around on one foot like an elated one-legged wallaby. Never was a compliment so well received.

With Julian taping up Andy Beattie's ankles and wrists, Nisbet, with adrenaline still anaethsetising his bruised body, dragged the gangster's brother over and he and Julian sat them back to back like comatose bookends. Deirdre went over to Bryson.

"Sit still. Let me have a look at that."

"Dinnae bother pet, Ah'll be fine," said Bryson. "Ah'll get it seen tae professionally."

She gave him a steely look in the eye. "I'm a nurse."

"Aw aye? Whit kind?"

"A pretty good one," put in Nisbet, for what it was worth.

She ignored him and took off her bomber jacket. Then the blouse came off and she put her jacket back on over her bra and buttoned it up.

"Nice tits!" said Mackenzie, balancing still on one foot.

"Thank you," said Deirdre, absentmindedly, starting to inspect Bryson's perforated knee cap.

"Shut yer trap Mackenzie," said Bryson. "Dinnae get too pleased wi' yersel'."

"Do you have a first aid kit around here?" said Deirdre.

Her voice had an in-charge quality about it which made everybody jump to attention.

"Well?" she said, like an impatient infant teacher to five-year-olds.

Matheson, for a second reverting to the obedient five-year-old he had once been, put the sandwiches down and scuttled back to the farmhouse to fetch the first aid kit.

Deirdre tore a sleeve off her blouse and began gently to mop the blood pulsing gently from Bryson's knee.

"This needs to go to hospital. There's a bullet stuck in your kneecap and I think the bone might be cracked in two."

"This is gawn naewhere near a hospital doll. Just dae yer best wi' it. Ye can see the bullet, can ye?"

She nodded. "It's not penetrated the bone too much. It's sort-of sticking out a little bit."

"Can ye get at it?" asked Bryson, his voice as cool as if it was only a case of removing a skelf.

Deirdre nodded.

"Well howk it oot please pet? It's gowpin' a wee bit."

"I can imagine it is," said Deirdre.

Matheson arrived with the first aid kit, a first aid kit of such splendour that only a wealthy lawyer could afford one. Deirdre used its stainless steel surgical scissors to try and grip the bullet to prize it out of Bryson's kneecap. Bryson sucked air in through his teeth as she did her best to get a grip on it, inevitably moving it slightly inside the wounded bone.

"That nips a wee bit, doll," said Bryson.

"It's not coming," said Deirdre. "It's stuck."

"Ye're daein' fine pet. Just gie it yer best go."

There was only a slight tightness in his voice.

"*What a hard bastard,*" thought Nisbet.

Then he looked at Deirdre in utter admiration. "*What an incredible woman!*"

She was like some Lara Croft heroine: a box-kicking - no, that's a rugby thing - a kick boxing, emergency medic, cool-headed, fearless ... ehm, total babe. Who wasn't his girlfriend. Apparently.

The copper-jacketed bullet had deformed considerably on its ricochet tour of the shed and had acquired some texture on the copper surface. After a few tries, Deirdre managed to get hold of the bullet with the points of the scissors, and gripping it as hard as she could, she levered the scissors up with the heel of her hand resting below Bryson's kneecap. The bullet popped out like a champagne cork, and flicked itself over Deirdre's shoulder. Blood flooded the hole. Bryson never made a sound.

Mackenzie chased the bullet down, wiped it with a used bit of Deirdre's blouse and held it up.

"Dadaaa!"

He put it in his pocket. What a trophy!

Julian, meanwhile, simply stared in queasy admiration. What a hard bastard Bryson was.

"Wee Mac!" said Bryson. "Ah think ye'll find that yon's mine's. Gie's it."

Mackenzie reluctantly handed the bullet over.

Deirdre continued to mop blood with the sleeve of her best blouse, then held a pad of the cotton fabric over the wound until the bleeding began to abate.

"You!" she said to Mackenzie. "Tear up the rest of that blouse and hand me some when I ask for it."

Mackenzie jumped on it and tore up the blouse while trying to get a look inside Deirdre's bomber jacket. She stopped and did up a couple more buttons.

"Aw!" said the frustrated and indignant Mackenzie.

A few minutes went by, but gradually, she had the bleeding under control and with Bryson lending a hand to hold some of her blouse on the wound, she reached for the first aid kit and began to prepare a dressing from the broad selection of bandages and dressings available. All of the men were standing around uselessly, staring in admiration at a professional at work - except for Mackenzie, who was still trying to get a glimpse inside her bomber jacket.

For his part, Julian had no interest in Deirdre's tits whatsoever, he was admiring Bryson's.

"That's a decent field dressing," she said at last. "But this needs to go to hospital. Now! It's a very bad wound." Then with a note of disbelief, "A gunshot wound."

"Listen pet, if Ah turn up at hospital wi' a bullet hole in mah knee, every polis in Scotland will be a' ower us in ten meenutes. Just bandage it up, Ah'll get it seen tae by somebody Ah ken. Ye ken how it is."

"I do not know how it is! I'm not a gangster, I'm a nurse." And nodding in Lockerbie's direction, she said, "Can somebody help that poor man up?"

"No chance," said Nisbet. He'd been standing around feeling a bit spare.

"Hey big man!" said Bryson, to Nisbet, "Who the fuck are you onywey? Are you the boy that was runnin' up The Mound? The boy wi' the red BMW?"

"Honestly," said Nisbet, "I have no idea what's going on. I've been run over - by my own car! Beaten up by the cops, kidnapped and nearly shot, and all I wanted to do today was take my girlfriend out on a date."

"I'm not your fecking girlfriend!" barked Deirdre, still focused on Bryson's knee.

"And what," continued Nisbet, "the hell are you doing with my prick of a father-in-law? Is he the bastard that screwed you? It wouldn't surprise me, he's a nasty, devious, crooked piece of shite."

"So it would seem," said Julian. "But he's been very cooperative in paying us back our money."

"Is that lassie yer girlfriend?" asked Mackenzie sidling up to Nisbet.

"No I am not!" said Deirdre.

"She's a wee cracker!" said Mackenzie.

"Yes, she is," said Nisbet. "A wee cracker, that is. But she's not my girlfriend. Apparently."

"Shut up Mac," said Bryson. Then to Nisbet, "So it's a family business this, swaggin' somebody else's swag? You, yer faither-in-law and yer ... not-girlfriend."

"No! I'm a bloody architect for Christ's sake! I've got nothing to do with him. I'm just married to his daughter, that's all."

"That definitely makes it a family affair," said Bryson. "Even if ye are two-timin' yer wife wi' yer not-girlfriend while in cahoots wi' her faither."

"Architect of a pretty nice little sting too, I would say," put in Julian. "Stinging two parties for the best part of half a million each - if it had come off."

"I have no idea what is going on around here, or what you people are up to. Me and my girlfriend ..."

"I'm not your fookin' girlfriend!" said Deirdre, even louder and angrier.

"That reminds me," said Bryson. "You twa Weegies, where are the diamonds?"

The Beattie twins, now with a hold on their senses, had been propped up back to back on the floor, and taped together like concussed Siamese twins. Julian had gone to town with the tape dispenser, orbiting them with Saturnian rings of Castlerock Systems-branded tape. They were two mummified Egyptians, slowly coming round after five millennia of slumber. They weren't liking their situation one bit.

Mackenzie, still feeling well hard, squatted, and ripped the tape off of Rab Beattie's mouth.

"Tell us where the diamonds are, or we'll waterboard ye tae a bliviom!" he yelled.

He pointed at Lockerbie, who was looking very wet and pretty rough with two, progressively darkening black eyes from the punch on the nose.

"Like whit we done tae him!" continued Mackenzie. "He pissed his pants ana'. Even Ah widnae dae that. Probably."

"Shut up Mackenzie," said Julian.

Nisbet interrupted. "They're in the car outside. Or what they think are the diamonds. The blue Ford outside," he said, as he took the bloodied scissors from the first aid kit and went over to help his ghastly father-in-law, for no reason other than his not-girlfriend had demanded somebody do it.

"Just leave yer faither's feet taped up big man," said Bryson. "In case he does a runner."

"He's not my father!" said Nisbet, almost shouting. "He's a psychopathic, sociopathic, narcissistic, piece of shite!"

"You missed out homophobic," said Julian.

"That too, more than likely," replied Nisbet. "If there's a mindless prejudice going a-begging, he'll grab it two-handed."

Mindless prejudice didn't seem to be all that contemptible from the Beatties' sectarian point of view, but neither felt the need to include Lockerbie in their van. Even if he had been similarly taped up.

Mackenzie was despatched to inspect the Beatties' Ford. He came back within seconds with Nisbet's overnight bag. He unzipped it, delved inside and withdrew the brown paper parcel.

"Da daaaa!" he said. "Oor diamonds!"

"Actually," said Nisbet emphatically, "that was meant to be a present for my girlfr … the lady here."

"Some prezzy for your girlfriend!" said Julian. "Four hundred-odd thousand pounds'-worth of diamonds."

He turned to Deirdre, "Your boyfriend must like you quite a lot, miss."

"I do," said Nisbet, glumly, more to himself than anybody else.

"He's not my boyfriend!" insisted Deirdre, but with less conviction than before. She was beginning to wonder if she'd got it wrong about Nisbet Sangster, again.

"He's very good looking," whispered Julian. He'd been eyeing Nisbet up.

"If you say so." She had to admit, that part was true.

"And he looks pretty fit. Nice and tall. Must be six-one, six two."

"Aye!" interjected the eavesdropping Lockerbie, unable to contain his loathing for Nisbet. "It's the highest ye'll ever see shite piled! -Two-time my daughter wid ye? Ya worthless bastard!"

Julian gave him a look of disgust. "You be quiet! Or I'll snog you!"

Then to Deirdre, he said, "Anyway miss, those diamonds, I'm sorry to say, technically, don't belong to you. So, I'm sorry miss, you can't have them."

Deirdre shrugged. "Diamonds are so ... common."

"Listen folks, you need to understand," persisted Nisbet. "This reptile over here is my arsehole of a father-in-law. He might be in on this scamming-you business, but I have nothing to do with him, or it. He's certainly capable of pulling something like this, he's a twisted, nasty bastard! Open that damned parcel! All that's in it is a perfumed candle set and a note from me."

"You are so full of shite!" shouted the immobilised Rab Beattie. "That's the packet wi' the diamonds a'right. Small parcel wrapped in classy broon paper. Exactly as it was described by wur client."

Matheson had been standing around feeling tense, and more than a little spare.

"Would anybody like a nice sandwich?" he asked, the only thing he could think of that might lighten the mood. The gunshots had scared the willies out of him and all these raised voices was upsetting him even more.

Everybody looked at him.

"Aye," said Lockerbie. "Ah widnae mind a sandwich."

At this stage in these weird proceedings, nobody seemed to think that a captive man who had been taped, waterboarded and punched, having an appetite for a cheese sandwich in the least bit weird. Nisbet had cut him free from his 3-legged chair and he was sitting on the floor, obediently, with his feet out in front of him. Matheson offered the tray of sandwiches to Lockerbie. He took one in each of his recently un-taped hands. Then like a greedy schoolboy at a buffet, took two more.

"Ta," seemed to be all that four sandwiches merited. He bit off half a sandwich and began chewing, open-mouthed, the masticated brown bread and cheese revolving like khaki shorts in a tumble drier.

"You're very welcome," replied Matheson, seeing no reason to let good manners slip, even though the sandwich recipient seemed to be a nasty piece of work who had apparently screwed him for a huge sum of money. His kind could be found at any corporate buffet, screwing it for all the free food they could get.

Julian saw the look of distaste on his father's face.

"Let me introduce you to my father, Roderick Matheson QC," he said, stepping over to Lockerbie. "You may need his services if you ever reappear after we've finished here today."

Lockerbie acknowledged this with the raise of a sandwich.

"Thank you Julian," said Matheson. Then to Lockerbie he said. "Yes, I'm a barrister, and I'm actually very good at my job. Let me demonstrate."

He went over to the Beattie twins. "Hello again gentlemen. Long time no see. Have a sandwich. Oh, sorry, your hands are still taped up."

"Hello Mister Matheson," said Rab Beattie.

"Beattie isn't it? Robert Beattie?"

The defendant nodded.

"I defended you a few years ago didn't I? Murder charge. The Crown offered Culpable Homicide, we pleaded not guilty. Jury went our way, if I remember correctly."

"Aye. Not guilty," said Rab Beattie.

"It was a close run thing. I thought you said that you were going to go straight after that?"

"Aye, Mister Matheson. But it's just no in mah nature tae go straight."

"Me neither," said Julian.

He got a bewildered look from his father.

"Well, it's been very nice to meet you again. Help yourselves to sandwiches. Pass them round Mac."

He handed the tray of sandwiches to Mackenzie in exchange for the brown paper package.

"I'll put the kettle on. And I think we need to take this package into safe keeping."

He stepped through the door and headed for the farmhouse.

"Open wide!" said Mackenzie to Rab Beattie. Beattie opened wide. "Choo, choo, choo! Here comes the train into the tunnel of – fucksake! Dae you need tae see a dentist or whit?"

A sandwich was shoved all the way into the Tunnel of Cavities. The tunnel closed around the sandwich and Mackenzie taped it shut. Beattie chewed, for the first time in his vulgar life, with his mouth firmly shut. Lockerbie was chewing in his usual manner, the second masticated sandwich on full view.

Andy Beattie declined a sandwich. The bewilderment and shame of having had a good kicking from a female Tim half his size had spoiled his appetite.

In the farmhouse, Matheson sat at the kitchen table, turning the package around in his hands. Were his diamonds in here? It was certainly exactly like the package he'd been expecting to receive a week ago. He took a sharp kitchen knife and carefully sliced open the package, meticulously cutting the sticky tape rather than the paper. He unwrapped it, painstakingly ensuring that the paper didn't tear. He did that with his Christmas presents too. It drove his hippy wife to distraction.

With the brown paper laid aside, he beheld a Ralph Loren box with a picture in the outside of a small candle set glowing romantically in a cosy room. It was a nice robust box, but then, you'd want something substantial in which to deliver diamonds. He opened the box.

On the top was a gift card reading, in neat, feminine handwriting, "To Staff Nurse McMartin, with Sincere Thanks and Best Wishes from Nisbet Sangster."

With his nerves jangling, he pulled out the contents. A perfumed candle set. The disappointment was, surprisingly, relatively easy to take, all things considered. He was getting more and more used to disappointment; it was becoming his new normality. He sighed, sagged forward and clunked his forehead onto the kitchen table, where it had spent much time recently. Oh well.

He remained like that for a few minutes, then got up and fetched a roll of sticky tape from the roll-top bureau on the sitting room. He put the gift card in his pocket, and taped the package back together again as neatly as he could.

Inside the shed, Nisbet looked with disgust at Lockerbie sitting, chewing with his mouth open, his ankles still taped and half a sandwich in each hand. He went over to Bryson and squatted down beside Deirdre. Bryson had the Desert Eagle in his hand, pointed at Nisbet.

"You *are* the boy wi the car," said Bryson, his tone matter-of-fact. "The red BMW."

"I have a red BMW, but it got stolen. Then I got run down with it. I ended up in hospital."

"Aye, that was Wee Mackenzie there. Bit ower zealous. But we wanted wur money back."

"I have no idea why you think I had your goods. I'm a free-lance architect."

"But ye were leggin' it when Ah came efter ye!"

"Where? When?" said Nisbet.

"On The Mound, a week ago."

A moment's recollection, then, "Oh that? I was racing a traffic warden to my car!" said Nisbet.

So much had happened in the last week, particularly to his head, that Nisbet had no clear recollection of the preceding events in the park or his race with the traffic warden.

Deirdre watched the interaction between the two. Nisbet was either a bloody good actor, or an idiot, or both. But, if he wasn't a gangster, he was quite a likeable idiot. There was something strange and deeply criminal going on here with all these gangsters around her. But she had to admit, Nisbet sounded genuine, like the nice, concussed man she'd nursed for a few days. Maybe he was just hyper-unlucky.

"I don't know what *his* involvement is," said Nisbet, indicating his father-in-law over his shoulder. "But he's a nasty crooked bastard. I take it you've been speaking to him."

"Aye. He had the money a'right. But he's gied us it back - wi' interest. And we've got enough on him now tae make sure he keeps his gob shut."

"I never had any of your bloody money!" shouted Lockerbie. "It's all a mistake. That was my hard-earned cash ye took! You're in cahoots wi' these bastards Sangster. Ah might have ken't ye were a criminal, ya useless, ungrateful bastard! You'll regret this for the rest of your life!"

"Excuse me a minute," said Nisbet to Bryson.

He stepped over to Lockerbie, with the intention of punching him on the nose. He drew his fist back to smash it into the nasty bastard's face. It seemed only fair. Lockerbie had blind-side tackled him, off the ball by emptying his house and setting his flabby lawyer on him. The hateful bastard deserved it. But he thought better of it. Nisbet just wasn't like that. Lockerbie couldn't defend himself, it wouldn't be right, even if he needed it. Better to have a square go, as Beastie Saunders would have called it, when the opportunity presented itself.

Lockerbie's eyes were fixed on Nisbet's fist as it hovered, apparently locked and loaded for a full-on punch in the face. He was expecting it.

The fist was lowered and Nisbet turned away.

"Aye, ye've no got the balls for it Sangster, ya fearty!" said Lockerbie. "Ye're nothing but a useless piece of shite! Ye're an ungrateful effin' waster. Efter a' Ah've done for you!"

Somehow or other, and so it seemed, with no apparent input from Nisbet, his fist hit Lockerbie on the conk.

He hadn't hit him as hard as he could have – Nisbet was quite a big lad - just hard enough to start another dribble of red snot bubble down onto Lockerbie's moustache. Despite the fact that Nisbet immediately regretted it, it did feel good. He went back over to Bryson.

Bizarrely, Lockerbie wiped the blood off with the remainder of a sandwich and took another bite. If the roles had been reversed, he'd have done an awful lot more to his son-in-law.

"I'll take that as a reasonable indication that ye dinnae get on wi' yer faither in law," said Bryson.

"He's, ehm, not a very nice person," replied Nisbet. "To say the least."

"That was the impression we got," said Julian.

They continued to talk it out. It was all too weird, even for Bryson, but the bloke seemed genuine.

The metal hinges of the Judas door screeched and Matheson stepped back into the shed.

"Gentlemen! And, of course lady," he said. "By the way, I do think you were magnificent earlier on, young lady. Such agility! Such grace! And such calm under pressure."

"Nice tits ana'," said Mackenzie, before he could stop himself.

"Mackenzie! Do be quiet, you Rabelaisian little reprobate," said Matheson.

"Whit the fuck does that mean?" asked Mackenzie of Julian.

"Rabelaisian? It means you're a course, vulgar, homophobic, dirty-minded, smutty, illiterate little prick," whispered Julian.

"It's a lifestyle choice," replied Mackenzie, with pride. He'd had a compliment from Bryson and still felt glowingly well hard.

Matheson turned to Deirdre, "I do apologise for my driver, Mister Mackenzie, miss. He is a valued member of our team, but occasionally a little vulgar. It's really difficult to get a full quorum of quality criminals who are also gentlemen these days."

Deirdre didn't answer. She couldn't fit the gentlemanly, polite, sandwich-serving Matheson in with the gun-wielding, violent thugs surrounding her.

Matheson continued, "Anyway, I've been thinking. This has all gotten a bit out of hand. There was obviously an attempt by somebody, probably this person ..." He pointed to Lockerbie, who was moodily masticating a mouthful of sandwich - cheese and pickle this time, "to swindle us out of our ill-gotten gains. Happily, we have now got our money back, *and* the diamonds into the bargain."

Matheson was adopting his courtroom persona, as if he was summing up to a jury, wandering around slowly inside the circle of combatants. He did a circuit of the Beattie brothers with his hands behind his back.

"Now, there is a risk of a continuing war of attrition developing between our three organisations. We have all come out of this with our pants merely singed, rather than on fire, so to speak. But we have suffered no great injury, except to my loyal grieve here. And so, I have a proposed solution! A gesture of good will."

He held up the brown-paper package. "I have here, a package containing diamonds to the value of, for round figures, four hundred and fifty thousand pounds. Diamonds, the title to which, we were expectant of taking. Notwithstanding having had our expectations fulfilled in that department, I believe that our guest here," he nodded towards Lockerbie, "has repaid the money he owes us."

"Ah never owed naeb'dy bugger-all!" mumbled Lockerbie, from behind a mouthful of sandwich. His instinctive belligerence was making a come-back now that his hands were free and he was topping up his blood sugar levels with cheese and pickle on Hovis wholemeal.

"My friend," said Matheson, "If there's one thing I cannot abide, it's people who speak, let alone shout with their mouth full. Do be quiet or I'll have you taped up again and waterboarded in the midden. Now, where was I?"

He gripped the lapels of his jacket as if he was in court.

"What I suggest, is that in order to be fair to all parties involved in the accused's swindle, and to avoid a range war, now that we have our money back, is this: that our poor London supplier gets his diamonds back. I assume that's who you're working for?"

"Indirectly, aye," said Rab Beattie.

"Very well," continued Matheson, "Accordingly: One, you, the brothers Beattie, will take the diamonds back to your employers and see that they're returned to your client. Two: we will keep our money. Three: this felon here," he pointed at Lockerbie, "can do whatever he wants, sure in the knowledge that a prison sentence awaits him along with his cronies in Edinburgh City Council, should he ever put a foot out of line again, either in our world or the property world. Is everybody happy with this?"

"That's pure mental!" said Mackenzie, still on a well-hard high.

"Shoot the bastards and keep the lot!"

"For pity's sake Wee Mac!" said Bryson. "Go and pit the fucking kettle on! Or somethin' else useful." Then to Matheson, "But it is a bit mental boss. If the boot was on the other foot, these bastards wid just keep the diamonds and waste everybody."

The Beattie brothers nodded glumly. It could easily have worked out like that.

"Be that as it may, and please trust me here Alec, we'll do it my way on this occasion," continued Matheson. "Is everybody happy with the proposed arrangement?"

He went to Rab Beattie and de-taped him. Beattie swallowed the last of the sandwich in his mouth, and the bit stowed in his cheek.

"Happy Mister Beattie? You get your client's package back and you clear out never to come west of Harthill again?"

"Aye," nodded Beattie. "Thanks Mister Matheson. Ah owe ye big time."

"This disnae feel right. Ye dinnae just gie gey-near hauf a million quid's worth o' diamonds away," said the naturally, criminally acquisitive Bryson, shaking his head.

He had professional criminal standards to maintain. But as always, he'd go along with the boss's instructions.

Julian was given the task of freeing the Beattie twins from their spiral of packing tape. Bryson took both guns, dropped out the magazines and shucked the rounds out of the chambers. He pocketed the bullets and gave the empty guns to Julian to pass back to the Beatties, with a further warning never to reappear in the east again.

The door was opened and two very contrite hoodlums headed, heads aching, for the door, empty guns in pockets, Rab with the box of diamonds in his hand.

"Excuse me one minute," said Deirdre. She strode over to Andy Beattie. "Beattie!"

He turned around and she hit him with a side kick on the side of the face. He rocked back on one foot and his brother caught him before he went down again.

"That's for calling me a Taig."

She side-kicked him hard in the belly. He bent over, winded.

"And that's for calling me a hoor, and this," she said, stepping behind him, "is because ye're a dirty, perverted creep!"

She kicked him in the nuts again, then calmly walked back to attend to Bryson.

"Good effort pet! Good moves! Where dae ye train?" said Bryson.

"None of your business!"

Nisbet stared in awe. She wasn't just a staff nurse, she was a female Bruce Lee.

Rab Beattie helped his giddy, crotch-clutching brother out through the Judas door and they headed for the car, Andy moving like Groucho Marx - minus the cigar.

Matheson watched them get to the car, closed the iron door and took over the conversation.

"Do you know why I gave them the diamonds?" he said.

"Total mystery tae me boss," said Bryson.

"The box didn't contain diamonds at all. It really was a present. A nice little perfumed candle set."

He handed the card to Deirdre.

She read it aloud, "To Staff Nurse McMartin, with Sincere Thanks and Best Wishes from Nisbet Sangster."

She looked at Nisbet, and misted up, this time, not bothering to choke it back.

"For me?" she said.

"It was just a wee thing. To say thanks. You know. It was really Angela that got it for me. Perfumed candles. Don't you like it?"

Deirdre's head was spinning. Was Nisbet Sangster a hoodlum? Or just a nice-but-persistently-unlucky, naïve and occasionally not-that-bright guy? All of that, maybe.

--------oOo--------

The OK Coral

The Judas door clanged shut behind the Beatties. Andy opened the boot of the car, lifted his hold-all and retrieved the spare magazines for the guns, He handed his brother the fully loaded spare magazine for the Desert Eagle and slid the full magazine into his Sig Sauer.

"Ah'm gawn back in there. Ah'm gawny shoot that wee Tim hoor," he said.

"Are ye hell!" said his brother. "They'll be watchin' oot for us pullin' some stunt. They'll see ye comin' And they'll be armed noo, nae doobt. And Ah've a splitting' headache, forbye. We've got the diamonds. Call it quits, a bum deal, dae better next time. Let's get back tae Wee Shady."

"Ah suppose," said his brother, reluctantly, his pride on fire from taking a kicking from a wee Tim wummin.

"And by the way, Andy. You need tae learn some respect fur women. An' a few better chat-up lines. That lassie didnae seem tae take tae you wan wee bit."

"Shut yer geggie Rab."

He slammed the boot shut, they got in the car and dropped the handguns in the footwell beneath their feet. They u-turned in the farmyard, headed down the drive and turned west for the one-hour drive back to Glasgow.

"Holy shit!" cried Campbell as they passed Matheson's drive. "That's the Beattie brothers in that Ford! Turn roond. Maybes they've retrieved whatever it was they were efter!"

McColl u-turned the car at the next road junction and they levelled off their speed, some fifty yards behind the Beatties' car. Both Campbell and McColl pulled out handguns, both snub-nosed revolvers.

"Flash them tae stop," said Campbell

The headlights flashed and McColl caught up with the Beattie's Ford.

Rab Beattie checked the rear view mirror. "Who the hell's that?" he said.

"Christ knows. A BMW. Unmarked cop car maybes. Better no run for it."

The headlight flashing continued from the car behind.

"It's no the cops. The blue light wid hae went oan by noo."

The Beatties retrieved their guns from the floor of the car and tucked them in the waistband of their trousers. Andy pulled into a lay-by and they got out as the BMW pulled up behind the Ford. Campbell and McColl got out, both armed, handguns held discretely in front of them, out of sight of any passing car but plain to see by the Beattie brothers.

"Round the blind side of the car wi' yer brother," said Campbell, raising his gun.

Rab Beattie walked round towards his brother.

"Ah've had quite enough for wan day," he said under his breath. "Ah'm no gettin' robbed by they twa pricks."

"Go for it!" said Andy.

They drew their guns, taking Campbell and McColl by surprise. Campbell got a shot off. He hit Andy Beattie in the chest. He went down on his back. Rab fired the Desert Eagle several times, hitting Campbell square in the chest. The bullet went straight through him and went through the side window of a passing Toyota estate, but not before Campbell got off a couple of shots at Rab Beattie. One hit him square in the chest and the other went through the ear of a Fresian cow in the field behind Rab, to the consternation of the dairy farmer when she came in at milking time.

Andy Beattie, still on his back, was spraying bullets up at Ed McColl, who was firing back. McColl went down, stone dead, shot through the heart. Rab emptied the Desert Eagle over the top of his collapsing body into the Patullo's passing caravan, going at Greg Patullo's usual, sedate towing speed. Four neatly-spaced holes were drilled along the top like some kind of new caravanning technical feature.

--------oOo--------

"Well, if you don't mind," said Nisbet, to Matheson. "Me and the girl will just be getting along now."

"Oh will ye?" said Bryson.

"Look, I'm just an innocent bystander, and so is she," said Nisbet.

"You've got your man right there." He indicated the still-seated and still-chewing Lockerbie. "We're leaving!"

He grabbed Deirdre by the arm and hauled her towards the door.

"Just let them go Alec," said Matheson. "Before this whole thing gets completely out of control,".

"I think we passed that point a while ago!" shouted Lockerbie.

"Shut yer gub!" said Mackenzie, his well-hard, miniature fists up on guard like a boxer.

"Nisbet. Dinnae leave me here wi' these bastards! Ah'm yer faither-in-law! Ah'm faimly!"

Nisbet didn't answer, he just gave the bastard a long look. Still holding Deirdre's arm he hustled her out the door, hoping not to get Muay Thai-ed on the kisser like Andy Beattie.

He clanged the metal door shut behind them, and still hauling her by the arm, said, "Run. Before they change their minds."

Behind them he heard his father-in-law's voice resonating on the corrugated iron walls of the shed.

"You bastard Sangster! I'll get you for this! You'll regret this for the rest of your life! Ya worthless piece of dog shite!"

Nisbet did his best to run, still lopsided on his stiff right leg, firmly dragging Deirdre by the arm. She put the brakes on, skidding to a halt on the rough gravel drive, and wrenched her arm out of his grasp. He stepped back, half expecting to get one of her Nike trainers round the ear or a karate chop to the throat. Instead, she took his hand and took off down the drive towards the road, dragging him limping behind.

--------oOo--------

"Jesus!" yelled Greg Patullo, and floored the pedal. The Toyota struggled up to sixty with the caravan following obediently.

"That will do dear," said Moira. "We're not hurt. Just drive at the usual speed."

"What the bloody hell was that? A gangster shoot-out or something. Head for a police station. Dial 999."

Moira fished out her phone. Damn! Middle of rural Fife, no signal.

They drove a couple of excited miles down the road, Greg Patullo torn between driving like a maniac to escape from their near-death experience, or wrecking neither the caravan nor his marriage. He managed to prize his terrified foot off the accelerator pedal enough to slow down to fifty and as they rounded onto a straight section of road, seventy yards ahead, he saw a young couple run across the road in front of them, thumbing them down. He'd just been shot at. He had no intentions of stopping for hitchhikers, not that he ever did.

But the man stepped out into the middle of the road with both his thumbs up. Greg Patullo hit the brakes hard, the caravan brakes engaged and the whole yoke stooped to a halt as he and his wife lurched forward into the embrace of their seatbelts.

The stranger leant his hands on the bonnet of the Toyota with a sigh of relief. Deirdre was in the back passenger door like a ferret down a rabbit hole, staking her claim to the back seat. Nisbet came around to the driver's side and bent down as a shaky Greg Patullo hit the button and whined the window down. His pulse was racing, having apparently just survived a shoot-out like the OK Corral and now he'd been kind-of forced to stop for a pair of extremely pushy hitchhikers.

"Thanks for stopping. It's very kind of you. We could do with a lift into the nearest town, if it's no trouble!" said Nisbet.

Without waiting for an answer, he got in beside Deirdre. A dog's face came between them from behind and licked them both.

"Bit pushy with the hitchhiking are you not?" said Moira Patullo.

Getting shot at *and* hitchhiker hijacked inside five minutes was spoiling the start of her holiday.

"Oh, I'm sorry," said Nisbet. "Bit out of practice with my hitchhiking technique. Hope I didn't, ehm, surprise you. Anyway, if you could just drop us somewhere near a bus or a train station, that would be lovely."

"Saint Andrews," said Greg Patullo. "We're heading that way ourselves. We've just been shot at!"

"Shot at?" said Deirdre. She looked at Nisbet, wide-eyed. Nisbet shrugged back. But it plainly had something to do with the Beatties.

Indeed, there was a bullet hole in the window beside her, and another on Nisbet's side.

"Good heavens!" said Nisbet, with his best attempt at genuine astonishment. "In rural Fife?"

Patullo described the brief scene of the gunfight they'd just driven by.

"Incredible!" said Nisbet. "What is the world coming to? I'm glad we missed that. We were, ehm, just visiting friends and, ehm ..."

"Our car broke down," put in Deirdre.

"So we decided to hitch a lift into, ehm - St Andrews?" Nisbet had no real notion of where in Fife they were.

Patullo looked in the mirror. "Hey, don't I know you?"

"I don't think so," said Nisbet, truthfully, and hopefully.

"Yes. I had you as a final year student. I'm sure of it. You're, you're, ehm - let me think ... Nezbet. Ehm, Thingummy Nezbet. Thingummy ... begins with an S."

"Yes," said Nisbet. "Thingummy Nezbet. Ehm ... Sammy ... Sandy Nezbet"

"That's it. Sandy Nezbet.

"Good student, as I remember. But you didn't have your head shaved back then," said Patullo. "you weren't bald back then."

Moira rolled her eyes. "Neither were you, as I recall."

"No, it's my new look," replied Sandy Nezbet.

He didn't volunteer his correct name. He was getting used to having Nezbet enforced as his second name and anonymity would do no harm for now. He leant forward and had a good look at the driver.

"Mister Patullo? Blimey, I'd never have known you."

"Me neither," said his wife.

"Well, you're wearing well, I must say. Eh, can we slow down a bit?"

The Toyota was doing nearly seventy, the caravan beginning to sway, swinging the tail end of the car from side to side.

Moira turned round to look at Deirdre. "Are you alright dear? You look as if you've been crying."

Deirdre hadn't given a moment's thought to how she might look.

"Oh, ehm, hay fever. And I banged me foot on something hard just before we left." She hadn't half banged her foot on something hard - Andy Beattie's skull. His balls weren't all that hard.

"Is this your wife Mister Nezbet?" asked Moira Patullo.

"No," said Deirdre. "I'm just his girlfriend." She put her hand on Nisbet's knee.

Nisbet's head flopped back onto the headrest. After a few seconds, he flopped it over in Deirdre's direction. She was looking back at him with those cornflower blue eyes of hers, a different look entirely from the looks he'd got in the shed.

A few miles further on, they got to the outskirts of St Andrews.

"I need to find a police station," said Greg Patullo. "We've been witnesses to something terrible, a gunfight or something."

"Yes, it sounds like it," said Deirdre. "Look, we don't want to hold you back. And we've got a train to catch. Just drop us off here and we'll walk to the station."

--------oOo--------

Rab Beattie struggled to his hands and knees. He felt like he'd been hit in the chest by an express train. He could hardly breathe. The right-hand side of his chest was making every movement agony. His ribs might be broken. He made it to his feet and helped his brother up. Campbell and McColl were lying stone dead in between the Ford and the BMW.

"Ah think mah ribs are broken. Ah cannae hardly breathe," croaked Rab.

"Me an'a'," grunted Andy, leaning on his knees.

His brother inspected the hole in his coat, and his shirt. A 9mm, copper-jacketed bullet fell to the ground. He put it in his pocket.

"They Kevlar vests were a guid buy, were they no?" he said.

"No half," croaked Andy. "But we should have bought the thicker yins. Ah think mah sternum's broken."

"Yer sternum? Ye didnae get shot in the arse did ye?"

"Let's get tae fuck oot o' here. Ah think Ah shot up a caravan. The cops'll be here ony minute."

They dragged the bodies of Campbell and McColl out of sight of passing traffic behind the BMW.

Rab Beattie wiped off the Desert Eagle and smeared it with the sweat from McColl's hand then wrapped the dead hand around the gun. His brother did the same with the Sig Saure, folding Campbell's fingers around it. They lifted Campbell and McColl's guns, got in the Ford and drove off.

They sat in silence for a few miles, driving sedately not to attract attention to themselves.

"See efter we get peyed fur this job, Andy," said Rab. "Ah'm gettin' a job in Tesco."

"Aye. That wisnae wur best move, going' efter the money. Kindae owe Mister Matheson fur letting' us go wi' the diamonds," said Rab. "That big geezer looked like he'd waste us soon as look at us. We definitely owe Mister Matheson."

"Ah owe that wee kung fu hoor. As soon as Ah …"

"Just forget it Andy!" insisted his brother. "Ye asked for it. Besides, she'd probably kick the shite oot o' ye again."

"That's the bit that hurts the maist, gettin' a kicking frae a lassie. An' a Tim at that."

"Ah wid hae thought the bits that hurt maist wid be yer baws," sniggered Rab. "Gied a kickin' by a wee Taig lassie! Ye better hope the word never gets oot, or yer reputation as a hard man is gawny take a kickin' an' a'."

They drove home slowly, avoiding potholes, the very texture of the road causing their bruised bones considerable discomfort. Wee Shady would have to wait until morning to get the diamonds.

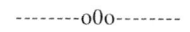

--------oOo--------

Hermens

The burner phone that McShaed had given Hermens went off, buzzing its way angrily along his desk. He watched it vibrate towards the edge, afraid to answer it in case it was bad news. He stopped it before it fell, and answered it.

"Yes?"

"Hello Eric," said McShaed. "We have your box of diamonds."

"Really? Well, that's wonderful. When can I get them?"

"Well, there's the small matter of getting your balance settled. Let me itemise it for you. To retrieve your diamonds was offered at ten percent of their street value,. That's fifty thousand."

"Yes, I understand," said Hermens. "I'll get the balance to you."

"Well, there's more," continued McShaed. "Unfortunately, there were some casualties along the way. You may have read something about it in the papers." Hermens hadn't. "No, I don't suppose the English papers are interested in Scottish affairs. Anyway, whilst in the process of retrieving your diamonds, two of my operatives had to deal with two armed hoodlums. Take them out, as they say in the movies. Purely in self defence, you understand. And it was a fairly public process so there may be some fall-out. Not that that affects you."

"Oh dear," said Hermens. The thought of somebody dying as a result of him taking action to get his money back was a little disturbing. But only a little. The elation at getting a result with the diamonds eclipsed that tiny bit of remorse immediately.

"So, I'm afraid that we need to bill you for the amount agreed were that sort of eventuality occur."

That hurt Hermens more than the thought of two hoodlums being taken out. After all, they'd asked for it. Probably.

"So, in short Eric," continued McShaed, "if we take account of the deposit which we've already received, there is an outstanding balance of seventy-five thousand pounds to be paid."

Hermens knew that something like that was bound to come, but it still sent a shockwave through him. He made an attempt at negotiating a discount.

"Come on now Eric. You've already had a substantial discount. I think Billy Bryce said that he'd only make the one charge if the population had to be reduced a little while retrieving of your goods."

McShaed was in business, and the fact that Campbell and McColl had been operating on their own cognisance and managed to get themselves killed by the Beatties simply rendered an opportunity for some enthusiastic billing.

He continued, his tone becoming a little colder: "So, I think, Eric, that we can agree that my organisation has expedited your work in a timely manner and within budget. Accordingly, a prompt settlement would be appreciated. As soon as we receive the funds, your package will be returned to you immediately."

Hermens protested again.

"I'll tell you what Eric. Since you've been a pleasure to deal with, I'm happy to offer you a prompt payment discount of five percent. I can give you until the end of the week. Happy? Excellent! Oh, and can you return the phone please?"

McShaed hung up. Hermens banged his forehead on the desk several times.

--------oOo--------

Bryson

"Ahm no gawn tae nae hospital," insisted Bryson to the equally insistent Matheson. "Ah'll get it seen tae masel'. Ah ken a guy in Dalkeith."

Julian insisted too. So did Mackenzie, although nobody noticed him. Eventually, Bryson gave in; he was outnumbered. Besides, to be fair, his knee was bloody painful.

"Ok boss, Ah suppose. But it's a bullet wound …"

"Well, we'll just have to say that it was an agricultural accident. We'll say that a hay cutter, blade doofur, thingumybob came flying off the hay mower's rotating how's-your-father, and hit you on the knee. It'll be fine. I'm a lawyer. I convince people for a living."

"Well, we cannae leave yon eejit here wi' Wee Mac. He'll need tae be properly restrained."

Bryson, one-legged, and with his torn trouser leg flapping around his expertly, Deirdre-bandaged leg, hopped over to Lockerbie. Julian and Mackenzie watched with admiration. Every hop on his good leg must have stabbed pain into his ruptured kneecap but he just took it.

"He must have a stratospheric pain threshold," whispered Julian.

"Naw," said Mackenzie, "he's just a pure mental hard bastard."

They both nodded at the undeniable, admirable truth of this.

Bryson beckoned Julian over and leant on his shoulder. Julian put his arm around Bryson's waist and gave him a bit of a hug. Mackenzie stared at that in consternation.

With blood occasionally dripping onto his Church brogue, Bryson looked down on the hapless Lockerbie.

"It's like this pal. Back on wi' the restraint. Cable ties this time. We've ran oot o' yer tape."

Lockerbie stared up at him, a defiant glint in his eye. His hands were free now. He looked at Bryson's knee.

"Dinnae even think aboot it," said Bryson. "Ah'm no in a good mood. Ah've a sair knee. An' Ah'm bored wi the water boardin'. Ye'll be the same yersel'. Ah could beat the shite oot o' ye wan legged wi wan haund ahent mah back. Ah think ye ken that. So be a guid laddie and sit at peace while Wee Mac fixes ye up."

Lockerbie nodded. At least it seemed that the worst of it was over and there'd be no more towel and bucket.

Matheson started to feel sorry for Lockerbie. The poor thing had two black eyes, two bruised and swollen cheeks, bruised elbows from falling over sideways, he'd pissed his pants, and worst of all, for him, his pathological ego had taken a beating. On the upside, his face was exceptionally clean.

The boss had Mackenzie fetch a four-legged chair to replace the one that had been shot. Lockerbie sat down obediently and was cable-tied in place.

"There you go," said Matheson. "My chauffeur, Mister Mackenzie here will look after you while we're away."

"Whit? That wee squirt? Guard me!?" Lockerbie's ego was offended that he only merited an insignificant wee pussnodule like Mackenzie to guard him.

"It's a good point dad," said Julian. "If you need a guard dog, you don't get yourself a cocker spaniel."

"Aye, very fuckin' funny Jools," said Mackenzie. But he was feeling so well hard, the insult didn't really bother him. He felt harder than Julian at the very least.

--------oOo--------

Deirdre and Nisbet

They hardly exchanged a word on the train. With umpteen oil workers heading south from Aberdeen in the carriage, all half-pissed, it wasn't quite the right place for it.

They got off the train at Waverly Station in Edinburgh.

"I can't believe what happened back there," said Deirdre, on the way to the taxi rank. "You need to tell me what happened."

"I'm buggered if I know. All I can think of is that my bastard of a father-in-law was mixed up, screwing with some very bad people and got out of his depth. And somehow, I got implicated with it. Maybe they were trying to get him when they ran me down, or something like that."

"The poor guy had a pretty bad time all the same," said Deirdre.

"Honestly? He was needing it," said Nisbet. "But I shouldn't have punched him."

Deirdre didn't think the less of him for it. She'd done a lot worse to Andy Beattie's balls.

"Look, I'm sorry you got involved. Really, really sorry. I wouldn't ever want anything to happen to you. And you were fantastic. It was you that saved us all from those two guys. I've never seen anything like that, the way you just … put him out of action. I could never do anything that."

"You did alright yourself," she said.

"Yeh, I nearly got everybody shot. Especially that arse Lockerbie. Anyway, I think maybe you ought to get off home. I expect you've had enough of me for one day."

"Don't you want to go to the police?"

"No way. I don't think those gangster guys in Fife would take too kindly to that, they look like a bad bunch. Shit, that big guy was hard, well hard. Plus, I don't want tazered and beaten up by the cops again. Come on, I'll get you a taxi home."

After a few seconds silence, Deirdre said, "Can I come home with you instead? I'm fed up going home to an empty flat. And ehm, well, you know … ." She couldn't think of the right words.

"Home with me? Well, yes, of course." He hadn't been expecting that. "I thought you didn't want to have anything more to do with me."

"No. I mean, yes. I'm sorry I said those things. It's just that I thought you were in on it."

"I don't think I'm clever enough for a life of crime," said Nisbet. "I'd have thought you'd have spotted that."

"Yep," she said, and nodded. "So, ...ehm ... can I be your girlfriend after all?"

Nisbet wanted to jump and punch the air, and shout "Ya beauty!" as if he'd just scored a winning try. But he was still too stiff to get off the ground. Instead, he said, "Yes, I'd like that more than anything."

--------oOo--------

Hospital

After an hour languishing in some considerable discomfort in the A&E reception and being chastised for bleeding on the nice clean floor, Bryson got triaged - after a child with a sprained ankle, a man with a salmon lure hooked onto his nose, and a drunk with nothing wrong with him.

Disappointingly, Bryson didn't get treated, he simply got his dressing changed, given a score higher than the salmon lure man and the drunk, and told to go back and bleed on the waiting room floor. But eventually, he got attended to by a nurse and a young surgeon.

"A farming accident you say?" said the A&E surgeon at Ninewells in Dundee, after much waiting by Bryson.

He cut the triage dressing away with scissors.

"Aye," replied Bryson. "A blade flew oot o' the hay mowin' tractor machine hingmy and hit us on the knee. Pure bad luck, so it was."

"We don't get many farmers coming in wearing Church brogues and Boss slacks," said the Doctor.

He was a little suspicious. The patient didn't look the agricultural sort. For a start, his hands might be big, but they weren't calloused. Staff at A&E were well briefed in spotting injuries that resulted from violent incidents.

"We were, ehm, just walking through the yaird when it happened.

Gawn oot for the evening."

"If I didn't know any different," said the doctor, "I'd say this hole in your knee looks more than a little bit like a bullet wound."

"Aye well it isnae a bullet wound," said Bryson, looking the doctor in the eye with his cold, hard-man stare. "Ferms can be dangerous places ye ken."

Then with the hard man eye contact understood all over Scotland, he said slowly, "It's amazin' how many people get hurt as a result of no bein' attentive tae their ain personal safety and wellbein' in the workplace."

Long, thoughtful pause.

"Indeed," said the doctor, deciding that suspending disbelief was the better part of valour. Not to mention additional paperwork. "Well, we'll get your knee stabilized, get you over to Admissions, and you'll need to be scheduled for theatre."

--------o0o--------

Leith

Instead of a taxi, Deirdre and Nisbet got the bus to Leith and sat holding hands like teenagers.

"I'm starving," said Nisbet. "It's a bit late to get a table anywhere. Fancy a bag of chips?"

"You sure know how to make a girl feel special," said Deirdre.

They ate their chips on the walk to the flat. Deirdre took the door key and trotted up the stairs as Nisbet followed stiffly, watching her legs and that beautiful, fit backside. As she put the key in the lock, the door swung open by itself.

"I suppose we did leave in a bit of a flurry," said Nisbet.

He shut the door and locked it, just in case of another gangster visit. His clothes were still scattered on the floor. He picked them up, threw them into the bedroom and headed for the kitchen.

There was a small kitchen table with two bent-wood chairs. On the table was a cute little guest welcome pack: a little basket of coffee, tea and sugar sachets, and tiny little milk cartons. There was some fruit, a bottle of wine and two glasses.

"Look! Ash does a nice job for his Airbnb guests, doesn't he? Would you like a coffee?" he said, lifting the basket of coffee makings.

Deirdre gave him a cute look, eyebrows raised, head to one side. She lifted the bottle of wine, unscrewed the cap, threw it over her shoulder into the sink and poured two full glasses.

They sat at the tiny kitchen table and sipped their wine while Nisbet had a few goes at processing the events that had culminated in their afternoon in Fife: his car getting stolen; getting run over by it; hospital; kidnapped by gangsters.

Deirdre topped up their wine glasses.

Nisbet continued puzzling it through. It was all very weird. Several times he apologised for getting Deirdre mixed up in it.

At last, she put her hand on his and squeezed it.

"Listen, never mind about that. We're safe now."

"Yes, mainly thanks to you and your box kicking."

"Kick boxing. Box kicking is what scrum halfs do."

"Yes. Kick boxing. Mooey Tie. Is that right?"

"Uhu."

She took Nisbet's mostly empty wine glass out of his hand, put it down beside the bottle and came around to his side of the table. She sat astride his lap and kissed him. It was a pretty passionate kiss, her hand on the back of his head.

His emotional pulse rate exploded up to a million hertz. He felt like the luckiest unlucky guy on the planet, something he couldn't really remember feeling for a very long time. Not this lucky anyway. Maybe he'd buy a lottery ticket if he *was* running a lucky streak.

Deirdre kissed him again, only more so. With her arms tight around his neck, she shuffled forward on his lap until she was pressed tight up against him. She hooked her ankles together round the back of the chair and pulled herself even tighter up against him. Right up against him, tight, like a limpet, her arms tight around him.

"Well I never," she said, wriggling her hips against him. "Who's a big boy then?"

This was the right thing to say.

She kissed him again. Yep. Luckiest guy on the planet. He slid his hand up beneath the back of her bomber jacket. Her skin was soft and smooth and he ran his fingers over the muscles of her back under her bra strap.

"*Fit, or what?*" he thought.

But then, he knew that. He'd recently see her wallop a guy, a thug, five or six inches taller than her, right on the chops with her foot.

He ran his fingers over the hooks of her bra strap. It was a nice idea, but he was still a bit unsure of himself. He didn't want Muay Thai-ed in the throat.

"On you go," she said, slipping the jacket off and dropping it on the floor. "Ye owe me a blouse, by the way."

She kissed him again. "And ye need a shave."

He unhooked the bra strap.

"We can go to Marks and Sparks in the morning."

"Harvey Nichols, actually. It was me best blouse. I wouldn't wear it for just anybody."

She slipped her bra off, hung it on the wine bottle and wrapped her arms around his neck again, rubbing her cheek on his scratchy face.

Slowly, he stood up with her clinging to him and headed for the bedroom, her legs wrapped around his waist.

"I like you an awful lot," he said, in her ear.

"I'm not sure what you mean," she said, in his. "Can you expand on that? Fill me in, so to speak – on the detail."

She clung onto him a bit tighter.

"Ok. Do you want my full PowerPoint presentation?"

"Yes I do."

--------o0o--------

10

Mackenzie

Matheson and Julian got back from the hospital after midnight. They'd sat for hours with Bryson in the A&E waiting room, reading - Matheson reading The People's Friend and Julian Hello! Magazine. Bryson read the Beano.

Meanwhile, Mackenzie had had hours, now that the main operators were out of the way, of Lockerbie belittling him. Snide, nasty, sneering and cruel, but Mackenzie didn't respond. He'd been told to mind the prisoner. And indeed he did. He did mind the prisoner, very much indeed.

Back in the big shed, much later, Matheson took charge. He had Mackenzie cut the cable ties securing Lockerbie to the chair and helped him to his feet. The cable ties on his wrists and the tape on his ankles were left in place.

"Now, Mister ehm … Sorry, I don't think were ever properly introduced. Anyway, let's get you back to Edinburgh," he said, sounding, and feeling up-beat, now that a relatively successful outcome had been reached.

He led everyone to the Judas door of the shed and spotted that Lockerbie couldn't get out with his ankles taped. The Judas door was small, set into the main sliding door, a foot above ground level. The huge main door was slid open and Lockerbie tried to shuffle out, his stride a mere two inches

"Can ye no just cut me free? I'm no exactly gonna run for it am I?"

Matheson swithered. "Well, I suppose …"

"No, you're not going to run for it," interrupted Julian. "Or do anything else. The tape stays put."

Despite having made this deeply unpleasant man's life a misery for a quite a while, Julian had not warmed to the homophobic bastard in the slightest.

Outside of the tractor shed the night air was cold. Lockerbie shivered. He hadn't dried off properly: wet shirt, wet underpants and wet trousers.

"My driver here will drop you off somewhere convenient," said Matheson.

He popped open the boot of the Mercedes and the light came on in the cavernous, empty space.

"Hop in, there's a good chap."

"I'm not travelling in there!" said Lockerbie. "Ah think Ah've earned some respect! You bastards have extorted hundreds of thousands out of me, and you cannae even treat me wi' respect! Jesus Christ! If Ah could get ma hands free, Ah'd …"

"See what I mean dad. Not to be trusted," said Julian. He turned to Lockerbie. "Get in there, or I'll find another way to deal with you. I still have a bucket and a towel, you know."

Bryson would have been proud of him. He was developing a talent for thuggery. Matheson was pleasantly surprised at his son's manly behaviour. Mackenzie shook his head. He just thought Julian was a wanker as well as queer.

Lockerbie gave in. He stared into the empty boot. At least he'd get home, he hoped. But with his hands cable-tied behind him and his ankles taped, there was no obvious way to climb into the boot. He'd had to bunny hop ignominiously towards the car like a child on a pogo stick, and merely keeping his balance in the dark wasn't easy.

"I'm afraid you have to," replied Matheson.

Julian gave Lockerbie a gentle push, forcing him to bunny hop round to the back of the car to stop from keeling over and planting his ugly face in the gravel.

"I don't think my colleague would appreciate your languishing on his immaculate leather upholstery," continued Matheson. "You've peed your trousers, you silly boy. It's only for an hour or so. Be a good chap and hop in."

Lockerbie remained stationary, his natural belligerence starting to find its feet again.

Mackenzie came round from behind Matheson and gave Lockerbie a firm shove. He fell into the expansive boot of the Mercedes. Julian tucked his feet in for him.

"Well done! Now, Mister Mackenzie here will drive as gracefully as possible. You'll be fine," said Matheson. "It's a very spacious boot and the car has excellent suspension.

"By the way, just in case you should ever chance to let slip anything regarding today's proceedings. Or slip into your old ways - those of the Rachmanite landlord - you might find this will come in handy."

He slipped a business card into Lockerbie's wet shirt pocket and shut the lid, stifling Lockerbie's protests.

Mackenzie set off in the big Mercedes. Having driven the slightly sozzled Matheson from the New Club to the farm many times, he had a mental map of every winding, hilly road, every speed bump and pothole between rural Fife and Edinburgh. After five minutes of enjoying the music of Lockerbie's groans, protests, threats and promises coming from the boot, he tired of it. He'd had to put up with that shit all evening. He fished out Bryson's "Shirley Bassey's Greatest Hits" CD and put it on. He turned it up loud.

"Jesus Christ Almighty!" cried Lockerbie, from the boot. "Shirley Bassey!? You nasty wee bastard!"

They got to Pilton during "Goldfingaaaah" and Mackenzie turned into a side street in the middle of the housing scheme. It was dark, but for the street lights, and the place was deserted. He opened the boot, took out his Swiss Army knife, and cut the tape around Lockerbie's ankles.

"Oot!"

The dazed and confused Lockerbie struggled to sit upright in the Mercedes boot with tied wrists. At last, he made it upright, looking around the view from the boot to see where he was.

"Where are we?" he said.

"You should ken," said Mackenzie. "Ye're rentin' oot yer shitehole hooses doon here. Colinton's only aboot five miles frae here, ye can walk. Ye'll be hame fur breakfast if ye set aff the now. It's a nice night, yer troosers will dry oot as ye go."

"You'll pay for this ya wee scumbag piece of dogshite!" screamed Lockerbie, managing to roll round onto his knees. He climbed out of the Mercedes' boot. At last on his feet, he demanded, "Get these things aff mah wrists."

"Ok. Gie me a minute," said Mackenzie. He retrieved a sports bag from the boot. "Dae ye ken whit this is?"

"Astonish me."

"This is ma "Gawn Equipped fur Crime" toolkit."

He held the bag open for Lockerbie to see his car theft equipment and a few other tools, including a crowbar. Lockerbie didn't like the look of the crowbar. To his relief, from the bag, Mackenzie fished, not the crowbar, but a pair of pliers.

"These'll dae for cuttin' they cable ties oan yer wrists. The boss says Ah've tae cut ye loose when Ah drap ye aff."

"Well, get on with it ya useless wee prick!"

"But you're thinkin' tae yersel', "Ah'll melt that wee guy when Ah get mah haunds free. Then Ah'll take the Merc." That's whit ye're thinkin', is it no?"

No answer from Lockerbie for a second or two. That was *exactly* what he was thinking.

"No. I won't do a thing. Just cut the ties and I'll be on my way, no hard feelings."

"Ok, just gie me a minute."

Mackenzie went back to the boot of the Merc. This time, he lifted out a plastic Asda bag of groceries.

"This is mah nan's shopping. Ye'll ken mah nan? Wan o' your tenants. Ah dae her shoppin' for her. She's eighty-odd."

"Bugger yer nan and bugger the auld hag's shopping! Just dae whit yer boss tell't ye and cut the bloody ties ya worthless wee piece of dogshite."

Mackenzie lifted a litre of milk from the bag of groceries, showed it to Lockerbie, and laid it gently on the ground.

"Mah nan's milk. She likes milk in her tea."

"Tae hell wi' yer nan's milk! Cut me loose!"

He kicked Mackenzie in the shin. It hurt like shit. But he ignored it. And basically, that settled it for Wee Mac. He stepped back out of range of Lockerbie's brogues.

He put his hand in the Asda bag and a half-kilo bag of sugar came out. He held up the sugar.

"Ma nan's got a sweet tooth. So dae you, apparently. Ye like sugar an' milk in yer tea." He held up the sugar.

"What the hell are you on aboot ya wee weirdo? Tae hell wi' yer nan. Ah couldnae gie two shites aboot yer nan. Or her sweet tooth, if she's actually got ony teeth left."

"Ok. Fair enough. Ah just thought you'd be interested in wan o' yer tenants, that was a'. Onywey, turn roond an' Ah'll cut yer wrists free."

Lockerbie turned round. He heard the pliers snap through the cable ties and his hands were free. Immediately, he spun round, fist arcing in the approximate direction of Mackenzie's face.

His face wasn't where it should be and his fist over-rotated on the follow-through. And before he could straighten up for a second go, arcing through the midnight air came Mackenzie's fist. In it, was the half kilo bag of sugar. In the dim street lights, Lockerbie didn't see it coming. The bag of sugar hit him very hard on the side of the head. He dropped vertically onto his hunkers and flopped onto his back, lights out.

Mackenzie held up the bag of sugar and chuckled inwardly. He felt even more well hard, he'd never knocked anybody out before. It was a good feeling. But he also felt that he'd done his civic duty on behalf of a load of Lockerbie's tenants.

"Dammit!" he said, looking at the bag of sugar.

The paper wrapper had burst at the bottom. Sugar was trickling out. He'd have to buy his nan another bag of sugar. He let it pour all over Lockerbie: over his thinning hair, around his neck, and a large portion over those parts of his slacks that were still a little damp with urine. Not damp enough he thought. He put the sugar down, lifted the milk, and poured it over Lockerbie's pants, then more sugar.

He watched Lockerbie gradually come to his senses. Slowly, he gathered himself together and raised himself up on his elbows.

"Ah wid think, by the time ye get hame, ye'll no be sae fond o' sugar and milk," said Mackenzie to the slowly waking Lockerbie.

He stood proudly over the groaning Lockerbie, as he imagined Bryson might after decking somebody. When it came to decking, his lifelong experience had mainly been as the deckee. It felt very good indeed to have laid somebody out. Especially a nasty piece of work like this.

Lockerbie began to groan himself up onto his hands and knees. Mackenzie bent over him.

"See, Ah might be just a wee naeb'dy. Ah ken Ah'm just riffraff. People tell me that a' the time. But at least Ah dinnae prey on auld folk and skint folk. You're nothin' but a bully, a nasty bastard. Dinnae expect tae get nae rent aff mah nan, by the way. Or we'll come efter ye – wi' the bucket!"

Lockerbie was trying to mouth a few psychopathic words to the little squirt. Mackenzie resisted the temptation to kick him in the ribs and walked away. He threw his toolkit and the Asda bag back in Bryson's Merc. He got in behind the wheel. It was dark, but he slipped on Bryson's Ray Bans nevertheless. He felt joyously well hard, and for once in his life, morally superior. The Merc schmoozed off onto Ferry Road and then, it being the middle of the night, Mackenzie gave it a loose rein. If there was one thing the wee shite could do, it was drive.

--------oOo--------

The Office

"I'd better check in at the office," said Nisbet. "Would you like to come? My secretary will be in. You've met her."

It was ten in the morning. They'd been taking time to enjoy one another's company, with some enthusiasm. Deirdre was curled up in his arms.

"Well, I'm still on a day off, so, nothing better to do," replied Deirdre, she hooked her leg over Nisbet's. "Besides, I can say hi to your secretary again. She seems really nice. She was very worried about you."

They squeezed into the small shower cubicle together. Another fifteen minutes of close proximity.

Drying herself, Deirdre said, "I've got a bruise on me foot."

"I'm not a bit surprised," said Nisbet. "But I bet that gangster's goolies are in a worse state."

Deirdre pulled her jeans on and fetched her bra and bomber jacket from the kitchen. She stood there, holding the bra and the jacket.

"Maybe I'd better go and buy a blouse before we go to your office. I'm feeling a bit ... under-dressed."

Nisbet looked at her for several seconds.

"*Jesus Christ Almighty!*" he thought, taking in the fit little body. "*You lucky bastard Sangster.*"

"You look pretty good to me," he said, out loud. "You look ... fabulous. But you might catch your death going round like that. Shall we go to Harvey Nichols and I'll buy you a blouse?"

He was a bit skint to stretch to a two-hundred quid Harvey Nicks blouse but he felt he'd buy her anything in the whole world.

"No, I was only joking. It was Next. Can't afford Harvey Nicks on my wages. I'll get something in Marks and Sparks and you can buy me something nice another time."

Nisbet opened the door to the offices of Nisbet Sangster, Architect, Engineer and Project Management and gingerly entered reception, expecting a dirty look from Angela for being late. Instead, when she saw Deirdre follow him in, she leapt out from behind her desk to welcome her.

"Oh, it's so nice to see you again," she said. "I think it's wonderful of the NHS to send a nurse home with a patient. I never knew they did that."

"Oh, it's, ehm, all part of the service," said Deirdre, giving Nisbet a funny look.

He shrugged innocently. They chatted for several minutes and Angela at last began to get the idea that Nisbet had been fibbing about a nurse being seconded to make sure he got home ok. It was midmorning. Where did the nurse spend the night? What had they been doing all morning? As if she didn't know – even if it had been many years since Angela and Colin, the dowdy civil servant had enjoyed much in the way of romance.

She got up and made coffee and biscuits all round and went into her big sister routine about how Nisbet needed looking after in the office as well. Not a word was said about their day out in Fife.

"Well, aren't you going to show me where you design all these skyscrapers and stuff?" said Deirdre at a pause in the conversation.

Nisbet's heart sank. His office always looked like a skip at the recycling centre. But he opened the door to find that Angela had been busy tidying up, and the place looked like a proper professional's studio for a change. He breathed a sigh of relief. He blew Angela kiss.

He looked around. He wanted to show Deirdre his workstation in operation.

"What did you do with my laptop Angela?" he asked.

"It's in the bottom drawer of the filing cabinet."

He opened the bottom drawer of the filing cabinet and lifted out his laptop. Then the brown paper parcel caught his eye. He lifted it out.

"Blimey! I'd forgotten about this," he said.

The events of several days ago in Princes Street Gardens played an ill-focussed slide show in his head. It made him dizzy.

"Jesus!" He turned to Deirdre, "You don't suppose it's a present? Like, maybe, a "perfumed candles" type of present."

"No," interrupted Angela. "That's the parcel that that poor man accidentally left with you in Princes Street Gardens. When he went off with your laptop bag," said Angela. "Remember?"

"Yes, I do now," he said, acting the daft laddie.

This parcel was bound to have had some kind of catalytic roll in the last few days. Sangster's parcel of doom.

He turned it over in his hand and gave it a rattle. Nothing. And no explosion from the castle wall either.

"Let's open it!" he said.

"You'll do nothing of the kind," said the morally scrupulous Angela. "It doesn't belong to you. In fact you can take it to the police on your way home. I'll hold the fort here, you need to go home and rest, and heal up properly." She smiled cheekily. "With the help of your private nurse here."

"I suppose so," said Nisbet. "I've still got a bad concussion and a bleeding submarine capsule."

"Sub-capsular bleed," said Deirdre.

Nisbet said, "Listen Angela, its Deirdre's day off and I'm still a bit bashed up. I think maybe I really ought to clear out and put my feet up. I can work from Ash's flat for a day or so. We'll drop the parcel off at the cop shop in Leith. If it isn't claimed in six months, it's mine."

--------oOo--------

Sangster's Parcel

Outside the office, Nisbet said, "C'mon, I'll buy you lunch. A nice lunch."

"I think ye owe me it," said Deirdre. "Too many bags of chips is bad for me figure."

They headed out of town, with Deirdre driving the big Jag SUV.

In the carpark of a country pub, Nisbet said, "I've got to know what's in this parcel. This has got to have something to do with all the crap that's been happening."

He started picking at it and at last, he made his way through the virtually impregnable layers of Sellotape, and gently tore away the posh looking brown paper to expose a box, luxuriously dressed in lustrous, shape-shifting, maroon silk. It shone in the spring sunshine that beat through the car windscreen. A box like this was plainly designed to hold nice things.

"Looks expensive," said Deirdre.

Nisbet wiggled the top as he slid it off. Inside, in matching maroon, was a velvet bag, held tightly closed by a silk drawstring tied in a bow. He loosened the drawstring and looked inside.

"Bloody hell," he said, and looked at Deirdre. "You're not going to believe this. Hold out your hands," he said. "Both of them. There's quite a lot."

She cupped her hands and Nisbet poured out a tablespoonful of sparkling white diamonds. It was only half of what was in the bag. There were dozens of small diamonds about half a centimeter across. Some were much bigger, and one or two were quite large, about the size of a pinkie fingernail.

"Jesus!" she exclaimed. "Diamonds! They can't be diamonds! Surely." She looked at Nisbet, "It's *their* diamonds! It's those gangsters' diamonds!"

They sat and stared at them, cupped in Deirdre's hands. They sparkled like white fire in the sunlight, glittering with every slight movement of her hands.

"What will you do with them?"

"Well, I'm certainly not taking them to the cops," said Nisbet. "I don't want tazered again. And can you imagine the can of worms that would open? And besides, well, screw them – they're just criminals."

"Who? The cops?" said Deirdre.

"No, those gangsters. But, since you mention it … Screw the cops and the gangsters. "

"You're going to keep them?"

"Bloody right! I think we're owed them anyway, you and me. And anyway, that older chap, lawyer-type guy seemed to think each of them had come out of their feud with a result. I wonder how you go about selling diamonds. There must be a good few grand's-worth here - tens of thousands, maybe more."

"If you can sell them, what would you do with the money?" asked Deirdre.

He thought for a minute.

"Dunno. Angela needs a new car. And I owe you a nice blouse."

He put his hand on her knee and looked her in the eye.

"Apart from that, right now, I think I've got everything I need."

Deirdre let the diamonds trickle into the lid of the cardboard box. She leant over and kissed him on his recently-shaved cheek.

"Ye're a nice man, so ye are, Nisbet Sangster."

--------o0o--------

Bryson

Alec Bryson sat back on his huge, overly-opulent leather settee, in his jockey shorts. One of his favourite Kylie Minogue records was playing softly in the background. His injured leg was stretched out in front of him, resting on a matching, leather-upholstered ottoman. His leg was encased in plaster all the way from his huge calf to his huge thigh. It throbbed like a ships engine, but it was ok, the hospital had fixed him up pretty good.

"It's awfy nice of you to look efter me like this Julian," he said. He patted the back of his boss's son's hand.

Julian rested his head on Bryson's other thigh and stroked the hairy lower leg.

"It's a pleasure Alec, an absolute pleasure. You'll need a bit of looking after until you're more mobile."

His hand ran up Bryson's hairy shin to his good knee. Bryson was surprised at this level of intimacy - he wasn't used to much in the way of warmth from his fellows in the criminal underworld. But he didn't mind. He really had taken a liking to the lad. He stroked the lad's hair.

"Aye, ye're a nice lad Julian."

--------oOo--------

Matheson

Roddy Matheson thanked his secretary for his morning coffee. He had to prepare for court this afternoon, but he always relaxed with the crossword beforehand. He'd learned that trick from his friend Aaron. He felt exceptionally at ease with the world. He'd come out of the fiasco of the last few days substantially in profit. His crafty son had not only got his money back from that nasty man that had screwed them, he'd screwed some extra from him as well.

Now, instead of the planned four-hundred-odd thousand pounds in diamonds, he had the best part of three quarters of a million pounds in digital currency. Not a bad result. He'd find another way to invest or disappear the money.

He picked up The Scotsman newspaper.

The headline read, "Crypto Currency Market Crashes." The strapline read, "Millions lose Billions on Bitcoin and Other Digital Currencies."

It went on, "After months of spectacular growth which has seen many small investors made rich beyond their wildest dreams, the price of digital currency tokens has crashed to an all-time low, leaving some larger investors virtually destitute."

Matheson stared at the headline, his pulse pounding in his temples. He stared blankly through the newspaper into the middle distance, his mouth open for several seconds while his mind spun incoherently. He sagged forward and his head thudded loudly onto the desk. A long and loud groan tapered off into the adjoining office.

"Is everything alright Mister Matheson?" said his secretary.

Several seconds went by before he replied.

"Yes. Everything's fine. Absolutely fine."

Tears dripped onto the practice's antique walnut desk.

--------oOo--------

Hermens

Eric Hermens signed for the FedEx parcel with some relief. It had cost him several tens of thousands to get his diamonds back. But at least he'd also got some pay-back. Two Scottish gangsters were dead, and, all-in-all, that seemed like a price worth paying. In fact, in some regards, it gave him quite a warm feeling. Two dead Scottish bastards of any kind would suffice.

He smiled to himself as he took the scissors and slit open the FedEx-branded plastic envelope. It had cost him more than most folk earn in two or three years, but he'd got his stuff back. Nobody was going to screw with Eric Hermens and get away with it. Especially not a bunch of ethnic, dialect-gibbering halfwits. Two dead Scottish gangsters? Hah!

With the contents of the FedEx bag in hand, he sliced his way through the bubble wrap and at last, held a parcel wrapped in brown paper and Sellotape.

It seemed they'd repackaged his diamonds. It was quite nicely done. Cautious and distrusting as ever, he opened a drawer and lifted his digital scales to weigh the contents. He'd know if even one carat was short. He picked away at the Sellotape and tore away the brown paper wrapping. Inside was a Ralph Loren box with a picture of a small candle set on the outside.

A small alarm bell went off in Hermens' head, but he shrugged it off. They'd probably simply had to repack them. He opened it.

Candles.

"Bastards! Bastards! Bastards! Dirty, thieving, swindling, Scottish bastards!"

His head thudded down onto the desk again. Tears of rage, hatred and deep, deep disappointment dripped onto the desktop. In an office four hundred miles away, a not-dissimilar pedestal desk was being dampened.

--------oOo--------

Rogoff

"How much did we make from that finder's fee," asked Aaron Rogoff.

"Oh, not a lot really. Twenty thousand finder's fee from the client."

"Yes, Actually, he's an old friend," interrupted Rogoff. "Roddy Matheson - you remember him, from university."

"Yes I do. Nice chap. Scottish." The word was sighed out, and carried with it the incredulity that anybody would ever want to identify as such.

A second's reflection then, more lightheartedly, he said, "Well, what's life all about if we can't help old friends? Oh, and we got fifteen thousand from the supplier. Actually, Aaron, the supplier was your young cousin, Eric Hermens."

"Well I never!" smiled Rogoff, with more irony than surprise. "What a small world."

"Not a bad little haul," said his friend.

"Oh, I don't know," said Rogoff. "It was quite a lot of work. It took what? Ten whole minutes in total to arrange. My hourly rate is higher than that."

He lifted the half empty, £38 bottle of Domaine Charvin, Châteauneuf-du-Pape and wiggled it over his friend's glass.

"Yes, thank you," said his friend, raising his fork to his mouth. "The veal's very good."

--------oOo--------

The Patulloes

Greg and Moira Patullo got the train home to Edinburgh - a holiday ruined. Their bullet-perforated caravan and car had been impounded by Fife police as evidence. They'd been witnesses to a firearms incident that had resulted in the deaths of two known Glasgow hoodlums. They'd given the police the name of a Sammy Nezbet who might have seen something. But on the whole, the police didn't give a shit: two Glaswegian gangsters were dead, apparently having shot one another. They had done society a civic service and well, the police had a huge backlog of non-crime hate incidents to investigate.

Greg sat at home in his easy chair with his laptop, checking Ebay for nearly-new caravans.

"I suppose we'll be able to claim on the insurance for the damage," said his wife. "But I wouldn't think that the caravan repair people are used to fixing bullet holes. They went clean through and out the other side. The police said it must have been some size of a gun."

"I know. We're lucky to be alive. In the meantime, we might as well get another caravan. Nobody's going to want a second hand caravan with bullet holes in it from a murder scene. And it'll leak even if it gets fixed. And I still want a holiday."

Bloody right he did - just in case he ever ran into that big bastard from Princes Street Gardens. Anybody who had lost the sort of money he had in that laptop bag must be going absolutely mental.

"Where are we going to get the money for a new caravan?" said Moira.

"It's insured," he said.

"I've looked at the insurance. It doesn't say anything about covering bullet holes."

Her husband was quiet for a minute.

"Sweetheart, I've got something to show you. Don't be angry, but I've been keeping something from you for a wee bit."

She looked him steadily in the eye. He'd been acting a bit weird for days: the comb-over and moustache disappearing; the new clothes. But she'd simply thought he'd had some kind of male menopause thing going on. She followed him into the office, where he explained his meeting with the big guy in Princes Street Gardens. He fished the laptop bag out and opened it.

Moira Patullo stared in wonder at the huge slabs of fifty-pound notes.

"Do you think we should hand it in to the police?" said Greg.

He waited for bad news. His wife was instinctively, thoroughly, and sometimes infuriatingly as honest as the day is long.

She stared at the money for a while longer. Her brain whirred as innate, instinctive, lifelong moral proclivity went toe-to-toe with decades of constricted domestic budgets and unfulfilled fancies for nice things. Things that money can buy.

"Well?" said Greg. "Do you want to hand it in to the police?"

"I'll get my coat," she said.

"What? You do want to take it to the cops?"

"To hell with that," she said. "Let's go and look at new caravans."

--------oOo--------

Ten days

Nisbet Sangster picked Staff Nurse Deirdre McMartin up at the hospital when she came off shift. Ten days had gone by. He'd hardly seen her: she was working her sensational little arse off at the hospital, and he was working his arse off on his contract with the city council. But she now had two days off – a weekend! Nisbet should be working the weekend through, but he would take any time off that he could, just to spend time with her.

"Nice car," said Deirdre, climbing into the passenger seat.

"Apart from the Nisbet-shaped dent in the bonnet," he said. "Hey, guess what! I've got my old flat back," he said. "Ash has got it all cleaned and painted. It looks brand new."

"Oh brilliant!" said Deirdre. "You'll be moving in straight away then. Are you going to show me it?"

"Not right now," he replied. "It's Friday evening, we're going to the rugby club for a pint. I need to, you know, insinuate myself back into the ehm ... rugby ... thing. And you can meet a few of the guys."

He let the Beamer glide out of the hospital car park and headed for the rugby club.

Nisbet Sangster held the door to the rugby club bar open, and Deirdre stepped in. It was quite busy, but when Deirdre walked in, it went very quiet as heads turned.

Nisbet followed her in.

"Good grief! How cute is that?" said Wee Hammy under his breath.

"What a wee cracker!" said Tam Gibb, under his breath, walking over with his pint in his hand.

"Whoever she is," said Beastie Saunders, "she's too good for him. Ah ken't his faither."

Wee Hammy strode forward to take Deirdre's hand. He gave it a gentle squeeze in his huge mitt. She squeezed his hand firmly in reply.

Impressed, he joked, "You'll be the new scrum half then? I'm Wee Hammy, but everybody calls me Wee Hammy."

"Wee Hammy, meet Deirdre," said Nisbet, absolutely glowing with pride. "Deirdre, meet Wee Hammy."

Hammy smiled his missing tooth at Deirdre.

"It's an absolute delight to meet you again Deirdre. I think we met at the hospital when we got flung out for disturbing the peace!" Then he looked Nisbet in the eye. "You are one spawny bastard Sangster," he said.

Turning his attention back to Deirdre, he said, "Deirdre, come with me and meet the wildlife. Meet Gibby, and Beastie. He proceeded to point out some of the other hard core near the bar.

"Can we get you a drink, Deirdre?" said Tam Gibb.

"Thank you," said Deirdre. "Pint of Guinness please."

Nisbet beamed with pride. A pint-drinking, gorgeous, sexy, rugby-intelligent girlfriend was the dream running between every pair of cauliflower ears in the championship.

"Niz? Pint?" asked Tam.

"No thanks Tam, I'm driving."

"Bloody wingers! Lemonade then? Cranberry juice? Gripe water?"

--------oOo--------

Six months

Nisbet Sangster trotted off the park half way through the second half. His lungs were bursting and his nose was bleeding profusely.

"Jesus! Did you see that?" he said on the touchline as rubber-gloved hands held his nose and began to wipe the blood from his face. "He kneed me in the face. Ref's as blind as a bat."

"Stand still." said the girl, continuing to wipe his face down while she held his nose. She wore an orange vest marked "Medic".

"What about a head injury assessment?" asked Nisbet, half hoping to do his bleeding from the sidelines. He was completely shagged out. He'd run his legs off, made a dozen hard tackles and counter-rucked himself to a frazzle. Playing at inside centre was a lot harder than loafing around on the wing waiting for a bluebird kick-pass.

"I'm bleeding like a stuck pig," he complained.

"Niz, you get a nosebleed buying a round," said the coach. "Get your game face on."

"My game face isn't usually bleeding! He kneed me in the face."

"Actually Niz, I think you faced him in the knee. Most people don't do a no-arms clear-out with their face. And we're out of subs, so you're on for the full eighty minutes."

Deirdre, held his nose while she finished wiping his face down. She shoved lint up both his nostrils to stem the blood flow and patted his cheek.

"Back on the park, sunshine," she said, patting his cheek.

"Fair enough," said Nisbet. He felt better just for having a two-minute breather. "I'll go and get the bastard."

"No you won't. Get yellow-carded and you're dropped!" said the coach.

"Ok. I'll be a good boy," said Nisbet as Deirdre wiped the last of the blood from his chin.

He ran back out on the park as if he was coming on fresh as a sub: he was fit, hard-muscled, and the desert island belly-bath coefficient was now at zero.

Today was his first start from kick-off for a very long time and he was going to have to work his arse off to keep his place. He ached all over. His girlfriend had just shoved half a pound of white stuff up each nostril. They were up 21-8 going into the final quarter, away from home. Life couldn't be better for Nisbet Sangster.

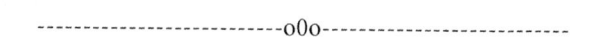

---------------------------o0o---------------------------

ABOUT THE AUTHOR

Born in Natal, South Africa, David Rice first came to Scotland as a political refugee. An innovator from an early age, he was the first, and is still the only white South African illegal immigrant to cross the Channel in a stolen rubber boat, getting a tow from a French Channel swimmer on the way.

With the ANC still hot on his tail, however, he kept moving, ducking in and out of seclusion in young offenders institutions and drug rehab clinics in far-flung corners of the empire. During this time, he journaled his travels and sold them for a pittance to any editor desperate to fill four column inches with anodyne drivel.

However, with an intense dislike of the muck they eat in foreign countries, he eventually made his way back to settle in Scotland where plain, but nourishing traditional foods like deep-fried Scotch pies and deep-fried pizzas form a healthy staple.

Washing this nutritious diet down with 7.5% wife-beater ale and lighter fluid shorts, while doing arms curls with the TV remote, he grew to be the fine figure of a man that he is today, with a Scottish record-low Systolic in the 180s and a liver like a red jellyfish.

He now lives on the wind-swept, midge-infested swamps of the Lang Whang, the interminably miserable road that struggles across the barren, gloomy and demoralizing moors that stretch between Edinburgh, Scotland's ancient capital and seat of Venezuelan-level, batshit-crazy political incompetency, to the equally ancient town of Lanark, the theoretical purpose of which, nobody has yet surmised.

When he is not writing in the native gibberish of Central Scotland, he just sits there wringing his hands, worrying when the police will show up.

THANK YOU

I'd like to thank you very much indeed for struggling through this story. I hope you enjoyed it, and if you didn't, well done for getting this far. And I'd be obliged if you could keep your opinions to yourself because I really don't need any bad reviews, thank you very much. If you did enjoy it, I'd be eternally grateful for a positive review because, well, it's flattering, and might help the book sell to others with the same poor taste in literature as you.

It is, of course, a work of fiction, or as the Americans would have it, complete baloney. However, some of the incidents that occur in this story are based more than a little upon my own experiences. I haven't had much to do, as far as I know, with gangsters, other than a few politicians, or huge sums of money, but peppered here and there are cameos and anecdotes based quite closely on things that happened to me, including, having discovered that gravity is not always your friend, languishing in hospital for a few weeks, – although I met my wife elsewhere And her name is not Deirdre. By the way, I was at school with a fellow whose first name was Nisbet. I do hope things turned out well for him but with parents heartless enough to curse their child like that, who knows. He has their genes after all.

I don't know if there'll be another adventure featuring Nisbet Sangster. After all, he seems to have knocked it off, what with getting the woman of his, and probably everybody else's dreams. And some loot. But, you never know – not much in life runs smoothly for a guy like Nisbet.

Best wishes, and much love,

David Allen Rice

Printed in Great Britain
by Amazon